GUARDIANS

SUSAN KIM & LAURENCE KLAVAN

GUARDIANS

An Imprint of HarperCollins*Publishers*

HarperTeen is an imprint of HarperCollins Publishers.

Guardians
Copyright © 2015 by Susan Kim and Laurence Klavan
All rights reserved. Printed in the United States of America.
www.epicreads.com

Library of Congress Cataloging-in-Publication Data
Kim, Susan.
    Guardians / Susan Kim & Laurence Klavan.
        pages   cm
    Summary: "In a world where teens die at nineteen and disease is rampant, Esther and her allies have created a haven within the District, the gleaming skyscraper that has become the center of all commerce; but as factions form and dangerous power emerges, the ultimate darkness is born from greed and Esther must save the citizens from themselves"— Provided by publisher.
    ISBN 978-0-06-211857-8 (hardback)
    1. Science Fiction—Juvenile Literature.   2. Action & Adventure / Survival Stories—Juvenile Literature.   [1. Interpersonal relations—Fiction.   2. Virus diseases—Fiction.   3.Mutation (Biology)—Fiction.   4. Science fiction.]   I. Klavan, Laurence.
PZ7.K55992 Gu   2015   2014027406
[Fic]—dc23   CIP
                                                                                                          AC

Typography by Michelle Gengaro-Kokmen
15 16 17 18 19 PC/RRDH   10 9 8 7 6 5 4 3 2 1
❖
First Edition

To Eugene, Dan, and Olivia—partners from an early tribe
—Susan

To my brothers, Ross, Drew, and Scott—then and now
—Laurence

PART ONE

PART ONE

ONE

IT WAS NEARLY DAWN.

Towering structures made of glass and steel stood in silent silhouettes. Beneath them, the rusted bodies of cars lay amid flattened cans, broken bottles, and the drifting tatters of filthy plastic bags. The poisonous sky, still dark yet tipped with the first streaks of yellow, was reflected as glints and flashes in identical windows that seemed to go on forever. Although the sun had not yet risen, the heat of December was already shimmering up from the cracked sidewalks, filling the canyon of buildings and making the air suffocating and lifeless.

Glancing around, the girl called Esther was satisfied that

there were no signs of life. Only then did she dare close her eyes as she savored both her surroundings and her momentary freedom.

She could barely remember the last time she had been outside. Her friend Joseph kept what he called "calendars" in his library, a jumble of numbers that allowed him to keep track of days, weeks, even months. By Esther's laborious reckoning, it had been six months since she or anyone else had been allowed to set foot outside of the District. That was how long the building that was once a mall had been their home.

Venturing outdoors was potentially deadly, and not just because of the possibility of an unexpected rainfall; Esther and her friends, after all, had made it this far without catching the fatal, waterborne disease that killed everyone by their late teens. The real danger lay in the bands of Outsiders who roamed the streets of Mundreel. Like animals, they were rumored to be savage and unpredictable. To guard against them, the revolving glass doors in the lobby were permanently locked in place, with wooden beams holding them shut. In addition, armed Insurgents were posted on the roof throughout the day and night, scanning the surrounding streets with binoculars.

The risk of being shot by one of them by accident, Esther knew, was at least as great as that of being set upon by an Outsider gang. She kept glancing behind her for a telltale glint of metal from the roof until she was certain she was well clear of the District.

Untouched by earthquakes, the building was an oasis of sorts in the devastated city of Mundreel. After the adults who

founded it had fled, the roof garden and storeroom of packaged goods provided them with ample food and clean water to
drink. True, the running of the District—tending the plants,
the water purifier, and the generator that gave them a meager
supply of electricity, as well as keeping up with repairs—took
time and effort. Because she knew how everything worked,
Esther had been put in charge.

But that was also a problem.

Given Esther's new responsibilities, it was virtually impossible for her to sneak away, even for a few hours. And ever since
she had begun to show signs of the baby she was now carrying,
her best friend, the variant girl named Skar, started keeping
track of her comings and goings with an especially keen eye.

Skar had always prided herself on making sure her friend
stayed out of trouble; that was one of the many ways she
showed her love. And Esther was also aware that variants, born
with male and female parts, had no experience of childbirth
and thought of it as a complete mystery. Skar clearly viewed
Esther's pregnancy with wonderment, even awe, and now
treated her friend like a precious and fragile thing in need of
special care.

Her concern made Esther grit her teeth with exasperation. She had grown up in almost total freedom, playing in and
exploring the scorched and abandoned streets and buildings
of her hometown of Prin. To now live such a restricted life and
under constant supervision felt like a prison sentence with no
end in sight. The girl felt restless, cooped up, and constantly on
edge being indoors day after day with the same people, unable

to hunt, ride a bicycle, or even run.

All she needed, Esther knew, *was just to be outside, on her own, for a single hour.*

Her partner, Aras, had been sound asleep, as was the child, little Kai. Only Aras's dog, Pilot, awoke as she silently laced up her sneakers in the darkness. He lifted his wolflike head in greeting and thumped his tail once on the carpeted floor before he curled up again and drifted back to sleep. Then Esther had made it down the ten flights to the lobby. She had previously located a side door that was fastened with a heavy chain. Although her belly was huge, she found she could still open it enough to squeeze through and into the early morning air.

With luck, Esther figured she would be back before anyone even realized she had gone.

Esther ran the way Skar had taught her years before, lightly and on the balls of her sneakered feet, slipping from one hiding place to the next. True, she was much heavier than she had been before; running felt clumsy and she had trouble seeing the ground, which made her footing precarious. Her jeans, belted low, were too baggy on her bony hips and threatened to trip her with every step. Yet it was a pure pleasure to move fast again, to feel her arms and legs working together in an easy, effortless way as the wind blew against her skin, ruffling through her dark hair.

As she ran, Esther scanned the horizon for any signs of Outsider activity, her eyes attuned to the silence of the city around her. She didn't stop until she reached the outskirts of

town, near one of the long bridges over the broad, dry expanse
that had once been a river. By now, the morning sky had grown
brighter, and as she pushed back the hood of her sweatshirt to
wipe the sweat from her forehead, she realized she was hungry.
Down the street was what looked like an abandoned supermar-
ket; with effort, she could sound out its name: *Pathmark*.

"Gleaning" was the way Esther and everyone else had fed
themselves until recently. It meant breaking into old stores and
homes and searching for packaged foods that were still edible:
sugar and salt, dried beans, honey, and coffee as well as plastic
bottles of water and soda. Special Gleaning teams continued
to go out once a week, accompanied by armed guards, to augment what they were able to grow; still, Esther hoped they had
somehow missed this place. She was about to approach when
she noticed the shattered front door. The store had most likely
been picked clean years ago.

But just as she about to turn away, she heard something
else.

A musical cooing in the distance started, then stopped. It
was answered by another. Silhouetted against the sky were several small shapes perched on an overhead wire strung between
tall metal poles. One of them took off and flittered to the
branches of a nearby tree.

Esther watched the birds for a moment. She had been so
intent on sneaking out that morning, she hadn't thought to
bring a weapon. Now she gazed about on the ground, looking
for a rock and wondering if she could launch it with enough
force and accuracy to hit one of the creatures. As if they could

read her thoughts, the shapes broke apart and, still calling to one another, took off into the air.

Resigned, Esther watched them disappear. Then something else caught her eye.

The one bird that had settled in the tree hadn't flown off. She could see it, a dark, formless form huddled upon a branch. It was a pigeon in a nest, its eyes bright and unblinking as it stared down at her. On an impulse, Esther stood underneath it and took hold of a low branch. Then she put one foot on the bark and attempted to hoist herself.

Climbing trees was something she had done since she was a small child; she could literally do it with her eyes closed. Yet this was the first time she had attempted it while pregnant. Her swollen midsection got in the way as she tried to hug the trunk, and when she began to bring her other foot up, she could raise it only partway before sliding back to the ground, skinning her hands and landing with a hard jolt. The baby shifted inside Esther, and she winced.

"Ow," she said.

The pigeon, alarmed, began cooing loudly and fluttering. Gritting her teeth, Esther attacked the tree again, grabbing a lower branch and pulling herself up with her arm strength alone before finding a foothold. By the time she made it even halfway up, she was sweating and the sun was visible over the horizon. As she drew closer to the pigeon, it tried to look bigger, its feathers fluffed out as it flapped its wings.

But she had reached her goal. The pigeon now dived at Esther in an attempt to drive her away; she brushed it aside as she pulled herself onto the branch and sat there, winded. Then she inched along until she reached the nest. Ignoring the cries of the agitated mother, she stuck her hand in.

There were five eggs, still warm to the touch; they were small, but to Esther, they were a godsend. Taking care not to drop any, she tilted her head back and broke one open into her mouth. It had a strange slimy texture, both thick and ropy, and she had to spit out a piece of shell; still, she was surprised how wonderful it tasted. Months ago, Aras had told her how to do this, and the idea made her want to gag. But now, she could not eat fast enough. The raw eggs satisfied a deep part of her, and even after she finished, she stuck her tongue into each shell fragment, trying to lick out what remained. Then she leaned against the trunk, savoring the feeling of being full if only for a moment, before taking hold of the branch and beginning the arduous descent.

But the effort cost her. She was halfway down when she felt another twinge, deep in her gut, and she hesitated.

It wasn't time. According to the primitive calculations she had worked out with the help of Joseph's calendar, she still had a long way to go. Yet even so, once she dropped to the ground, Esther decided it would be wise to hurry back to the mall.

By now, it was much later than the girl had anticipated; the sun was well into the morning sky and climbing higher, making her feel exposed and increasingly vulnerable. She had taken a winding route, which she now regretted; it wasn't clear which was the shortest way. She decided to stay on the river's edge, which would at least bring her back to the center of town.

From there, she would be able to spot the roof garden and find her way home.

But haste was making Esther careless. In order to avoid the main road, she began taking shortcuts down unfamiliar side streets. She saw a building that looked vaguely familiar, and on an impulse, she cut around it, assuming she could follow the small road that lay beyond it and through to the other side. But several steps in, she realized that the path was in fact an alleyway, dark and narrow. It was cluttered with looming mountains of trash: an abandoned car, a stripped sofa, and heaps of plastic bags and bottles. And only when she made it to the end did she realize there was no way out.

Esther stopped dead in her tracks. She was about to turn around and head back to the street, but she hesitated.

Someone else was in the alley with her.

The hair on the back of Esther's neck was rising before she even saw what it was. In the dim light, a dark shape scuttled from one pile of garbage to another as if hiding. As she picked up a low vibration that she realized was the sound of growling, Esther could see a pair of eyes glittering out at her.

It was a wild dog.

Esther exhaled with relief. Wild dogs were dangerous only in packs. Alone, they were cringing, pathetic creatures that roamed the street at night, hunting rodents and scavenging any food they could find. But why was this one out at dawn?

She took a bold step forward. Normally, such a minor act of aggression would be enough to send the animal fleeing.

Inexplicably, this one staggered forward, seemingly pulled by an invisible force.

"Go on!" Esther shouted, clapping her hands. "Get out of here!"

But the dog continued to advance. It was filthy, and its bony sides twitched and jerked as if covered with fleas. Confused, the girl took a step back and then another. Again, she felt a deep twinge and she winced. Then the dog stopped and seemed to sink to the ground. To her disbelief, Esther realized the creature was crouching low on shaky haunches not out of fear but for another reason.

It was preparing to attack.

Esther's eyes flickered around in search of a stick or piece of metal with which to defend herself. Unexpectedly, she was hit by a powerful contraction that she couldn't control, one that forced a cry from her lips and brought her to her knees. This apparently signaled weakness to the dog and gave it the opening it was waiting for. Esther threw her arms in front of her in a vain attempt to shield herself as the animal launched itself across the dark alley. In that split second, she could see its jaws open and yellowed fangs bared.

A sharp twanging sound rang out behind her. At the same moment, the dog froze in midair and, with a single yelp, dropped to the ground. In the silence that followed, it lay shuddering on its side, its legs kicking. Only then did Esther notice the arrow shaft buried deep in its chest, and the black blood pumping around it through the matted fur.

Esther whirled around. Standing at the mouth of the alley

was a small figure in a drab tunic; its weapon was still lifted as the air vibrated with the echo of its firing. The creature was androgynous and bald, with strange lavender eyes, and covered from head to foot with elaborate scars and tattoos.

"Skar!"

Her friend put down her bow and came forward. As Skar helped her up and the two hugged, Esther only just realized how close she had come to serious harm. She felt a wave of shaky relief. *She had been stupid*, she realized with fresh remorse, *to go out by herself*, and now she waited for Skar to rebuke her. But as was her way, the variant girl said nothing that would make Esther feel bad.

"That one," was all Skar said, gesturing at the dead animal with her bow. "If you ever see a wild dog out during the daytime, especially by itself, stay away. It has the sickness that animals get." She shuddered. "You are lucky it didn't bite you. That is a terrible death."

Esther felt guilty: She had exposed not only herself and her unborn child but her best friend to this danger. And all because of her impulsiveness, which she could never control.

"Thank you," she said, touching Skar's shoulder. The next part was harder. "And I'm sorry."

Skar shrugged. "Many people depend on you now," she said. "You must be careful for everyone's sake." She was about to speak again, when her expression changed. "Esther," she said. "What is the matter?"

Esther didn't reply. She was seized by another terrible contraction deep inside her. She felt helpless to resist; she had no control over her body. "I don't know," she said between clenched teeth.

Skar was regarding her with an openly worried look. "Do you feel well enough to get back inside? It is only perhaps another half mile."

Esther took a deep breath and nodded. She was already self-conscious about having put the two of them at risk; the last thing she wanted was to bring any more trouble to her friend. "I think so."

She set off at a brisk pace, as Skar tagged along close behind, keeping a concerned eye on her. But after several blocks, Esther was hit by another clenching sensation that was so bad, she had to stop and lean against a building until it passed. Several steps later, it happened again.

Flushed and in discomfort, Esther bit her lip. She was determined to ignore her pain and make it safely back to the mall, especially since she could see how rattled Skar was becoming. A cool and fearless warrior who had just taken down a maddened dog, Skar seemed to be unnerved by not only what was happening to her friend but her own inability to help. Esther wanted to reassure her. But before she could take another step, she gasped as something inside her seemed to give way. A moment later, hot liquid burst forth from her. Within seconds, it soaked her jeans and splashed onto the pavement.

Helpless and apologetic, Esther turned to Skar. "I think it's started."

Skar could only nod. She looked close to panic: Her face was pale beneath its elaborate tattoos.

The two girls were exposed where they stood, in the middle of a long block surrounded by giant buildings. Making a quick decision, Esther indicated a lobby that lay beyond a large window frame, edged by broken glass. BMO BANK OF MONTREAL was the meaningless phrase on the giant sign above the door.

"In there," she instructed.

Inside, a long metal counter set with cracked glass panels ran along one wall, separated by partitions. It wasn't ideal, and the marble floor was dusty. Still, the space was cool and relatively secluded; it would shelter them for the birth. As Esther fumbled to undo her belt, she glanced at her friend's face. Skar looked terrified.

"It's okay," Esther said. She remembered a childbirth she had witnessed long ago and knew to squat low, grasping the edge of the counter in front of her. "Just be ready to catch the baby when it comes."

"All right." Skar could barely speak.

For Esther, there followed an hour or two of discomfort during which the contractions came more and more frequently. After a while, they were like an earthquake, sending rippling shock after shock across her body. Esther tried to push as hard as she could, realizing with a kind of awe that it didn't matter: With or without her help, the baby was going to come out on its own.

At long last, it happened. With an immense rush, something slid out of her and into Skar's waiting hands.

The relief was exquisite. Although she was trembling with exhaustion, Esther instructed Skar how to cut the umbilical cord with her knife and clean off the baby's mouth. Then with shaking hands, she reached out and took her child.

It was bawling in a high, reedy voice, its arms and legs impossibly thin and precious. Her fears over, Skar crowded close, cooing in wonder at the tiny thing.

"Look," she whispered. "It's perfect."

And it was, Esther thought.

Pregnancies were rare, and the birth of a living child was nothing short of a miracle. She thought back to her late partner, Caleb. This baby was a living testament to their love, a legacy he would never see. Her emotions were so strong, they seemed to blind her as she cradled the precious being close.

But beside her, Skar had grown quiet. And as she wiped the infant clean with the edge of her sweatshirt, Esther saw why.

Only now did she notice the child's eyes, so unusually large and set so far apart. The tiny, flattened nose, barely nostrils etched in a broad face. And the sex itself: small, misshapen, not really belonging to either boy or girl.

Esther drew a deep breath as she glanced up at Skar, who looked grave. The question was already forming on Esther's lips, and yet she said nothing, for she realized she already knew the answer.

Her child was a variant.

Esther couldn't speak. Her mind was whirling.

She had known for a long time that variants were human. Although they were born different for reasons no one understood, inside they were the same as norms; they were all people.

Yet she was alone in daring to think this.

For some reason, the profound connection between norm and variant seemed to be a shameful secret that very few on either side chose to acknowledge. In fact, any other girl in her position would have abandoned her child without hesitation and had it taken in by other variants to be raised. Esther had seen that happen once, back in Prin.

But that possibility didn't even cross her mind. Instead, Esther's arms tightened around the infant in an automatic and protective way.

Skar seemed to understand what she was thinking. "What will you do?"

Esther was already fumbling with her shirt; the baby was crying, and she had only just realized it was probably hungry. "I'm keeping her."

"Her?"

Esther smiled. Variants, she knew, raised their young without gender until they were ten; then each child was allowed to choose his or her sex in a special ceremony. "I can't help it. Maybe she'll change her mind when the time comes. But it's what she seems to me."

Skar smiled back, a dimple flashing in her cheek. "Me, too." Then, once again, her expression grew serious.

Esther thought she understood. Back in Prin, her neighbors, even her older sister, Sarah, had viewed variants as the enemy, with fear, disgust, and contempt. When the earthquake forced them away from their home and they had all taken off for Mundreel together, Skar had been the only variant among them. It had not been not easy for her. Even though she never spoke of it, Esther sensed that on the road, Skar had experienced more than a few examples of the townspeople's ignorance and hatred.

But all at once, Esther was distracted from the idea. She was preoccupied by a strange new feeling, something that suddenly seemed far more important than anything else.

Her baby was nursing.

TWO

BY THE TIME ESTHER AND SKAR RETURNED TO THE MALL, THE SUN WAS well overhead. Following her friend's advice, Esther took care to wrap her sleeping child in a tattered towel she found in a subway entrance. Flattening themselves against a neighboring building, they both kept an eye on the guard, who was watching from the roof. Only when he turned did they hasten across the street.

The girls peered through the side door and waited until there was no one in the lobby. Once they had slipped indoors, Skar kept lookout as they ran to the windowless stairwell at the far end of the hall. There, they slowly made their way to

Esther's home on the tenth floor, the girl leaning on the banister every few minutes.

The mall itself was made up of open levels that occupied the bottom four floors of a large indoor courtyard, including a basement. Above were seven more stories, each filled with dozens of windows that revealed darkened hallways beyond. High in the ceiling, a brilliant glass panel let in sunlight, which streamed past the strange man/bird sculptures that hung at various points. Most of the mall's inhabitants—Esther's small band and the three dozen or so Insurgents—chose to live on the lower levels, in various stores and restaurants that were scattered throughout the commercial space. Only Esther and Aras opted to live higher up, in one of the offices on the top floor. Their room was close to the roof garden, where Esther spent most of her time. It was also clean and quiet, its enormous window looking out on the city and the nearby mountain.

Esther and Skar emerged on the top hallway without running into anyone. Then they stopped.

"I should go," Skar said.

Esther was hoping her friend would come with her. She had not realized how worried she was about her partner's response; if Aras rejected the child, she would need Skar's support. Then she shook off the feeling. As hard as it was, this was something she had to do by herself.

Esther's tread was light on the thick beige carpet. Still, Pilot was already waiting for her at the door, his tail wagging, when she walked into their room. Inside, she could hear Aras moving about.

"Where you been?" He appeared at the door, his lean and handsome face etched in worry beneath the dark glasses he always wore. His right hand extended, brushing the air for her. "Skar went out after you, but it's been a long time."

Esther hesitated, then took his hand. Her heart was pounding; Pilot was already sniffing the dangling edge of the towel with great interest. "I know." Her voice faltered. "I've got someone I want you to meet."

She undid the cover and guided Aras's fingers to the sleeping baby. When he first felt the soft, warm creature, he recoiled as if touching fire. Then a smile stole over his face. He brought his hand back and continued his gentle exploration of the tiny being, barely skimming her delicate skin as he traced the curve of her cheek, her pink ears, the soft dome of her head.

"And you . . ." He turned to Esther and his hand rose to her face, cupping her chin. "You okay?"

"I'm okay." Then she swallowed. "But there's something else."

The baby was starting to awaken; she squirmed a bit and let out a miniature yawn, showing pink gums. Esther took her partner's hand and directed it to the features of the child's face. Aras's palm hovered over them.

Then he stopped.

After a moment, he went back and tapped her flattened nose, her bulging eyes. His fingers flickered over the rest of her body, checking her with a quick thoroughness that made Esther's stomach clench. Tense and anxious, she was watching her partner, trying to read his thoughts.

"Is it—" he started to say at last, but Esther cut him off.

"Yes," she said. "She is."

There was a silence that seemed to extend for a lifetime. *Wasn't he going to say anything else?* Esther wondered. She loved and depended on her partner, the blind boy who against all odds had led her and her friends to not just safety, but a new life in Mundreel. Theirs was a relationship based on mutual loyalty and respect. Yet for a moment her trust in him wavered and she hated herself for it.

Aras held out his arms. With her heart pounding so hard it hurt, Esther handed the child over.

With the utmost care, Aras gathered her up. Then he bent forward, brushing his lips against her soft forehead.

"Our baby," he said.

Esther was so relieved, she only just realized how exhausted she was; her knees nearly buckled. But Aras was crouching low, showing the infant to Pilot.

"This our little girl," he was saying. "And you got to do everything you can to make sure she safe. Got that?"

His tail thumping as if in agreement, the dog nuzzled the baby.

"Now," Aras told Esther, "let's go introduce Kai to his little sister."

Later that morning, the four dozed in one bed, with Pilot on the end as sentry. Two-year-old Kai had been delighted with the tiny creature and wanted to show her all his toys; yet soon, the excitement had tired him out. Her arms now around both children, Esther slipped in and out of consciousness; it was a delicious feeling.

Then she realized that next to her, Aras lay awake.

"What if it was just us?" He spoke as if addressing the ceiling, his voice soft. "The three of us. Four, I mean."

"What do you mean?"

"If we found our own place. Away from here."

Esther was touched. She knew that before he had lost his sight, Aras had been a guide, making his living taking travelers to where they wanted to go. He considered no one place his home; he had been long accustomed to his freedom and felt even more restricted in the District than she. And he was a loner at heart, ill at ease among others. That he wanted to create a new home for his family was the most loving thing she could imagine.

"It'd be all right to go," he added. "Everything run pretty good here."

It was true. Under her supervision, the garden was flourishing; there was more than enough to feed everyone. The clever drainage system in the greenhouse roof collected rainwater, which, after being strained and purified, was safe to drink. And down in the mall, most of the stores were still intact and stocked with all kinds of items, luxurious and untouched: clothing, shoes, jewelry, housewares.

Yet Esther felt such peacefulness lying there with him and the two children; if she could have preserved the moment forever, she would have done so. It had taken them all such hard work and terrible sacrifice to get where they were, to finally reach a place of safety and security. And they now had a baby, one who would require special care to raise. Should they really abandon the District and go away on their own?

As if reading her mind, Aras kissed the top of her head.

"Well," he murmured. "It something to think about."

He nestled close to her, and within minutes, his breathing grew slow and regular.

Yet Esther stayed awake for much longer, staring out at the yellow sky.

The next day, Esther asked her friends to gather in her room.

"This is Sarah," she said. The baby lay bundled in her arms, dozing. "She's named after my sister."

Joseph, comfortable with just his cat, Stumpy, beamed with delight as he hovered over the baby, not daring to touch. A smile fell upon the ravaged face of Skar's partner, Michal; she adored all little ones and couldn't wait to coo over the child. Even Silas, so tough and hardened by the age of nine, asked if he could hold her. Once he did, he stood gazing down upon the tiny face, a foolish grin on his lips.

"Remember," Esther now reminded them, "you're the only ones to know. Don't tell anyone else."

All nodded with solemnity. Then, one by one, they drifted off, allowing Esther and her family their privacy.

The suggestion to keep Sarah's birth a secret had been Skar's. Not telling Eli had been the hardest part for Esther; of their original group from Prin, he was the only one whom she had not invited to this small gathering. She had felt a pang, but in the end concluded that Skar was right. For months, Eli had separated himself from the old circle and been spending more time downstairs with the Insurgents and their leader, Gideon, who was now in charge of the guards.

"Of course you must tell our friends," Skar had said. "That is as it should be. But as for Gideon and his people . . ." She did not complete her thought.

At first, Esther had been exasperated by her friend's suspicions. True, the Insurgents were a warlike people; there were still signs of their initial rampage after breaking into the District: shattered windows, scorched walls, bent railings. And certainly Esther had been distrustful of the headstrong Gideon from the start. Yet she could not forget that the Insurgents had been instrumental in securing the District; she and her friends couldn't have taken over the mall without them. What's more, in the ensuing months, Gideon had been nothing but helpful and kind to Esther and her friends.

Still, Esther had to admit, *she trusted Skar better than anyone she knew.* She didn't need to be reminded that while hatred of variants came from a childish place of ignorance and fear, it was still a very real emotion, one that was both dangerous and unpredictable. If her old friend didn't think it wise for others to know about the existence of something as precious as her child, neither could she.

Sarah would be safe from prying eyes, kept where she was; the Insurgents never came upstairs. Esther also decided to ask Silas to bring Eli a special message, one she knew would eventually make its way to Gideon.

Her child had been born dead.

She hoped it would be for the best but still had to wonder: *Had anything good ever come out of such a lie?*

"Who's there?"

Annoyed, Gideon let out his breath. He had been leaning against the cold white basin, so intent on the girl across the room that it took him a few moments to even hear the pounding on the locked door. It echoed across the dingy tiles, the metal stalls, and the shining expanse of mirror.

The Insurgent girl stopped removing her clothing. Her name was Nur, and even though she was nearly naked, her pretty face showed only irritation, not alarm. Gideon knew why. No one was aware they were involved, seeing each other like this. He didn't want anyone to know, while she, he guessed, wouldn't have minded if the whole world found out.

"Who you think it is?" she whispered, not being quiet enough.

Gideon frowned. "I don't know. Don't talk so loud."

There was another pounding on the door. "It's me," said a voice. "Eli."

Gideon considered. Eli knew when to contact Gideon and when to take care of things himself. He would only interrupt if he felt it was truly important.

"Wait!" Gideon called.

With a brusque nod, he indicated one of the stalls. Nur glared at him, but nevertheless had begun to head in when he suddenly called her back with a snap of his fingers. He gestured down at the scattered items of clothing she had left on the ground. With a look of annoyance, she bent down and snatched them up. Then she disappeared into the metal booth, climbing up on the strange white chair within so that her legs wouldn't be visible underneath.

Unlike Nur, Gideon was fully dressed. He smoothed down the front of his shirt and glanced in the mirror. His reddish hair was brushed back from his pale forehead, and his gray eyes were without expression. Other than a faint flush rising along his cheeks, he looked normal. *Good,* he thought. As for Nur, he knew she would wait for him.

For the fleeting second that Gideon thought about the girl, it was with a mixture of arousal and disgust. Then he crushed all feeling. As ever, he only watched her; the thought of actually touching her, like anything having to do with the body, filled him with repulsion. When he and the Insurgents lived on the streets of Mundreel, he had even deprived himself of food and water, going for days without ingesting anything. *It only made him stronger,* he thought.

Just as a third and most insistent knock began, Gideon reached the door. He unlocked it and let Eli in. The boy didn't even try to look around. *He was not only dutiful but discreet,* Gideon noted with approval. He would make a fine second-in-command, if Gideon were ever in charge.

"What you want?"

"It's about Esther," Eli answered.

At the mention of the name, Gideon pursed his lips; now he felt angry that he had responded so quickly. He and Esther had come to the mall as equals, with Gideon leading the ones Inna and the other adults had dubbed "Insurgents." Yet, once inside, he had been reduced to being little more than an enforcer, supervising boys who kept guard against any Outsider who dared approach. Meanwhile, Esther had taken on what he considered the petty and mindless business necessary to run the District—the farming, water purification, and maintenance—and become the boss.

It took no great intelligence to tend the garden or sweep the halls or patch windows, Gideon thought; it was mindless drudgery fit for females and small children. Yet every day his position grew weaker while Esther's became stronger. Without even seeming to try, she attracted others to her; even his own people, now scattered and intermingled with Esther's, were dependent on her. The idea that a mere girl—at sixteen, a full year younger than he was, scrawny and awkward and not even that pretty—could command the respect of people she barely knew mystified Gideon. It infuriated him as well.

He had been nothing but polite to Esther, biding his time as he waited to find a way to take over. But he was getting impatient.

"What *about* Esther?" he snapped at Eli.

"Her baby," said Eli. "It was born dead."

Gideon registered this, then shrugged. The news meant nothing to him; after all, the same thing happened to most babies. Yet he couldn't help but notice that the other boy seemed upset by the news. He knew that Eli and Esther had once been close; from what he understood, Eli had even asked her to be his partner long ago.

"Too bad," he said, trying for sympathy.

Beyond his occasional desire to watch Nur, Gideon almost never felt longing for anyone. On the rare occasion he did, he had long since learned how to deal with it. Scattered across his torso and upper arm were faint, raised scars from when he locked himself alone in his tiled room and used a knife to tease and then break the surface of his skin. Cutting himself like this brought him a deep feeling of calm.

Gideon was about to dismiss Eli and allow Nur to escape her hiding place. Then something interrupted him.

A faint sound came from the distance. It was a ragged shout that was followed by more voices. They sounded agitated and angry, and Gideon could hear the distinct sound of shattering glass.

Alarmed, Eli glanced up. But Gideon had already pushed past him and was running for the lobby.

When Esther first heard the shouts, she was in her room, putting Sarah to sleep. She ran to the corridor, where she pressed herself against the window in a vain attempt to see what was happening on the ground floor. Then she raced to the stairwell and bounded downstairs.

As she entered the main lobby, she saw that a large crowd had already gathered. A group of terrified Insurgent guards stood clustered by the side doors, trying to hold them shut. One panel had already been smashed in the scuffle; glass shards littered the marble floor. Perhaps two or three dozen

Outsiders were shouting and shoving, attempting to force their way in.

"Who's on the roof?" From where Esther stood, she could see that Gideon's face was flushed with anger as he screamed at his guards. "Who let them get so close?" There was no answer, and in his fury the boy pushed his way through the crowd. Esther had already joined him, and when she finally emerged, she saw the Outsiders face-to-face, separated by only a cracked piece of glass. She was braced to see a band of vicious marauders. Instead, she was so startled, she caught her breath.

The Outsiders were children—little children.

Although a handful of them were in their teens, most of them were no older than ten or eleven. Many were younger, not much bigger than Silas or even little Kai, swallowed up in the filthy hooded robes they wore as protection against the sun. And they were all clearly starving, their outstretched hands filthy and shaking. As the children shouted in hoarse and ragged voices, they revealed toothless and blackened gums, and the sound of their cries made Esther's insides wrench. They were near death, all of them . . . and they were begging for food.

Gideon had yanked a guard close and was attempting to fumble something out of the boy's waistband. Esther grabbed his arm.

"What are you doing?" she shouted.

"We scare them off. If they don't run, then we shoot to kill."

Vehement, Esther shook her head. "No. Just give me ten minutes." Skar had materialized next to her; and at her questioning look, Esther nodded. "Let's go." She tapped one of the Insurgents, a boy named Tau, and he joined them. Then the three began pushing their way back out through the crowd.

"You get more guns?" Gideon had to shout to be heard.

Esther didn't even look back. "Not guns." Then she and the others took off.

With Tau not far behind, the two girls matched each other stride for stride, elbows pumping as they raced to the metal door at the end of the lobby. Then all three burst into the dark stairwell, and, taking two steps at a time, they sprinted upward. Several flights up, Esther thought she could hear the door clanging far below; someone else had clearly joined them. And yet she didn't slacken her pace.

When the three emerged onto the roof, Joseph and the others looked up at them, startled.

"What's happening?" Her old friend's long face was flushed in confusion. "We heard something happening outside." But Esther had already seized two baskets, which she handed to Skar.

"We need help," she said. "I'll explain later."

Working quickly, she and the others loaded three baskets with food: tomatoes, squash, carrots. By the time Esther had filled two buckets with clean water, she could see out of the corner of her eye who had arrived on the roof. Gasping for breath, Gideon stood there, his face flushed.

"What you doing?"

Esther didn't answer. "You start with those," she said, nodding at Skar and Tau. They each picked up a basket and headed for the stairs, ducking past Gideon.

Esther had already grabbed the buckets, their precious contents sloshing, when Gideon approached her. "But wait . . . that ours."

Only then did she glance at him. "They're dying. And we've got enough to share."

Gideon made as if to stop her, but she slipped away and reentered the stairwell. The containers were heavy and she didn't want to waste a drop; still, she was able to outrun Gideon in the dark.

By the time Esther made it back down, the situation on the ground floor had grown worse. Someone had pushed a few benches against the doors; several of the guards were now leaning against them with all their might. But this only seemed to make the Outsiders even more frantic as they redoubled their efforts to force their way in. As people screamed, the ones in front of the mob were in danger of being crushed to death. One of them, a boy who looked no more than six or seven, was pressed so hard against the door, he had been lifted completely off his feet. Unconscious, he dangled against the glass as if pinned there, his thin arms and legs drooping.

Esther and her people had already made their way through the crowd. "Open the door!"

"What?" One of the Insurgent guards gestured outside. "They get in here, they kill us all." But Esther shook her head.

"If we feed them, they'll back down."

By now, Gideon had arrived. The guard's eyes, wide with terror, flickered over to the boy for confirmation.

Gideon hesitated; perhaps he could feel that everyone was staring at him, including Esther. Then he shrugged. "All right," he said to the boy. "But only her." Then he raised his voice. "Go ahead. Let her out!"

Clearly uneasy, two of his people pulled back one of the benches, allowing Esther to slip through the gap in the chained door. She carried one of the buckets in her arms as if for protection; it splashed against her, making the front of her T-shirt glisten.

The Outsiders drew back and grew silent.

At first Esther hesitated. Now that she was outside and alone with them, she felt a sudden stab of fear. There was only one of her and dozens of the Outsiders. Although they had stepped back, she could still feel the heat rising off of them, smell the dust and desperation that rose from them like a cloud. Even though they were young, they vastly outnumbered her. If they attacked, she would have no chance to fight back, none at all.

She tried to speak, but the words caught in her throat. Swallowing hard, she raised her voice so that all would hear.

"Here," she said. "It's clean." For a moment, she was not even sure whether they understood words, and so she demonstrated, hoisting the bucket and taking a sip. "This is for you."

There was silence; no one moved. Then a girl next to Esther, her hair filthy and matted, reached out a trembling hand. With unexpected delicacy, she took hold of the rim and tipped the container as she bent forward to drink. When she lifted her head, wiping her mouth, Esther could see the lump in her thin throat rising and falling as she swallowed. Then the girl smiled.

Esther passed over the bucket. After a second, the Outsiders took it: boys and girls, some so little they needed help drinking. A few lunged forward, shoving and elbowing, but most did not. Most waited their turn and accepted the gift of a single sip of water before handing on the bucket so that everyone could share.

By now, Esther had retrieved the other bucket and the baskets that Skar had passed to her. Although they had clearly never seen anything like them, the Outsiders seemed to understand that the fruits and vegetables were meant to be eaten. It wasn't much: just a single tomato or beet per person, maybe a carrot or a few radishes. But they began devouring it all, the sounds of their ravenous biting and chewing filling the air. More than a few were crying, silent tears carving clean lines on their filthy faces.

"Eat slow," cautioned Esther. "Chew it carefully, or you're gonna get sick."

The containers were empty, and only then did Esther turn to head back inside. Behind the cracked glass, she saw that Gideon and his people were staring at the scene before them in utter shock. When she slipped her way in through the door, even the Insurgent guards parted to make a path for her.

In the silence, one boy's voice spoke up. "Now we got less."

"Then we'll grow more." Esther felt resigned, but not apologetic.

The others nodded, considering it. Then as they watched Esther go, they smiled and whispered among themselves.

Baffled, Gideon turned away, replaying over and over what

Esther had just done and how she had been received.

Yes, she had squandered their precious stores of food. But without using force, strength, or even common sense, Esther had not only defused a potentially deadly situation, she had done so by winning the affection and respect of everyone around her. He didn't know how she had managed it or if she even knew what she was doing. But Esther clearly possessed something he didn't: the knack to win the hearts of the foolish, the weak, and the desperate. In other words, the majority.

For the first time, he saw her as possessing something that had always eluded him. Something he craved more than anything: authority.

As Esther began to head upstairs, Gideon ran to catch up with her. Keeping his voice down, he spoke in the tone he always used with her: one of warmth and sincerity. "You right," he said. "We feed them, we ain't got need to fear them."

His flattery had never failed him before. As he knew she would, Esther smiled back at him with gratitude.

THREE

A FAINT RUMBLING FILLED THE AIR.

At first, Joseph was too absorbed to notice. He was nearing the end of an exciting book, its yellowish pages pleasantly musty. A group of young boys had been abandoned on an "island," a piece of land surrounded by water. Although many of the words were strange to him, Joseph understood enough to figure out that there was a battle going on: between the good boy, Ralph, and the bad one, Jack.

This was the fourth time Joseph had read the book, one of the few left over from the fire set by the Insurgents that had nearly destroyed the mall's library. It had taken him this long to decide that it was a made-up story; although it seemed so believable, it wasn't real, like the many newspapers he had saved and read over the years. In fact, those were the stories that truly seemed fantastical; after all, they described a terrible disease, the Spanish flu, which had poisoned the earth's water and killed off so many people. That seemed far more unreal to Joseph than the events of this book, which spoke a kind of truth.

Then he felt something bump against him. The noise had grown more persistent, and this time, he felt a soft paw tugging at his jeans.

"Stumpy!" he exclaimed.

Putting aside the book, he scooped up the tabby cat that was milling between his legs. She was small yet determined, with gray and orange markings on her round and indignant face. Joseph glanced at the four watches on his wrist and recoiled. It was much later than he realized.

"Sorry," he said to the cat as he stood, reaching for her carrier. "Time for your breakfast."

When they had first arrived at the mall months before, it had been virtually impossible for Joseph to feed his cat. The building was kept so clean, there were no vermin; and since they weren't allowed outside, there were no places for him to set squirrel traps, either. Thanks to Silas, he discovered that the parking garage downstairs, where garbage and other noncompostable waste were thrown, was filthy and teeming with rats. Although Joseph hated leaving his home on the fourth floor, he admitted that some things couldn't be helped, no matter how distasteful. Now he and Stumpy made daily pilgrimages to the basement.

Joseph groped his way down the dark staircase that led to the lower floors, the padded leather carrier bumping against his side. Then he slipped through the main atrium of the mall. As he passed, he noticed there was a commotion going on by the front entrance. Unfamiliar people were gathered outside, thin and filthy faces pressed close to the glass.

Joseph recalled Esther mentioning it at dinner: Outsiders were now regularly coming to the mall looking for help. She was giving them food and water, which struck Joseph as the right thing to do; as with Stumpy, one was obliged to help those who couldn't help themselves. But after a few weeks of handing out provisions, it seemed there was now a problem with the arrangement, a question of whether there would be enough to go around. Even as he picked his way unnoticed down the last steep stairway, the one with grooved metal steps and rubber handrails, Joseph could hear distant voices raised in anger and confusion.

Rattled, he decided to ignore the conflict. *People were more complex yet less interesting than cats*, he thought. As he headed across the food court, past tables and benches embedded in the tiled floor and the dim recesses of restaurants beyond, Joseph could tell that Stumpy could already sense where they were heading. At the dented metal door, he fumbled with the key and felt her shifting forward in the carrier, eager to be set free.

Opening the door to the garage was always an unpleasant shock; no matter how much Joseph tried to prepare himself, the stench was so powerful, it was like a blow to the stomach. But Stumpy didn't mind. Before he could even finish unzipping her bag, the plump tabby had wriggled her way free and taken off into the cavernous darkness.

Joseph closed the door behind her and waited, checking his watches. As he always did, he marveled at the hunting efficiency of cats; he never had to wait more than ten minutes for Stumpy to locate, kill, and eat her food. After fifteen had passed, he opened the door, expecting to find her waiting just outside, licking her chops.

She wasn't there.

Joseph called her name again and again. Then, exasperated, he closed the door and waited some more. But after ten more minutes had passed and she had still not shown up, he realized with a sinking feeling that he had to go in and find her.

Joseph had never been inside, for it wasn't only the smell that bothered him. He knew that the garage had once held terrible and dark secrets, had been where the adults had hidden their dead, and he was nervous about what he might see. He was also aware that the rats that lived inside were large and fierce. Although Stumpy was an inimitable hunter, he didn't like taking any chances.

Joseph took a deep breath. Then he opened the door, propping it so it wouldn't slam shut. He fumbled in his pockets; to his relief, his hand closed on a slim plastic firestarter. He clicked it, and the small flame that blossomed out of one end gave him courage. He lifted it high as he stepped into the garage, his other hand trembling as he pressed it against his mouth and nose in a vain attempt to block out the smell.

The light threw deep shadows across the immense space. As the object grew hotter in his hand, Joseph saw that he was surrounded by towering mountains of garbage, heaped to the ceiling. Despite the hellish squalor, the trash seemed to be roughly sorted: dented cans in one pile, moldering heaps of flattened cardboard in another, tattered shopping bags in a third. Extreme anxiety made him sensitive to the tiny sounds that came from all directions: the skittering of claws, an occasional sharp squeak, the shifting of objects. The air seemed heavy and poisonous, a thick blanket of rot that caught in his throat and made him gag.

"Stumpy?"

He saw a dark object skulk low to the ground, and a pair of eyes glittered at him. Was it her? As he held up his light, he saw to his horror that it was an immense rat. He stumbled back and stepped on something soft that squished beneath his sneakered feet. Leaping sideways with a shout, he felt the firestarter scorch his fingers and he dropped it, plunging the garage back into darkness.

Joseph was shaking all over. Finally, he was able to scrabble around on the ground and locate the firestarter. He clicked the tiny wheel once more and raised it.

He saw something huge glinting in a distant corner that threw off its own illumination, green and oddly beautiful. Curious, Joseph moved closer in order to investigate. It was a large heap of something he didn't recognize. He reached out a hand and his touch triggered a tiny avalanche of sliding pebbles, twinkling in the meager light. But they weren't stones. Picking one up and examining it, Joseph realized that it was a minute piece of glass, clear but deep green, the color of leaves and grass. It was irregularly shaped but smooth-cornered, about the size of his thumbnail.

Broken glass was a part of their world; it was as common as air. And Joseph knew it often came shaped this way: in pieces that were small and uniform as opposed to sharp and jagged. Yet he had never seen any glass as rounded as this or in such a pretty color.

On an impulse, Joseph scooped up a handful and slipped them into his pocket; the fragments were dusty, but cool and pleasing to the touch. Only then did he notice Stumpy, sitting a distance away, washing her face with an impressive lack of fear or interest. When he picked her up, her stomach was distended and she let out a small belch.

"Don't run off like that," he admonished.

By the time he made it back into the food court, he had forgotten all about the fractious strangers outside; he was too busy thinking about the treasure in his pocket. But as he trudged to the main level, he could hear that the struggle was still going on. He hesitated, the carrier back on his shoulder.

He saw that Esther, Skar, and a boy were holding baskets that were partly full of food from the garden. They seemed to be waiting. Nearby, Gideon was arguing with someone who stood outside, a scrawny girl with matted hair. As Joseph watched, Gideon turned to Esther, a look of concern on his face. He tried to keep his tone polite, but Joseph could tell it wasn't easy.

"She already got food," he said. "I'm sure of it." Joseph couldn't hear what Esther was saying in reply, but he saw a look of uncertainty on her face. Skar and the boy rested their containers on the ground, as the crowd appeared increasingly restless.

Joseph thought he understood what was going on. And as he did, a new thought came to him.

"Excuse me," he said in a faint voice.

No one heard him, which was just as well; Joseph was still struggling to pin down his thinking. But as he fingered the glass in his pocket, the idea he had, so vague and unshaped, blossomed and began to grow clearer and sharper in his mind. "I said, excuse me!"

It was practically a shout. Gideon and Esther stopped and turned around to take him in.

Esther was surprised by her old friend asserting himself. She couldn't imagine what Joseph could have to suggest, but was happy to give him a chance. She was eager for *any* help at all these days.

Her attempt to feed people outside the District was already floundering. Every day, more and more Outsiders showed up, desperate and demanding; and while most were happy to wait their turn for what little food and water there was, a few had begun cheating the system by means of deceit, theft, and intimidation. Gideon had been nothing but helpful, assigning his guards to try to supervise the handout. Still, it was almost impossible to police who had received the day's allotment and who had not. What was meant to be a fair distribution was quickly turning into one that was hopelessly disorganized and even chaotic.

By now, the Insurgent leader was gazing at Joseph. Given how shy the other boy was, it was probably the first time Gideon had heard him speak or paid him mind at all. But before he could say anything, Joseph, gazing at the ground and rocking back and forth, continued.

"I didn't mean to listen," he said, "but I believe I know what your problem is." Glancing around, Esther tugged on Joseph's arm to step aside from the crowd. He shot her a look of gratitude; she knew he couldn't bear to be surrounded by people, especially strangers. After a moment's hesitation, Gideon followed them, squelching obvious impatience.

It was only once they were by themselves that Joseph went on, wringing his hands as he spoke. "You're trying to distribute food in a fair way. One piece per person is fair." Both Esther and Gideon were leaning close to hear, and Joseph hastened to speak louder. "The problem is, it's hard to keep track that way. People come back for seconds or even thirds, when there are others who haven't had any."

Gideon seemed about to discount him, but Esther listened with an intent expression, nodding. "So what do we do?"

His face flushed, Joseph hesitated as he fumbled in his pockets. Then on an impulse, he drew something out which he held forth. "Here," he said, his hands trembling.

It was a handful of the green pebbles, brilliant in the sunlight.

Gideon tried to repress a dismissive sound but could not

entirely. "Glass," he said. "What that suppose to do?"

Joseph glanced at Esther, not him. "We give everyone one piece," he said. "It's much easier to distribute. Later, they can exchange it for a piece of food. One pebble, one tomato. Or one carrot. Do you see?"

Esther chewed her lip, thinking. "And that would be more fair."

Joseph made an expansive gesture. "I think so. More flexible, too. For example, someone can give his pebble to his partner. She can come here and with her own, exchange the two for two pieces. Or people can save them up and use them when they want."

Esther frowned. It was so unlike anything she had heard of, she wasn't sure what she thought. She was about to say something, but to her surprise, it was Gideon who spoke first.

"It don't got to be food." He was no longer considering Joseph; he was gazing off, as if at something important in the distance.

"No," Joseph answered in a voice so muffled, it could barely be heard. "I suppose it could be water, too."

"Or clothes." Without asking, Gideon reached out and took the pieces of glass from Joseph and weighed them in his hand, clicking them together. He seemed to be talking to himself, as if thinking out loud. "Shoes. Firestarters, firebowl." Then he looked up. "Or protection, maybe. Or even place to sleep."

Now it was Joseph's turn to be confused. "I don't understand," he mumbled. "You mean each of those things—clothing, a firebowl—could all be exchanged for one piece of glass?"

Still not looking at him, Gideon held up a hand for silence. "Not one. Maybe two, three. They worth more than a carrot."

The redheaded boy was so confident, Esther couldn't help but feel encouraged, too. Still, the idea of procuring anything with something as meaningless as a piece of glass was new and strange. Whenever people needed something, they mostly Gleaned it themselves. Back in Prin, everyone worked for Levi, who paid them with packaged food and clean water. It was that simple, that direct.

"What do you think?" she finally asked Gideon. "Do you really think it could work?"

Gideon moved his head back and forth, as if weighing the possibilities. "We try," he said at last. "I make a plan. You get folks to do it. You good at that. We a good team."

As she took the handful of glass from him, Esther tried to think what could go wrong with the idea. *At the worst,* she thought, *we could go back to the old way.* Then she smiled; the feel and color of the smooth fragments pleased her, too. "Let's try it."

Gideon nodded to her in a deferential way. Then he turned to Joseph, at last acknowledging him.

"Where this from? They more?"

Joseph swallowed. "There's a mountain of it," he said. "Down in the garage."

It was late afternoon and shadows were beginning to fall upon the streets.

Ever since Esther had begun feeding the Outsiders, the strict safety rules had been eased. Guards no longer patrolled the roof around the clock, and people within the District were now free to venture outdoors. Few took advantage of it; most were still too frightened. Although it was a beautiful day, Esther and Aras found themselves alone as they took a rare walk with the children.

There was something, he said, that he wanted to show her.

Covering Sarah with a scarf, Esther secured her to her back with the cloth sling that had once held her brother. As for Kai, he seemed astonished at being outdoors. The enormity of the blasted cityscape made him gaze about in wonder and he would dart off to explore the things he had no memory of, things that were extraordinary to him in their newness: rusted cars, streetlamps that resembled dead trees, piles of rubble. With Esther walking alongside Aras, Pilot was allowed off his leash. Still, the dog continued to keep a watchful eye on Kai, herding him back to the others from time to time.

It was a pleasure to be out in the open as a family. Esther didn't like living in secret, especially since it wasn't a secret to be ashamed of.

By now, they were a mile or so from the mall, in an unfamiliar part of town. Aras lifted his head and seemed to gaze around before indicating that they take a right. Even without Pilot, Esther knew he could orient himself by counting blocks.

Soon Esther noticed that they were on a side street she had never seen before. "Where are we?"

"We on a street with an empty lot on the corner?"

"Yes," replied Esther, puzzled. But Aras had already whistled for Pilot, who bounded to his side. Attaching the dog's chain, he clicked his tongue and the animal led him down the block, to a row of three-story buildings. Esther called Kai to her side and took his hand. They watched as Aras approached the structures, counting under his breath as he ran his hand lightly along the black metal fence that stood in front.

Then he stopped and turned back to her. "This a brick building with a red door?"

"Yes," said Esther again. Wondering, she helped Kai step over the trash and broken glass that littered the sidewalk. In front of her, Aras was trying the handle of the middle house. To her surprise, it turned and the door opened.

"Come on," he called over his shoulder.

It took Esther a moment for her eyes to adjust to the relative dimness. In fact, sunlight was pouring in on all sides through windows that were miraculously unbroken. It revealed that they were in a small hallway with vibrant yellow walls and rich carpeting underfoot.

Esther was as stunned as Kai, who clung to her. "What is this place?"

Aras turned to her, a shy smile on his face. "It nice? Silas say so, but I wasn't sure. All I know is that nobody ever broke in here. It clean, right?"

Wordless, Esther took his hand and squeezed it tight.

The place was small but beautiful. True, the mall had its own kind of splendor—soaring spaces filled with gleaming steel, brass rails, and immense overhead lights made of twinkling glass—but this was more to Esther's taste. The floor was made up of broad wooden beams that still held a faint golden

glint. A large mirror and the beveled glass ball at the foot of
the staircase reflected the four of them, as well as wooden wall
pegs, from which two coats still hung.

Without a word, the four investigated the rest of the house.
Downstairs was a living room, with crumbling magazines still
held in a wicker basket by the sofa. The furniture was simple
yet pleasing: wooden frames set with cushions in deep blues
and greens. There were even ornaments on the mantelpiece:
a glass clock with frozen hands, a small animal made of dull
metal, and photos of smiling people long dead. Beyond it was a
dining room; a bowl in the center of the table still displayed the
faint and dusty smudge of whatever it had once held long ago.
The kitchen was a wonder of bright surfaces in candy colors:
pale greens, yellows, and blues.

True, dust lay heavy everywhere, and muffled sounds from
inside the walls and the brick chimney in the living room
revealed the presence of mice or nesting birds. But other than
that, the house was eerily immaculate. It was as if the previous
owners had just stepped away for a few minutes, leaving everything in place until they returned.

Upstairs, Esther and the others explored the three bed-
rooms, the closets, and the tiled room with the tub and
porcelain chair. Towels that matched the dark pink of the carpet hung on the rods, and a shriveled shard of soap still lay
in a dish on the marble counter. One flight up was the top
floor, a single room that was bright and sunny. The walls were
painted with large and colorful flowers, and ancient toys and
dolls spilled from several oversize baskets lined up beneath the

curtained windows. With a happy cry, Kai rushed forward and seized a stuffed animal, sending up a cloud of dust.

It was, Esther realized with a sense of wonder, *going to be their new home.* But that was not all.

With Pilot left to guard the boy, Aras felt his way back down the hallway and led Esther up the final small flight of steps. It ended in a door made of heavy, tinted glass. When he opened it, warm air rushed in as he and Esther stepped out.

She gasped. Low walls separated the attached roofs of all three buildings; together, they made up what seemed like an immense expanse, open to the yellow sky. Aras put his arm around Esther's waist and squeezed.

"For our own garden."

Esther heard his words, but it took her several moments to process them. When she did, she was stunned by what he was proposing: After they moved into this house by themselves, they would build their own greenhouse, a miniature version of what stood atop the District.

Turning away, Esther realized that the entire conversation was starting to make her deeply uncomfortable. "I might want to wait," she said. "To go."

"What you mean?"

"There's something," she said uneasily, "I have to do first."

"Something? What that?"

Aras's tone was already confrontational and Esther chose her words with care. Although she loved what she and Gideon were doing and found their new responsibilities thrilling, she sensed that her partner might not understand. So she kept her explanation simple: she needed to make sure that the distribution of food and water back at the District was fair. For the first time, she described the glass fragments to him and how they would be given to all of the Outsiders, to use in exchange for what they needed.

Aras had his head down as he listened. "And this your idea?"

"No," she admitted. "It's Gideon's."

"Gideon." Ever since he had met him when they took over the District, Aras had never trusted the boy; there seemed to be a world of meaning in the way he spoke his name. Then, without another word, he abruptly turned. Making a clucking sound to Pilot, he strode off.

"Aras!" But by the time Esther had collected Kai and followed her partner downstairs, he was nowhere to be found. She noticed that the front door was hanging open and, looking out, saw that Aras was already half a block away. He was walking fast, the gap growing longer between them.

Esther knew that Aras's silences meant more—and were more to be dreaded—than his words. With a sinking feeling, she too stepped outside and closed the door behind her and her children with a final click.

Overhead, the pale sliver of a moon appeared in the skylight. It shone down through the clear panes, past the many layers of the mall, filtering through to the basement level far below.

Alone in the restaurant called Chipotle that was his home, Gideon sat at one of the dozen tables that was bolted to the ground. He caught the moonlight in his hands, toying with a single piece of glass. He turned the fragment so that it cast green glints on the walls around him.

Yet he was not admiring its beauty.

He was thinking instead about the new system and the sort of power it could bestow upon him. The more he considered it, the more he was astounded by its vast potential. Although Esther had initially suggested that they simply distribute the glass to the Outsiders, he soon realized that this was a foolish idea; it would be the same as giving away their food and water for nothing.

But what if people were to work for it?

There were plenty of chores in the District that needed to be done every day. The Outsiders might also Glean valuables—packaged food, bottled water, whatever they could find—and bring those in to exchange for glass. He could even arm and train a group of the oldest and strongest, to create a small army.

Gideon shivered. Mundreel was enormous, and the idea that he might have found a way to harness all the power of its people was nothing short of exhilarating.

The possibilities were limitless.

When Gideon and his fellow Insurgents lived on the streets of Mundreel, barely existing as living skeletons, he too had once been like the Outsiders. He had loathed the privileged adults who lived inside the District, obsessed about how he could destroy them and punish them for their arrogance. When they finally broke in, he and the others had tried at first to ruin everything they could find in the building, to trash the mall's glittery goods.

But now Gideon found that he felt no differently about those outside from how the adults had once about him. He too was revolted by the grotesque faces on the other side of the glass, appalled by their desperation and helplessness. The idea that he could possibly make use of them struck him as ironic, and a small smile crossed his face.

True, for the new system to work, he would need Esther and her talent for persuasion. He had once seen a toy, a wooden man that dangled from strings. If you held the strings just so, the man would dance and wave, as if it were alive. That would be his new relationship with the girl. She would engage with and communicate to the crowds, and he would be the unseen force behind her.

A sudden noise pierced the surrounding gloom and Gideon glanced up. At the same moment, his hand went to the club he often kept by his side. As he hoisted it, he heard the sound more clearly: a rapid clicking of nails on tile approaching from across the darkened food court, accompanied by panting and the jangling of a chain.

"Who—" he was about to say.

Then a monster flew at him.

A snarling, drooling creature from a nightmare lunged and snapped at him, its jaws open, its breath foul. With a terrified cry, Gideon fell back in his seat, scrabbling to get away. As he tried to escape beneath the table, the thing came closer, its growling horrible.

Crouched on the floor, Gideon realized it wasn't a monster,

but an animal. It was the blind boy's dog, the boy, Aras, who was Esther's partner. Gideon brought down his hands, his heart still thundering.

There was a whistle and the animal retreated.

"Sorry to bother you," Aras said.

Gideon didn't answer and got back to his feet. He was already regaining his composure as he dusted off his knees. Annoyed, he assumed the boy had stumbled into the room by mistake. His dog was now sniffing around, going from one corner to the other.

"So this where you live," Aras said at last.

"That right," Gideon said.

Aras made a clucking sound and without hesitation, the dog returned to his side. The animal was benign now, not threatening. *Impressive how well it was trained,* Gideon thought.

And that wasn't the only impressive thing about Aras. He had met him when they first broke into the District, but the two had kept their distance ever since. The blind boy wore sunglasses, even though it was dark. His hair, in strange, matted locks, fell halfway down his back. The sight of Aras made Gideon shudder. He couldn't bear defective things; to him, the blind were about as useful as an ugly girl or a broken bicycle.

Yet Aras was no weakling. The more Gideon studied him now, the more formidable he sensed the other boy was. The idea that Esther shared her bed with him gave him a disgusted fascination.

Aras seemed to be in no hurry to leave. He found one of the tables and sat down on its molded plastic bench. Then he stretched out his long legs and the dog curled up at his feet. Gideon realized his room had been Aras's actual destination, after all.

"I would have thought you would live nicer," Aras remarked.

"No," Gideon said, still uneasy. "This all I need."

"Really?" Aras said. "Maybe you think you could use a girl around the place. Most boys do."

Gideon didn't respond, unsure of what he meant. He noted that Aras's upper lip was curled into the smallest of smiles. "But you better choose a girl," continued the blind boy, "who ain't somebody else's."

Gideon stared at Aras until the comment struck home. He and Esther—some sort of *romantic* connection?

"That stupid!" he snapped, louder than he had intended.

Aras continued, unfazed. "See, me and Pilot are the same. We can tell things that don't smell right. Sometimes even before people know it themselves. That's one good thing about being blind."

Aras got to his feet, the dog shaking itself with a jangling of its chain. The boy approached him now, the animal guiding the way. The beast still was unnerving and Gideon had to force himself to stay still.

Aras stopped Pilot with an effort, the dog panting, champing at the lead. "Don't worry. He ain't gonna hurt you *now*. But he's got an even better memory than me."

He released the chain and Pilot lunged at Gideon. Instead of biting him, he reached out his muzzle and nosed Gideon's bare leg, as if memorizing his smell. His nose was cold and wet, but it was his teeth Gideon feared; he braced himself and forced himself not to tremble. After a few seconds, Aras pulled the dog away.

"Get some rest," Aras said. "You might need it."

He made a clucking noise at the dog, which led him toward and out the door. Gideon stood motionless for a minute. Then, his flesh tingling, he sat back down again.

Normally, Gideon would have dismissed such an episode. The idea that he had any interest in Esther was not only absurd, it was distasteful.

Still, what did it say about the girl?

Gideon had always believed that the blind boy was Esther's most powerful ally. The two had a relationship that seemed like a fortress, unshakeable and strong. But Aras had just made it clear that he was jealous of Gideon and suspicious of the time he spent alone with his partner. While ludicrous, such mistrust was intriguing as well. For if Aras didn't have faith in Esther, that meant there was a fundamental weakness between them, a crack in their seemingly perfect union.

And weakness could always be exploited.

But how? he wondered.

Despite Aras's parting words, Gideon was too excited to sleep all night.

FOUR

ELI AWOKE WITH A START.

He had been sound asleep, and, for a few moments at least, he had been happy. This much he remembered, although the details were already fading fast. When he realized he had been dreaming of Esther, he felt a flare of embarrassment, followed by irritation. Ever since she had partnered with Aras, the girl was as good as dead to him; he had made a private vow to try not to speak to or even think of her again. Yet she continued to haunt his fantasies, no matter how hard he tried to banish her from his thoughts.

But something else had startled him awake.

Eli blinked. A figure was standing on the threshold of his room, its features indistinguishable in the early morning light. As he struggled up on one elbow, Eli saw to his surprise that it was Gideon.

Although Eli acted as Gideon's assistant of sorts, this was the boy's first visit. Still, Eli admired him deeply. He often watched him when he thought no one was looking and even tried to imitate his nonchalant way of standing, his cool bearing. From the start, the Insurgent had seemed his total opposite. Nothing ever seemed to rattle Gideon; unlike Eli, he never wavered or doubted or appeared to feel any pain. He had certainly never been made a fool by the love of a girl like Esther, of that much Eli was certain.

Eli scrambled to get up and offer his guest a seat.

"It okay," said Gideon. He didn't sit in the chair, but leaned against the counter, his expression unreadable.

Eli nodded. Without being aware of it, he too settled his weight against the wooden barrier that ran halfway across the side of the store; like Gideon, he hooked his thumb in the loop of his jeans and affected a careless look. After a few moments of silence, however, he began to feel self-conscious: He knew his hair was rumpled and that he was still wearing the T-shirt he'd slept in. He cleared his throat and glanced around, wondering why the boy was there and what Eli could do for him.

"What you know about Aras?"

The question was abrupt and took Eli by surprise. "Aras?"

"You know him awhile, right?"

"Yeah." His reply seemed more like a question than a

statement, and he winced at how uncertain he sounded.

"So? What you think?"

"Well . . ." Eli licked his lips. He sensed that Gideon wanted something from him, and although he wasn't quite sure what it was yet, he wanted to provide it. "When we were on the road, coming to Mundreel . . . I guess I didn't like him much. Not at first, anyway."

Gideon nodded. "Why not?"

"He was—well, he pushed people around. Told us what to do. Like he was better than everybody."

"You say 'at first.' What about after?"

"Well . . ." Eli kept glancing at Gideon to gauge the effect of his words. "After that, I saw he knew what he was doing. He was a good guide."

Gideon snorted. "He blind."

"I know. But still—"

Gideon shook his head as if dissatisfied and Eli felt unnerved; although he had only spoken the truth, he had failed. Yet what exactly did Gideon want to hear?

"I got to know more." The other boy spoke with muted exasperation. "Anything you know about Aras."

Eli felt even more desperate to comply. "Well—I mean— well, he has a dog."

"I *know* that," Gideon said, ice in his voice.

It was getting worse by the moment. "Then I don't know what you—"

"He like girls?"

"Oh. Well, yeah. Esther."

"Besides Esther!"

"Not that I saw."

Gideon leaned back. Eli noticed that he was working his right hand into a fist, then relaxing it. The boy stared directly into Eli's eyes. The flash of gray made Eli dizzy, as if he were falling.

Eli forced himself to look away.

He felt torn. It was true that when Aras partnered with Esther, he had hated the blind guide more than he had thought possible. Yet even at his darkest moments, Eli still retained a grudging respect for the boy who had gotten them where they wanted to go, often by risking his own life. Although Gideon now wanted him to reveal something negative about his rival, Eli couldn't bring himself to lie.

"I'm sorry," he said at last.

Gideon stared at him a second more; then, with an abrupt nod, he turned to go.

Eli followed him out, his heart pounding; never had he felt so helpless and full of regret. And then he remembered something.

The guide had had an odd habit on the trail to Mundreel. Over the years, Eli had seen other boys do it once or twice, but none as frequently as Aras. Eli sensed that in private, Esther had discouraged the practice; certainly, Aras stopped altogether once the two became close, and that had been months ago.

Revealing this now to Gideon would be a kind of betrayal . . . wouldn't it?

And yet it was true.

All of a sudden, Eli felt good.

"Wait." Gideon was already halfway down the hall, but at the word, he stopped. "There *is* something."

Gideon turned around. The intensity of his gaze gave Eli a strange feeling of excitement. *He, Eli, was the only person in Gideon's world right now.*

"What?"

Eli answered, nearly breathless.

"Aras," he said, "used to smoke something."

In the late afternoon, Aras sat alone in the open space of the basement food court. He and his dog had ended up there after yet another endless day spent roaming the halls of the District. Long polished tables and matching stools with swiveling seats were bolted to the tiled floor in orderly rows, providing a momentary oasis of quiet. He heard Pilot snuffle nearby, his chain clanking behind him.

Ever since Esther told him that she wished to remain in the District for the foreseeable future, Aras had attempted to take refuge in these long walks. There had never been much work for him in the garden, and he couldn't bear to be still, so he spent his days wandering the ten floors of the immense building, working his way downstairs, then back up again, then back down.

Even so, he felt as if he was going crazy.

Aras had never been one to ponder motives or emotional complexities. Even before the attack that had left him blind, he had lived his life based on instinct and action. Yet for the first time, he was being asked to deny those very impulses, the wordless, urgent voice inside him that told him again and again that he had to get out.

He was staying for Esther; he would have done so for no other. But as the days dragged by and she spent longer and longer hours away from him and their children, questions began to nag at him: *Why wouldn't she leave with him? What was taking so long?*

And worst of all: *Did her decision to stay have anything to do with Gideon?*

She and the Insurgent now spent long hours alone together, every day. When Aras and Esther had first met Gideon, neither of them liked or trusted him, yet she now spoke of him with admiration, even affection. Aras thought back to his recent visit to Gideon's room and wondered what the other boy looked like. Certainly, he had seemed as cold, unfriendly, and calculating as always. But he had also evinced a kind of toughness that might be considered attractive. He also possessed something Aras could never regain.

Aras could not help but think back on his first partner. Min had abandoned him soon after he lost his sight. Esther, of course, was different: She did not care about such things, and in addition, had never known him any other way. Moreover, Aras was comfortable in his own skin; he rarely felt self-conscious. Yet for the first time, he wondered how he might compare with Gideon if the two were lined up.

Then he shook his head.

Aras hated this kind of thinking; it made him feel not only

wretched, but weak. Yet he didn't know how to discuss his suspicions with Esther. He didn't have the words.

With any other girl, he would have left long ago and not looked back. Aras couldn't do that now; he loved Esther and Kai too much. They had a new baby as well, a daughter who would need special care and attention.

His right hand began twiddling at his side. His thumb ran over his second and third fingers, the way it did when he was nervous or worried.

He caught himself doing it and forced himself to stop.

It was as if Aras were rolling himself one of the special papers he had promised Esther he would never again smoke.

Then he sensed something.

Pilot had returned to his side, but he tensed and stood. His chain collar jangled as a low growl emanated from his chest, and Aras automatically reached for his lead.

"He gonna bite?"

The soft voice was unfamiliar: a female, perhaps in her mid-teens.

"No. It's okay, boy." Aras made a low clucking sound in his throat and with reluctance, the dog settled back down.

"You Aras?"

Aras hesitated. It was an innocent-enough question and the stranger appeared to be alone and harmless; still, experience had taught him to be wary of people he didn't know seeking information. "Why you want to know?"

"It okay," the girl said. "I seen you with Esther. I'm Nur."

He nodded, stiffly, even as he sensed the girl climbing

unbidden onto the stool opposite him.

"Don't come down here much," she remarked. "But it nice to get away."

"That so?"

A rustle of clothing indicated that she shrugged. "Sometimes it more lonely when you with others."

Aras exhaled. He was surprised to find that in the past few weeks, he had often felt the same way with Esther. Still, he wasn't about to share that with a stranger. "So I've heard."

"Your dog is pretty. Some say they better friends than people."

Aras agreed with this, too, but still said nothing. He was distracted by the flowery scent that arose from the girl's skin and hair. Although it was obviously fake and from a bottle, he decided he liked it; it had a sweet and delicate quality that went with her voice.

Despite himself, he found that he was opening up.

"The District can be—I don't know." He gesticulated with one hand, struggling to find the right words. "Too big. Worse than outside. Outside, you can always find your way. Here, you can just be . . . lost."

The guide sensed the girl shift in her seat. She must have leaned over the table that separated them, for he could now feel her breath tickle his face. The sensation was intimate, yet not unpleasant: far from it. "That how I feel."

Talking to Nur reminded Aras of the old days, when he still had his sight and used to guide people to their destinations. Often, he would grow close to one of them like this:

talking late at night, just the two of them, in soft voices. Then they would part. He would carry the private moments they had shared, yet never see them again. It became their secret.

He tried to shake off the feeling, but it was too late.

The girl's words were already acting on his mood. The District, which up until now had felt merely oppressive, suddenly seemed stifling, as if the giant glass-and-steel walls were literally closing in on him. He yearned to be outside again, alone on the road with Pilot.

Aras only became aware that he was once more rubbing his fingers together back and forth when Nur placed a hand on his, to stop him. The unexpected touch felt like fire crackling through his skin, and he jerked back.

She laughed. "Don't be nervous."

"Ain't nervous," he replied, self-conscious.

"If you are," she said, "I got something that help."

Aras wasn't sure if she was teasing or being serious. "What's that?"

"Don't think I can say."

Aras shrugged. "Sure you can. No one else here."

He felt the leash being tugged from his hand; she was pulling it gently. "Here," she said, "let him go. He ain't going nowhere."

Aras did what she suggested and let the lead drop. His hand was taken by Nur, who opened it and placed something within his palm. Even before his fingers closed over the crinkling square of paper and the small pile of dried leaves and seeds, he knew what it was.

"Go on," she said.

Aras was motionless. Then, as if in a dream, he took it in both hands and rolled the object with a few quick, expert motions. He tightened it by twisting and pinching both ends. Then he hesitated.

"Why don't you lick it?"

He did, sealing it. The act felt familiar yet forbidden, both good and bad. "I ain't got a firestarter," he whispered.

He felt an object pressing into his hand: slim and plastic, the size of his thumb. He was already fumbling with the tiny button, trying to get it lit, when she took it from him with soft hands.

"You join me?"

Aras didn't let himself dwell on the right or wrong. All he knew was that smoking had always helped him whenever he was worried or upset. He remembered the feeling of peace and detachment that the drug used to bring and realized now that he wanted it. In fact, he couldn't remember anything he had wanted this badly in a long, long time.

And, he reasoned to himself, *it would just be this once.*

"I won't say no," he answered.

Days later, Esther was up late, waiting for Aras.

After over an hour of cajoling, singing, and stroking Kai's back, she had finally coaxed him to sleep. Yet as soon as he was down, the baby awoke and started to fuss. After feeding her, Esther began to drift off herself. Then Kai woke up once more.

"Please," she begged him, to no avail. The boy was marching

around the room, imitating soldiers in a book that Joseph had showed him.

As she had for many nights now, Michal—with her patient, childlike nature and understanding of little ones—had come to the rescue. Scooping him up in her arms and whispering a story in his ear, she had paced the room with him until Kai finally fell asleep, this time for good. She settled him in his bed and pulled the covers up before turning to go.

"You'll be back tomorrow?" Esther had asked helplessly, and Michal nodded. Esther felt guilty about how much she depended on the other girl and wished there were something she could do to repay the favor. Yet unspoken between the girls was the understanding that Michal would be there every night, to help out while Aras was missing.

He was not really gone, of course. Yet for days now, Aras had been coming home so late that he was practically useless as a parent. Invariably, he was hazy and reeked of the bad-smelling papers he used to smoke on the road, on their way to Mundreel. Esther found it impossible to talk to him at such moments. He would ignore her, flopping down on a chair or on the ground itself. Within moments, he would be sound asleep.

And he was in this condition once again when he stumbled through the door.

"Evening," he said. Pilot followed him, a little tangled in his lead.

"Keep your voice down." Esther didn't mean to speak sharply, but she noticed that both children stirred at the noise.

"Sorry."

On the road, Esther had made it clear to Aras how she felt about his smoking. She hated how the drug changed him into a different person, one who was foolish and apathetic at the same time. Now, with two little children to take care of, his smoking seemed worse than before, much worse. As he made his way to a chair, Esther smelled something else on him. She thought she caught a whiff of flowers: the bottled scent that some of the Insurgent girls used. Was that possible?

"I think you should know," she faltered, "that I don't like this."

"Like what?"

"What you're doing."

"Better not think about it, then." Aras slumped in his seat and turned away, his face in his hands.

"I'm talking to you."

"Didn't think you was talking to Pilot."

Esther bit her lip. He had not spoken to her like this since the very beginning, before they had grown to know and care for each other. But she refused to back down.

"Where do you go? How come you're never here?"

At this, Aras let out a loud and incredulous laugh. "Me? Where do I go?" He raised his voice, not caring that Esther was trying to shush him. "Where do *you* go? Where are you all day?"

His shouts awakened Sarah. In a second, she started to fuss, then whimper, then scream. Moments later, Kai awoke and he, too, began to bellow.

Esther put a hand to her forehead. She was honestly perplexed; it hadn't occurred to her that Aras might be angry. Yet what he was saying was true: With a sudden pang of guilt, she realized she had forgotten all about his plan for them to move.

It was true that figuring out the glass system that would feed so many new people was taking far longer than she had thought. Yet what made Esther feel guilty wasn't so much the work she was doing: It was her sudden realization that she enjoyed it. She found herself thinking about the problems she faced even late at night; they were the first things she thought of in the morning, as well. She didn't want to go . . . at least not yet.

All of this flashed through her mind as Aras stood up and loomed above her, shouting over the screams of their children. *"How come you spend so much time with that boy?"*

"Gideon? We're working together. You know that—"

"Is that all? How come you spend all day alone with him?"

Esther was stunned by what Aras was implying. "I . . . I don't know what you're saying," she stammered, flustered.

"Don't you?"

Esther was so appalled, she couldn't speak at first. "There's nothing between us. . . . How can you say that? He's like a brother. . . ."

But Aras was sneering at her now, with his eyebrows raised. "Maybe I ask his guards what you do all day. Bet they know a whole lot."

Esther felt as if she had been slapped across the face. "If you don't trust me," she shot back at last, "why don't you just leave?"

"Maybe I will!"

The children's voices were like a hammer to Esther's head. Still, she was shocked to see Aras actually turn toward the door, pulling Pilot with him.

"Aras—" she said. "I didn't mean that. Look, don't . . ."

But he didn't respond or even turn her way. Instead, he headed for the door, the dog following with what seemed deep reluctance. Esther grabbed his arm as he passed, but Aras yanked away.

After the door slammed, Esther stood alone in the room, trembling, amid the din of the children's cries. She was tempted to run after the boy; it was late, and he was in no condition to wander around by himself. Still, she was exhausted and sick of fighting, and she needed to get Kai and Sarah back to sleep.

Esther reached down into the crib and picked up the baby. Bouncing Sarah on her shoulder, she soothed her until her wails subsided. Then she sat down next to Kai and stroked him with a gentle, tickling touch, something he loved.

Within minutes, a blissful silence once more fell over the room.

In the darkness, Esther got into bed alone, but could not sleep. Tossing and turning, she stared at the ceiling, trying to remember something crucial she could not pin down. Only when the night sky began to brighten did she finally realize what it was.

Aras's partnering tie had been missing from his wrist.

The following afternoon, Aras stood in the doorway of the room he shared with Esther. In stark contrast to the night before, his home was now deserted and silent.

Although he was not expecting anyone to be home, Aras still felt odd that Esther wasn't still there, waiting for him. He couldn't blame her. After their fight, he had stormed downstairs and out into the nighttime streets of Mundreel. At the time, he was so angry he had sworn he was leaving for good.

But hours later, Aras found himself waking up in an unfamiliar storefront that he didn't even remember entering. It was already late morning: Hot sun poured in through a broken window as Pilot licked his face and whimpered. The boy needed several moments to piece together what had happened the night before, and when he remembered his angry words, he winced, wishing he could take them back.

With Pilot leading, Aras had no trouble making it home to the District. As always, the dog knew where to go and in fact seemed eager to return home. The boy was happy to let him lead; his head was pounding and his throat was so dry, it hurt.

Now, as he stood in their room, Pilot lapping noisily from his bowl in the corner, Aras realized that he couldn't continue like this. He had to stop smoking again, and this time, for good. His children depended on him too much. And although he always found it difficult to express himself, Aras also knew he needed to get past that. He had to be frank with Esther; he had to talk to her.

They were partners, after all.

That was when Aras realized that his partnering tie was missing. He checked his wrist and the length of his arm quickly and then slowly and methodically. Although he had little memory of the evening before, he couldn't believe that the tightly knotted band could have fallen from his wrist without his notice. Yet there was no mistake: The frayed cloth band had somehow vanished.

Full of shame, Aras shook his head; it was yet another sign he had let things go too far. *He would make it up to Esther,* he thought. He knew she was working; he would have to wait to speak with her until that evening.

On an impulse, he crossed to the box where they stored their clothes. He sorted through the contents by touch, finally identifying the thing he was looking for. It was the shirt Esther had given him months ago, her first gift after they had partnered: soft, with buttons that went halfway down the front. As Aras exchanged it for what he was wearing, he smiled. He remembered that she had told him he looked handsome in it and that the vivid blue looked good against his dark skin.

Putting it on wasn't much, he knew: It was just a gesture, a simple way of saying he was sorry. Aras meant to do more to make things up to Esther: a lot more. He was putting the box away when he felt Pilot get to his feet behind him.

Turning around, Aras didn't understand why the dog didn't growl, nor why he felt a flicker of dread. Then he realized what had caused it.

He could smell the scent of fake flowers.

Nur had never been this far upstairs before.

She was taking a risk, for she knew it was critical that no one discover her connection to Aras. Yet the blind boy hadn't shown up to meet her that morning in their usual smoking place. When she'd told Gideon, he had grown angry. *It was taking too long*, he said; it was time to deal with the problem another way. She had begged him to be patient. After all, several times she and Aras had touched and even almost kissed. But on each occasion, the boy had pulled away.

All she needed, she promised Gideon, was one more chance. Then Aras would leave Esther for good.

Nur wasn't speaking out of pride alone. The idea of seducing the blind one had been hers, the easiest way she could think of to destroy Esther and ensure Gideon's lasting gratitude. Yet now she was surprised to find that she had developed a kind of affection for Aras. Then again, it would have been impossible for her not to like the boy at least a little, having spent so much time with him smoking, talking, and opening up. She wasn't exactly sure what Gideon had in mind for him were she to fail, but she sensed it wouldn't be pleasant. For Aras's welfare, then, Nur thought it was worth making a final attempt.

What's more, Nur had a flicker of curiosity to see how he and Esther, the leader of the District, lived.

Yet now she was here, she was disappointed to see how unimpressive the room was: just another drab office with bedding on the floor and various belongings stacked neatly by the window. On the far side, Aras stood with his back to her, as if deep in thought; he didn't seem to realize she was there. Then, with surprising speed, he turned and strode toward her.

"What are you doing here?"

After a pause, Nur answered, trying to sound light and carefree.

"You didn't come. I wonder where you are." She paused again. "You okay?"

"I'm fine."

"Because I hate if you . . . mad at me."

"Never said I was."

Now she was by his side. "I save some," she whispered, "for you." She tried to force a smoking paper into his hand.

Aras pulled away and shook his head. "Let's forget it," he said. "I been doing too much of it, anyway."

He stepped forward, as if to escort her out. Thinking quickly, Nur touched his forearm to stop him. She had to stand on her tiptoes, for he was so tall. Balancing herself against him, she reached up and kissed his cheek.

Aras started, yet didn't move. "Better not," he said in a rough voice. "I told you that before."

"But why?" Her voice was as soft and pleading as she knew how to make it; she had never known a boy to turn away. "You know I like you. Don't you like me?"

She took a chance. Taking him by the shoulders, the girl

leaned forward again and, straining to reach, tried to kiss him on the mouth. She got no help from Aras, who turned his head, his arms by his side.

"I said don't do that!"

A flare of anger spread through Nur.

She was not accustomed to being rejected or to being addressed with such hostility; such a thing had never happened to her before. It suddenly dawned on her that Aras was attempting to end the situation—not just the smoking, but their friendship as well.

That possibility hadn't crossed her mind.

Her cheeks now flushed with humiliation, Nur drew herself up with as much dignity as she could muster. *Not,* she thought with unexpected viciousness, *that Aras could have even seen what she was doing.*

Without another word, she turned and fled down the hall.

He had his chance, Nur thought. Yet she was surprised to find tears stinging her eyes and splattering down onto her robes as she yanked open the heavy metal door. With a brusque gesture, she rubbed them away.

She had done what she could. Now it was no fault of hers what would happen.

Nur wasn't surprised to find someone waiting for her in the darkness of the stairwell, his upturned face a question in the spill of light. Gideon had obviously sent backup to deal with Aras, in case her efforts failed . . . which they had.

"He all yours." Nur nearly spat out the words. "I done with him."

Then she turned and clattered down the stairs.

* * *

As Eli stepped out into the hall, he left the door propped open. A tremor shook his body, beginning with his hands and passing through his torso.

He hadn't realized how nervous he would be. Although he knew Esther and the others were upstairs on the roof, he felt much too visible, exposed by the bright afternoon sun. To counter his anxiety, he forced himself to recall how much he despised Aras: for his superiority and arrogance, and most of all for stealing Esther away. But no matter how hard he tried to stoke his righteous anger, his hatred wavered and then faded altogether.

He found it much easier to think about Gideon and how badly the boy wanted this.

The Insurgent leader had promised much to Eli for this favor. He would guarantee him not only extra rations, but something even more precious: his gratitude and lasting respect. Gideon had made it clear that if Eli was successful in carrying out this task, he would be in his debt: an unbelievable prospect that still made Eli giddy with happiness.

Now everything seemed to be heading inexorably to this end. Eli didn't think he could stop it if he tried.

As Eli moved down the hall, checking each door, his footsteps were muffled by the deep beige carpeting underfoot. Still, a jangling sound revealed that someone had heard him.

Pilot stood motionless by an open door at the end of the hall, his ears cocked.

"Who's there?"

As Aras appeared behind his dog, Eli froze in place. For a guilty instant, an impossible thought flashed across his mind: The blind boy could see him. Then he shook off the feeling as he began to move down the hall, his sweaty hand gripping the handle of the metal stick with the heavy wooden club. To his relief, the dog seemed to have recognized him, as Gideon assured him he would; although he continued to watch him, he made no threatening move.

Gideon told him the chore would be easiest if he worked quickly, without thinking. So as he stepped toward his target, Eli swung the weapon once, as hard as he could. At the last second, however, he couldn't help but flinch, and the blow, aimed at Aras's temple, hit his forehead instead. Still the single crack of wood hitting bone was shockingly loud, and Aras staggered backward before slumping to the ground.

It was done. Eli put a hand to his mouth and reeled backward.

He too felt as if he was going to black out; he was lightheaded and his heart pounded madly. Then he noticed Pilot, and his adrenaline spiked even higher, snapping him back to alertness. The dog had lowered to his haunches, growling, his fur rising in spikes along his back. Then he sprang with unbelievable speed.

Terrified, Eli lashed out blindly with his club, raining blows on the animal in an attempt to ward him off. He felt rather than heard the repeated thuds as he made contact again and again with ribs, bone, teeth. Finally, he knocked the dog to the ground with a final blow, where he lay whimpering, his chest heaving up and down.

There was no time to lose.

Eli dropped the club. Then he bent over and blotted up the single drop of red that had trickled from Aras's bleeding face to the floor. Grunting, soaked with sweat, he grabbed the body by the ankles and began to drag it down the hall and around one and then a second corner.

In the middle of the third section of corridor were the twin sets of metal doors: "the elevators," Joseph called them. Although there were no handles, Eli knew what to do. As instructed, he pulled a metal tool from his back pocket, inserted the sharp, flat edge into the seam, and used it to pry open the panels an inch or so, enough to get his fingers in. Then he managed to pull back one door. He didn't look down; a great black hole loomed below.

Eli yanked Aras's leaden body as close as he could, turning him so his back pointed toward the opening. As a result, he found himself inches away from the dead boy's face. Aras's dark glasses had tumbled off and for the first time, Eli saw the pale, raised scars across his eyelids and the bridge of his nose. The markings stood out on the dark skin, making him seem vulnerable and oddly young. Blanching, Eli had turned away and was about to push him in when a sudden spasm shook his hands.

To Eli's horror, Aras was struggling to sit up. *Was he alive? How was that possible?*

With a cry of terror, Eli fought back.

He wrestled Aras with one hand as he frantically felt around behind him for a weapon, any weapon. *He had left his club back in the hall,* he realized too late as the other boy clawed at him with desperate strength, the two of them teetering on the brink of the abyss.

With relief that was nearly hysterical, Eli felt his fingers close on the small metal lever he had used to pry open the door. At that instant, Aras's hand landed on his face. But his touch was soft as his fingers scrabbled across Eli's features, reading them with swift assurance.

Then the blind boy gasped.

"Eli?"

Eli went numb with shock. To erase the moment, he brought the weapon from behind him and cracked Aras across the head as hard as he could. The boy slumped, but his hand fell to Eli's arm and stayed there, twitching.

Shrieking, Eli kicked at Aras's ribs to free himself. As he scrambled to his feet, he rained more blows on him, knocking the boy backward into the dark.

Eli stood, quivering, at the brink of the shaft. For what seemed like forever, the only sound was his harsh and ragged breath. Then, dimly, he heard a faraway explosion that seemed to shake the entire building. After a second to collect himself, he tossed in the metal bar as well.

Eli wiped his soaked face with the back of his hand, staring at his shredded shirt. He knew he wasn't finished, not quite yet. He had to get rid of the club and make certain there were no signs of the struggle. Last but not least, he also had to dispose of the dog's body. Yet when he returned to the place he had left it, his mind froze.

Pilot was gone.

Panicked, Eli glanced around. No one had returned; the hall was as silent as it had been before. Working quickly, he smoothed away the tracks he had left when dragging Aras's body, disposed of the club, and closed the elevator panels. Then he saw it: a telltale trail made of darkening flecks of blood, almost too tiny to see, that led in a crooked path down the hall and through the open door to the stairway.

Eli hesitated for a moment. Then he shook his head. *It was only a dog, after all.* And the worst part was over. His job was done.

He was about to leave when he noticed something odd about his hands. Frowning, he held them close to his eyes. They were stained a dark brown, the color of rust. Although he rubbed at them for a moment, he couldn't seem to remove the marks.

He realized what it was, of course: blood. Aras's blood. For a moment, Eli stood stock-still, trying to fight down the hysteria that was rising from deep within.

Then he took a deep and shaky breath. He would be fine. He would wash off the marks and no one would ever know what had happened.

And Gideon would be so pleased to hear the news.

Eli headed to the stairs. The last thing he did was pull away the stick he had left to prop open the metal door. It swung shut and the hallway was once again silent.

FIVE

THE SMELL OF SCORCHING FOOD FILLED THE AIR.

"Watch it," said Silas. Reaching across Esther with a fork, he speared a piece of flatbread that was in danger of catching on fire and shot her a concerned look. "You okay?"

"Yeah," Esther mumbled. "Sorry."

Bleary, she squinted her eyes hard and shook her head in an attempt to wake herself up. She was helping prepare breakfast but had been close to nodding off several times as she knelt over the firebowl. Picking up the basket of sorry-looking bread she had just cooked, Esther tried to stand but stumbled, dropping the entire contents onto the ground.

Skar was already at her side. "Why don't you sit?" she murmured as she stooped to pick up the blackened food. "I can take over."

Numb, Esther could only nod as her friend slipped into her place. As Esther crossed the roof where she and the others prepared and took all their meals, she could sense a few of them looking up from their plates and glancing at her with sympathy.

She looked awful, she knew; her eyes were bloodshot and deeply ringed, and her skin was ashy. It was no surprise; Esther had barely slept in days. The fighting with Aras had kept her from closing her eyes for more than a few moments at a time. But last evening had been the worst.

For the second night in a row, Aras hadn't come home at all.

After Esther fed and put Kai and Sarah to bed, she had waited. She stayed up for hours, her bare feet silent as she paced back and forth across the carpeted floor, her ears keyed in vain to the familiar jingle of Pilot's chain in the hallway. Then she sat on the floor with her back pressed against the cold wall. Other than the soft sounds of her children sleeping across the room, no noise arose from the cavernous mall below. She had watched the moon travel across the night sky through the huge windows until it disappeared. The dark expanse grew light with dawn, and still Aras had not returned.

Now Esther fussed over the baby, trying not to meet anyone's gaze. She knew the others were aware of Aras's absence. Joseph, for one, was openly staring at her with a look of consternation. But the last thing she wanted was anyone's sympathy.

What she needed most of all was to see her partner again. As concerned as she was for their relationship, she was also sick with worry. Aras was adept at navigating the world without sight, but she knew anything could happen, especially if he was smoking again.

Once Esther made certain that Kai had finished his bread and fruit and that Sarah had drunk her fill, she got to her feet. After asking Michal if she would watch over the children, Esther slipped downstairs.

As she feared, the long, dim hallway was empty. The sunlight pouring in at the windows on either end revealed only the beige carpeting, embedded with the faint impressions of countless footprints. Esther and Aras's room was empty, too.

Although there was much work to do on the roof, she had no other choice: She had to search for him. Her children were safe for now, although the thought of Michal's constant generosity again gave her a pang. Esther headed for the staircase and began the long and arduous process of checking the entire building.

She went down to the levels directly below their living quarters, places she and the others had barely visited: long, dim hallways identical to their own, lined with anonymous doors made of the same blond wood. Many of them were still locked. The few rooms that she could enter seemed to be preserved in time, their dusty desks and chairs frozen in place and their surfaces orderly with wire baskets still filled with yellowing paper, containers full of pens and pencils, framed photographs, and strange machines and contraptions whose purpose she could not begin to guess. Even the air seemed from another era. It was clear no one had been inside for many months, perhaps years.

By the time she made it down to the top floor of the mall, she saw it was already bustling with activity. The glass system had just started two days before. Even though the remains of shops still carried some clothing, food, and mysterious items of entertainment and recreation, the majority of goods had now been moved out and placed on tables in the main hall. Beside them was food from the garden, vegetables and fruit in baskets and boxes. As she and Gideon had planned, everything had been made to look as appealing as possible, to attract buyers with pieces of glass.

More than a few workers stopped to greet her; some whispered as she passed by, their expressions shy and grateful. She saw that there were many unfamiliar faces at work: sweeping the floor, repairing a broken window, tending the generator. Clearly, these were Outsiders, now toiling for glass. Gideon had suggested this arrangement, and it seemed to be working; everyone appeared happy and busy, and the place gleamed. Still, that was not what mattered to Esther; at the moment, she had only one thing on her mind.

She gave her well-wishers an automatic smile and kept going.

But it was no use. A thorough search of the basement level, including even the foul garage, revealed what she had already feared: Aras was nowhere.

She stood alone and uncertain what to do next. What if Aras was not hurt or lost but staying away on purpose? *If she had any pride,* she thought, *then she should go upstairs and act as if nothing were out of the ordinary. Aras was bound to return at some point. If he was attempting to punish her, she would not give him the satisfaction of seeing how worried he had made her, how miserable.*

That was something she would have done if she were younger. But Esther understood from bitter experience that pride was not only childish but foolish. It meant you assumed the other person would always be there no matter what, a belief that was foolhardy even in safe and prosperous times. Life was too uncertain to ever take anyone for granted or to harbor anger against someone you loved. And as she thought this, she realized she still had one place left to look.

The house. Their house.

Esther slipped out of a side door and took off. Although Aras had led her and the children the one time they had gone, she still had a good sense of direction and knew which way to head. Esther was surprised by how good it felt to run: It was mindless yet exhilarating, as if she were fleeing her troubles. She put on speed and covered the distance so quickly, she nearly overshot the street she sought. Only at the last moment did she recognize the abandoned lot on the corner, and she skidded to a stop.

Breathless, Esther approached the small building, her heart pounding. She forced herself to be calm and not to get her hopes up as she took hold of the doorknob. Then she stood inside the front entrance. It looked untouched since the last time they had been there, but she still strained her ears to hear if anyone was at home.

"Hello?"

The silence was stark; even the mice or birds had stopped their activity inside the walls and chimney. Without hesitation, Esther ran through the house, quickly checking each room. The idea that Aras was waiting for her up on the roof grew stronger until it became a kind of magical belief. Her heart pounding, Esther flew up the final small staircase and paused before pushing open the heavy glass door.

He wasn't there.

As Esther stood staring out at the empty expanse, disappointment and exhaustion hit her like a physical blow. Then she heard something downstairs: the banging of a door.

"Aras?"

Esther was already at the door, cocking her head to hear better. *Yes,* she realized with a jolt of hope, *someone was definitely downstairs.* "Aras!" She bounded down the steps two at a time, racing down the hall and rounding the corner, and thundering down the final stairs. Her relief was so enormous, she could not keep a huge smile from her face.

And then she stopped.

A stranger was standing in the front hallway, wrapped in sheets worn as protection against the sun. When it pushed down the hood from its face, Esther saw with a sense of crushing disappointment that it was no one she knew: only a girl about her age, pretty, with thick, wavy dark hair and big eyes.

"Esther," she said.

The visitor was clearly from the mall; there was no other way she would know Esther's name. But how had she managed to find her way there? As if reading her thoughts, the girl spoke.

"I'm Nur. I saw you go and I followed." She smiled. "I got a bike, and you still go faster."

It was true; Nur's cheeks were bright pink and she was out of breath. Yet despite the stranger's friendly words, Esther was on guard. Now she vaguely remembered having seen her before: She was one of Gideon's Insurgents. "What do you want?"

Nur's expression turned serious. "I got to talk with you. Away from the others. It personal." She hesitated. "It about your partner."

Esther froze. Nur crossed to the stairs and sat on the lowest one. She glanced down as she pulled the robes out from under her feet. She didn't seem to want to look Esther in the eye. "He friend with my friend."

"Who's your friend? What's his name?"

Nur shot her a look. "*Her* name." She busied herself again with her sheets as Esther took in the meaning of her words. "Ruth."

A girl.

"Where is he?" she finally asked.

"That what I try to say." Clasping her hands in her lap as if for courage, Nur stared straight up at Esther for the first time. "They both gone. Together."

Esther blinked; the words made no sense. "Gone?" she said stupidly. "What do you mean?"

"Gone." Nur lifted her hands in the air. "Last night they go. I don't know where. But it for good. My friend told me."

"Your friend . . ."

"I tried to stop her," Nur added. And she seemed genuinely sorry; her face was flushed and her eyes bright. "Ain't right to steal someone's partner. But she don't care. She say they in love."

Esther swallowed; when she tried to respond, her throat was so dry it was nearly impossible to choke out the words. "I don't believe it." But as she spoke, she saw something out of the corner of her eye, a spot of color. She whirled around and realized what it was: a ragged bit of cloth lying as if tossed in the corner of the front hallway. Even as she crossed to pick it up, she knew what it was, and at once, Esther gave a low cry.

It was Aras's partnering tie.

Esther reached out and her fingers closed on the familiar strip of cloth, the twin of what she wore on her own wrist. As she pulled it free and crushed it against her face, she could hear nothing else but the sound of her heart, hammering within her chest, and all she could feel was anguish.

"How long was it going on?"

Nur shrugged as if to say, *What did it matter?* "Long enough."

Esther could only nod, her face expressionless.

Another girl . . . That would explain the late nights, the long silences. The fights. The smoke and perfume. With a fresh shock, she recalled their last encounter, their angry words. *She had dared him to leave. And now he was gone.*

She thought of Kai and little Sarah . . . and for the first time,

Esther experienced a flare of rage. Aras had abandoned not only her, but two innocents who needed his love and care. And all for someone else.

Nur had risen and was standing in front of her, her face full of pity and another expression Esther couldn't name. "You all right?" she asked, placing a hand on Esther's arm. Esther shook it off.

"Why did you tell me this?" Despite her efforts, Esther's voice broke.

"Because. You our leader. And you got to know."

There was nothing left to say. Nur pulled her hood back up over her face and slipped out the door.

Esther was left standing in the shell of what was to have been her home, a refuge she had avoided accepting. How much of this was her fault? She felt something new, a dizzying sense of guilt.

She waited until the clanking of Nur's bicycle faded away.

And then Esther broke down and cried.

Gideon was alone in his locked office, tallying up his glass pieces. He trusted no one else to count them, not even Eli.

Every day, several of Gideon's Insurgents brought in the pebbles, heaped in cardboard crates, and dumped them on the tiled floor. Thanks to the system of calculation he had asked Joseph to teach him, Gideon now knew exactly how much he was paying out and how much he was taking in.

He paused now to admire the quantity of fragments. They were piled in glistening heaps, catching the light that streamed through a translucent window and casting a greenish glow on the white tiled floor. It wasn't their beauty he was contemplating; the glass was essentially a pile of trash. What was remarkable was that he alone had given value to something so worthless. It had started as nothing more than a hunch. But the system was already starting to flourish.

It turned out that these glittering pieces of green could make others work for you and get you what you wanted. In short, the pebbles could give you power.

Gideon had seen the way Esther convinced the others to embrace the new system. Instead of calling a large meeting, as he would have done, she had gone person by person, talking to people both inside the District and out. Esther used simple words and short sentences. She also allowed the others to ask questions, which she answered with patience. By doing so, she had managed to win over even the most stupid and fearful. It had taken her more than a week, but by the end, everyone accepted the new way without question.

It was clear that people responded to Esther as they never would to him. If anyone could persuade even more to come around to his way of thinking, it was she. With her influence, he would soon be in the position he wanted.

And now that Aras was gone, so was his final obstacle.

There was a knock at the door.

"Who?" Expectant, he set aside his notebook and flexed his fingers, his hand cramped from clutching the pencil. There was silence and then a girl spoke.

"It's me." At the sound of Esther's voice, Gideon smiled.

Gideon had watched Esther experience what it was like to live without a partner. In secret, he had observed her as she worked in the garden and around the mall. At first, she behaved as if nothing had happened—displaying more stubbornness and grit than he would have predicted.

It was, in its own way, admirable.

Still, the new reality had begun to take its toll on her, as Gideon knew it might. He could see it in the sadness that tugged at her face, the way she struggled to police her son, Kai, the air of distraction she had when he worked with her late into the night. The day before, one of his guards had reported that Esther had faltered while toiling on the roof, even breaking down in tears.

He found her vulnerability exciting, and a new idea came to him.

He had called her and she had come. As Gideon glanced in the mirror, he ran his fingers through his hair. Satisfied with how he looked, he collected his thoughts. Then he crossed the room and unlocked the door.

As Gideon let her in and closed the door behind her, Esther wondered why he had asked her there. She shot him a questioning look.

"I hear you been sick," he said.

Puzzled, the girl shook her head. "No. A little tired, maybe. But I'm fine. In fact, I . . ."

"I know what happen." Gideon spoke in a meaningful way. Then he added in a softer voice, "I mean about Aras."

At the mention of her partner's name, Esther flinched. Then

she felt her cheeks burn hot.

For many days, Esther had not spoken with anyone, not even Skar, about what had happened. Although her friends had certainly noticed the boy's disappearance, they were too discreet to bring it up, and, stubborn as always, Esther clung to the belief that he would return. She forced herself not to think of the girl he had left her for; she knew no details and wondering what she was like only tormented her. Yet even if Aras's new lover was more feminine and beautiful than she, Esther was convinced that Aras still loved her and the children.

Surely he would come back.

In the meanwhile, she had thrown herself into work, getting up early to head to the garden and staying there until well past sunset. During the evening, she busied herself with Kai and Sarah. Esther had declined any help from Michal; as much as she loved Skar's partner, she couldn't bear her pitying glance. What's more, the children took so much energy to mind, they proved a welcome and exhausting distraction.

Only late at night, after the children were long asleep, did Esther perform what had become a secret nightly ritual. Days after Aras's disappearance, she remembered a dusty box of white candles she had stashed at the bottom of a closet. Although cracked and dry, they still burned well, and each night, she lit one and set it in the window.

The solitary flame was a signal to Aras, wherever he was, that he was welcome back.

Yet as the days turned into weeks and her supply of candles began to dwindle, Esther finally had to admit the truth that she had been fighting all along:

Aras was never coming home.

Ashamed, she now stood in Gideon's office and pretended to examine the ceiling. She hoped that the tears that had sprung to her eyes wouldn't spill down her cheeks; she hated for anyone to witness her misery, most of all Gideon. To her relief, the boy turned away, as if he hadn't noticed.

"What he done ain't right," he remarked. "Smoking that stuff, running off with that girl. That bad. We all think that."

At first, Esther recoiled. Then she exhaled; it was inevitable that rumors would have spread by now. "Yeah." She swallowed hard, relieved that her voice didn't shake too much. "Thank you."

"It okay." Gideon turned and spat on the floor. "But that kind of trash ain't worth it. You deserve better."

Humiliated, Esther gave a frozen nod. She supposed, as usual, Gideon was trying to be nice; still, she wanted nothing more than to get away from him as quickly as possible. Although well-intentioned, he was only making things worse: His sympathy and kindness ground into her heart like broken glass.

She turned blindly to the door, but Gideon followed.

"Dwelling on it ain't gonna get things done," he said. "People need you. You got to move on. Question is, how?"

Esther had been fumbling in vain with the lock. Now with a sigh, she turned and faced him.

"I don't know. What do you think?"

Gideon shrugged. He was standing so close, he loomed

over her. "I think you need a new partner."

Esther shook her head. "I'm not looking for one."

Then the boy did something peculiar. He sank to his knees so that their faces were nearly at the same level.

Had he fallen sick? Alarmed and perplexed, Esther glanced around for help, but his guards were nowhere to be seen. Then Gideon did something even more bewildering.

He took her right hand in both of his.

Esther found herself staring down at the sight. Despite his height, his pale hands were small and square, with broken fingernails and a faint scar that ran across one knuckle. She felt as if her mind were not quite working; nothing seemed to make any sense.

"Are you . . ." She could barely form the words. "Are you asking me to be your partner?"

"Things here working good," Gideon said. "The new system. The glass. But ain't one person who can run it himself. Herself."

Esther was aware that a smile of disbelief was flickering across her face. Realizing that it probably seemed rude, she tried to control it. When she finally spoke, it was in a grave voice. She felt as if she was explaining something to Kai.

"But I don't love you."

Gideon shook his head, as if impatient. "Ain't important. Besides, there ain't much time. Got too much work to do." He glanced at the floor as if examining the tiles. "And who knows? Maybe something happen between us."

As Esther took in his words, she found she was appalled by such cold practicality.

To her, a partnership meant nothing without love, deep friendship, and shared desire.

Caleb had been the first boy she had ever cared for, and she had adored him with all of the fire and passion of youth. Her feelings for Aras were as deep, yet they were the seasoned emotions of someone older: Their bond had grown out of the many hardships and triumphs they had faced together on the road. Both boys had been a part of her, and she of them: They had been her friends, helpers, and lovers.

Yet what had love brought her?

When Caleb was killed, Esther felt as if her heart had been torn from her chest; the pain had nearly destroyed her. Now Aras had left her as well, but of his own accord. He had cheated on her with another girl and abandoned their family for good.

Maybe, Esther realized with a sudden wave of sadness, *she was done with love. For it had only brought her heartache and despair.*

Was it such a bad idea after all to treat partnering as a sensible decision of shared labor? After all, both she and Gideon were well into middle age: Esther was already several months past sixteen. There was so much work to be done and so few years in which to do it. Perhaps her days of passion were behind her.

Gideon was watching her closely, as if reading her thoughts. "And," he said, "we got responsibilities. To others."

Esther could only nod. "We do."

"Think of all the people here." He paused, as if for effect. "And your child."

"My *children*."

Esther spoke the word deliberately, all the while watching Gideon: His response would mean everything in the world. "I have a daughter. She didn't die like I said. Sarah's alive. And she . . . she's a variant." She swallowed hard. "I know most people would tell me to give her up. But I won't."

If the boy had any reaction to her news, he didn't show it. Instead, he nodded in a sympathetic way.

"That good," he remarked. "Mother got to take care of her baby. Even if it a"—he hesitated for an instant as if stumbling over the word—"a variant. I take care of her, too. Same as her brother."

At that, Esther exhaled.

She could not deny that this was the strongest argument he had made so far. Esther knew she couldn't continue working all day and trying to tend her children in her spare time. It wasn't fair.

Kai and Sarah deserved better. And they needed a father.

So when Gideon pulled her into his arms, Esther allowed it to happen. She felt as if she were watching it from across the room; the boy was awkward and not quite sure what to do, and she was utterly passive. When he took her face in his hands, she was reminded of the way she would hold Kai when attempting to wash his neck. Then he cupped the back of her head and drew her close.

He pressed his lips against hers as if in a question. His kiss was hard and dry, and the breath from his nose made the ends of her hair flutter. Esther kept her eyes open and felt nothing inside: no affection or stirring of desire.

Yet neither did she feel disgust.

It was something Esther had never experienced before. By not moving, by not pulling back or pushing Gideon away, she understood she was making a decision, perhaps one of the biggest in her life. She would normally have despised such inaction. Yet she was so sick at heart, so tired of emotions, that she no longer cared.

Gideon released her. He cleared his throat.

"Then it settled. We be partners."

"Partners," Esther repeated.

The word had taken on a whole new meaning.

SIX

ESTHER OPENED THE FIRST BOX.

Inside lay a stunning necklace made of silver metal and clear blue stones. When she held it up, colorful little beams danced across the wall and ceiling. In the large central room on the top floor, the dozens who surrounded her exclaimed with admiration.

"You like it?" An Insurgent girl named Naomi leaned forward with an eager smile.

"Yes. Thank you." Esther began to set the object back into its container, but Naomi took it from her and draped it around her throat. Esther had to sit still while it was fastened in place.

Then the ones closest to her clustered around, murmuring their envy and approval. One even thrust a mirror close, so that she could see and admire herself.

The trinket was indeed beautiful, Esther had to admit. Yet she felt awkward, not only because of the lavishness of the present, but because of the very public way in which it was presented.

Partnering was usually a simple and private affair. A boy and a girl, or two people of the same sex, made a personal vow to love and take care of each other, using a strip of cloth to bind their hands together. The partnering fabric would then be torn in two and worn by both partners at the wrist from that day onward. The idea that partnering might entail onlookers, finery, or any sort of celebration struck Esther as unnatural and deeply embarrassing.

When Esther had agreed to become partners with Gideon, she'd assumed they would perform the basic ritual right away or perhaps later that evening. Yet from the beginning, the boy had had different ideas.

Gideon wanted a more elaborate ceremony, one that would be held in public, in front of everyone who lived in the District. Joseph had looked through his books and magazines and found out that such things were indeed once common. What's more, people used to hold smaller ceremonies that led up to the main event. In one, guests were expected to present lavish gifts—clothing, jewelry, and other adornments—to the girl.

A shower, it was called.

At first, Esther had refused. In such harsh times, she shrank from the idea of special treatment or useless gifts. Furthermore, she didn't really care for such things. She had always worn the same things every day: a T-shirt or hoodie, jeans, tattered sneakers. Her only ornament was a braided leather necklace that Skar had given her back in Prin.

But Gideon had proven to be stubborn. "You the leader," he said again and again. "You special. People should treat you special. They want to."

In the end, Esther had decided to trust him, though, in truth, she simply didn't care enough to keep arguing. Gideon had promised to take care of everything. And so now she found herself surrounded by piles of presents that contained far more finery than she had ever owned in her life: necklaces, earrings, sweaters made of a creamy material, wristwatches, colorful gloves that felt softer than Sarah's skin.

As she opened each gift, Esther tried to have a good time. The items, after all, were undeniably beautiful and sleek, and since each one was hidden in a box or plastic bag or wrapped in cloth or paper, they were fun to open, as well. Throughout, Michal sat by her side, her eyes sparkling as she selected which one to open next. "This one," she would say as she handed Esther a new item. Then she would watch, enchanted, as Esther took out yet another bracelet or scarf or pair of shoes. "That one."

Esther was aware that all of her guests were taking in the ritual with greedy eyes; other than Skar, there was no one present who would not have traded places with her. And because her reactions were also being observed closely, Esther tried to look enthusiastic about receiving each gift. Yet after the seventh or eighth one, her cheeks began to feel strained from smiling so much and her words of thanks started to sound insincere to her own ears. The only present she liked outright came from Silas: a pair of tapered drinking glasses, elegant and light green.

"These are good," she said sincerely, meeting Silas's eyes in thanks. The boy smiled, gratified that he had made the right choice—or swiped them from the right place.

Soon, the shower was over; and Esther had to admit, all of her guests seemed as if they had had a good time. After they left, Michal stayed behind and offered to help carry the presents back to Esther's room, but she declined.

"You've already done so much," said Esther, squeezing her arm in thanks.

In truth, Esther was exhausted. She wanted nothing more than to return to her room for a few precious moments of solitude before Joseph returned with Kai and Sarah, whom he had been tending on the roof.

Yet she was surprised to find someone waiting for her inside. A small figure wearing a short robe stood at the far end of the room, her back to the door as she gazed out the window at the afternoon sky.

At the moment she saw Skar, Esther felt the excitement of the party dissolve.

Throughout the shower, Esther had been keenly aware that her friend had not uttered a word. Although she had stood in the background watching, Skar had not once leaned in close, nor exclaimed at any present, nor had she laughed or even smiled. *In fact,* Esther realized now with a pang, *her closest and oldest friend had not even given her a present.*

"You think it's a mistake," Esther blurted out.

Skar turned in surprise. "What?"

Esther shook her head. "You don't even have to say anything," she said. "I know you think it's wrong."

But as her friend approached her, she looked only puzzled. "What do I think is wrong? That you are partnering with Gideon?"

Though Skar was expressing no negative opinion, Esther still felt as if she were being judged. "He's not so bad," she retorted, her voice louder than she meant it to be. "We want the same things—and we know what we have to do to get them. We both know we can't do it by ourselves. We can help each other."

Skar nodded. "That is good. That is important."

Esther glanced past her friend and felt her face flush. Right in front of Skar, stuck on the windowsill, was the end of a white candle: It was the last one Esther had lit for Aras, two nights ago. Skar had probably not even noticed it, nor would she understand what it meant if she had. Still, Esther wrenched up the lump of wax and stuffed it in her pocket.

"I'm doing what's best for my children. And for the District." *Was she talking to Skar,* Esther wondered, *or to herself?*

Skar nodded. "I understand," she said. "All that matters is that you are sure of your reasons and that your eyes are open."

Somehow, Skar's lack of condemnation only made it worse. As if sensing this, her old friend smiled. "I did not come here to argue, Esther," Skar said, "only to give you this. I felt shy in front of all of the others."

She held out a small object, unwrapped, in the palm of her hand. It was a tiny stuffed bear, no bigger than her thumb, with a metal tag in its ear.

To those who had rewarded her with luxurious items, the gift would have seemed a childish trifle. Yet it wasn't—not to Esther. As her fingers closed around it, she felt her throat tighten.

"Thank you," was all she said.

A female voice broke into Gideon's thoughts.

"Am I doing it right?"

He turned and looked at Nur. She was posed on a makeshift bed in the corner of his office, covered only by a diaphanous scarf tied around her neck that extended to her knees. In a few hours, Esther would wear the same item, a veil, at the partner-ing ceremony; Gideon had seen girls do the same in Joseph's magazines and had secured one for that very purpose. Yet in a moment of happy inspiration, he had decided that Nur should wear the item first, in private. That way, he would be able to keep the teasing memory fresh in his mind throughout the day.

"Put your arms up," he said, demonstrating. "Like that."

The girl did as he asked, yet without enthusiasm. Then she sagged and curled up on the cushions, refusing to go on. She turned her face to the wall, pulling the cover up and shielding herself with it.

Gideon stood over her. "What wrong?" he asked.

Nur shrugged, refusing to say.

"You still mad about Esther?"

Nur still would not look his way, and he noticed a pout had formed on her lips.

"I told you," he said, "how it going to be. It won't mean nothing."

He was met with silence, and Nur closed her eyes, as if the words hurt to hear. Gideon was growing impatient. Still, he knew the girl had a point: She had taken a risk by helping him with Aras. And good work, he knew, shouldn't go unacknowledged.

"Everything stay the same with us," he said. "I promise."

Nur's eyes remained closed. Then they fluttered open. She looked up at Gideon and, to his surprise, didn't look all that grateful. There was something else in her expression: entitlement.

"I *want* it to change," she said.

Gideon didn't know how to respond. He was unused to this kind of spirit from Nur, who always did whatever he wanted. Now she leaned toward him, the sheet falling down. The scarf had bunched up around her neck so that nothing covered her, but she didn't seem to care. "I want it to change *now.*"

Although he towered over her, Gideon felt an unexpected flicker of fear. Before he could back away, the girl reached out and grabbed his leg.

As her fingers curled around his thigh, Gideon's flesh shrank from her touch. This was the closest she had ever come to him, and his heart began to beat so fast it hurt. Yet he forced himself not to yank away as a sudden thought came to him.

Maybe Nur could be of help.

He was aware that on the partnering night, one was expected to engage in physical contact. He had tried not to dwell on what exactly this entailed, yet he suspected there would be no avoiding it. *And it could be a good thing.* Physical intimacy with Esther could eventually forge a stronger bond between them.

He certainly didn't intend to perform the disgusting act that he had heard so much about; that would be out of the question. Yet Gideon thought he could manage *something.*

And Nur could be his way to practice.

"All right," he heard himself say now, the words sounding harsh. "Come here." Then he softened it. "Please."

Nur smiled, surprised. But instead, she lay back, her hair flowing in a soft mist across the blanket.

"No," she said. "*You* come *here.*"

Gideon swallowed, with difficulty. Then he took a step forward. Tugging at the knees of his jeans so as not to wrinkle them, he descended, stiff and awkward.

He knelt beside her, fully dressed and unsure what to do next. After a few moments, Nur reached up. Wrapping her arms around him, she pulled him down on top of her.

Their bodies were now pressed together. Gideon was surprised: Nur's naked skin was soft and warm. He smelled her hair and was pleasantly reminded of flowers. Her proximity almost felt nice.

But slowly this feeling began to fade. The boy began to have trouble breathing. The longer he lay in Nur's arms, the more he felt suffocated; her grip was growing as tight and deadly as a rope wrapped around him.

It was all Gideon could do to extricate himself. Digging his fingers into Nur's hands, first gently and then with increasing panic, he began to pry them loose. It took forever. At last, he wrenched free of her, panting as he sat up.

"That enough," he barely managed to say.

He wiped away the sweat that covered his forehead as he scrambled to his feet. Then he glanced back down.

Nur was staring at him, not angry or offended, but with a quizzical look on her face. *As if he were a freak,* Gideon thought with irritation.

"Don't worry," he snapped. "I give you something. Just wait."

He was already fixing his hair in the mirror when Nur muttered something inaudible in response. The next noise he heard was the slamming of the door.

Gideon didn't care. All in all, he had done the best he could. And the experience would help him with Esther, he had no doubt.

He locked the door and tidied the bedding. Then Gideon tapped a drinking glass upon the edge of a sink until it broke into four jagged slices. He used one piece to cut himself, on his upper shoulder, where it wouldn't show.

Hours later, the ceremony was about to begin.

The atrium was already crowded with dozens of guests, wearing new and elegant clothes taken from the District's many stores. The gentle sounds of their murmuring echoed through the vast hall, past the strange half-man, half-bird sculptures that hung high overhead and up to the skylight. Everyone had arrived early and now stood where they had been ordered to, except for one.

Esther was four stories up, pacing back and forth in a darkened hallway. She had put on the clothes Gideon had told her to wear: a white lace dress with a full-gathered skirt and high-heeled white shoes that bit into her feet and made her stumble. She was wearing most of her new jewelry, as well, which weighed down her throat, arms, and hands; together, the chains and bands felt heavier than both of her children carried together.

From where she stood, she could see Gideon looking around for her. Wearing black pants and a matching jacket, he was easy to spot on the ground floor of the mall. It was lit by what seemed a thousand candles, the tapers filling the space with an eerie glow, one that Esther knew could be seen for at least half a mile in the night sky, through the enormous windows.

"This way, everyone outside look in," Gideon had told her when he described the design he had invented. "My boys make sure no one gets near. But strangers find out about us and go tell the others."

The hall was bisected by a long and narrow red carpet that extended from one end of the space to the other. On either side were the spectators, both Insurgents and Esther's friends, their faces receding and advancing in the flickering flames. Everyone faced a simple wooden platform at the end of the carpet, framed by an arbor that was decorated with vines from the roof.

To Esther's eye, all of these elements cobbled from partnering ceremonies in the ancient past seemed not only garish, but unreal. She was surprised that Gideon would have approved them and not asked her opinion. Yet that was not why she had taken refuge far from the gaudy display.

She had come up here to be alone with her thoughts—to remind herself that the point of this partnering lay not in any strange ceremony but in her children's security and the work that remained to be done.

Her alliance with Gideon, she kept telling herself, *would make it easier. It would change everything for the better.*

With that thought in mind, Esther drew a deep breath. Then she started downstairs.

From the far end of the carpet, Gideon saw her. With a look of relief, he made a single gesture to her from across the room. As if in a dream, Esther made her way toward the foot of the red carpet, lifting her skirts and stepping with care in her slippery shoes. As she did, people moved aside for her, mumbling in admiration.

Esther was aware of the familiar faces in the crowd: Joseph with Kai, Skar, Silas, the female Insurgent Nur; Michal had stayed upstairs with Sarah. Then she sensed someone staring at her: It was Eli, whom she had not seen for weeks.

He looked pale and drawn and his eyes were heavily ringed, as if he had not slept in a long time. Seeing her old friend, Esther felt a pang of regret. How might things have been different if she had accepted his offer long ago, back in Prin? Their eyes met for only a second. Then, with surprising violence, he shuddered and glanced away.

A young female Insurgent now came forward and handed Esther a candle. She fumbled with a firestarter and, after a few tries, managed to light it. Giving a nervous glance down the aisle at Gideon, the child lifted the veil, which Esther had draped around her neck, and then shook it out. She fluttered the delicate fabric over Esther's face.

"Please," the girl said. "Go ahead."

Holding the candle, Esther proceeded down the carpet. She had to keep the lighted candle far enough away so that it did not ignite her veil, which obscured her vision, making the environment shimmery and even more unreal.

When she stepped up onto the platform, hot wax dripped down the candle and onto her fingers. Esther was glad for the unexpected pain, for it suddenly made her more alert.

"Here," Gideon said.

He held up one arm and indicated that she do the same. Then he drew from his pocket a silky cord, which he draped loosely around both of their wrists.

Then he began to speak.

"I promise I respect and take care of you . . ." The boy spoke quickly, his restlessness apparent. The loud words rattled together and began to blend, becoming an incoherent stream. Startled, Esther realized that they were not Gideon's words; they had been taken from one of Joseph's books.

Esther thought of her other partnerings, with Caleb and

Aras. *How different they were from this ritual!* The first had been done in a stable, the two of them hiding from those who pursued them. She and Caleb had made up the vows themselves, clumsy words that were nevertheless from the heart. The promise she had exchanged with Aras had also been simple, a genuine declaration of not only love and hope, but faith.

There had been so many reasons against both unions. Caleb had been a fugitive, hunted down by the townspeople of Prin. Aras was blind and reclusive, a bitter loner who distrusted people. Pledging her life first to one and then the other, Esther had not had the support of her family or community, yet she had done it anyway. And she had never regretted either for a second.

Now she gazed at Gideon from the corner of her eye. Unlike the others, he was a good prospect; any girl present would be honored to take him as a partner. There were a dozen reasons why she should be happy to be standing there: good, solid reasons that would make sense to anyone with half a mind.

And yet through the haze of the smoke on either side, Esther suddenly saw the faces of the two boys she had loved. Everyone else seemed to vanish. Their ghosts had become the only guests, peering at her from the past.

Esther looked up. Gideon was staring at her expectantly, his vows over, waiting for her to begin. His eyes held only impatience and expectation, not kindness, affection, or even concern.

With a pang, Esther suddenly realized she could never call this boy her partner. She could not bear to spend the rest of her life without love. As foolish as that made her, she could not help it. It was who she was.

She tore the veil from her face and let it fall to the floor. She yanked the partnering tie off her wrist and threw it to the ground as well.

Esther did not remember escaping, yet found herself halfway down the carpet, running. As she went, she kicked off one shoe, and then the other, ripping the delicate leather straps that bound them to her feet. She tore the heavy gold and silver from her wrists, fingers, and throat as well, and flung them from her as if they burned her skin. On either side, gaping faces, gleaming in the candlelight, turned to watch her go; and their indistinct whispers grew louder until they became a wordless roar.

But Esther didn't care. All she knew was that she was free.

And as she ran, she grew lighter.

PART TWO

SEVEN

AFTER THE PARTNERING CEREMONY, THERE WAS A SWIFT AND SUDDEN change.

Esther and Gideon kept their distance, and she hoped that any bad blood between them would soon fade. Yet everywhere she went, she was now greeted with a new restraint by Gideon's people. Instead of acknowledging her with their usual smiles and small talk in the hallways or on the roof, the Insurgents averted their eyes. Even the girl Nur, who had told Esther about Aras, moved quickly away when she spied her.

Soon she realized that the problem was far worse than she had imagined.

Four days after she spurned Gideon, Esther was standing on the roof with a small team of workers. The central drain in the glass ceiling had become clogged, and a pool of rainwater, deadly yet precious, had built up in the squared-off depression surrounding it. Since it was such a dangerous job, Esther had volunteered to fix it herself.

Wearing rubber gloves and holding a bucket, she stood balanced high atop a precarious ladder, kept in place from behind by two of the Insurgents, a boy and a girl. The pipe leading down from the ceiling had to be unscrewed and cleaned out. The trick was to capture the water before it could splash on anyone.

"Hold it steady," Esther called down. "I'm undoing it."

Using an oversize wrench, Esther attempted to rotate the metal fixing. It was much tighter than she had assumed, and she had to set the bucket down on the top step and strain to turn it with both hands. Gritting her teeth and pushing with all of her strength, she was relieved when the metal cuff finally began to move. Water started beading at the join, and she grabbed the bucket to catch it; it would be important to control the flow in a slow stream. But as she gave the wrench a final tug to increase the stream, her weight inadvertently shifted sideways. As the ladder lurched, she dropped the tool with a clang and only just managed to right herself, grabbing the bucket at the last second.

Her heart pounding, Esther drew a shaky breath.

It was a miracle that she hadn't fallen, or dropped the container, or been splashed by any of the water. She was about to say something to the ones helping when she noticed that the boy was looking away. To her shock, she saw he wasn't even pretending to be of use; his hands were tucked in his pockets. As for the girl, she had one hand draped casually on a rung, offering no support as she stared back up at Esther with an open look of insolence.

Anger bloomed in Esther's heart and she could feel her face flush. When she glanced around, she noticed that the other Insurgents working in the garden had stopped what they were doing to watch. Every one of them had the same expression as the girl: one that was not merely unfriendly or mocking, but eager somehow, as if they were all waiting to see her physically hurt.

Her cheeks now burning with rage, Esther dismissed the two workers with a curt nod. Then she walked to the stairwell with stiff and self-conscious steps as the others parted before her in silence. Shortly, Esther returned with Silas and Michal. Within an hour, the three of them managed to fix the clogged drain without further incident. Esther then added the salvaged water to the purifying tank, where it would be boiled and strained for future use. But the whole time, her mind was churning.

Gideon's people were punishing her for having rejected their leader. With deliberate carelessness, the two Insurgents had risked her life; she could easily have been injured or even killed.

She had been lucky this time. But what about the next?

Such behavior could not be repeated. As she finished clearing the drain and helped Michal put the ladder away, Esther realized she needed to consult someone with a cooler head to figure out what to do.

At the same moment, Skar was pushing a broom through the grime on a marble floor. Unlike the others, the variant girl enjoyed being on one of the cleaning teams. To her, the job was so easy it didn't feel like work. Skar had never used things like polishing cloths, mops, or cleaning creams before. Making the District sparkle was like a game.

She was rounding a corner, following a small pile of dirt and grit. Then she stopped. She heard a soft, two-toned whistle above her, the secret signal she and Esther used to share when they were little.

Skar shot a quick glance at the other workers on her team. They were farther down the hallway, kneeling at a railing they polished with old T-shirts dipped in tins of cream. Skar set down her mop without a sound and took off on her bare feet.

"What is it?" Skar asked once she had joined Esther and made certain that they were alone.

Esther was so agitated, she spoke quickly, not finishing sentences and jumbling her thoughts; Skar had to lay a hand on her friend's to make her slow down. But even before she fully comprehended what the other girl was saying, Skar had a sense of what the problem was.

Moreover, she wasn't surprised.

Skar was the only one who had understood the terrible

miscalculation Esther had made by rejecting Gideon. *The whole thing was a mistake from the beginning,* she thought ruefully.

Among the variants, partnering was a practical matter. It was approached with less sentiment, less need of affection. If her first partner, Tarq, had treated her with more respect, she would have made her relationship with him work somehow . . . although, of course, she was thankful to have broken with him and found happiness with Michal. Yet most norms couldn't imagine being partnered without attraction and love.

Skar thought that her friend had been impetuous to agree. Was it because her heart had been broken by Aras? Skar didn't know and would never presume to ask. Whatever her motivation, it appeared that Esther had agreed to partner with Gideon on the spur of moment, assuming the situation would work out; it was the way she did everything. It was why Skar was often exasperated with Esther and why she secretly admired her, as well. For while Skar seemed fierce, she alone knew she was far meeker than the norm girl and more loyal to convention.

Still, risks had their costs . . . and it seemed as if Esther was now being forced to pay. Breathless, Esther finished her story. "Do you think they're acting on their own?"

"We can't know."

"So what should I do?"

"Do?"

"How do I make them stop?"

Skar considered for a long moment before she spoke. She had been silent before, out of respect for propriety. "In our tribe," she said at last, "the most foolish thing you can do is make an enemy. But once you do, you have to apologize. And then you have to do something for him."

"Like what?"

Skar shrugged. "Give him something he wants." She paused. "But it must be something precious."

Esther scowled; she had been clearly expecting a different answer. Skar knew that strategizing had always been the girl's weak point. Over the years, she had been learning, but not fast enough.

"But I didn't do anything wrong," Esther said. She sounded petulant.

"Others might not agree."

Still stubborn, Esther shook her head. "It wasn't my fault. He shouldn't have asked me in the first place."

"Maybe not," said Skar. "But it was your choice and you agreed. And then you changed your mind."

"I don't care," Esther shot back. Two spots of color had appeared in her cheeks. "I don't owe anyone. I can take care of myself. I don't need anyone's help. In fact, I . . ." A sudden thought seemed to strike her and she faltered.

Skar gave her a questioning look.

"Sarah," said Esther at last. "I told him."

Skar nodded. Gideon knowing about the baby's existence put things in an entirely different light. In the past, Esther might have felt fine taking on the entire District as her enemy. But putting her daughter in danger was something else.

"Think about what I said." Skar reached out and squeezed Esther's hands in sympathy, her little teeth showing in a smile of support. "You have made a mistake. But perhaps it is not too late to set things right again."

Two days later, Esther stood in Gideon's doorway.

Without any advance word, she had walked down to his dwelling on the basement level. It had taken her this long to mull over what she would say. She now stood hesitating and cleared her throat.

The boy lay on his meager pallet, eyes closed. Esther saw that he had no mattress, cover, or sheet; his bed was no more than a single blanket laid on the hard tiled floor. He appeared thinner than when she had seen him last.

"I just wanted . . ." Esther started to say, before swallowing her words.

Gideon's eyes opened. He sat up and stared at her, expressionless. The silence grew to an uncomfortable length and still he said nothing. *Clearly*, Esther thought, *this was not going to be easy.* "I just wanted . . . to say I'm sorry."

Gideon flinched, as if struck. He stood and, turning his back on her, pulled a sweater on over his T-shirt. He had no doubt gotten the garment from one of the stores in the mall; it looked soft and fine. Though the weather was as warm as ever, he made a point of tugging the sleeves down past his wrists. Esther thought she had noticed scars or bruises there but wasn't sure.

"All right," he said. He did not face her.

Esther sensed that she was being requested to leave, but she was not finished.

"It wasn't because I don't respect you," she said. It was miserably hard for her to speak the words, but she forced herself to be as sincere as she could. "It was on account of . . . well, I rushed into it too fast."

Gideon nodded and waved his hand once as if dismissing her. "That nice, but it ain't necessary."

But Esther took a chance and advanced farther into the room.

Gideon turned to face her, surprised and wary. Then his eyes narrowed. *Was it bruised feelings? Suspicion?* Esther wasn't sure. Of all the boys she had known, Gideon was the most opaque. She wasn't sure what emotions he felt or when he felt them. Still, that was no excuse not to continue.

"Your people," she said, ". . . some of them. They tried to hurt me."

Now Gideon glanced up with what appeared to be genuine surprise. "They did?"

Esther nodded. "Nothing happened. But . . . it might have."

The boy shook his head, staring past Esther. Then he found her eyes again. "That ain't right. I make sure that don't happen again. You got my apology."

Esther was relieved to find out that Gideon had not been involved. Now she could raise her most important point.

"I have an offer for you," she said.

"You gonna give me the gifts?"

Although it was only a joke, it stung. Esther's immediate impulse was to tell him the truth: that she had never wanted the presents in the first place and had already given them—even

the partnering dress—to Michal and the others. But she bit
back her retort and smiled, as well.

"If you want," she said, keeping her voice even. "But it's
something else. I think you should have your own part of the
District. The mall will be yours, the market and the other three
floors around it. Me and my friends will stay at the top, to work
the garden. We'll send food down every day, to keep providing
for those who need it, using the glass system. You and I will
keep to ourselves and do what we do best."

It had been a difficult decision Esther had made, and on her
own. It was wrenching to lose half of the District, like giving
up part of herself. Yet she believed there was nothing else that
Gideon would want more. *It must be something precious*, Skar had
said.

Esther saw the expression shift on Gideon's face. She had
clearly taken him by surprise. He seemed to be tallying up the
good and the bad of it. Then he turned away again.

"Maybe," he said, "we help more folks that way." Then he
hesitated. "Well . . . I think about it."

Esther had done her job. She gave the boy a smile that she
trusted looked sincere and headed to the doorway.

It had gone better than she had feared. She was relieved
that Gideon didn't seem angry, nor did he appear to bear her
any ill will. She hoped he would accept her offer. If he agreed
to what she had proposed, they would each have autonomy,
and that would be the best for both of them.

Esther turned back one last time. "Please think about it,"
she added. "It'll be equal. And fair."

Gideon smiled now. "That," he said, "is always the most important thing to me."

Only an inch of liquid remained.

Alone in his room on the third floor, Eli hoisted the greasy bottle by the neck and drank it all, the familiar burn searing his throat and making his eyes water. Then he sat back on his bed and waited for the diffuse warmth to soften the harsh lines of memory.

After he had killed Aras, Eli found himself haunted not by his thoughts, but by sensations. He could still hear the crack of the club, see the single drop of blood, and, worst of all, feel the dead boy's fingers on his face. The sense memories filtered through to his dreams and forced him awake night after night, his heart thundering and a scream boiling up from deep within. Sleep had become all but impossible.

At first, he had tried to take solace in Gideon's approval. His idol had opened up to him, made him more of a confidante, taken meals with him. Yet to his dull surprise, Eli found he no longer cared. Even when Gideon praised him, Eli was distracted by the itching of his palms, covered with reddish stains that only he could see.

But one thing seemed to help.

For months, Eli hadn't given a thought to the bottles of harsh drink locked in a closet down in the basement; the one or two times he had tasted it with the adults, he had spat it out. Yet during another sleepless night, he had remembered the small room, as well as the keys that unlocked the door. The stuff had been as nasty as he remembered. But after a few long swallows, it lost its sting. And soon, a dreamy relaxation took over his body and eased his mind.

The only problem was that it took more and more drink to get to this peaceful place. At first, Eli had brought back several bottles; too soon, they were gone, and so he returned to stock up. Now he was nearing the end of his stash.

Recently, Eli had grown to hate being with people. Although only he and Gideon knew what he had done, he could still feel the eyes of others watching him, hear their whispers behind his back. He sensed he was being judged, not just for what he had done to Aras, but for what he was doing to mask his pain.

Yet the idea of being without the drink made him panic. And so, with difficulty, Eli now got to his feet. He only just remembered to bring his keys.

Weaving, he stumbled out of his room.

He only hoped he wouldn't run into anyone he knew.

After Esther was gone, Gideon finally unclenched his fists. Without knowing what he was doing, he had broken the skin on his palms with his nails. Yet he hadn't noticed.

For days, all he could think of was Esther's behavior during the ceremony. He had done so much to make the union happen: planning, scheming, not to mention the risk he had incurred to himself by getting rid of Aras. The thought that it would all come to nothing—and so publicly!—was almost more than he could bear.

Gideon didn't believe for a moment that his heart was

broken. Instead, he realized he had lost not only the alliance he so desperately wanted, but also face . . . and that meant losing power. And that was far worse.

For days, Gideon had weighed how best to pay Esther back. He had spread word to his people that by rejecting him, Esther had disrespected them as well. She had already felt the sting of their displeasure. The treatment had worked better than he could have dreamed. Even now, he had pretended to be magnanimous and forgiving, and, like a fool, she had believed him.

Yet her proposal had taken him completely aback. Had she not known what she was offering? People were desperate to have what was in the mall, and there was no limit to what they'd be willing to do to get it. Now he alone would determine what price they paid, without any interference. He would have a region—a kingdom—to himself.

Gideon wondered if in fact Esther was being genuine, whether she could possibly be that guileless. *Did she really believe his act . . . or was she playing him for a fool?* He knew he had to be careful to assess her next moves, in case she was engaged in a long and devious game—one he was determined to win.

Then he looked down and gasped. Lost in his thoughts, he had squeezed his hands shut again. Blood was starting to ooze from his palms.

EIGHT

With the District divided in two, Esther felt a new freedom.

She could now go about openly with Sarah on her back. She no longer had to live in constant fear that the Insurgents or workers from outside would overhear her baby's cries from the stairwell. And with the easing of her anxiety, she found more time to play with Kai.

Gideon had waited for a full day to respond. Then he had had one of his guards come and tell her that he agreed to her plan, with certain conditions. Her people were to be gone from their dwellings by the end of the day.

Skar and the others had packed their meager belongings

and moved up to the top floor. Silas helped Joseph carry his books up and they set about transforming one of the rooms at the end into his new library. The rest spent most of their time up on the roof, working in the garden or tending the water purification system.

With Aras gone, Esther found she was grateful for the company, especially after the sun went down. She and her friends prepared and took all their meals together in the conference room. After dinner, she would put the children to bed, and then they all would sit around talking and laughing by the dimming light of the firebowl until late.

It was the happiest any of them had been for a long time.

Thanks to the immense expanse of glass that spanned the entire roof, Esther and the others were no longer terrified of the faraway rumble of thunder and flashes of lightning that sometimes appeared above their heads when they were working. In fact, Esther began to take pleasure in staring up at the poisonous drops hitting the panes and watching them trickle down toward the center drain.

It was true that she and the others were now more confined than ever. While they weren't actually prohibited from visiting the lower floors, they no longer felt welcome. Esther's people didn't even have to bring down the day's produce every day. Without asking, Gideon would send several workers each morning to pick up the loaded baskets and to return the empty ones by sundown. Before leaving, they would hand Joseph a bag of glass fragments, the day's payment for their work. He would then take pains to distribute them evenly among the five of them.

There seemed to be more new people every day, eager to work for Gideon or bring in goods they had Gleaned, all in exchange for a handful of glass. As a result, the District seemed to be flourishing below, or at least Esther imagined it to be.

The peace acted as a balm for all of them. Without the turmoil of the District to distract them, Esther hoped that she and the people she loved would continue to thrive for a long, long time. She even felt some of her hurt and sadness about Aras begin to fade.

Esther now knelt on the hot tarred roof, collecting food for lunch. As she pulled slender yellow squash from their vines, she took care not to dislodge their roots from their water containers. She put the last vegetables in her bucket and felt the sun beating down on her head through the overhead glass; it was a pleasant, drowsy feeling.

She was getting to her feet and easing her back when she noticed something odd.

Squinting, Esther crossed to one of the large tubs across the aisle. Thin wire cages propped up the sprawling green vines with tiny yellow blossoms that grew in profusion, two rows of containers that ran as far as the length of the building. Each vine supported heavy, rounded tomatoes, at varying stages of ripeness. The ones that caught Esther's attention were pale green, meaning they still had several days to redden.

One tomato dangling low from its wire support seemed to have a small dark spot near the stem. As Esther reached out and pulled the fruit close in order to examine it, she realized it wasn't a blemish but a blackened hole. At the same moment, the tomato exploded in her hand with a dull splat. With a cry of disgust, she saw that it had rotted to the core, as foul-smelling pulp dripped between her fingers.

Wiping her hand on her jeans, Esther examined a second tomato from the same plant, and another. Then she moved to the next container and the one beyond that. Each fruit she examined had the same small hole at the top . . . and each one was ruined. It was only then that she noticed a tiny worm that clung to the tattered leaf of a plant. It had a dark brown head and a soft, fat body that gave no resistance when she killed it.

With a sinking heart, Esther began to sort through all of the plants, picking off every rotted tomato she could find. There were dozens. Whenever she saw a worm, she pinched it off as well, her stomach clenching in disgust. She wondered how the pests had made their way into their greenhouse in the first place and whether they had already managed to spread.

Soon, Esther had filled eight oversize plastic bags with rotted fruit and killed dozens of the wriggling grubs. The amount of ruined food was shocking; it was a sizeable part of a day's yield that would have fed dozens.

Yet that was not the worst part. Although she was relieved that the larvae had not spread to the other plants, Esther reeled in sudden understanding of how fragile the entire system was. She and the others had taken the bountiful crops for granted and assumed that with hard work, they would always be there. Yet she now realized that a single catastrophe was the only thing that stood between everyone in the District and hunger.

Esther got to her feet. Glancing down, she noticed that her jeans were covered with green smears where she had wiped her hands, and she shuddered.

"No! No no no no no!"

Esther could hear Kai's wails echoing from the stairwell. Moments later, Joseph emerged, attempting to carry the little boy, who was red-faced and struggling. She knew that her son's petulance was probably from hunger; it was lunchtime.

"I think he wants something sweet." Joseph's long face was also flushed and he was perspiring. "He doesn't seem to want his mashed yams."

Esther didn't blame the child. Although she and the others had grown used to the boiled and roasted vegetables and fruits that now made up most of their diet, Kai still loved salted flatbread, hard candies, and, best of all, soda whenever she could find it. She tried not to indulge him too much, but it was hard not to when he refused to eat anything else.

Putting aside her worries for the moment, Esther took Kai by the hand and went down to her room to see if there was anything there. She found a small glass jar of honey called Golden Blossom, but it was empty. Unscrewing the top, she stuck a finger inside anyway, trying to scrape up even a taste of the sweet stuff. Then she handed the lid to the boy to suck on, but after a moment, he flung it away and burst into fresh tears.

Scooping him into her arms, Esther ran down the hall and explored the supply room where they kept their emergency stores. Under her supervision, the tall metal shelves had been stocked with provisions that rose nearly to the ceiling: not only

boxes and bags of salt, coffee, and dried beans, but also packets
of dried food, jars of preserves they had canned themselves,
and extra bottles of water and vinegar. But a quick search
revealed nothing sweet: no honey, no sugar, no soda.

For a moment, Esther despaired. Then she had an idea.

Going back to her room, the girl went over to her meager
belongings, piled on a chair in the corner. She sorted through
them and found what she was looking for: a large sock tied in a
crude knot. She undid it and poured some of its contents into
her hand.

Glass pebbles glittered in the sunlight. They were her share
of the payment they each received every morning for the
farm's produce. Until now, she had never thought about them
or bothered to count what she had. As far as she knew, none
of her friends had, either. But it dawned on her that she might
be able to use some of it now to procure some honey or candy
for her boy.

She hesitated. Not knowing how much she would need,
Esther ended up stuffing a handful into her jeans pocket before
taking Kai back to Joseph. Begging him to watch the child for
another few minutes, she took off once more for the stairwell.

Esther wasn't prepared for what greeted her when she
emerged on the ground floor. She and the others had not been
downstairs for several weeks, and during that time, Gideon had
transformed the mall.

The noise alone was astonishing. Dozens of emaciated
Outsiders, some wearing new articles of clothing, jewelry, and
sunglasses that looked at odds with the filthy and bedraggled

robes they still wore as protection against the sun, pushed past her, shouting and arguing. Everywhere was the sound and glinting flash of glass fragments changing hands, as well as the feeling of impatience and frenzied energy.

Outsiders were already standing in a long, restless line, clutching Gleaned objects they had brought to trade: not only packages of food and bottles of water and soda, but also clothes, tools, furniture, housewares. One carried an immense table lamp, thick with dust; another held a pair of cracked white boots with metal blades on the bottom. They all waited for the two Insurgents who sat at a long table, a glittering pile of glass shards heaped to one side. Each item was examined and assessed, and after much arguing, a few pebbles would be counted out and given as payment.

Elsewhere in the mall, even more people were using their fragments to trade for items that were on display. Table after table was heaped with merchandise, more than the eye could take in: clothing, sunglasses, wristwatches, jewelry, shoes, vegetables and fruit from the roof garden, and extraordinary stores of packaged food. Old objects mingled with new, and pieces of junk lay next to other things that seemed pristine and untouched.

As Esther picked her way along, strangers crashed into her, pushing and arguing with one another. Babies cried; shrill laughter rang out. Esther noticed Outsiders were sweeping the floor, dusting the fixtures, and washing the walls of the ground floor, jobs that had once been done by Gideon's Insurgents.

Carried along by the mob, Esther soon found herself crushed against a table display. All of the items were heaped in a disorganized pile, watched over by one of Gideon's people. It was a boy she knew from before whose name was Rahm.

"What you want?"

Although his tone was friendly, Esther was so disoriented she had trouble speaking for a moment. "Do you have anything sweet?" she asked at last. "Honey, sugar?"

Without hesitation, Rahm plunged one hand into his goods, sorting through them with rapid assurance. Then he pulled out an object. It was a flat, round can the size of his palm, with a pretty flowered border. When he shook it, it rattled.

"Lemon drops," he said.

Esther took the object, marveling at it; she had never seen such a charming thing. "Thank you," she said. She was about to turn away when Rahm rapped his knuckles on the table.

"You got glass?"

"Oh." She dug down into her front pocket, pulling out some of the fragments she had remembered to bring. "How many you want?"

"Eighteen."

Esther frowned. She could only count to ten, but still, she knew that eighteen seemed an unusually large number. She fumbled with the pebbles for a moment, trying to figure it out. "Here," she said at last, pushing everything she had at him. "Take it all."

She turned to go, but was called back again. "Ain't enough," he said.

Esther was astonished. "What do you mean?"

"Ain't enough." Rahm pushed the pieces one by one, count-ing to himself in a labored way under his breath. "It eighteen. This only fourteen."

"You mean you want more?"

Rahm seemed exasperated, as if he had been asked this kind of question many times before. "Four more." He held up his fingers to demonstrate.

But Esther refused to be intimidated. "I thought a tomato was one glass piece."

Rahm shrugged. "That ain't a tomato."

"I know. But eighteen is a lot. How come?"

"It what Gideon told me to charge."

"Just for this?" A thought dawned on Esther and she picked up another object at random: a soft green scarf. "Well, how many for this?"

"That—" Rahm's eyes flickered; he appeared to be search-ing his memory. "That thirty-one."

Esther indicated a cap with a brim that read ST. LOUIS CAR-DINALS. "This?"

"Nineteen."

Next, it was a box of salt. "And this?"

"Eleven."

"Eleven . . . for salt? But why?"

Rahm shrugged. "It make people work hard. That what Gideon say. This way, anyone can get anything." He hesitated, then added, "That is, if they not lazy."

A flare of indignation spread through Esther's chest as she picked up the small tin one last time. "So I can't have this."

"Not 'less you got four more."

Outraged, she slammed the object back on the table. "Where's Gideon? He should know what you're doing. You're asking too much."

Rahm shrugged. "He the one told me."

Esther felt the heat rise in her face. "I don't believe you. Where is he? I need to talk to him."

Then out of the corner of her eye, she saw another boy step close. To her disbelief, it was an Insurgent guard, his hand on a club at his belt. Rahm had clearly summoned him somehow, in case he was needed.

Shaken, Esther backed away as several strangers crowded to take her place. Struggling to make her way past the crowd, she didn't look up until she heard someone calling her. It was Silas, who stood a level above her, his face quizzical.

"Wait there!" he called over the commotion. Moments later, she could see him working his way through the crowd with ease before joining her. Without needing to ask, Esther knew why he was downstairs and despite herself, almost smiled: The boy was a born thief and couldn't stay away from so much temptation. "What you doing here?"

Esther shook her head; the entire experience had put her in a dark mood. "I need something for Kai. . . . He won't eat."

"You get anything?"

"No." Esther still couldn't quite believe it. "They wanted eighteen pieces for candy. Something anyone could get outside for free." A thought came to her. "And that's where I'm going to find it."

She was already moving through the crowd as Silas tried to catch up. "You can't," he called after her, but she ignored him. Finally, he caught up with her at the front door and grabbed her elbow. "It's all picked clean out there. Ain't nowhere left to look."

Esther threw up her hands. "I've got no choice. I've got to feed Kai."

"But you don't know where to go."

Esther thought about it: He was right. Silas was in charge of Harvesting gasoline, gathering fuel from abandoned vehicles and buildings to power the generator; this had been one of their daily chores back in Prin. Silas had bicycled his way through most of Mundreel and, by now, knew his way around better than any of her friends. "Then show me," she said.

Silas hesitated, then gave a quick nod.

Together, the two slipped through the front door, past a crowd of Outsiders who were desperate to get in with their newly Gleaned goods.

The merciless sun was directly overhead, so both Esther and Silas pulled up their hoods and put on the sunglasses they always carried. Then Silas nodded down the street, and they took off at a quick trot. Esther, who could run almost as fast as Skar, had to slow her pace in order for Silas, only nine, to keep up.

They ran side by side in silence for several minutes. To her chagrin, she saw that they were passing the house Aras had picked out for them. After they had left it behind and traveled for what Esther estimated to be three or more miles, she could see that her friend had begun glancing around, checking for landmarks. "This way," he said at last, and they swerved down a narrow street.

She saw what he was looking for halfway down the block. It was a group of small storefronts, set in from the sidewalk. Hung above them were signs written in strange symbols of gold and red that she did not recognize.

"I saw these the other day when I was Harvesting," said Silas, panting. He bent over at the waist to catch his breath. "But I ain't had a chance to check them until now."

Esther had already moved close to one of them and squinted to look in one dusty window. The only thing she could make out were the odd statues on the sill. One was a bald man, fat and smiling, who sat cross-legged. Another was a strange creature that looked like a colorful snake, with wings on its back. Nearby, a white cat seemed to be staring back at Esther; it was sitting up on its haunches with one paw raised as if in greeting. Nothing was disturbed, which made it a promising place to Glean, and Esther felt her hopes rise.

"Don't look like nobody broke in yet," said Silas as he joined her.

It took them a few moments to find what they needed: a heavy chunk of masonry in a nearby alley. Older and stronger, Esther alone could carry it. It was craggy with dried mortar, yet she still had to throw it several times as hard as she could until the window finally broke with a resounding crash. She and Silas then climbed in, taking care to avoid the jagged glass edges.

Dust motes rose in the sunlight that now streamed in the small store, revealing empty shelves and counters that had been Gleaned long ago. Disappointed, Esther picked her way through the trash-strewn aisles, as Silas moved farther in.

"They got in through the back," he called.

To Esther's disbelief, the same turned out to be true for the neighboring stores and the ones on the next block, as well. In all her years eking out a living from abandoned storefronts and restaurants, she knew that there was always something to Glean if you looked carefully enough: a few packets of sugar, a handful of dried beans. Yet by the time they finished searching all three buildings, it was well into the afternoon and they had nothing to show for their efforts.

Esther pushed back her hood to wipe the sweat from her forehead, which was now gritty with dust.

"I guess we should head back," Silas said, resigned.

Esther thought of Kai and Sarah with a pang; she couldn't bear the thought of returning empty-handed. "You can head back if you want. But I want to try a little longer."

Silas hesitated. "That case," he said at last, "I got one more place to look. If you're willing."

Esther nodded. As they took off again, Silas changed direction, now aiming for the northern part of the city, toward the mountain that loomed on the horizon. Esther noticed that the grade of the streets had changed; they were now toiling uphill. Soon, she could see the central part of Mundreel beneath them in the distance, the sun glinting off the tall buildings made of glass and steel. They were now in a part of the city Esther

had never entered before, a place of small three-story buildings
with peeling and splintered wood set close to one another.

The streets were deserted, yet Esther had the distinct sense
that they were being watched. She would spin around, but the
empty windows and doors showed nothing: not a flicker of
movement, no faces hiding in the shadows.

Finally, they stopped when the road in front of them ended.

She was about to speak, but Silas flashed her a warning
look. Instead, she held her tongue and gazed about.

Esther heard it first: a faint whispering no louder than the
wind blowing through the leaves of a tree. Out of the corner of her eye, she saw something materialize in the darkened
doorway of a house, as insubstantial as a wisp of smoke. The
apparition stepped into the light, and she could see what it was:
a boy Silas's age, dark skinned and impossibly thin, with eyes
that seemed gigantic in his narrow face. Behind him was a girl
who looked at most nine, with fine, dark hair that stood in vivid
contrast to her pale skin. She was clutching what seemed like a
filthy bundle of rags, but when it moved, Esther realized with
a shock that it was an infant.

More and more Outsiders appeared. There were too many
for Esther to count, and still they kept coming, children of
every age. All of them were dirty and so malnourished, they
were little more than skeletons draped in cloth.

Esther felt as if the breath had been knocked out of her.

"They won't hurt you." Although Silas kept his voice low, it
seemed loud in the silence. "You can ask them."

"Ask them? For what?"

"For sugar. Maybe they know where to look. Where they get stuff."

His answer was so innocent, Esther blushed, for it was clear that these children had no idea where to look; they had no food, no water at all. And as she stood there, she suddenly understood what should have become apparent when she and Silas had searched store after store in vain for something sweet.

It used to be possible to scrape out a living by Gleaning. It wasn't easy and the pickings were meager. Yet it was something. But now that Gideon had altered their glass system, all that had changed, for there was now nothing left to take. His prices were so high, he had essentially forced everyone in Mundreel to clean out the city, to scour every building for its remaining goods and bring them to the District. There they'd be exchanged for a tiny amount of glass and sold again. If Outsiders wanted to eat, they had to be involved in the unfair process or else be left behind.

The plan had been intended to help them, but it had only made them suffer. It was a betrayal of everything Esther and Gideon had agreed upon.

Impulsively, she spoke up. "Come with us." Esther raised her voice and addressed everyone within earshot. "We have food and clean water. Enough for you all."

She could sense Silas shooting her a quizzical glance, which she ignored. Esther knew better than anyone how little there was to spare back at the District. Yet right now, any objection seemed unimportant, a little mark in a notebook that didn't make sense. The reality was here, right in front of her. And most important, she wanted Gideon to see with his own eyes the effect of his scheme.

To Esther's surprise, however, her words had no impact. A few looked frightened or suspicious. But most of them had no reaction whatsoever. Their faces remained blank and withdrawn.

Only the dark-haired girl holding the child spoke up. "I come with you." After a pause, the boy behind her stepped forward, as well.

"Me, too," he said.

No one else volunteered. Before she left, Esther made a point of noting where they were. *She would return later,* she thought, *with food and water. Maybe that way she could convince them to trust her.*

It was easier walking back to the District since it was mostly downhill. Still, Esther and Silas had to stop every block or so to allow the girl, Saith, and the boy, Uri, to catch up. Saith clung to the child in her arms and refused to let anyone else hold it, even though she was clearly tired and stumbled from time to time. Esther learned that it was her little brother, Gera. She found herself admiring the girl's loyalty and stubbornness. It made Esther happy to have her near.

For his part, Uri was silent, so much so that Esther assumed he couldn't speak. Then, suddenly, he raised a hand and pointed to one side. "We walk that way; it quicker."

His voice was so soft it was hard to make out what he was saying. For a moment, Esther wondered if he was quite right

in the head; he was indicating a path that led in a completely
different direction, and what's more, he had never been to the
mall and had no idea where they were going. She dismissed his
words and continued to lead the others on their way. Yet soon
she realized that the road she had taken them on was a dead
end. As they retraced their steps and headed the direction he
had first indicated, she spoke up.

"How did you know where we're going?"

The boy Uri shrugged, a quick gesture. "You go where the
tall buildings at. This way lead to the big road. It quicker that
way."

He was right. Thanks to his shortcut, Esther and the others
found themselves on the main street that led to the center of
downtown. They were home within minutes, and Esther found
herself marveling at the boy's quick wits.

By now, it was late afternoon and Outsiders had begun
streaming out of the District in swarms. In addition to small
containers of water and food, many of them also carried or
wore items they had clearly just traded or toiled for: new clothing, housewares, or trinkets. The air was full of laughter and
chatter as they showed one another their new belongings. In
the commotion, it was easy for Esther and Silas to slip the newcomers into the building.

Although Saith and Uri were fading badly, Esther needed
them to make one last stop. Shepherding them before her, she
made her way through the lobby and up to the floor where
Gideon's office was.

Standing in front of the door were two guards, boys she knew.

"Is he there? I have to see him."

One acted as if he hadn't heard and the other only glanced down at her for a fleeting moment.

"You ain't allowed in."

Esther flushed.

Next to her, she could sense Silas and the others quail, yet she refused to back down. Keeping her temper in check, Esther raised her voice. "It's important. He's got to come out and meet these two. He's got to understand what's going on outside."

The two refused to even respond. It was only when Esther attempted to push past that one of them moved; he blocked her hard with his shoulder, knocking her to the side. Esther, her stomach knotted with anger, turned back to the others.

"Let's go," was all she said.

The long stairwell proved difficult for their guests, especially Saith. Silas held up a firestarter so she could see where she was going, but the light didn't help. The little girl clung to the banister and at one point nearly dropped the infant. Without thinking, Esther reached out to take him, but the girl pulled away.

"No," Saith said. "I got him."

By the time the five of them emerged on the top-floor hallway, the air was already filled with the smell of dinner. Esther was about to lead the strangers to a room of their own when Skar appeared, looking concerned.

"Esther!" she exclaimed. "We were all worried where you two were."

Esther spoke a few private words to her oldest friend. Then she and Silas led the strangers to the large room where her friends had gathered. As they stood in the doorway, the chattering and the clatter of silverware stopped as everyone noticed the newcomers.

"This is Saith and Uri," said Esther. "And Saith's little brother, Gera. They're going to stay with us for a while."

Joseph made room on his side of the table and already Michal was pouring water into two goblets. The entire table watched as the strangers approached the table. Then the boy and girl seized the glasses with both hands and drank with frantic thirst. After a few moments, Saith attempted to give the remainder of her water to the child.

"Come on," Esther heard her whisper. "Try to drink."

In the meantime, Esther made certain that the newcomers had enough to eat. Since the portions for the rest of them weren't that large to begin with, she scraped her entire share onto their plates as well. Out of the corner of her eye, she saw Uri examining the boiled squash and potatoes, spearing some on his fork and sniffing it.

Joseph sat next to him, watching. "It's vegetables," he said at last. "I know they smell strange, but they're safe to eat."

"They from the ground?"

Startled, Joseph blinked. "Normally, yes. We grow them on the roof."

The younger boy seemed to be thinking. Then he nodded.

"Animals eat them," he said as he put the entire forkful into his mouth and began to chew, "so it safe." Tickled by the boy's obvious intelligence, Joseph smiled.

Saith, however, hadn't touched her portion. She was still focused on the child in her arms, murmuring over her brother as she tried to get him to drink.

Michal, who had a deep love for and understanding of all babies, no matter how fussy, had been watching with sympathy from the far end of the table. Now she picked up a spoon and stood to bring it over.

"Here," she said. "Maybe he drink out of this."

But the sound of her voice seemed to startle Saith. She turned to Michal so quickly the edge of her hood caught the child's blanket and yanked it aside. Michal gazed down at the infant with a smile that faltered.

Then she let out a gasp.

Flustered, Saith tried to cover up the baby again, but it was too late. Michal, Esther, and everyone else had already glimpsed the child. In that moment, they could tell it was not an infant, but a little boy, a toddler tiny for his age. Even so, that was not what Saith had been trying to hide all along.

It was the glassy stare. The cheeks flushed with fever. And worst of all, the lesions, purple and the size of a thumbnail, scattered across the child's face and arms.

The boy had the disease.

No one spoke for a moment.

Then everyone except Esther and the strangers stood up as one, some chairs scraping on the carpet and falling to the ground. Their faces pale and drawn with fright, they stumbled backward from the table in their haste to get away. Skar yanked Kai by the hand. He knocked over a plate that broke with a dull smash, and Sarah, bundled to Michal's back, woke with a start and began to cry.

Esther had seen the ravages of the disease; they all had. The sickness spared no one, not the smallest child nor the strongest teenager. A single drop of water could kill the healthiest person within days, bringing with it the familiar bone-crushing fatigue and headaches, searing fever, and telltale sores. Soon, delirium would set in. The suffering the illness brought was so great that death often seemed to come as a relief.

Her hood pushed back, Saith gazed up at the others with a look of defiance and sadness.

Then she met Esther's eyes. "If I said," the girl said, her voice husky, "you wasn't gonna let me near."

She was right.

Everyone was terrified of the sick. The custom was to drive them away, to let them die on their own, for the healthy feared that they too would catch the disease from breathing the same air. Even now, Silas and Michal were each pressing an arm to their faces in an attempt to cover their mouths.

Saith lifted her chin and stared at Esther in open challenge. Esther didn't blame her; the girl had no hope or chance left. She even found herself smiling at the other's stubbornness, which reminded her of her own.

"You make us go now?" Saith said.

From where she still sat, Esther could feel the heat radiating off the child in Saith's arms. "No," she said. She had not planned her answer; in fact, she was almost as surprised by it as Saith seemed to be. Then she made up her mind and turned to the others. "They're staying."

A look of concern passed among her friends. Even Skar looked doubtful. "Esther—" she began. Stubborn, Esther shook her head.

Esther knew what it was like to nurse the dying. She had done so several times, first with her sister, Sarah, back in Prin. Then she had taken care of two of the adults from the District, sponging them off to give them some relief from the fever, propping them up so they could drink sugar water from a spoon. It allowed the ill a modicum of peace and even comfort. It was, she felt, the least she could do.

In all three cases, no one else dared to come near the sick except Joseph, and even he did so reluctantly, wearing a scarf wrapped around his mouth and nose. Yet Esther had taken care of them all and had even buried her sister after she died.

And she had not grown ill.

Her friends, she knew, were aware of this. And yet they were all still frightened, as if rumors were more persuasive than reality.

"There is nothing to fear," Esther said.

Yet none of them volunteered to help her.

She would do this by herself.

Esther gave Saith and little Gera their own room, across the hall from her own. Then she set about fetching a bucket of water, clean bedding, and some of her clothes. Because no one else would help, little Kai carried some towels and contributed one of his stuffed animals, a tattered creature with a long nose and oversize ears. He seemed fascinated by the other boy and even reached out to pat him on the stomach. *He was,* Esther realized with a pang, *the same age as Gera.*

Late that night, Esther came back by herself to see how the two were doing. Saith was already fast asleep in a pile of blankets, her dark hair vivid against the white pillowcase. Gera lay next to her, still wide-awake. His dark eyes, enormous in his pale face, glittered as he gazed up at Esther, his breath quick and ragged.

Esther reached down to touch his forehead; the fever had subsided a bit, as she knew it often did at night. On an impulse, she leaned over and picked him up. As light as he was, he clung to her with surprising strength. Esther settled herself on the ground with care, sitting close to his sister so she wouldn't be frightened if she awoke and found him gone. Then she rocked him in her lap, brushing his hair back from his forehead with a gentle touch.

It was how she soothed her own children when they couldn't sleep, and once again, it worked. Within moments, Gera's eyelids fluttered shut and his breathing grew soft and even. And still, Esther continued to stroke his face.

She awoke with a start; she wasn't aware she had fallen asleep. The room was filled with the pale, gray light of early morning and as she stretched her limbs, she found she was stiff from having spent the night curled on her side upon a hard floor. She realized Gera was no longer in her arms and that the bedding next to her was empty as well.

"Saith?"

Then Esther saw her. On the far side of the room, the girl stood motionless in the receding gloom, gazing out. When Esther drew next to her, she saw Saith was staring at the deserted city with unfocused eyes. The girl was clutching Gera, and even before Esther could ask, she saw how rigid the child was.

She knew the reason.

Esther hesitated. For a moment, she thought of comforting Saith, of opening her arms and enfolding the grieving girl in an embrace . . . for she too knew what it felt like to lose those you loved. Yet she noted Saith's silence, her proud and stony profile, and her dry eyes.

I suppose she needs to mourn in her own way, Esther thought. And so she slipped away without a word, closing the door softly behind her.

Back in her room, Esther stood gazing down on her own children, both sound asleep. She was overwhelmed with emotion: not just love but gratitude for the luck that had kept them both safe so far. Yet it struck her for the first time that, in fact, luck had very little to do with it.

Kai and Sarah were healthy for two reasons: because they lived indoors and had plenty to eat and drink.

Gera hadn't. And now he was dead while they lived.

It was as simple as that.

Esther had barely known the boy, had only held him for a few hours, yet she could still feel the warmth of him in her arms. He was a child who had lived such a short time and then died, leaving someone to grieve alone. A great sense of sorrow and anger filled Esther at the thought of all those who suffered: not only the sick, but those who were left once they had gone. As she herself had been.

And then something odd happened: Esther discovered that she was forming words within her mind. She could hear them as clearly as if she were addressing someone next to her.

If you let me, she thought, *I promise to help as many as I can.*

She had no idea to whom she was speaking. It wasn't the memory of Caleb or her sister, Sarah. It wasn't even her mother, who existed as only a fragment of a memory. She was addressing something bigger, a force that lived in the earth and trees and sun, an invisible power that lay far beyond human experience, one that could make sense of light and dark, day and night, life and death.

The words brought Esther peace, a feeling she had not known in a long time. She suddenly understood that she was strong, much stronger than she had grasped. It had been one thing to feed a few hungry people. Now she realized that she could make a bigger commitment, a grander plan.

She would no longer concern herself with Gideon; from that moment on, whatever he did would be his affair. Instead, Esther would focus only on the problems she could do something about, things that were within her control.

Of course, it would take not only work but shrewdness and patience, qualities she had in short supply. When she tried to calculate how many beds they could fit on the floor below them and how they would bring the sick and injured back to the District, her mind reeled at the size and scope of her vision.

Yet Esther had faced seemingly impossible odds before; from experience, she knew that what she lacked in practical knowledge she more than made up for in resourcefulness and a stubborn will. All she needed was the slimmest trace of hope. Then she could not be stopped from doing what she knew in her heart was right.

As if she could understand, Sarah laughed and babbled as she awoke, her tiny legs kicking.

NINE

THE DAY OF TRADING AND WORK WAS OVER. FROM A HIGHER FLOOR, Gideon stared down at the crowds.

Outsiders continued to stream into the District each day, carrying Gleaned goods and pockets full of glass pieces. The more people came, the higher the prices went up. Sometimes Gideon had them raised on the same day, even as he lowered the amount paid for labor and Gleaned goods. Gideon was fascinated by how compliant the visitors were, how readily they agreed to whatever was demanded. He knew that sometimes they purchased things simply because someone else wanted them. And that person only wanted them because

Gideon had assigned them a high price.

Gideon was aware that the amount of glass was finite. His people had carried the entire mountain of oddly colored fragments from the garage; there were no more left. Yet by paying the same glass out piece by piece and then receiving it back the same way, he was able to generate not only a steady stream of new items coming in, but also an endless supply of labor.

It was, he thought, *magic.*

Yet he knew that the system was fragile.

He had seen a temporary slowdown in produce from Esther's garden and heard rumors of some kind of pestilence. It hadn't lasted, but what if it had? People only wanted worthless trash—a lamp that needed electricity, a useless coat made of dark, sleek fur, a heavy wristwatch with hands that wouldn't move—when their bellies were full. His entire system depended on a steady supply of food and drinkable water.

At the moment, trading in bits of glass was a novelty. But all it would take was someone to question what was going on. If enough people refused to play by his rules, the entire structure would collapse within days.

Gideon began to think ahead. He had to find something else to sell.

From the far end of the hall, he saw a figure stumble toward him.

It was a boy making a great effort to walk but weaving nonetheless. Gideon thought that the person might be suffering from the illness and as he made a sudden lurch toward Gideon, he intended to ward him off.

Then he realized it was Eli.

Gideon's underling staggered back a step. As he blinked, a confused look of recognition crossed his face. "Gideon," he said, as if to himself. He tried even harder to affect a rigid and proper posture, but it was impossible.

Gideon sighed. There were no sores or lesions on Eli; he didn't appear to be dying. He was only acting as he had since they had dealt with Aras: irresponsibly.

After the blind boy had been eliminated, Eli had been transformed. Now he behaved in an odd and absent manner, and his skin and clothes gave off a sharp, unpleasant aroma. For some reason, he had gone from being a trustworthy, even exemplary helper to someone Gideon couldn't depend on in the least.

Today was a new low. As Eli fell forward and clung to Gideon, Gideon averted his face to avoid the noxious odor coming from the boy's mouth.

"Sorry," Eli kept saying. "Sorry, sorry."

Gideon pushed him away and Eli stumbled back. A look of discomfort crossed his face. Then without warning, Eli buckled at the waist and proceeded to vomit all over the marble floor.

Gideon backed up, appalled. He turned his face to avoid the miserable spectacle, but nothing could keep the stench from invading his nose. He felt the shaky touch of Eli on his arm and he recoiled in disgust.

"Please," Eli said in a raspy voice. "Help me home."

Gideon refused to touch the other boy or let him grab hold. Instead, he deigned to walk to one side as Eli felt his way along the hall to his room. Once inside, Eli collapsed face-first onto his mattress, one arm hanging limply onto the floor.

Gideon prepared to go. Then he noticed that the other boy was reaching under his bed, scrabbling for something, which he pulled out. It was a rectangular glass bottle, nearly empty save for an inch or so of brownish liquid that sloshed near the bottom.

Gideon stared at the object and finally understood. He had seen this kind of drink in the past, a rare commodity that was fought over whenever it was found. The few times his Insurgents had drunk it on the outside, it had made them loud and foolish, not to mention incapable of work. Gideon couldn't fathom why anyone would deliberately put himself at such a disadvantage; he had refused to even touch it. To him, it was as dangerous as the stuff Aras had smoked.

"Want some?" Eli asked.

Gideon shook his head. "It poison."

Eli shrugged. Then he uncapped the bottle and finished it off. "You should try it," he said. "It feels nice. Only I reckon you don't like to feel that way." Eli snickered a little.

Gideon ignored the barb, something the old Eli would never have delivered. Instead, he looked down at the boy with new interest as Eli struggled to screw the top back onto the bottle.

"Why you want it?" Gideon asked. "If it make you sick?"

Eli stopped and thought for a moment before responding. "It makes me feel so good, I don't remember I feel bad."

Gideon took this in. "Where it from?"

"Bet you'd like to know." Eli said the last to himself, his tone again snide, but Gideon heard.

"Yeah," Gideon said seriously. "I do."

He loomed over the other boy, his eyes cold. Eli looked up at him and, for the first time that night, seemed afraid.

Minutes later, a shaky Eli was leading Gideon down to the basement and an inconspicuous-looking door, not far from the garage. Using a key ring that he had stolen from the adults who had once run the District, Eli unlocked it. Inside was a large, windowless room filled with stacked wooden crates, each containing bottles.

"They drank it at dinner." Eli's intoxication seemed to be wearing off; now he was ashen faced and bleary. "I saw where the old people kept it."

The labels all had different, unpronounceable names, but one word stood out: "proof." Gideon began examining the crates, counting the bottles they held. There were at least eight hundred, he reckoned, and took a moment to jot down a few numbers in a notebook he always carried in his back pocket. Then he turned to the other boy.

"How much you give to have it?"

"You mean glass?" Eli seemed confused. "For a bottle?"

"No." Gideon made a quick calculation, holding up a flask and guessing how much it contained. "For a drink."

Eli furrowed his brow. "I dunno. As much as I had to."

Gideon smiled to himself. It was uncanny: Eli was always of help, whether he intended it or not.

"Here," Gideon said, and held out the bottle. "Take it."

Later, after Eli had passed out on his bed, Gideon slipped

the ring with the collection of keys from the snoring boy's
pocket.

He could, Gideon thought, *make much better use of it himself.*

If she learned of it, Esther would disapprove, of course. So
he would be careful: A select number of customers would be
invited at first, and after that, others by word of mouth.

The more Gideon thought of it, the better he liked the idea.
Creating a forbidden air would heighten the value of what he
was planning. The basement, after all, was a place of darkness
and shadows. Where better to create a place where people
could enjoy a disreputable pleasure?

Once they paid for it, of course.

The hallway that lay beneath the one Esther and her friends
occupied was identical in its layout. The nine rooms were
spaced evenly along the outside of a rectangular corridor,
including a large office with double doors made of golden
wood. Sealed windows along the inner wall looked down on
the atrium below. Although the air tasted stale and dust clung
to the furniture after decades of disuse, the carpet was soft,
thick, and comfortable to lie on. After Esther had helped push
the desks and chairs against the walls, she and her friends
brought down armloads of blankets and pillows.

Each room, she figured, could easily hold three people.

Esther had remembered where Saith and Uri lived. When
she went back the next morning with supplies, she was relieved
to find that people began to open up and trust her. In fact, it
soon became painful having to choose among them, for this

time, she could have easily brought many dozens back. Still, she decided to keep her focus on those in the direst condition. Working with Silas, she began transporting the sick and the frail to the District, one or two at a time.

By the third day, all of the spaces had been taken.

Most of the Outsiders had injuries, wounds that most likely had been brought about by Gleaning buildings that were dilapidated and unstable: broken fingers and ankles that were swollen and red, deep gashes on the arm or leg that wouldn't heal. Still others were wracked by ailments that refused to go away: a rattling cough, stomach pain, fever. Esther tended to the ill early in the morning, cleaning their wounds as best she could and fetching them water. After working in the garden, she would bring down a meager lunch, usually vegetables and either porridge or flatbread she had prepared. Then she would come again one last time before bed, to provide supper.

To feed so many new mouths, Esther knew she couldn't rely on the rooftop farm alone; any sudden drop in supply would have brought unwanted attention from Gideon. Instead, she filched what she could and tried to augment it by dipping into their emergency stores. Each time she went into the closet, however, she deliberately kept her eyes down; she couldn't bear to see how quickly she was working her way through their precious reserves. At some point, they would run out altogether and she would be forced to find a way to deal with it. But for now, there was enough, and that was all that mattered.

Usually, Esther took her own meals with the newcomers. At first, she did it to save time, but as the days passed, she began to enjoy their company. With regular food and care, the Outsiders became less timid and savage seeming.

Esther was especially glad that Saith had blossomed under her protection. No longer remote, she had grown vivacious and sweet natured, always flattering Esther and making the older girl laugh. Soon, the newcomers would be well enough to decide what to do: to leave the District or join the others in working the garden. Secretly, Esther hoped Saith would stay.

Only a handful of the strangers had the killing disease. Although Esther now understood that it was impossible to catch it from simple face-to-face contact, she knew that the others weren't convinced. As a result, she kept the dying together, in a separate room at the end of the hall. She couldn't save them, but at least she could offer regular meals, some comfort, and a safe place to sleep for their final days.

One morning, as Esther entered one of the sick rooms, she recoiled at an unfamiliar smell, unpleasantly sweet and heavy. The odor seemed to come from a young girl she had brought in two days earlier, one whose leg was badly cut. As she did with all such injuries, Esther had wiped off the gaping wound to clean it as best she could, then wrapped it in an old T-shirt. But now when she undid the cloth, she was appalled by the swollen skin, the yellowish discharge, and the angry, red-edged flesh.

"You need to clean it." Esther was surprised to see Joseph standing at the doorway, watching. Up until now, no one from upstairs had ventured down to see what was going on, much less offer a hand. Her old friend sounded apologetic, as if interrupting. "If you don't clean a cut properly, it gets infected."

"Infected." Esther had no idea what the word meant. Yet she was desperate. She followed Joseph upstairs, where he headed to the supply closet. There he rooted around until he came up with an oversize plastic jug that sloshed when he lifted it.

Doubtful, Esther took it from him. She was familiar with the clear liquid, which was labeled HEINZ DISTILLED WHITE VIN-EGAR. From experience, she knew that it was sharp tasting and unpleasant. It could be drunk without ill effect if there was nothing else around, which was the only reason they kept it on hand. Still, Esther wasn't exactly sure what he expected her to do with it.

"Use this to clean her leg," Joseph said. "And anyone else who's bleeding." He seemed serious, and so Esther shrugged off her uncertainty and brought it downstairs. It *was*, she thought, *worth a try*.

Yet from the shrieks of the girl moments later, Esther wondered if Joseph knew what he was talking about. The vinegar seemed to burn the flesh and her patient struggled and kicked, sobbing with pain. But the discomfort faded quickly and Esther was soon able to rebandage the leg. To her relief, the strong smell helped to mask the stink.

Esther didn't expect anything beyond that. Yet to her shock, the next morning she found that the swelling had gone down. By evening, the wound had clearly begun to heal.

Esther found Joseph in his room, reading by torchlight. He was so intent he didn't notice her, and, accustomed to his ways, she kept quiet and crouched to let his cat, Stumpy, smell her hand and rub against her. After a few moments, he glanced up and saw her.

"How did you know that?" She didn't waste time in small talk. "About the vinegar, I mean. How did you know it would work?"

"Oh." Joseph was startled by the question. "I read it." He spoke as if that explained everything.

It was only then that Esther, baffled, glanced at the books that surrounded him. Joseph used every available space for the reading material he had been able to gather over the past few months. He even slept under a table that was piled high with dirty and mildewed volumes, newspapers, and magazines. To Esther, they were not separate items but a single, indistinguishable mass.

In Prin, Joseph had owned a library that was many times the size of this one. Her sister had also owned books; when Esther was little, Sarah had read aloud to her charming and mysterious stories of fairies and talking animals and children going on magical journeys. When they left Prin, Esther had brought along one of her sister's volumes: a battered copy of *The Wonderful Wizard of Oz*. Hearing Joseph read the story had been one of the few pleasures of their difficult trip.

Now what he said made Esther's mind reel.

Esther was aware that some books contained maps, and that those could be useful from time to time. Their former nemesis Levi had long searched for one that would help him locate the hidden springs of Prin. Beyond that, however, she had never considered the notion that reading could have a function beyond entertaining little children and passing the time.

Joseph had already crossed to the windowsill, which was heaped with disorderly stacks of reading material. "It's here somewhere," he called to her. Pulling out one dusty spine after another, he muttered to himself as he read the titles out loud.

"Got it!" he said at last. His face flushed, he returned and presented Esther with a worn book.

"You mean it's in here?" Esther was astonished. *If this one slim object could explain how to heal wounds,* she thought, *what other valuable secrets might it contain?* She was overwhelmed by the possibilities.

But when she took it with eager hands, Esther found she couldn't even sound out the title, much less understand what it meant: *101 Home Remedies.* She tried flipping through a few pages, but the dense black print swam in front of her eyes in a meaningless jumble. After a few minutes, she gave up.

"I'm sorry." It was not the first time Esther had felt both frustrated and embarrassed having difficulty deciphering even the most basic of sentences. But Joseph was gazing off, deep in his own thoughts.

"I'm teaching Uri to read," he said at last. "He asked me."

Esther nodded with chagrin. Even though Uri's intelligence had been apparent to everyone from the start, he was even younger than Silas.

"If you'd like," Joseph added, "you can join us."

Esther hesitated.

She had a clear memory of her sister, Sarah, attempting to teach her. Night after night, the two girls sat at the table in the apartment above STARBUCKS COFFEE. Sarah had printed out the alphabet on a sheet of brown paper. As stubborn in her own way as the younger girl, she had been exacting and strict, and Esther had reacted with typical resentment and defiance.

It had been, Esther now recalled ruefully, *a disaster.*

Yet this was a new situation. Esther was not being forced to do anything; she would be choosing to learn, for a very real reason. *And if a little boy like Uri could be taught to read,* she thought with a flare of competitive feeling, *why couldn't she?*

"I'd like that," Esther said at last in a shy voice. "If you don't mind."

And it *was* different now.

Joseph's kindness and patience made every lesson a pleasure and eased Esther's anxiety. Uri already worked at a far higher level than she could ever hope to reach. By the time Esther could make her way, shakily, through a book of fairy tales, he was reading books about things she found incomprehensible: *The history of medicine. The space race. The early days of the internet.* Yet Joseph didn't even seem to notice any difference between his two pupils, and so she quickly lost any self-consciousness. His pleasure in words was infectious, and he took pains to pick a diverse and unusual selection for both students to read, proving to Esther once and for all that books were, in fact, as distinct as people.

For the first time, Esther understood what her sister had tried to instill in her so long ago: Reading was a source of not only pleasure and comfort, but knowledge. And because of that, it seemed wrong that only a few of them—Joseph, and now Uri and herself—had access to it.

If she could learn to read, Esther thought, *then anyone could.* If more people knew how to decipher a publication, they could take the experience away with them, to share with others. As their knowledge spread, everyone would benefit: not only those who lived on the top two floors, but all the people who lived in the District. And perhaps everyone in Mundreel, as well.

Esther had an impulsive thought, one that was unformed yet so audacious it made her smile. Perhaps it was not enough to merely shelter and care for the sick. What if she could somehow help others—just one or two, whoever was willing or interested—to learn to read, as well?

She had no idea how such a proposal would be met or if such a thing was even possible. Yet the more she thought of it, the more it seemed like something worth doing.

TEN

THERE WAS A RESOUNDING CRACK AND THE BOY, AGED THIRTEEN OR SO, reeled backward.

Blood began streaming down his flushed face. When he put his hand up and saw that it was covered in red, he let out a furious roar and charged at the one who had hit him with an empty vessel. But he slipped on the wet tiled floor and pitched forward. Clutching his attacker by the shirtfront, he dropped with a thud. There, the two wrestled on the filthy ground, crashing into tables and chairs as the air filled with the fumes of spilled proof and encouraging shouts of laughter from onlookers.

Ever since Gideon had opened the secret room, it had

been like this every night. In short, his plans had succeeded far beyond anything he could have imagined.

It started as a rumor: Proof was available downstairs. Within a day, word had begun to spread and the place began drawing people: mostly boys, but some girls as well.

First out of curiosity and then with greater avidity, they drifted down singly and in twos and threes to the food court in the basement. There, they approached the armed Insurgent who stood guard in front of a locked door at the end of the hall, not far from the storeroom. Behind it was a windowless room.

Inside was a network of rusted pipes that led to a huge vertical drum that was discolored by dust. On a nearby table lit by torches, Nur dispensed drinks from various bottles that were either clear or colored amber, dark red, pale yellow, or blue.

Gideon had asked her to run the place, owing her something as he did. He was also guilty that he no longer called on Nur for her personal services and had been avoiding her in general, even though she often came looking for him. Ever since their disastrous encounter before his partnering ceremony, he had been repelled by her presence; he couldn't see her without feeling her clawing arms. And once she learned how to count, he had to admit that she had turned out to be a surprisingly competent and shrewd worker, one of the best he had.

It was Nur's idea, for example, to dispense the proof in small servings, no more than a single sip that she herself policed. Since she charged only three fragments, it seemed cheap to her customers, who had initially come out of curiosity. Although most choked and made faces when they first tasted the fiery stuff, the low cost made it easy to buy another and still another. By the second or third visit, one swallow never seemed like enough and thus it kept people asking for more—so much so that a boy could easily hand over nine, twelve, even fifteen pieces in a single evening without even being aware of it.

By the end of the first week, Nur was bringing in close to two hundred glass pieces every night. That number nearly doubled by the second week. Even after she had taken her cut, the amount of which Gideon never asked after or questioned, that made proof by far the most successful item in the District, more so than even food or water.

Yet the success brought risks, as well.

At first, only Insurgents came to drink. These were people Nur knew well, boys and girls she had lived with and who would comply when she asked them to pay up. For all of the loudness and foolish behavior brought on by their drinking, the crowd was mostly orderly. Yet that started to change as more and more strange faces began appearing.

The Outsiders were gaunt and filthy. They were only children, the same as everyone else, but living outdoors and scrabbling to survive had made some of them unpredictable, argumentative, and even violent on occasion, especially after a few sips of proof.

Nur watched the boys, strangers to her, who were now struggling on the floor. She had become accustomed to such fights; at least one broke out every night, and she was always quick to break it up if it looked like it was getting out of control.

Warily, she watched for a moment as the two rolled on top of each other, knocking into walls and furniture. A torch fell over, which she was quick to set straight.

Then one of them, the boy with the gash on his forehead, seized a metal chair and threw it at the other. It glanced off his shoulder and flew straight at the table where Nur was standing, along with her bottles and bucket of glass. Narrowly missing her, it crashed against the wall behind her with a deafening clang.

"Hey!" she shouted.

Furious, Nur jumped around from behind her station and came straight at them. Although she was small, she was fearless as she waded in between the two, yanking one up by the collar. "Stop it!" she screamed in his face. She turned to the other and attempted to grab his fist, which he had pulled back to deliver a blow. "That ain't allowed in here!"

In her new domain, getting yelled at by Nur made most boys, even the inebriated, sheepish and compliant. But the stranger just stared her down, his eyes mean and watery. Then, to Nur's shock, he gave her a violent shove. She flew backward and crashed against her table. She could hear the explosion as her container of glass fragments hit the floor. Several bottles tipped over and their contents began to glug out. In the next second, frantic patrons lunged at the flow, attempting to lap it up.

Helpless, Nur scrambled to one side.

All of the customers were on their feet and pushing one another, shouting and throwing punches in their eagerness to get a free drink. They didn't even seem to care about the glass fragments they were skidding on and trampling. When Nur saw people grabbing new bottles and attempting to open them, she ran to the door.

"Help!" she screamed at the boy who stood guard outside.

Eager for action, the guard, a hulking sixteen-year-old, waded back inside with her. As he pushed his way through the mob, he began swinging his weapon, a club with the words LOUISVILLE SLUGGER printed on the side. The air was soon filled with the sickening sound of wood cracking against flesh and bone as people screamed. The ground underneath grew slick with puddles of spilled proof mixing with blood. Even so, others continued what they were doing: raiding Nur's supplies, attempting to drink what they could, and stuffing any bottle they found beneath their robes.

By the time it was all over, an unnamed boy, stinking of drink, lay unmoving on the dusty floor that was littered with broken bottles. Many others had been injured, some badly; they had all stumbled away or been carried out by their friends. Now Nur crouched next to the body, picking up glass fragments that were sticky and flecked with dark red. She had to steel herself to check under him for any that were missing. Shuddering, Nur forced herself to concentrate on counting even as she could hear the boy's breath grow fainter and fainter and then stop altogether.

Wiping her hands off on her jeans, Nur took the bucket of glass and stood, refusing to look down as she went from torch to torch, extinguishing each one.

There was nothing left to steal. Yet out of habit, Nur made certain to lock the door behind her.

No one seemed to know who the dead boy was. Because no one would claim him, Gideon ordered the body dragged to the garbage room and tossed into a far corner for the rats.

He was bothered by the violence, not out of any feeling for the child or those who had been injured, but because of the effect it might have on his newest and most popular attraction. By Nur's count, she had lost seven bottles in the melee.

Gideon cursed the idiot of a guard who had acted in such a clumsy and stupid way. *It was a mistake,* he realized too late, *to have used the boy for such a delicate job when all he brought with him was size and strength.* The guard groveled and wept, tears staining his ugly face as he begged for leniency, but Gideon banished him from the District for good. *And even that was too generous,* Gideon thought with contempt.

Then Gideon made a decision.

When he had been living on the outside, he had heard rumors of a notorious enforcer. According to Insurgents who spoke of him, the boy was an expert at weaponry, skilled at bringing order to lawless areas and pursuing and eliminating troublemakers. He was said to work for whoever would supply him with the best food, water, and shelter: variant or norm, it didn't matter. He would even switch sides in a single town if the terms suited him. Gideon admired such lack of sentiment. If only half the things people said about him were true, the boy seemed to possess the traits that Gideon most admired: practicality, shrewdness, and steeliness.

With any luck, the fighter could be enlisted to help out.

Gideon sent out five of his best runners with instructions to cover the city. He hoped that through word of mouth, his invitation would reach its intended target.

Soon, to his delight, it had.

Two days later, Gideon was told that someone was waiting for him on the market level. No one had seen him arrive. When he came out, Gideon saw a stranger standing alone amid the milling crowd. He was sniffing a handful of what looked like figs and talking with the girl who was selling them.

It wasn't difficult to pick him out.

The boy looked old, perhaps seventeen or so, and was what Gideon assumed girls found handsome: tall, lanky, with an aquiline nose and watchful eyes. Yet what stuck out most of all was that everything about him was pale. He wore a white shirt and white jeans, both of which were impossibly clean. His face was dominated by a pair of blue mirrored sunglasses, the only note of color. The cap that he wore, with a number 37 stitched on it, was white; and when he pulled it from his head to scratch his scalp, Gideon was surprised to see that a shock of white decorated his dark hair.

"Trey?"

The boy didn't turn. "Let me finish here."

The visitor leaned in to whisper into the girl's ear. A blush came over her face and she giggled. He dug out several pieces of glass from a back pocket and pressed a few into her palm. The girl's blush deepened and she grinned a thank-you. Then she turned to help another customer.

The boy had a grand sense of himself, and this could be both good and bad,
Gideon thought. Trey studied one of the figs and bit into it,
savoring the taste. Then he returned the leftover pebbles to his
jeans. "Glass," he remarked as if to himself. "First time I used
it." He spat out a stem.

"Yeah?" Gideon said. "Where you get it?"

Trey's eyes flickered up at Gideon and, behind their reflec-
tive cover, looked him over. "Outside. Off a dead boy."

Gideon nodded, glad to hear that his influence was spreading. "I'm Gideon." He didn't extend a hand; he never did.

"What you want? I want to get going before it too hot."

Gideon could not help it; he was distracted by the boy's
strange appearance. He gestured to his hair. "Why you look
like that?"

"Maybe I seen a ghost." Trey chewed and swallowed.
"Maybe I *am* one." He put his cap back on and, when he smiled,
Gideon saw that his teeth were unusually white, too. "Why you
call for me?"

"To work here," Gideon replied.

"Do what?"

"Keep order."

Trey shrugged. "I ain't one to stay in one place long."

"I make it worth it."

"What with? Glass?" His smile was scornful.

Gideon kept his voice even. "It going to be the way now,
everywhere."

Trey shrugged. He was already looking around, appraising
the marketplace. Although it was crowded and noisy, people

were behaving in an orderly way; they waited their turns to trade and buy, paid what was asked, and didn't argue. "Things look pretty peaceful."

"Ain't here I mean."

As he descended the staircase with the grooved metal steps to the lower level, Gideon was surprised that Trey didn't follow. When he turned to look, however, he was startled to discover that the boy was right behind him. To his consternation, Gideon had never heard his footsteps.

As if reading his thoughts, the pale boy smiled. "Don't worry," he said. "I'm always right there."

They headed across the food court in silence. Gideon opened the door at the far end, revealing the large room where proof was sold. When the boys entered, Nur was polishing the bottles that lined the table, dressed in a formfitting top and jeans.

The stranger doffed his hat again, exposing his partly white mane. "Trey," he said. He extended a hand and, when Nur placed hers in his, kissed it with delicacy. She started, not sure what to make of him, and, blushing, withdrew her hand.

As Gideon explained the purpose of the room, Trey didn't appear to be listening; he kept his eyes on Nur, who smiled back in a self-conscious way as she continued working. Yet he was clearly paying attention.

"I seen the stuff drunk before," Trey said, "but not in a place like this. This new." He seemed appreciative, then thoughtful. "Bottles should be *that* way." He pointed. "Away from the door.

And tables go that side. So she see who come in and go out. Safer."

Gideon nodded, impressed by the suggestions. "I give you twenty pieces a week. Plus food and a room. How that sound?"

Trey nodded his approval, but Gideon wasn't finished with his interview. "What weapon you use?"

Trey chewed his lip. "What I always." He pulled something from near the ankle of his jeans and held it out: a small white pistol with a blunt muzzle.

Gideon smirked. "That?"

"It may be little, but it do the job." Trey put the weapon back. Then his eyes fell on someone across the room. "Who that?"

Gideon had been ignoring the boy who sat in the corner. Eli was asleep, head down on a table next to an empty bottle. Gideon looked at him with a flare of both disgust and embarrassment. He had probably begged some proof off of Nur, who had taken pity on him.

"Introduce me," Trey said.

"Eli." Gideon crossed the room and kicked at his foot. "Eli. Wake up."

Eli awoke with a grunt. He blinked, getting his bearings. He saw that Trey was holding out an empty bottle. With a fuzzy smile, Eli stood and took it into his quivering hands.

"Now stand down there," the stranger said.

Still barely conscious, Eli agreed. He wandered down to the far end, past Nur, who ceased what she was doing to watch.

"That good," Trey called. "Now hold it up . . . beside your head."

Eli stopped. He did what Gideon instructed. The bottle trembled next to his temple.

"For true?" Gideon himself was a little alarmed. "What if you miss?"

Trey shrugged. "Miracles happen."

In one motion, he whipped out the small weapon, aimed it, and fired.

It made an astonishingly loud bang in the windowless room. Both Nur and Eli screamed as the bottle exploded in Eli's hand, the shards spraying by his face and into his hair. He dropped to the floor, a trickle of blood running down his cheek, moaning in terror.

"He okay." Trey's voice was dismissive as he put back his weapon. "He ain't hit."

"I saw," Gideon said, taken aback.

"So. We good?"

Gideon smiled. He even let Trey shake his hand, an intimacy he never allowed anyone.

"We good," he replied.

Despite the prevalence of illness, the mood on the upper floors was festive.

By now, the Outsiders viewed Esther with a kind of awe; she had not only saved them, unbidden, from a slow and certain death, but also treated them with kindness and respect. As patients grew stronger, Esther brought them into the library, where Joseph read out loud to them. The stories, fanciful tales of imaginary characters, were popular enough; but to her surprise, the idea that the words themselves were somehow recorded on paper seemed even more remarkable.

Esther had assumed only a few would be interested in learning. Yet by the second day, nearly all had stayed behind to pore over the tiny black marks that they could not decipher. Seeing their hunger to learn, Esther and the older boy had begun to teach all of them how to read for themselves.

Yet one of them now watched her with an intensity that arose not from gratitude, but from overwhelming curiosity.

Although Saith could neither read nor write, she possessed an instinctive cunning that was almost animallike. She had always understood without thinking the basics of a certain kind of survival: who was in power, whom to fear, and whom to ignore. She had survived off these skills, for although not powerful herself, she knew how to flatter and ingratiate herself with those who were. In the best cases, they would in turn protect and take care of her; in the worst, they would at least spare her the brunt of their violence. And now Saith realized that Esther possessed unquestionable authority.

That in itself was a mystery to Saith. Until then, she had only witnessed power of a specific type: the cruelest and most brutal person using physical intimidation to subdue and punish everyone else. Although barely nine, she had seen many such tyrants rise to power for a day, a week, a month, until they were challenged and defeated by someone even more savage (for there was always someone waiting to take a turn).

Saith had never once seen a girl like Esther in charge of anything.

It was true that Esther possessed a wiry strength. Saith had seen her lift an injured boy much larger than she was and then carry him for a long distance. Yet Esther didn't appear to be a fighter and in all other ways was unintimidating. She carried no weapons; even her voice was soft.

More intriguing to Saith, Esther was direct in her manner, openly emotional, and impulsive in word and action. At first, Saith assumed it was a game the older girl was playing, a way to keep her real intentions hidden. She had not trusted Esther's show of sympathy when her brother, Gera, died; from experience, she had assumed Esther was attempting to manipulate her grief for reasons Saith did not know. It had made her deeply suspicious, and for days she hated the older girl.

But soon Saith realized to her astonishment that it was no act: Esther was guileless. Yet she was also the undisputed leader of the small community atop the District. Growing stronger each day, Saith began to spend her waking hours observing and studying her.

How did Esther do it? Saith wondered.

Saith had made sure to win over her affections; by now, she knew she was one of the older girl's favorites. Esther had been down that morning to bring coffee and water for the sick. As usual, Saith was waiting to help her carry the tray and bring drinks to those who couldn't get up. As Esther smiled at her with what seemed like real affection, Saith said nothing, but ducked her head in a bashful way that she knew made her appear younger than she was. Then she had collected the empty cups and handed them back.

Now Saith watched as Esther headed down the hall and disappeared through a metal door. On a whim, she decided to follow.

The girl found herself in a dark and echoing stairwell, the air stifling hot. Groping her way forward, she discovered the metal banister as well as steps made of cement that led in both directions. Esther and the others, she knew, lived on the floor above. She crept her way up, leaning on the rail, for she was still weak and could be short of breath. Reaching a landing, she fumbled for the bar of the door and pushed it open.

Saith emerged onto a drab hallway carpeted in beige. Not seeing Esther, Saith wandered down the corridor, peering into each room. They were all unoccupied yet filled with humble belongings: bedding, clothes, shoes. She was nearly at the end when the last door opened and someone stepped out, nearly bumping into her.

Saith drew in a sharp breath.

The creature was bald and dark skinned, wearing a shape-less sack. Its limbs were covered in a welter of scars and tattoos, and its face, Saith thought, was hideous: bulging lavender eyes set on the sides of the head, with slit nostrils and tiny, pointed teeth.

It was a mutant.

Although she was much shorter than the other, Saith drew herself up to her full height, trembling with indignation. "How you get in?" she hissed. "What you steal?"

The creature blinked at her, as if it didn't understand. Then it had the audacity to give a faint smile, its eyes crinkling at the corners.

"If you're looking for Esther," was all it said, "she's on the roof."

Without answering Saith's questions, the mutant slipped to one side. With no sign of haste, it sauntered past Saith and down the hall. Trembling with anger at its insolence, the girl watched it go. Then she made up her mind.

Esther had to be told right away what had happened. True, it didn't seem as if the mutant had stolen anything; its hands were empty. Yet it had clearly broken in and needed to be reported and punished. Even if it managed to escape, Esther would at least know that Saith was on the lookout for trouble.

Saith headed back to the stairwell and climbed the final flight, her heart pounding with righteous fury. She pushed open the heavy door at the top and stepped onto the roof. For a moment, she was stunned by not only the brilliant sunlight but also the suffocating heat and the profusion of growth that surrounded her. The garden seemed to go on for miles in all directions. Others were moving about, holding baskets and tools, talking quietly among themselves. But Saith only had eyes for Esther. She glimpsed her at the far wall, a bucket in one hand as she talked with someone.

"Esther!" Saith could not convey the news fast enough. "Esther!"

The older girl turned around as Saith ran to meet her. Esther's companion turned as well, and when Saith saw who it was, she stopped in her tracks.

It was the mutant.

"What's wrong?" Esther had already seized the younger girl by the hands and crouched to talk to her. "And what are you doing out of bed?"

Saith said nothing. She felt as if she had been punched in the stomach, and she lowered her eyes, even as she quailed under the mutant's even gaze.

"N-nothing," Saith managed to stammer. "I . . . I had a bad dream." Her confusion was so great, she found herself on the verge of tears. Then she let out a childish sob. "Scared."

Esther gathered her in her arms, and for a moment, Saith shut her eyes and luxuriated in the attention. She found herself almost believing her own lie as Esther patted her on the back. "Don't worry," she said. Then the older girl pulled back.

"Saith," she said. "I want you to meet my best friend. Skar, this is the girl I told you about."

Saith finally looked up and met the mutant's stare. There was no anger or hatred in the lavender eyes, just an opacity that unnerved Saith. The creature smiled in a polite way, revealing her little teeth. Saith smiled too, but only out of nervousness. She had a wild and fleeting hope that the mutant hadn't recognized her, but it was dashed by what the creature said next:

"We already met."

As she often did with Esther, Saith hunched her shoulders and opened her eyes wide to make herself look younger and smaller. She started babbling obsequiously: *She had been dreaming. She ran upstairs; when she saw Skar, she mistakenly thought she was a being from her nightmare. She was foolish for having made such a stupid mistake; how could she mistake someone so distinguished as Skar for a monster?*

Saith knew she was exceptionally good at making things up on the spot. Esther listened to her story with an amused and sympathetic smile, and even Skar nodded once, as if in forgiveness.

Inside, however, Saith's mind was whirling.

Esther's best friend was a mutant. That meant he, she, or whatever it called itself was a person of consequence in a position of influence. Yet how could that be? A mutant in power would be an abomination, like a dog standing on its hind legs and talking.

Then a girl, heavily veiled, wandered up to them, towing a boy by the hand. Saith recognized the child as Esther's son, who had once tried to play with her brother. For a moment, she couldn't breathe; she was filled with bitterness and pain at the sight of the child, alive and laughing while her beloved Gera lay dead in the ground.

Then a cry caught her attention.

The hooded girl was holding something else in her free arm, something bundled in a dark blanket that had begun to squirm.

"Here," the girl said. "Sarah wants her mama." Esther reached out her arms and took the child, murmuring into its neck as she bounced it up and down.

In the bright sunlight, Saith clearly saw: the bulging, wide-set eyes. The slit nostrils. The hairless skull.

Like her best friend, Esther's baby was a mutant.

Saith drew a sharp breath. At first, her mind was unable

to take in what she was seeing. It was bad enough that Esther treated the mutant Skar as an equal, free to roam the halls unescorted. Yet what she was seeing now was so sickening that Saith felt she must be dreaming, caught up in a repulsive nightmare.

Esther was making no secret of her affection for the tiny monster; to Saith's horror, she even brought her face close to its deformed features and nuzzled it. For Saith, the shock of witnessing that kiss was like a physical blow.

How was it even possible for a human being to give birth to it? What father had been responsible for such a demonic offspring? Fighting a wave of nausea, the little girl now saw Esther in a whole new light, as something that was filthy, unclean, and utterly repellant.

Still, it suddenly made certain things clear to her: why Esther chose to live up here, far from the others downstairs. And why she chose to have a mutant as her second-in-command.

Saith didn't know how many people knew about Esther's shame, but she guessed it was very few indeed. If so, the information could prove to be useful.

She suspected that someone else might want it.

Days later, Esther sat on a dusty couch, fidgeting.

She was alone in the living room of the house Aras had chosen for them. She had not come back to lacerate herself with painful memories; instead, she was waiting with impatience for someone to show up. Esther had been there for so long, she was beginning to think that no one was coming. Just when she was about to return to the District, she heard a fumbling at the front door.

When she stepped into the front hallway, Gideon stood there, removing his sunglasses.

"It been a while," he remarked.

Esther gave a brief nod and said nothing.

"What this about?" To her surprise, the boy seemed nervous, his eyes darting around but not meeting hers. "Why can't you say it at the District?"

"I've been *trying* to reach you." Then she bit her tongue; she had something important to discuss and didn't want to be sidetracked by bickering. "I wanted you to see this place for yourself."

Only then did Gideon bother to look up, giving the entrance and living room a cursory glance. "So?"

"Not here. I want to show you something upstairs."

She turned to go. When she didn't hear him follow, she glanced back and was surprised by his expression: He looked guarded and wary. "Come on," she said, unable to keep the trace of impatience from her voice. After a moment of hesitation, he followed her as she walked with sure steps through the living room, the dining room, and the kitchen that lay beyond. Then she entered the small stairwell that stood behind a door, climbing to the next level before reaching a smaller flight that ended in a glass door.

Esther turned to him. She was so excited she found she was able to forgive the boy, both his tardiness and his insolence.

"Here it is," she said before turning the handle and pushing it open.

Gideon had been on his guard when he had first received word that Esther wanted to see him. The complicated directions and obscure location of their meeting only deepened his suspicions. He had even been tempted to bring two of his boys with him and had only decided at the last moment that doing so might make him appear weak.

Gideon was convinced that Esther had somehow found out about the basement. Only the week before, he had decided to put Nur in charge of a new business that promised to be even more successful than the room where proof was sold. From the moment he walked in, he had braced himself if not for a literal ambush, then at least some kind of confrontation. But to his shock, she showed no indication of doing that. If anything, she seemed as if she had some kind of wonderful secret she wanted to share. *Clearly,* he thought, *she had no idea of what he had been up to,* and for the hundredth time, he was relieved that her silly work tending to the poor had distracted her from the important business he was doing downstairs.

As he followed her through the strange and shabby-looking little house, he wondered what her secret could be. She led him to a glass door on the top floor and pushed it open as if some rare treasure lay on the other side.

But there was nothing. Instead, Gideon found himself stepping onto a bare roof, one that was hot and dusty. Confused and irritated, he turned to her. But she had already wandered off, gesturing as she spoke.

"Don't you see?" Esther turned around, her eyes sparkling. "We're running out of food. There isn't enough to feed everyone. But what if we built a greenhouse here? We could set up a water purification system, too. Joseph knows how to do it . . . I know he does."

Gideon blinked as he absorbed her words. Then he let out a short bark of laughter. "That impossible. And even if you do it, this place too small."

Esther was already shaking her head. "This would only be a test . . . to see if it works. If it does, we can build more. There are places like this all over Mundreel—hundreds of them. We can teach people how to work the garden, how to fertilize the crops and purify the rain. That way, they can support themselves and not have to depend on us."

Gideon smiled; he felt as if he were tolerating the foolish chatter of a child. "It crazy. You can't teach Outsiders to farm. They animals . . . they can't think. How they gonna run a garden?"

Esther turned to him, her expression serious. "I think they can," she said. "But that's not what I'm asking you. I was hoping maybe a crew could work here with me." She paused.

"So?"

"I think they should be paid for their effort. You're in charge of that."

"If this such a great plan, why they need pay?"

"Because it's fair. Remember we talked about that when we made our deal?" She said this pointedly and Gideon glanced up at her. "I've lived up to my half of the bargain. I don't question

what you've been doing. And I don't ask for anything." Esther
let out a deep breath. "But I'm asking now. Will you help us?"

Gideon paused.

With sudden clarity, he understood what Esther was proposing and realized that it wasn't stupid at all. In fact, it was
revolutionary—in the most dangerous sense of the word. She
was suggesting that they take the means of procuring food and
drinkable water, something that he currently controlled, and
put it in the hands of the mob: the ignorant, undisciplined,
and foolish hordes who roamed not only the District, but the
streets beyond.

If he allowed it to happen, there would be no more need
to work for glass; people would be able to support themselves
instead. Business would no longer be conducted on the main
floor of the District, but on every rooftop where anyone
could grow enough plants to survive. And Gideon's system,
the one he had spent so much time perfecting, would eventually become outmoded and then disappear altogether. Leaving
Esther the undisputed leader of the entire city.

He couldn't allow that to happen.

"Don't need to waste my glass on your foolishness." Gideon
spat on the tar paper between them. "I already know it ain't
gonna work."

Esther started to say something, but he had turned and
headed back to the door. He didn't give her enough time to
catch up; he fled down the stairs as if being pursued. Only
when he was back on the street did Gideon manage to resume
his air of studied indifference, putting on his sunglasses before

remounting his bicycle. He could sense her watching him, a pale face at the narrow window beside the door.

He ignored it.

As he took off, Gideon was aware that his heart was pounding. Once again, he found himself confounded by Esther. Was she acting naïve on purpose in order to trick him? Or was she really as simple as she seemed?

He shook off his uncertainty. After all, his little trip had made one thing clear: Esther knew nothing about what he had been up to. And that was the most important thing of all.

For now, the secret of the basement was still safe.

ELEVEN

SKAR HAD BEGUN TO SUSPECT THAT SOMETHING STRANGE WAS GOING ON in the District.

She had taken to standing at the hallway windows, the interior panes that faced inward onto the complex. Pressed against the cool surface, she gazed down as best she could, past the immense objects made of glittering glass that dangled from the ceiling. It seemed to her that there were more disruptions than she had ever recalled, especially in the late afternoon and early evening. Occasionally, she could hear loud voices, raucous laughter, and the unmistakable sound of fighting that carried faintly through the open air.

Several times, Skar tried to share her concerns with Esther. But her friend was always too busy to pay much attention.

"That's Gideon's concern," she said once. "I have too much to do."

There was no one else with whom Skar felt comfortable sharing her doubts. As her partner and confidante, Michal was the obvious choice. Yet despite—or perhaps because of—the hardships she had suffered in her short life, Michal hated serious discussions and remained lighthearted and carefree. Skar usually loved Michal's sunny spirit, which contrasted with her own tendency to brood and worry. But at times like these, she found herself frustrated by her partner's frivolity.

"Why do you want to stir up trouble?" It was late at night, and Michal was standing in front of their mirror, trying on the elegant veil that Esther had worn during her partnering ceremony. The girl tied it around her golden hair, binding it back; then, frowning, she draped it across her mutilated features. Satisfied with the results, she gathered the ends around her throat and secured them in a bow. "People like all the pretty stuff there is to buy. So do I. . . . I wish we got to go down there."

"True," Skar replied. She had always enjoyed watching her partner try on ornaments and show them off, but tonight, she was in no mood. "Esther gave Gideon the freedom to do what he wanted. She is only interested in her own plans. But I'm worried that something bad is happening."

"So stop worrying. Do something."

Skar realized that her partner was right. It was no good

brooding and keeping her suspicions to herself; she had to find out for certain whether or not she was right. Yet that was not so easily done. Skar herself could not go down and find out what was going on; as the only variant in the District, she was far too noticeable.

Spying had been a common practice among her people, an effective way to see what rivals were planning and to prevent attacks. As leader, her brother, Slayd, had orchestrated many such missions and kept their people safe as a result. When she was little, Skar had watched him countless times and learned. Now it was her turn to put into practice what she had picked up.

Hours later, after Michal had fallen asleep, Skar slipped down the hallway, the carpeting cool and soft under her bare feet. Although it was pitch-black, she knew the layout well, and moved silently three doors down. She gave a soft tap on the door, then turned the cool metal knob.

Moonlight poured through the curtainless window. Silas was already sitting up, squinting at having been awoken so abruptly, his hair standing on end. Although he looked surprised to find Skar standing in front of him, he knew better than to say anything.

"You are a good stealer," Skar said, without wasting any words. It was true: The boy had broken into many buildings, plundered corpses, and been adept in a world that sometimes required nefarious action.

Silas blushed and began to protest. "I ain't stolen nothing! Not from here, anyway. So if anybody says, they're lying. I—"

Skar put up a hand. "I am not here to punish you."

Silas stopped. His eyes, wide and unblinking in his thin nine-year-old face, watched her carefully.

"I want you to steal something for me."

The boy relaxed; he even chuckled. "Why didn't you say? That's easy. What do you want?"

Skar's voice was serious. "Information."

It wasn't hard for Silas to blend in on the main floor of the District.

By midmorning, the mall was packed with eager customers. From above, it looked like a sea of dirty, billowing robes that were belted at the waist and draped around heads. Similarly attired and wearing mirrored sunglasses, Silas squeezed his way unnoticed through the crowd as people crushed against booths, examined merchandise, then stood in line to haggle and buy things with their pieces of glass. He skirted past other Outsiders who were working: sweeping the floor, replacing windowpanes, or lugging cans of gas to the generator.

It was so easy to get around, Silas marveled; *maybe too easy.* Because as Skar had suspected, he was beginning to think that the real problem, if there was one, wasn't to be found on the ground level.

Silas found himself gravitating toward the twin metal staircases that led to the lower level. That was where he had once followed Joseph's cat and found a room full of garbage and a human skull, where he had learned what the adults had eaten in order to survive.

Still, Silas liked challenges. *And this one,* he thought, *seemed like it would be a lot more fun.*

Yet making it downstairs proved to be much more difficult than he had assumed. Standing at either side of the glass-encased stairs were four Insurgents. Two openly held clubs, and Silas was certain that the others had weapons hidden in their pockets and beneath their robes. Pretending to examine merchandise, he watched as a boy approached them. One of the guards patted his robes and spoke a few words to him. The boy took out a knife and handed it over. Only then was he allowed past.

As one of Esther's friends, there would be no way for Silas to simply barrel past. He would have to be more clever than that.

His unique talents were about to come in handy.

Silas swiveled around as if making up his mind what to buy and saw he was facing a particularly busy stand. People crowded around a table that was heaped with the usual welter of goods: shoes, packets of food, bottles of water, furnishings, clothes. Taking advantage of his small size, Silas managed to snake his way through to the front. There, he saw a tangled pile of the small objects that strapped to the arm: "wristwatches," he had heard them called. Joseph owned several that he wore every day, Silas knew, and was forever fussing over them.

A girl of about twelve was laboriously counting out what seemed like an endless amount of glass. Her new purchase, a watch made of gold and silver metal, was already fastened to her wrist with a pink band.

To anyone who was watching, the little boy who stood beside the girl was gravely examining the selection of shoes for sale. In reality, Silas was reaching up one thin hand. With fingers as light as silk, he tugged at the end of the leather strap until it pulled free of the tiny loop that secured it. Then he bumped into the girl.

"Hey!" Silas whirled on the surprised person behind him. "Stop pushing!" He then turned back to the girl, who was now glaring at him. "Sorry," he said. But in that one moment, Silas had managed to pull at the strap on her wrist and release it from the metal pin that held it in place.

The wristwatch dropped into his palm.

Without drawing attention to himself, Silas moved away as swiftly as he could. Moments later, he heard exactly what he wanted.

"Hey! My watch! Stop him!"

As the girl's screams echoed through the giant marble atrium, all of Gideon's guards sprang into action. From every corner of the mall, they ran forward, shoving people aside and drawing out their weapons. But Silas had already slipped the watch into the hands of an unsuspecting boy, younger than he. Perplexed, the boy was now holding it up in the air . . . but before he could stammer out an explanation of what had just happened, the mob descended.

Silas ran past the crowds who were racing the other way. He felt a brief flicker of guilt for the innocent boy, whose screams were even now being drowned out by the sounds of his beating. Then he shook it off. The twin staircase in front of him was momentarily unguarded. Silas flew down the steep, grooved metal steps, taking two at a time, his hands skimming the hard rubber banisters.

When he reached the basement, Silas ground to a halt. Then he slipped around a corner.

Across the food court, he saw a crowd of people gathered together outside a closed door. It was mostly older males, standing in a restless line. The door was cracked half-open. Flickering light and thumping, rhythmic music wafted out from within. The sounds were completely unlike the gentle tones he had remembered the adults dancing to when he and the others first came to the District.

Whenever anyone exited the room, a new one was allowed in. Those who emerged acted strangely: red faced and glassy eyed, they stumbled and clung to the wall. A few of them laughed for no reason at all and more than one had been sick, the fronts of their robes stained with vomit. As they passed the corner where Silas hid, he could smell the overpowering liquid that the adults used to drink on occasion. The one time Silas had tasted it, he'd found it so unpleasant he had spat it out onto the floor, to the laughter of the leader Inna and the others. *Still,* he thought, *those stumbling by seemed to enjoy it well enough.*

"Next! Keep moving!"

A boy supervised the goings-on; he stood on the threshold releasing old customers and bringing in new. To his shock, Silas saw that it was Eli. He had not seen the older boy in many weeks, not since the District had been divided. His friend seemed transformed, and not for the better: He was pasty faced and sickly and had dark circles under his eyes.

At that moment, Eli propped the door open to talk to someone and noise, light, and smoke, the pungent kind Aras once used, poured out. Silas ducked back, to avoid being seen. But for that instant, he had been able to catch a glimpse of the murky room, lit by flickering torches. He noticed that tables were crowded together, and people sat around them, drinking from glasses. Heavy and insistent music throbbed, competing with a clatter of voices that were talking, laughing, shouting. Then Eli escorted in another boy and the door closed behind them.

Although more boys and a few girls were heading toward the guarded room, Silas noticed others walking in another direction, continuing farther down the hall. He slipped in after two of them, boys who butted each other with their shoulders, as if sharing a private joke.

"I heard a lot about this place," Silas heard one murmur. "It just open up."

"Me, too. Can't wait. Just hope I got enough." Silas could hear him jangle a few pieces of glass around in his pocket.

"How do I look?" The first attempted to comb his tangled hair with dirty fingers, then turned to the other for an appraisal.

"It don't matter," the other one said, and laughed. "She got to like you, right?"

Silas caught up to them as they came to the end of the next corridor. Ahead were two narrow doors, outside of which a smaller group of boys congregated.

Silas hid behind a pillar he suspected was too close for

comfort. He feared he wouldn't have any time to see what was going on before being discovered. Still, he had no choice.

After several minutes, one of the doors opened and a boy emerged. He did not seem affected by drink as Eli and the others had, although he was grinning. Silas peeked inside the room, which was narrow and dark, perhaps a former closet. In it he glimpsed what looked like bedding heaped on the floor. Standing above it, a girl in a white T-shirt and tousled hair was pulling her shorts back up. She had an absent expression and her face was pale.

Standing outside, as if supervising, was the Insurgent girl called Nur.

"Next," she said.

As another boy paid her with glass, went in, and shut the door, Silas drew back behind the column. Although he didn't know what he had just seen, he had a tight feeling in his stomach. He hoped Skar would be able to explain when he described it. Then he glanced up.

Someone was approaching.

A teenage boy was coming down the hall. He wasn't headed to the room in question; Silas could tell by the way he walked. There was nothing either eager or aimless about his gait: Cutting his way through the crowd, he seemed intent on reaching Silas, upon whom he had locked his gaze. He was dressed in white and, as he came closer, Silas could see a streak of white in his hair, too.

He could also see a gun.

Without missing a step, the older male had leaned down and

in one fluid motion pulled a weapon from near his ankle. Now only feet away, he lifted it, taking aim at Silas's chest. Those on line outside the rooms hadn't noticed and continued to talk and laugh.

Silas shrank back and, by instinct, threw an arm in front of his face, knocking his hood back as he froze in fear. He locked eyes with the older boy, who stopped and, all at once, seemed unnerved. His expression, which had been stony, softened; Silas could swear he almost smiled. Still, he kept the gun raised.

And fired.

The explosion echoed in the hallway, causing a commotion from those standing around. Silas, who had squeezed his eyes shut in terror, heard the zing of the bullet as it whizzed past his ear; he opened them only when he realized he hadn't been hit. As he looked around, stunned and confused, he saw that several feet behind him, bright red bloomed against the wall, dripping down in rivulets.

A moment ago, it had been a rat.

Silas stared up at the gunman, still petrified. The boy in white met his eyes and gave a single impatient nod that clearly meant *go.* Silas forced himself to move, turning away and fleeing back the way he had come, toward the double stairs.

He didn't dare look behind him.

Trey tossed what remained of the dead animal on the tiled floor.

Gideon recoiled. "What that?"

Trey shrugged. "You got pests."

Gideon pursed his lips. "You come here for a rat?"

"What I meant is you got somebody snooping around. Downstairs."

There was a moment before Gideon replied. "Who?"

"Don't know. He got away."

The two boys were alone in Gideon's tiled office. Trey was inspecting his own clothes for any trace of the rat's blood or gore. Mostly, though, he wanted to avoid the other boy's eyes because he was a bad liar. He didn't lie often—he didn't have to, at least not about missing his target, for he rarely did. But the gunman didn't kill small children. That was the only rule he had and no one needed to know it. *Let Gideon think he had failed,* Trey thought.

"Got away?" Gideon's voice was sharp. "How that happen?"

Trey shrugged again. "Like everything else in this life. No reason."

Gideon turned away. But what he said next surprised Trey.

"Esther up to something."

Puzzled, Trey could only nod. He had heard Gideon talk about this girl before, whoever she was; he seemed to blame her for everything bad that happened. Trey had been rejected by his share of females before; he merely moved on to the next, for there were always more. He couldn't understand the boy's obsession with one person or his inability to let go.

"She aim to destroy me." Gideon had turned back to face him, although he seemed to be speaking to himself. "Ain't happy with what she got. She try to squeeze me out."

Trey located a fleck of dirt on his sleeve; he had to use his fingernail to work it loose. He suspected that Gideon was going to ask him to do something, something that had to do with this girl Esther. *Avenging a broken heart seemed a foolish waste of his skills*, Trey thought. But Gideon was the boss, and so Trey would do whatever he wanted.

"You want me to get rid of her?" he said at last.

Gideon shook his head. "Not now," he said. "Maybe later. But right now, she too important. People like what she do upstairs. I hear it." Gideon thought for a minute. "Just get her to stop spying. Lean on her. Use your little gun, if you got to."

Trey considered this. He figured Gideon was exaggerating the situation. Still, this Esther obviously had spirit. Most girls could be undone by a smile or a few sweet words; maybe this one would be a challenge.

"I got a better way," he said. "Girls like me." He winked, but Gideon didn't smile. The gunman sighed; the boy was all business, no fun.

"Maybe this Esther lonely, I mean," Trey said. "Maybe she need a boy to take her mind off her worries."

"And that boy would be you?"

Trey shrugged. Gideon's eyes swept up and down Trey's body in a way that made him feel odd. Yet Trey realized there was only calculation in it, as if he were a piece of jewelry or clothing to be priced.

"You tell me stuff about her," Trey said, "and I carry the facts in case I need them. Like my . . . little gun."

He smirked, but Gideon's expression was serious. "I know plenty about her." Trey let the other boy speak: Esther had a mutant child. Her partner had left her for another girl. There were other details that he dutifully noted. When Gideon was finally finished, Trey noticed that Gideon was out of breath and red in the face.

"We good?" the boy in white asked.

"Yeah," Gideon said.

"Then it settled."

But Trey wasn't finished. *When people wanted things,* he thought, *they were at your mercy.* He smiled now, his teeth gleaming.

"But it's gonna cost you," he said, "extra."

Esther sat on the top step of the dark staircase, Kai in her lap.

It had been a while since she had had time alone with her son. Sarah was in their room, tucked up in her crib. The rest of those needing her care were at long last asleep. There wasn't a sound in the entire District; everyone was gone or settled for the night. Esther hadn't even felt the need to bring a torch with her. She and the boy rested in the stillness, which seemed peaceful and unending.

She heard something before she saw it.

Someone had entered the stairwell far below. Alert, Esther peered through the darkness, all of her senses straining; after a few moments, she saw the distant flicker of light throwing deep shadows. As whatever it was approached, she saw that it was pale and moved in a deliberate way.

For a shocked second, Esther thought of Pilot, Aras's dog. *Had the animal returned?*

As the shape grew nearer, it became more distinct. As

Esther's eyes adjusted, she realized it was no dog but a boy she
had never seen before. He was a little older than she was, seventeen she guessed, and dressed all in white, which gave off a
soft glow by the light of the candle he held. When he rounded
the final landing and saw her, he stopped as if expecting to find
her there.

"Evening."

Esther nodded, not responding, Kai stirring a bit in her
arms. The boy had a strange white streak in his hair, too.

"I'm Trey," he said, and climbed to the top.

"Esther." The boy was nodding even as she spoke. He
fumbled in his pocket and drew something out. It took her
a moment to identify it in the flickering shadows: It was the
round tin of the lemon drops she had once tried to get for Kai.

"Care for one?"

"I don't have enough glass." Esther was surprised to find she
was still annoyed.

"It don't cost you nothing. It's mine." He opened and
offered the tin. When she didn't touch it, he reached in and
placed a piece of candy into her hand. The brief touch was
startling; his slender fingers were unexpectedly soft. "Actually,
that ain't true. It's yours."

As he handed her the round can, he smiled, and Esther had
to admit, he was handsome when he did it. She found herself
smiling, too, even though she didn't want to; she still didn't
know who this boy was or what he wanted. Neither accepting nor rejecting the gift, she placed it on the step below her,
the child stirring in her arms. Kai had woken up, although she

wasn't as annoyed by this as she normally would be.

"What are you doing up here?" she asked.

"Stretching my legs. I get restless sometimes, downstairs."

"You work for Gideon?"

"If he's the one who hired me. Stiff boy? Never smiles?"

"That's him." Esther laughed now; it felt like forever since she had done so. This stranger who had emerged from the dark seemed like someone from a dream. Maybe he was. In any case, for a moment at least, she relaxed.

"I sell things. Like this." He indicated the tin. "And this. Watch."

Trey dripped hot wax on the landing and stuck the candle in it. Then he took something from his breast pocket and held it out. Esther examined it: It was a small metal rabbit, with a tiny white knob that protruded from its side.

By now, Kai was wide-awake. "What's that?"

Smiling, Esther held the boy away. "We've seen toy rabbits before."

"But not like this one." Trey twisted the button, which made a faint clicking sound. Then he leaned forward and set it on the ground. To Esther's amazement, the metal animal scurried forward a few steps, paused, and then jumped in the air. It spun in a circle, ran in a new direction, then leaped again.

Kai stared at the vision, openmouthed, then lunged at the toy. "Give me!"

Although Esther held him back, Trey picked up the rabbit, crouched down, and presented it to the boy. Kai squealed with delight, then proceeded to examine it with both hands.

"Are you sure?" Esther asked. She, too, was enchanted, although she managed to keep a straight face.

Trey shrugged. "He can have it."

There was silence for a while, as Esther assessed him. Then she asked, "How come you wear white?" It was an impertinent question, yet she found she didn't care.

"Maybe I'm a ghost," he said, and smiled, his teeth white, too. When he saw Esther's quizzical expression, he grew serious. "I'm just passing through," he said. "Had a little trouble. I'm trying to leave it behind. Ain't easy."

"What kind of trouble?" *This Trey encouraged openness*, Esther thought. She was asking him questions she would normally keep to herself.

"With a girl." He shrugged, looking off. "She run away with someone else. Bad feeling here." He thumped his chest once, to illustrate. "Don't seem to go away no matter how far I go."

Esther was surprised to hear this. It was odd that such a confident—even arrogant-seeming—boy had the same problem she had. Kai was reaching out for Trey, and she had to rein him in.

"I know how you feel," she said.

"Do you?"

"Yes."

"That's hard to believe, pretty girl like you."

Esther blushed. "It's true, anyhow."

"He must have been crazy."

Esther didn't know how to answer. Brooding about Aras seemed silly now, in the face of so much true suffering, seeing what she did each day. Still, in the quiet hallway, with no one else around to provide perspective, she felt the pain again. Knowing this boy had gone through something similar helped.

"You mind?" He indicated the stair beside her. Esther made room and he sat down, stretching his long legs in front of him.

Trey couldn't help it; he kept looking at Esther. He had expected another kind of person: if not the diabolical schemer Gideon had described, then someone bold and experienced. Instead, he found a girl who was sincere, direct, and self-possessed. She didn't flirt, nor did she wear artificial colors on her face or tight clothing that showed off her body. In fact, Esther almost looked like a boy at first, with her slim frame and short, tousled hair. Yet she was pretty in a way that made you want to glance at her twice. It made Trey feel funny about what Gideon had accused her of, and the lies he was about to tell her.

Kai escaped Esther's embrace and moved into Trey's lap. Trey let the boy crawl on him, not minding, even enjoying it. Kai grabbed his nose; Trey made a monster face and growled. The boy squealed; Trey laughed. Then Kai settled into a ball in his arms and fell asleep again. Trey rocked him.

Esther studied his profile as the little boy began to get drowsy. *There was something about Trey that was utterly appealing,* she thought. *Small children didn't like just anybody, after all.*

"Was she pretty, your girl?" she asked.

"Oh yeah. I thought so." He waited. "But maybe it wouldn't have worked out anyway."

"You can't know that."

Trey had to shake off his feelings about Esther. He was about to speak the false words he had prepared and needed to keep a clear head. "True. But it's what I tell myself. See, my girl was a . . . well, what some people call a mutant." He swallowed hard, aware of her eyes on his face. "Maybe that shock you. But I loved her the same as if she was a norm. Others didn't like the . . . you know, the marks on her. The tattoos and such. To me, that's ugly thinking. But people do what they do."

Esther said nothing, only listened. But the smile froze on her face and she could feel her spine tense up. Trey wasn't looking at her; he was peering into the darkness.

"Anyhow, we had a hard time. So maybe it for the best. She went off with one of her own kind. Can't say as I blame her, but still."

"What was her name?"

Trey paused and bit his lip before answering. "Lavie."

Esther watched her son, as he lay in the boy's arms. She had an impulse to take him back but didn't obey it. Then she glanced down to Trey's crossed legs and his idly swinging sneaker.

She saw what looked like a small weapon strapped to his ankle. Then, on the step near it, the round candy tin had some lettering on it, along with a faded picture of fruit. Esther squinted to see. It read LAVIE.

"I better go," she said quickly, and stood.

"Something wrong?" Trey glanced up at her, a flash of concern in his eyes. *As if,* Esther thought, *he was afraid he had made a mistake.* She opened her arms, gesturing for her son.

"Maybe," she said.

Trey glanced down and saw the container. He grunted and kicked it, lightly, to the side, cursing himself for his blunder. He hadn't been able to use lazy charm and cheap tricks against this girl; Esther was too smart, too observant. He surprised himself by his next thought: *And maybe that was a good thing.*

"Look, I . . . ," he began, and stopped. The door in the landing above them creaked open and both of them glanced up, blinking in the unexpected light that spilled down on them.

Skar stood, holding a torch overhead. "I am sorry," she said. "But Sarah is crying and we did not know where you were." Her lavender eyes held Esther's for a second, then flickered over to the boy.

Without a word, she stepped closer to her friend, as if for protection.

"The boy—now?" Although her voice was firm, Esther's outstretched hands had begun to shake.

"Hold on." The light had awakened Kai, who squirmed in the boy's arms. Trey retrieved the tin and took out a piece of candy, which he gave to him.

Esther brought her arms down, slowly. The hair was standing up on the back of her neck, and her body trembled with the desire to run. *Had Trey been sent by Gideon?* If so, then Gideon had surely told Trey what to say to her. She shuddered at the thought that she had been so nearly taken in.

Even so, she was struck by the boy's actions. He still held

her child and was now stroking his head with what looked like true gentleness.

"That's a good little fellow," he whispered. Trey hoisted Kai up under the arms. Before he could place him on his feet, Esther reached forward and seized him, holding him close.

"Good night," Trey said. He was gazing at her, a faint smile on his face.

Esther's nerves were still jangled. She thought of the boy's lies and the gun he kept by his ankle. Yet his expression was soft, as if he were about to apologize. *Had everything he'd said and done been insincere and duplicitous?* Suddenly, Esther didn't think so. But she put the feeling aside.

The two girls watched him disappear down the stairs. In a moment, only the soft tread of his sneakers could be heard fading into nothingness.

Once she was sure they were alone, Esther turned to Skar. "That boy. He—"

But Skar gave a brusque shake of her head and held a finger to her lips. Then she pointed upward, indicating that they should talk on the roof.

The garden was silent and still warm from the day's heat. Esther waited until the door was closed behind them before she told her friend what had just happened.

Skar listened, her head down. "Gideon."

"I'm afraid so." Agitated, Esther could not keep her voice as low as Skar's as she frantically paced back and forth. Kai, who was dozing off in her arms, awoke with a start.

"It sounds like this boy was trying to win your confidence.

To see what you were up to."

Esther's voice grated with frustration. "But why *now*?"

Skar didn't say anything at first. To Esther's surprise, her friend, whom she had once thought incapable of lying, averted her eyes as if hiding something. Then she looked up with an expression that seemed almost defiant.

"I have something to tell you."

Astonished, Esther could only listen as Skar told her about Silas: how she had approached him late at night. How she had asked him to infiltrate the lower levels of the District. How he had managed to trick his way down to the lowest level, to see what Gideon was hiding.

"You asked him to spy on the mall? Without even talking to me first?" Esther wasn't sure if she felt more shocked or outraged.

"I tried to talk with you," Skar retorted. By the light of the torch, her eyes were bright. "But you did not listen."

"*I always listen to you!*" Again, Esther forgot to keep her voice low. Yet instead of backing down, Skar grew as stubborn as her friend.

"Gideon is doing terrible things," she said. Unlike Esther, Skar kept her voice down, yet her words were relentless. "In the basement. There are special rooms down there. You do not understand what he is selling to people. To boys—"

"I don't have time for this." At the thought of Gideon, Esther grew even angrier. "I asked him for help, and he turned his back on us. So I don't care what he does."

"But you do not understand. He—"

"No," retorted Esther. "Let him just do things his way. That's the only way we can get along, him and us. I'm not going to judge him." She drew a shaky breath. "After all, variants used to be judged, too."

As soon as she said it, Esther realized her mistake. Skar's eyes flared dark with anger. "You cannot compare us! Variants are nothing like Gideon . . . nothing at all!"

She had already whirled around. "I'm sorry!" Esther called, a pang in her chest. "Come back!" But Skar was already halfway across the roof, heading for the door.

Esther exhaled. She could feel her fury dissolving; now all she felt was regret for having lost her temper, as she had done a hundred times before . . . but never at Skar. *The variant girl,* Esther knew, *was a careful and deliberate person; she always had a good reason for doing and behaving as she did.* If she had gone behind Esther's back, that could only mean she felt she had had no choice. And that said far more about Esther than it did about her.

Full of contrition, Esther took off after Skar.

In the moonlight, a lone figure wrapped in a blanket watched as Esther disappeared down the stairwell.

Saith had not intended to eavesdrop. She had been sleeping, as she often did, in the guards' lookout. The narrow piece of roof had been empty ever since the District opened its doors to Outsiders, and once she had discovered it, the little girl took refuge there since she found she couldn't bear sharing a room with others. Yet she had been awoken by Esther's voice raised in what sounded like anger.

By instinct, she slipped behind a row of greenery and listened intently as Esther and Skar argued. She stayed there long after Skar left and Esther ran after her, pondering what she had heard.

At first, the quarrel had given her hope that the friendship between Esther and the variant was at an end; both girls had seemed so angry. Yet the moment it was over, Esther seemed full of self-reproach, calling after the other girl. Disappointed, Saith realized that the two had a stronger bond than she had hoped.

She would never get as close to Esther as she wished.

And so Saith abandoned that plan as easily as she had formed it; her thoughts now turned in a new direction. What Skar had mentioned about the District seemed far more promising. Although Saith did not quite hear all that was said, it seemed clear there was action downstairs: desperate people coming in every day, things being sold for glass. And it sounded like there was one person in charge of it all: someone named Gideon.

Saith made up her mind.

There was no point in flattering and manipulating Esther any longer. It would lead nowhere, and frankly, Saith was already tired of the farm, the hall of sick people, and all that was upstairs.

She gently laid the blanket down on the ground. Then without looking backward, she turned to the stairwell and headed down into the inky blackness.

TWELVE

THE NEXT DAY, TREY SAW THE LITTLE SPY AGAIN.

It was apparent that the child had neither heeded Trey's warning nor appreciated the fact that the older boy had deliberately chosen to spare him. Instead, he was even more brazen than the first time, weaving his way in and out of people who filled the basement of the District. Trey watched him with disbelief mixed with pity. *If the boy had learned anything,* he thought, *it was only to disguise himself a little better and blend more into the crowd.*

Still, he ran right into Trey.

Silas looked up and recoiled. Skar had told him not to spy anymore, but he had done so anyway; being told not to do something had always had the opposite effect on him. Yet this time he realized he had pushed it too far.

He saw Trey freeze, unsure how to proceed.

Then Trey gripped Silas by both scrawny arms under his billowing robe and half lifted him in the air, pulling him close. Silas didn't bother to fight back; he prepared himself for the worst.

Trey leaned in and whispered, his voice low and urgent. *"This the last time."* Then Trey released Silas, nearly flinging him to the floor.

The boy gazed up at him, shocked. As relief swept over him, he scrambled to his feet and took off, racing for the nearest stairs.

Trey watched him go, uneasily. He hoped the boy would bring Esther the message, so she'd hold off from spying. Gideon wouldn't let it go about Esther, Trey knew; it was only a matter of time before he realized that nothing had changed. And although he wasn't sure why, Trey felt he had to protect the girl. He had always served anybody, no matter how cruel or corrupt; he had taken no sides, as long as he was paid. Now that seemed unacceptable. Trey had a few minutes to get his story straight before reporting back.

Then he turned and found himself staring into the face of Gideon.

His employer had clearly witnessed what had just happened. His eyes flickered back to Trey in a question. Trey felt himself blush, the first time he could ever remember doing so.

"Why you here?" He hoped his belligerent tone would put

the other boy on the defensive. "You checking up? You don't trust me?"

Gideon shrugged. "Should I?"

"You hire somebody, you let them do their job. And since you open that other room, my job is two times what we agreed on. Maybe it should cost you more."

Out of the corner of his eye, Trey saw Eli, who was staring at them in open curiosity; Trey shot him a harsh look, and the drunken boy glanced away.

Gideon ignored Trey's words. "That little one name Silas. He Esther's boy." Gideon was following Trey through the basement, raising his voice to be heard. "He the one you see before?"

Trey stopped. It was unavoidable; they had reached the small rooms near the end of the hall, where the girls were sold. Here the crowd was so great, it was hard to get by; Nur and her guards had a hard time policing them. Gideon was at his back, his mouth nearly pressed against Trey's ear as they squeezed past.

"You let him go again? After you seen her?"

"I do what I think best." Trey couldn't help it; his voice shook a little.

"That right?"

"That right."

They were now alone, their footsteps echoing in the dark and barren end of the food court. Trey felt sweat prickle at the back of his neck, another new sensation. He craned his neck to see how far they were from the others: *Too far,* he thought.

That the other boy had caught Trey letting Silas go was bad enough. But what made it worse, much worse, was that Trey had all but guaranteed Gideon that the spying would end. And he had already lied to him. He claimed to have charmed and seduced Esther, sweet-talking her into not only confessing her forays into the District but also promising to call them off.

Trey knew that Gideon wasn't stupid, and it took no great leap of the imagination to surmise that Trey had let Silas go just now because of the girl. Still, Trey couldn't come out and confess his unexpected feelings for Esther and her child; he could barely admit them to himself.

He had always liked little children because they were innocent. They said what they meant and believed what you said; they loved without motive, without guilt. Esther was no child, yet she had the same kind of honesty and openness. He had learned that, upstairs, she helped the sick and desperate. She did it without gain for herself, not because she thought she could get something from it. Trey had met good people before, yet they had been invariably weak or foolish. Esther was neither; and the idea of betraying her bothered him more and more. But to tell Gideon this, he sensed, would be a fatal mistake.

"So it ain't true, what you say?" Gideon pressed.

"What I tell you?"

"About Esther. It all a lie."

Trey started to make something up, but before he could speak, Gideon spat on the floor. "Never figure you as soft." His voice was full of contempt. "Maybe you think she sweet. But she ain't."

Trey glanced up. From the tone of his voice, Gideon seemed more a spurned lover than anything else.

"You get out," Gideon said. "Hear me?"

Although he said nothing, Trey couldn't keep from sneering. Gideon was short for his age and bone thin, with no muscles to speak of; his neck was like a barren twig. It would have taken Trey no great effort to kill Gideon where he stood, and for a moment, he was tempted. But as the idea flickered across his mind, he could hear in the near distance the clamor of the boys outside the rooms.

What Gideon provided was not merely popular; it had become the very life and blood of the District. He had grown too powerful to kill and get away with it.

"I hear you," Trey said in an even voice.

Hours later, Gideon stood in his tiled office, his eyes closed to ease his throbbing head.

He couldn't bear to think of what might have happened between the assassin and Esther. Instead, he concentrated on what he knew for sure: that Trey's departure had left him two very real problems. There would be no one taking care of order in the District. And his enemy was still upstairs plotting against him.

Was it his imagination, or were there fewer people buying proof and girls ever since Esther had started caring for the sick and teaching others to read? Were people turning against him and what he offered, siding with her?

He was so preoccupied, he didn't hear the knocking at the door.

"Go away." Gideon assumed it was Eli. He had little patience for the boy and his pathetic needs and was in no mood to hear his drunken questions about Trey.

But the knocking came again and was more persistent. Gideon sighed and turned around. When he unlocked the door, he saw no one at first. Then he glanced down. He was astonished to see a child standing before him.

She was no older than eight or nine, and tiny for her age. With delicate features and pale skin that seemed almost translucent, she had dark curly hair that framed her face like a halo. She looked like an expensive doll or a toy, and as finely made. Yet she stared up at him with eyes that were shrewd, fearless, and strangely knowing.

Gideon let out a bark of incredulous mirth. "What you want?"

"I want to talk," the creature said.

Again, the boy laughed. He started to close the door in her face, but she had already slipped inside.

"Out," he instructed. She shook her head, even as Gideon reached forward and gripped her by the bony shoulder. "I told you, out."

"I'm Saith," she said. "And I can help."

Gideon hesitated. Then with an abrupt move, he released her. "What you mean?"

She shrugged. "Depends. You need sellers?"

"No."

"Gleaners?"

"Every day, I got more than I need."

"I see." She glanced around the Spartan room, at the white tiled walls and metal stalls. "You need someone count that?" She nodded at a heap of green glass that glittered in the corner.

Gideon was impressed. "You count?"

"No. But someone teach me, I learn." Saith looked back up at him with a cool gaze. "I learn anything."

Despite himself, Gideon was amused by the child's arrogance. "That nice. But I ain't needing anything."

He had already taken her by the shoulder again, to push her out. But Saith held back, her pretty brow furrowed in a frown.

"Ain't nobody don't need things." She slipped from his grasp and moved out of reach. "Even the ones got everything."

"What *you* know about that?"

"Plenty. I watch it all my life."

Gideon hesitated. The girl's weird confidence was impressive. Still, what could he do with her? "You ain't strong enough to help. 'Less you got a gun and can use it."

To his surprise, the little girl smiled.

"Oh," she said, "it ain't about guns. Who can fight, can kill. It about who knows things."

Gideon grunted. "How you mean?"

Saith took a step closer. "There other ways to control folks," she said. "I see what Esther do. I been upstairs."

The boy paused a minute.

"You interested now," Saith said.

"Yes," Gideon had to admit.

"I seen her baby. The mutant. You know it's a mutant?"

"Yes," he said, taking a seat.

She came close. Gideon was aware she had even placed her hand, a tiny, slim paw, on his arm. He didn't shake it off. Her voice was soft, insinuating. "I know how to make her do what you want."

Gideon didn't scoff; her manner forbade him. He studied the little girl again. "I listening," he said.

Saith was gazing off, her eyes clouded in thought. When she smiled, the boy noticed that her teeth were white and a dimple flashed in one cheek; her innocent appearance was strangely at odds with her knowing words. "I hear what you do . . . downstairs."

At that, Gideon felt a new flare of rage at Esther and her spy, the boy Silas. He leaned forward.

"I think," she said at last, "we give them something even gooder."

And with that, Saith winked.

Several days later, there was a commotion on the main floor of the mall.

Like the other information he had conveyed, Gideon had arranged to release a rumor in a judicious way. At first, he told only his favorite vendors, whom he instructed to provide hints to just a few key customers. At every step, people were urged to keep the news strictly confidential . . . and so naturally, it soon spread throughout the entire building.

Most people were both too suspicious and too stupid to trust anything resembling an official announcement. Yet overhearing something from people you didn't trust or even know was a completely different matter. Gossip made even the most scurrilous report believable.

A girl had come to the District who was either witch or prophet.

She could see the future.

She had visions of an afterlife.

Watching from the fourth floor, Gideon could almost *see* the exciting news fly from one person to the next. It fascinated him, this glimpse into the strange workings of the ignorant mind, the avidity and glee with which people hoarded then shared what was to them precious: the promise of something better than this short and painful life.

Saith had told him this would happen. She was right.

She spent the entire time hiding in his office. Because no one could know of her, Gideon was the only one who slipped her food and water. He also procured for her clothing: a fine silken robe of white, a silvery scarf that she draped over her hair. She gave specific instructions, and he fulfilled them to the letter. Then she spent the remainder of the time resting and preparing herself for her first appearance.

Soon it would be time.

THIRTEEN

A BOY STOOD BEFORE ESTHER. HIS NAME WAS NOAH, AND IN HIS SWEATY palm he held out a single object. The others who had been learning how to read were already on their way out the door, talking and laughing.

Noah was heavier than the others, big for his age, which was about twelve. He had had a brief stay in the sick rooms with an injured ankle; then he had started coming to Esther's classes.

From the beginning, Noah struggled to learn. In fact, his stumbling and halting attempts reminded Esther of herself. Today, she had helped him sound out and write the letters of his own name for the first time. She had seen his eyes brighten with pride and a smile of discovery sweep across his face.

For this, he was now offering a piece of glass.

Esther had always made it clear she didn't want anything in return. "Please," she told him now. "I said no."

The boy didn't move, only looked at Esther with a furrowed brow.

"But," he said, "you deserve it."

"And I told you," Esther said, her patience ebbing, "that's not the point of this."

Noah put the glass piece back into his pocket. Still, he didn't leave. Then, to her shock, he sank to the floor and threw himself at her feet.

"Thank you." His voice was muffled. "Thank you."

For a fleeting moment of pure confusion, Esther thought he was sick. Then as the boy clung to her calves, she became flustered and appalled. Trying to keep her temper, she reached down and unwrapped his fingers from around her legs. With an effort, she pulled him upright again.

"That's enough," she said, her face flushed.

Noah looked at her, truly baffled. She knew that the boy was slow compared to the others. But what he said now astounded her.

"But that how we thank Saith."

Although Esther said nothing, her mind was whirling. "All right," she said in an even voice. "But that's not how we do things up here." As the words sank in, Noah glared at her with resentment.

After the boy had left, Esther let out a long breath, surprised at how unnerved the encounter had made her.

Since Saith had disappeared, Esther had heard many speak of the younger girl with awe and reverence. That alone was disturbing. But what bothered Esther most of all was that as a result, fewer people were coming to the ninth floor: The little girl claimed to alleviate their ailments by a simple touch. Even Noah had not waited for his ankle to heal and had opted for Saith's approach instead.

This worried her. The more Esther read and the more she spoke with Joseph and Uri, the more she was convinced that the only things that cured illness and injury were rest and knowledge, not superstition and magic. She had also heard of predictions the girl had made, performances she gave, and devotions she encouraged. Yet Esther suspected that real prayer was a personal matter, a private dialogue between one's soul and a greater power.

The young girl was clearly working with Gideon now—that much was certain. Esther went over and over it in her mind: Had there been some clue she had missed? Was there any way to have realized that the little girl's desire to please had in fact masked bold calculation and ruthless ambition?

Esther tried to put the whole situation out of her mind, for she had other things to attend to. It was even later than usual due to her work with Noah. For although she spent each day working, Esther always made sure to tuck Kai and Sarah into bed.

Tonight, as often happened, she was too late: They were

already asleep. Michal, who had dozed off beside the children, stirred at Esther's touch.

"Thanks," Esther whispered.

Michal gave a sleepy smile. As she stretched, something fell unnoticed from her lap. Idly, Esther reached down and picked it up.

"What's this?"

When Michal saw what it was, she gasped. She tried to seize it, but, her curiosity aroused, Esther held it back and tried to examine it by the moonlight.

It was a doll baby, no bigger than her hand, made of light brown plastic. Whatever hair it once possessed had been plucked out; tiny, empty sockets covered the bald skull in a neat pattern instead. It wore a crude outfit, obviously hand-stitched from a piece of brown cloth: a baggy and shapeless tunic.

"Give it back." Michal's voice was louder than she probably intended, and Sarah flinched in her sleep. "Ain't no need to see that."

"But what is—"

Then Esther fell silent. In the dim light, she saw that the doll was covered with scars and symbols carved deeply into its plastic limbs.

Like a variant.

A deep chill ran down Esther's spine. "Where did you find this?"

Michal shook her head. "It was here when I come. Lying on your bed so no one could miss it. I was going to throw it out."

"Did you see anyone come or go?"

"I wish I had."

Michal was trembling, and Esther realized it wasn't just for Sarah's sake. After all, Michal and Skar knew firsthand what it meant to be the object of derision and hatred; the doll must have felt like an especially painful and personal attack. Esther moved forward and placed a hand on the other girl's shoulder.

"It's okay," she said.

She hugged Michal, who clung to her for a moment. Then, adjusting her veil, the girl slipped away, back down the hall to the room she shared with Skar.

Alone, the meaning of the doll hit Esther like a physical blow. It had clearly been left as a warning and perhaps even a threat.

Still clutching the hateful object, Esther stepped outside of her room; she needed time to think. Then she recoiled.

Standing at the far end of the dark hallway, silhouetted against the night sky outside the window, was a small figure, gleaming in immaculate white like a ghost. It seemed to be waiting for her.

"Saith," Esther said.

She had recognized the girl at once, even without seeing her face. Yet as she approached, Esther noticed that Saith had in fact changed.

Wearing silk robes that gave out a faint glow, the little girl stood with her back straight and a faint smile on her lips. Her hair was newly brushed and radiated around her pretty, doll-like features like a soft cloud. The scent of roses and jasmine wafted from her skin. She seemed to have aged years, not weeks. But when she spoke, her voice was still that of a little girl, high-pitched and ingratiating.

"You got my gift," Saith said. "That make me happy."

Esther had forgotten she still held the revolting doll. She almost threw it on the ground but managed to hold herself back.

"I made it," Saith added.

"I couldn't have done it," Esther replied, and that much was true. "I never could sew. That's what my sister always said, anyhow."

"Your sister, Sarah?"

With a sinking feeling, Esther realized she must have mentioned her sister at some point and Saith had remembered. *What else had she revealed about herself without thinking? What other information had she unwittingly supplied?* With reluctance, she nodded.

"That why you call her that. That nice."

Esther said nothing, just kept her eyes on the young girl. Saith held the gaze, then eventually glanced to the side.

"I'm glad you trusted me to show me your baby," she said.

Esther refused to look away. "I did trust you."

Saith kept going. "People talk about you all the time. When they come to me. They say such nice things."

"I'm glad." Esther's voice was flat.

"But you know what funny? No one mention little Sarah. No one."

Esther felt chilled.

"Don't be scared," she heard Saith say. "I bet people still like you even if they know you got another baby. And it a *mutant*."

At the hateful word, Saith giggled.

Despite herself, Esther could remember the child's appeal. There was something clear and piercing about her gaze, whether sincere or not. And like before, she seemed so sweet and eager to please. Yet it was clear that Saith had hidden behind this innocent-little-girl image when in fact she had never been one.

Still Esther said nothing. As if impatient, the little girl reached forward and, without asking, took back the doll. She cupped it in her hands and rocked it; the gesture seemed like a nasty parody of love.

"Maybe one day I forget no one know. And I just let it slip out." Saith glanced up, her black eyes glittering like coal. "That would be bad. Maybe people might not like it. They get angry. What you think?"

"I don't know," Esther said. "You tell me."

"Maybe I ask Gideon what he think." Saith smiled. Then she expelled her breath, as if surprised, and glanced down. "Oh no," she said. "Look what I done."

She had twisted the head off. Now she let the pieces fall to the floor and kicked them to the side. "Well. I like to see you, Esther. I think about you."

The little girl gave one last smile. Then she turned to the stairwell and was gone, leaving nothing but the scent of flowers.

"I'll be thinking about you, too," Esther said, to no one.

* * *

That night Esther couldn't sleep. After hours of tossing and turning, she slipped out of bed. The hallway was dim, lit by the window on the far end, and the air in the stairwell was unusually cool. She sat upon the steps, her mind whirling with thoughts about Saith.

How seriously should she take the child's threats? she wondered. *She was just a little girl, after all; was it just a malicious prank? Or was there something more sinister beneath her words and if so, why? Had Saith in fact been set up to do it by someone else . . . namely Gideon?*

Esther did not know how long she sat there. But all at once, she heard a far-off door close and the sound of someone approaching from far below.

The figure made the light of Esther's candle waver. When she saw who it was, she drew a quick breath and the flame ducked and danced.

It was the boy with the white streak in his hair.

Even as she tensed up and readied herself to escape, Esther had to admit that she wasn't completely unhappy to see him. She knew that Gideon was mounting some kind of campaign of intimidation against her, sending Saith and this boy. She knew Trey had no scruples and would kill for pieces of glass. Yet for reasons she could not explain, she trusted him.

Was it the look of regret he had given her the night they met? The way he had played with Kai? It was as if Trey were at odds with himself, aspiring to be better than he was. Even his white stripe of hair suggested there was someone older and wiser inside, trying to get out. *It was silly,* she thought, *but true.*

"Evening," he said. When Esther nodded a greeting, he indicated the step beside her.

"Mind?"

Esther made room for him on the cement step. "Don't think I don't know why you're here."

"And why's that?"

"Gideon sent you."

"It was just my job." Esther began to respond, but he cut her off. "And I don't work for him no more. He don't even know I'm here."

Trey now moved his hand and dug in his pocket. He took out a palmful of glass pieces, which sparkled in the meager light. "It's all junk, anyhow." He let them spill at his feet and they rolled and bounced down the stairs and over the edge, disappearing into the darkness below.

He had spoken without guile, Esther thought. Taking a chance, Esther decided to speak the truth as well. "I don't know what Gideon told you. But what Silas is up to wasn't my idea."

Trey didn't answer, just shrugged. He seemed mesmerized by the candle stuck to its holder of hardened wax, watching the yellow flame bend and flicker. Yet it was clear from the expression on his face that there was something else on his mind. He looked serious, even grave.

"Look," he said, "I hear about the girl. The little one downstairs? She's up to something bad. It ain't safe for you anymore. Or your children."

At the mention of Saith, Esther looked up sharply. "Is she working with Gideon?"

Trey nodded. "Once that boy gets something in his head . . ." He didn't elaborate. "He got fierce feelings about you."

Esther sighed and looked away again. "He wanted to be my partner. But that doesn't mean he's got feelings."

Trey shook his head. "You broke his heart. If that possible with him."

"I guess everybody's got a heart." Esther turned back and looked the boy in the eyes.

"It's true." He reached out a hand as if to touch her, then let it fall on the step. They sat like that in silence for several moments. "Look," he said at last, "I got room for two. Four, with your kids." He paused again. "Maybe Gideon hired me. But I'm on *your* side, Esther."

Esther drew a deep breath.

Saith and Gideon were intending to come after her or Sarah—it was only a matter of when and how. Trey was offering her and her children not just a safe escape, but perhaps something more: a chance at a life together.

It would be so easy, she thought with a real pang, *to go away with him.*

And yet she hesitated.

She thought about the people who even at that moment were sleeping a floor below them. There were only five of them, Outsiders whom Esther had brought to the District. She had fed and washed them by hand, was teaching two of them to read. In one case, she had saved a boy from certain death . . . and there would always be more, for the world was full of the sick and dying.

None of her friends, Esther knew, *shared her intense desire to help.* If she were to leave tomorrow, no one would take over her work.

Esther remembered the private pledge she had made to whatever higher power existed: She would try to help others as best she could. And now that Saith was threatening to destroy all that she had started, could she truly turn her back on it, just to save her own skin?

"I thank you," she said. "But . . ."

"Don't say no right off. You ought to think about what I said. Still, there ain't much time."

"I can't. I'm needed here."

There was a pause. Then he nodded. "Well," he said, "I better be gone, then. Before I'm found."

Esther said nothing. She could feel him pulling away from her, concealing himself again behind his hard exterior as he got to his feet.

Before he did, he turned back, surprising her. His sudden movement snuffed out the candle. In the dark, Trey pulled Esther to him. He kissed her, and his mouth was soft and warm; she had not been kissed like this since Aras left. Then he let his lips trail to her neck, where he buried his face, taking in the scent of her.

Slowly, he let go.

"Maybe I'll see you again," he said. "It can be a small world sometimes."

He took the stairs now, vanished into the black. As his white form drifted from view, Esther heard him say:

"Take care of that little boy."

Then even his footsteps faded away.

When she returned to her room, Esther was able to sleep, at least for a little while. Then she heard the door open as someone came in and sat on the edge of her bed.

In the moonlight, she could make out Skar's profile. "Michal told me about the doll," her friend whispered.

Esther let out her breath. Ever since the two girls had made up after their fight on the roof, they had been closer than ever.

"Did you know?" Esther asked at last, as she sat up. "About Saith?"

Skar was silent for a moment. "I knew something was wrong from the beginning. But I thought she was just a silly little girl. Now I realize that was a mistake."

"It was my mistake, too." Esther bit her lip. In whispers, she told about Saith's visit and the threat she had made against Sarah.

Gideon, she was certain, *was behind it all.*

"How can I stop it?"

Even as she spoke the words out loud, Esther realized she was asking the question of herself. For it had finally become clear to her that ignoring what was going on downstairs and tending to her own business had been a mistake. Running away with Trey would not have helped; in fact, it would have made things even worse. Her willingness to turn a blind eye had allowed something terrible to grow and flourish; something that now threatened to end everything she had worked for.

She only hoped it was not too late to act.

Skar was deep in thought. "There is one thing you have that she doesn't," she said at last. "It may not seem like much, but it might turn out to be greater than all of this little one's lies and badness."

"I know." The sudden realization struck Esther. "I know what it is." In the moonlight, she saw her friend turn to her with a questioning smile.

"The truth," Esther said simply.

Joseph glanced over Uri's shoulder, squinting to make sense of what the younger boy was reading. Then, as he had so many times, he gave up.

The two now spent most mornings alone in the library, for as the days passed, fewer and fewer students came to the tenth floor. Joseph understood in a vague sort of way that it had something to do with what was going on on the lower levels. He was saddened by the change, for he found he enjoyed teaching. Still, the unexpected freedom gave both him and Uri endless time for their beloved books.

Uri in particular had been keenly focused on his reading. For the past few weeks, he had been working his way through a stack of yellowed and crumbling magazines and journals, often referring to thick books, including a dictionary, that were piled up next to him. The titles of the articles were incomprehensible to Joseph: He couldn't even pronounce most of the words, strange things like "immunology," "resistance," and "waterborne pathogens." Yet Uri had been staying up late each night, even falling asleep over his books. Joseph brought him food and water several times a day and had to remind him to eat.

Although Joseph was much older and had been reading far longer, it had been clear from the start that Uri had the better mind of the two. While Joseph loved to read, it was purely for pleasure; he had little understanding of topics like math or science. The more time he spent with Uri, the more this had started to make him feel self-conscious; his maps and clocks and childish stories were no substitute, he sensed, for what Uri read. It was the kind of knowledge that really mattered.

Still, Uri seemed oblivious to any difference between them and was always happy to share what he learned. And knowing that he had been the one to teach him brought Joseph a genuine sense of pride. Joseph was the oldest of them all, thanks to the spring of uncontaminated water beneath his home in Prin; yet this was the first time the older boy had ever understood what being a parent must have felt like. He had been a mentor to Esther, but this was new. Uri was not merely following in his footsteps but surpassing him.

Now if only he could understand what the boy was talking about!

Uri was reading as he usually did, his head propped up on both fists as he gazed down on a thick book with tiny black print. Scattered across the table in front of him were various articles that he had carefully clipped from magazines. He didn't even seem to notice when Stumpy lay down on the pile, scattering some with her tail. Stroking her in an absentminded way, the young boy finally looked up.

"You ever hear of smallpox?"

Abashed, Joseph shook his head. Lately, many if not most conversations with the boy began this way: with a word or question that left him completely baffled.

"It was a disease that killed lots of people. But there was another disease like it, only not as bad. You got sick . . . but then you got better again. They called it cowpox."

Joseph perked up. He knew that cows were a kind of deer, and he always enjoyed hearing stories about animals. "Really? What was the cow's name?"

Uri blinked at Joseph as if perplexed by the question. "I don't know." Then he continued. "Anyway . . . if you got cowpox, you didn't get smallpox. That's called immunity."

Joseph was doing his best to follow, but was starting to become confused. "Cowpox," "smallpox"—the strange words felt like they were getting tangled in his ears. He stared at the floor and concentrated as Uri continued. "But not all diseases work that way. The killing disease . . . the one that comes from water? It's different."

Although he didn't understand, Joseph felt he had to say something. "It's not like smallpox?"

Uri shook his head, staring off into space. "No . . . it doesn't have a related disease. See, there was so little time . . . the sickness hit so fast and everybody died so quick. But some people started doing experiments on immunity, since nothing else seemed to work." He tapped the faded journal that lay in front of him. "One of them thought immunity was simple. That maybe it came from contact with open lesions." He looked up at Joseph and gave a rare smile. "Repeated contact."

Joseph nodded. He was glad that Uri was excited by the information, but he wasn't sure why. Even his cat looked confused. Stumpy was curled next to the book, one paw draped on the exposed page, her yellow eyes half-shut.

"I think we should tell Esther," Uri said.

"You do? Why?"

"Because. She might want to know." When he turned to Joseph, the older boy was surprised to see that Uri's face seemed to glow. "It will be a gift. To say thank you for everything she's done. For—"

He was interrupted by a noise. Silas stood at the door, breathless.

"Ain't you heard?" he said. "Everybody got to go to the market. Now."

Even as Silas spoke, Joseph could hear faraway doors and the murmur of voices in the stairwell. "What for?" Joseph asked.

Silas shrugged. "It's Esther. She got something to say and she want folks to hear. Everyone."

Joseph wondered what it could be about. By the time he struggled to get Stumpy into her carrier and he and Uri entered the stairwell, he could hear others picking their way downstairs in the dark ahead of him. Joseph could make out the voices of Silas, Michal, and a few of his students. Others were unfamiliar to him, and he assumed they were sick people also making the effort.

When Joseph emerged on the top floor of the mall with Uri

trailing behind, he was regretting that he came. The main level of the District was teeming with even more crowds than usual; the sound was deafening. Across the floor, he saw Silas, Skar, and Michal with Kai, huddled together by the railing. Uneasy, he scurried over to join them, Uri following on his heels.

Looking out over the mall made Joseph dizzy. There were far too many people to count, perhaps even more than two hundred, crowding the steps and the lower landings. Behind them all, he thought he could see Gideon, although he wasn't sure.

All of a sudden, the noise quieted.

Joseph looked around. Then he saw that everyone was staring at Esther, who stood alone on the other side of the fourth floor on a wide central stairway. Even from where he stood, he could see that his old friend was nervous.

"Excuse me." It took the entire hall to grow silent for people to hear her. She cleared her throat and began again.

"Some of you know me," she began. "Some don't, although I think you've heard talk about me. I'm Esther. And I live with my friends up on the top floor. We work the garden. I help people who are sick. And my friend Joseph and me—we teach people to read."

From where he stood, at the mention of his name, Joseph felt as if he was going to faint. Yet no one was paying him any attention. A faint murmur rippled through the hall. Esther waited until it subsided before she spoke again.

"Anyone who wants to learn can come. It doesn't cost anything. And there's something else."

Esther rubbed her face with a sleeve, as if brushing away sweat. "Maybe some of you heard I had a baby, only it died. Well, that's not true." She bent over and, for a moment, disappeared from view. When she reemerged, she was holding something in her arms. "I want you to meet her. Her name's Sarah."

The murmurings grew even louder as Esther lifted the bundle so that everyone could see. Then she undid the blanket, revealing the baby's face.

"In case you didn't know, she's a variant. She's my little girl and I love her."

There was a collective gasp, followed by a moment of silence. Then all at once, people began talking. Esther had spoken in a clear and deliberate voice, yet it seemed that not everyone had heard her; now her words were being relayed person to person as swiftly as fire through a field of dead grass. Joseph could not perceive what was being said, but he sensed agitation, even hysteria, in the raised voices. With mounting panic, he saw people begin pushing and shoving to get closer.

The noise became deafening as the crowd surged around Esther, and she vanished from Joseph's sight.

FOURTEEN

CARRYING HER BABY, ESTHER PICKED HER WAY DOWN THE STAIRS TO THE main level. Within moments, she was mobbed by both acquaintances and strangers. The noise and jostling soon awoke Sarah; as she blinked open her lavender eyes, people exclaimed and murmured among themselves. When she yawned, revealing tiny pink and toothless gums, a ripple of harsh laughter spread through the group.

There was a hostile and reckless feel to the crowd as they pushed and shoved to get closer. Esther recoiled from the jeering faces.

Had she made a terrible mistake?

Even though she was terrified, Esther knew that any show of fear or uncertainty would be a signal to the others to attack. And so she kept her head high and greeted those who approached her, answering all of their questions, no matter how hurtful or ignorant.

Everyone continued to whisper and laugh, and more than a few made cruel jokes that were loud enough to be heard by everyone. Yet more and more, it seemed the crowd had begun responding to Esther's straightforward and unashamed approach. If the prevailing emotion on people's faces had at first been revulsion, it was soon curiosity. There were few enough infants around and so many seemed moved just by the sight of a baby. Some of the older females even wiped their eyes.

Within half an hour, most had wandered away, eager to get back to the business of working, buying, and selling. Soon Esther and Sarah were alone and making their way to the far staircase, to go back to their home on the top floor with the rest of their friends.

No one had seen Saith there except Gideon.

The little girl stayed until the last of the curious were gone. Then, moving quickly, she slipped away. She was not, Gideon noticed, heading to her room in the back of the fourth floor. Nor was she joining the others who now thronged the market. Instead, she went straight to the twin staircases that led downstairs to the secret rooms.

The little girl in white strode past the boys with the fearsome weapons guarding the entry without even acknowledging them. Bowing and touching their heads in respect, they let her pass. Then, gathering her robes, Saith pattered down the metal steps without a sound.

Gideon followed.

Saith did not head for either the drinking room or the small closet where Nur supervised the girls. Instead, she moved past them, into the dark and abandoned section of the food court, her white clothing gleaming in the murky air.

Gideon saw her turn down a narrow hallway. She stopped halfway down and fumbled inside her robes; he could hear the sound of keys. Then she unlocked the door and pushed it open, disappearing inside the parking garage.

Curious, the boy continued.

Gideon stepped inside the cavernous space with distaste, for although this was where Joseph had discovered the glass, he had no sentimental feelings about the foul and rat-infested room. Still, he wanted to see what business Saith might have in here. He lifted his arm to block his nose from the dreadful smells that arose from the mountains of waste tied in black plastic bags; he could hear nothing but the scurrying and squeaking of vermin. Taking out a firestarter and clicking its tiny wheel, Gideon lifted it high so he could look around. And across the echoing space, he finally saw Saith.

She stood with her back to him, apparently not having seen him enter. As he approached, Gideon was surprised to discover that she was shaking, her shoulders heaving. He was unused to such behavior, and it took him a moment to understand what was happening.

Saith was crying.

Just then, it seemed she finally noticed the flame's glow, for she whirled around. The firestarter had grown hot in Gideon's hand and he let it drop, plunging them both into darkness. Yet in the second that Saith was illuminated, the boy had been stunned by the look of rage that contorted her face, carving deep lines across her forehead and around her eyes.

She looked ancient.

"I sorry." Gideon was startled enough to give an automatic apology. But it became apparent that Saith's anger was not meant for him.

"You see how she do?" Saith seemed barely able to control herself. In the dark, he heard her take in deep shuddering breaths and stammer as she struggled to form sentences. For the first time since he had met her, the little girl seemed at a loss for words. When she spoke, it was in whimpers, making her sound more like a wounded animal than a human. "How she bring that little mutant and show it off? And because she do, everybody think she good. Everybody love her more." Saith choked with hatred, and a fresh sob erupted from her. "She know what I planning. But then she turn it around. Now she laughing at me. She laughing at *me*."

Gideon did not know how to reply. He too had been infuriated by Esther's cunning. Although it seemed impossible, she had somehow deflected what could have been a dangerous, even deadly situation and used it to serve her own ends. But he had never been one to express extreme emotions; to him, revealing your anger made you all the more vulnerable to

others. He realized that perhaps this was why Saith had sought
out a place where she could vent her feelings in private. He was
beginning to be in awe of the girl's unbridled fury and, for a
fleeting moment, was glad she was not his enemy.

"Nobody," she said, "laugh at me. Nobody."

Gideon had relit the firestarter. Saith's nose was pink and
her face shone with tears; the boy noted that she displayed no
shame about it. Instead, she held her chin up high and kept
her tiny fists clenched by her side; her black eyes glittered like
coals.

"So what do we do?"

"I know," she said at last.

"What?"

"You see." Saith smiled and in an instant, she was transformed once more back to the little girl she was. To Gideon,
the sight was even more unnerving than her rage. "Then she
sorry."

The first new law went into effect the following morning. It
was insignificant, Gideon noted, a simple extension of what
had already been in place. As a result, few commented on the
new regulation even as word of it spread throughout the mall.

Before, only the guards had bowed to Saith when she passed.
Now everyone was required to do so, and not only when they
approached her at her altar or thanked her for her prophecies.
Whenever anyone saw the young seer in the District, he or she
was to shield his eyes by touching his forehead with the fingers
of both hands, lower his gaze, and duck his head.

In short, no one was to look at Saith directly.

In addition, Saith had started walking around accompanied by armed guards. Although the two boys did nothing, their silent presence reminded others of the new law and helped ensure that it was obeyed.

And that was only the beginning. Several days later, Saith disappeared.

She was neither in her quarters nor at her special altar, nor could she be found anywhere within the District. That morning, the sky darkened and the air grew heavy; it seemed to heighten the fearful mood inside. As anxiety began to grow and spread throughout the mall, people began searching for the girl in every conceivable place: in abandoned stores, hallways, and storage spaces. By late afternoon, the heavens broke open in great blasts of lightning that lit up the skylight as thunder shook the District to its foundations. For two days, heavy rain poured down, lashing at the windows and keeping everyone indoors.

Gideon had no idea where she was. As the days passed, he grew more curious about when she would return, fascinated to learn her reasons for vanishing.

Then a week later, from inside his tiled office, Gideon heard the excited calls throughout the District.

"She back!"

"It Saith!"

"Saith is here!"

When he emerged, he saw people heading toward Saith's altar on the fourth floor. He joined the growing mob that thronged outside the small room, jostling to get in. On all sides, boys and girls pressed their fingers against their temples, gazing downward as they bowed again and again. Gideon had to work his way through the crowd before he managed to catch a glimpse of Saith.

What he saw took his breath away.

The young girl was almost unrecognizable. She sat cross-legged on the floor, a guard on either side. She had cut off nearly all of her hair; what remained was a fuzz that lay close to her bony skull. And she had lost significant weight off an already tiny frame. Now she looked skeletal, her gauntness accentuating her enormous dark eyes. Her skin was so pale it seemed translucent, as if lit from within.

Before, Saith was just another little girl. Now she looked ethereal, otherworldly . . . like something not quite human.

And that, Gideon realized, *was the whole point.*

He took stock of everything else she had done in order to heighten the effect. She had discarded all of her finery; there were no more gold and silver chains draped around her neck or heavy wristwatches on her arms. She no longer emitted the scent of roses and jasmine. And instead of the voluminous white robes and metallic sandals she used to wear, she now had on a simple black T-shirt, so huge it fit her like a dress, loose and baggy. Her exposed legs and arms, paper white and as thin as twigs, stood out in shocking contrast.

When everyone had gathered, the majority spilling out into the hallways because there was no room inside, Saith crooked a single finger. At the gesture, one of her two guards clapped his hands once, compelling the crowd to order.

And then she began to speak.

Her voice was higher and fainter, lighter and more singsong than it had been only a week before; Gideon had to strain to make out what she was saying. One by one, everyone around him grew silent as well, mesmerized by the tale she told. It was pure nonsense, the boy knew, a story he assumed she was making up on the spot. Yet after a few moments, even he had to admit that he felt caught up in its spell.

A week ago, Saith had been praying to the Beings, who, she explained, had created the world. But late that night, she was surprised that the voices did not respond. When they still did not answer her prayers in the morning, she left the District to seek them out and discover why they were no longer speaking to her. That day, a great storm came that drove her to seek hasty shelter in an abandoned store. She felt her way through the dark building and soon fell asleep in a corner. Yet when she awoke, there was enough light for her to realize that the roof was partially missing. To her horror, she discovered that while she was sleeping, she had become drenched in rainwater.

At this, many gasped, their eyes still averted. Saith waited until they stopped before she continued.

Within two days, Saith became seriously ill. She developed a fever so bad she thought she would die from the heat alone. When the sores came and spread over her body, she knew that the end was near. And yet she continued to pray to the Beings, asking them for help.

On her deathbed, they finally spoke.

They told her that the sickness was their punishment of all who behaved in a sinful way. It was intended to destroy those who chose not to believe. For only the pure and the righteous could hope to live, to bear healthy children, and to survive past their youth.

After the Beings spoke, the fever went away. Within hours, Saith found that her sores had healed and for the first time in days, she had an appetite. Yet she had learned her lesson: to renounce all vanity. To turn her back on pleasure, on self-indulgence. And to worship the Beings with every breath she had within her.

That was the way to survive the disease.

Saith gladly put aside the trappings of immodesty, for she now understood they were dangerous: her rich clothing, her jewels, even her hair. The Beings had saved her, but for a reason: She was to spread the word of salvation.

When she finished speaking, there was silence. Most in the crowd had their heads still bowed. But Gideon noticed that more than a few were peering up, a look of doubt upon their faces. Two boys whispered to each other, and another laughed. Without glancing at them, Saith raised her voice.

"Some don't believe." She lifted her arms and displayed them, palms upward, and those closest to her let out a gasp. That prompted the others to peek through their fingers. Even from far away, anyone could see that the inside of her white limbs were dotted with faint yet distinct purple blotches: scars left by the deadly lesions of the killing disease.

Gideon wondered what the blemishes really were: daubs of mud? Or perhaps Saith had squeezed one of the tubes of dried color that some females used to darken their lips. *It was even likely,* he thought, *that the girl had deliberately cut or burned herself to create the necessary marks.* But he was alone in his speculations. Around him, everyone else had broken out in murmurs and exclamations of shock and excitement.

It was impossible, he could hear people saying; *no one had ever survived the killing disease. Yet Saith stood there in front of them, alive.*

"Follow me," she said. She was smiling. "And you ain't gonna die."

Overnight, all forms of ornamentation were outlawed. That meant no jewelry, wristwatches, belts, scarves, or even sunglasses. The robes and headdresses that people wore over their jeans had to be either white or black; a ban on any sort of pattern, color, or embellishment was enforced. With Gideon's permission, Saith expanded her personal guards to a small army of a dozen of the strongest Insurgents. She took pains to pay them well, and they returned her generosity with unquestioning loyalty. They roamed through the mall, using force to collect items, which they would later destroy in immense bonfires in the main hall. The air would be filled with the stink of melting plastic and burning leather as giant flakes of soot wafted high.

Yet to the people of the mall, losing their personal goods was just one of the painful requirements to come.

Saith decreed that the sexes were to live separate from one another. This meant that families were broken apart: brother was forcibly separated from sister, partner from partner, and parent from child. *The mingling of the sexes led to bad thoughts,* she decreed.

Throughout, Gideon watched with a kind of awe. Saith was making the rules capricious and subject to change without warning. No one knew what to expect, and therefore everyone lived in constant fear of breaking a law they hadn't even known existed. Many complained, although not out loud; a handful even began meeting in private to discuss how to fight back against Saith and her harsh decrees. Yet the girl prophet heard about their plans before they could even be formed, for she also paid handsomely for information. If anyone was even suspected to be a troublemaker, Saith's guards would pay a visit in the middle of the night.

After that, no one would ever hear from that person again.

One ruling met the greatest opposition: It banned all the activities in the basement.

Gideon had given Saith free rein when it came to making rules; he and the girl were a team, after all. But, in private, he tried to argue her out of this one. He reminded her that the lower rooms were the greatest source of glass in the entire District. Yet she pointed out that the lost profits could be made up for in another way: Her guards would simply seize the possessions of anyone made to disappear. Reluctantly, Gideon agreed that this might work. And so under Saith's supervision, both the drinking room and its locked supply closet were emptied. Hundreds of sealed bottles were removed and brought outside, where their contents were poured into the gutter. The stench filled the street for hours.

A day later, Nur was stunned when guards arrived at the twin closets where her girls plied their trade. She assumed there had been a mistake and attempted to talk reason to them. But pushing her aside, they went through her belongings, gutting the rooms.

All of the girls she supervised were led away at gunpoint. Then the boys pulled out the stained bedding and set it on fire, not even bothering to block Nur's attempt to escape. They knew as well as she that the dual stairways were heavily guarded upstairs and that there was no other way out.

In her desperation, Nur ran into what had been the drinking room. There she found Eli, who sat slumped over a table, asleep. By now, he was little more than a shadow that could not or would not do anything to save her. He didn't even seem to understand that the drink that had sustained him for so long was now forbidden.

Two guards seized Nur. As she screamed, they held her down and sliced off her long brown hair, flinging the locks onto the ground. Then they dragged her up from the basement. As they paraded her through the main hall, everyone gathered to watch from all sides of the mall and gazed down from the balconies. Now that Nur was out in the open, newly shorn and in disgrace, many jeered at her, catcalling and spitting.

She was finally brought upstairs to Saith, who sat in her altar room. At first, the older girl was defiant, her head held high. When she saw that Gideon was there, however, her bravado wavered and she threw him a look that was both terrified and beseeching. Then a guard smacked the back of her head, hard, and Nur touched both hands to her forehead as she gave a deep bow. Tears splattered on the marble floor at her feet.

The little girl stared at Nur with an unreadable expression. "It true what they say?"

"What that?"

"You in charge of girls who sell their bodies. To boys. That true?"

Nur continued to keep her gaze averted, but her cheeks flushed. "Maybe you ask *him*," she said under her breath. "It was his idea."

Saith's face darkened. She was about to speak when Gideon cleared his throat. He leaned forward and whispered in her ear. Saith responded with heated words, but he persisted, holding his ground. Then at last, with what seemed like misgivings, she nodded.

"I Shun those other girls," she said. "But you lucky."

To her confusion, Nur was led from the room. She was given a black sheet to wear and a place to sleep on one of the halls reserved only for girls.

In the early morning, Nur was told she had been given a new job. She was to be Saith's assistant, nurse, and cook.

Nur knew that Gideon had spared her life. Yet for the girl who once had so much vanity, there could not have been a worse punishment.

Like everyone else on the top two floors, Esther was aware that something significant was going on downstairs in the mall.

She could hear her few remaining students whisper about the new and restrictive rules: the change in clothing. The forced separation of the sexes. The actual worship of Saith. Yet if they noticed Esther was listening, they would stop talking and break apart from one another at once.

It was impossible not to notice that many of them dressed differently now: in black or white robes, unadorned by jewelry, watches, sunglasses. The girls either cut their hair short or tied it back beneath a hood. Yet all of these new rules were just the outward signs of a bigger and more sinister change.

Even though Esther and her friends were effectively sealed off from the lower floors by windows that looked down over the atrium, she could smell smoke arising from time to time in the stairwell. And on two recent occasions, she had awoken to the sound of faraway screams.

Esther knew what was happening. She had thought showing everyone her child had defused a deadly situation. Now, not to be outmaneuvered, Saith was taking her aggression to a whole new level.

Esther would have to confront Gideon and the little girl before it was too late. But first, she would have to find out everything she could.

This time, she called on Silas herself.

FIFTEEN

SILAS ADJUSTED THE BLACK SHEET SO HIS FACE WAS OBSCURED. THEN HE made his way down the staircase to the main floor of the mall.

The little thief had taken extra precautions. He had been caught by the assassin with the white streak in his hair not once, but twice. Why the older boy hadn't killed him was something Silas would never understand. Still, he had learned from his close encounters. And now that Esther had enlisted his help, he felt an even greater need to prove himself.

Like the others, Silas had heard rumors about the changes downstairs. He knew enough to wear a black hooded robe fashioned from several bedsheets, as well as to confine his spying to the lower two floors, where only boys were allowed.

Yet nothing could have prepared him for what he saw when he emerged.

The market that had been a bustling center of commerce was now completely different. Gone were the mobs of people and the endless rows of tables heaped with clothing, housewares, luxury items, shoes. Now, a dozen or so male customers stood on a silent and orderly line. Identical and anonymous in robes that were either white or black, they waited to purchase only two things that were on sale from a single vendor: food or water. There were no more glittering luxuries, like the watch he had once stolen. Silas recognized produce, squash and potatoes, that he himself had helped pick that morning.

Armed boys no longer stood guard at the head of the dual staircases leading to the basement; what few pedestrians there were now were free to move up and down between the bottom two floors. Because there were no crowds in which to get lost, Silas had no choice but to join the line. He had brought along a handful of glass in case he needed to buy something. As he approached the table, he suddenly noticed something else on sale.

A loose stack of paper was piled to the side. Nearly everyone on line was buying one.

When he made it to the table, Silas selected a bottle of water and a bunch of radishes. On an impulse, he took one of the sheets of paper and added it to his pile, as well. Only when he handed over his glass fragments and took his items could he examine it. A drawing done with pencil, crude and childlike, showed a girl with large eyes and short hair.

Around him, others were folding up the pictures and slipping them into their pockets. Silas did the same. Then, as he made his way to the basement, he heard something odd.

A dull drone filled the air. Although it was faint, it grew louder as whatever it was approached.

Silas glanced around. To his surprise, nearly all of the other boys, including the vendor, had stopped what they were doing and stood as if rooted to the spot. In unison, everyone closed their eyes and raised their hands, pressing their fingers against their foreheads; then all began bowing again and again in the same direction. They faced the far end of the hall, where the rounded stairwell spiraled down from the floors above. Everyone's lips moved as they mumbled something Silas could not make out. It matched the tone and rhythm of the noise, which the boy suddenly realized was the faraway sound of many people chanting.

Without missing a beat, Silas copied their gestures, facing the stairs and moving his lips as if joining them. Yet he kept his eyes open enough that he could observe what was going on.

Silas noticed that one boy refused to join in, a heavyset child who seemed a few years older than he was. He could tell at a glance that it wasn't intended as an act of rebellion. Silas remembered Eli's partner, Asha, who hadn't been right in her mind. She was more like a toddler than someone in her teens and this boy was no different. His face slack and his gaze turned inward, he seemed to be talking to himself. Laughing at nothing, he repeatedly flicked his fingers against his thumb, one at a time, as he rocked back and forth.

Without knowing why, Silas felt a stab of dread for the boy.

Meanwhile, a slow procession had emerged on the fourth floor and was making its way down. Dozens of females cloaked like the boys in black or white crowded the staircase, covering their faces, bowing, as they chanted loudly. They appeared to be following someone. But although Silas strained his eyes, he could not make out who it was.

By the time the ensemble made it to the ground floor, all of the boys had crowded forward to join them, if at a distance. Silas went with them, uncomfortably aware that everyone around him had a strained, expectant expression, their faces reverent. The person at the head of the group, a tiny figure draped in black, picked its way across the marble floor of the giant atrium to what Silas knew had once been a fountain. It climbed inside the large tiled receptacle, now empty of water, then turned to face everyone as it took a seat on the fanciful structure inside, pushing back its hood as it did so.

With a start, Silas realized it was Saith. He could not believe that the little girl he and Esther had rescued from the streets of Mundreel had become what she was rumored to be. And with this comprehension came the sudden understanding of what the people around him were chanting:

"*Forgive us, Saith. Clean us, Saith. Heal us, Saith. Save us, Saith.*"

With her newly shaved head and air of total authority, Saith was almost unrecognizable. Yet she still had the same sharp features and huge black eyes that, even now, seemed to be trained on him.

Silas shrank back, glad he was heavily cloaked. Still he made certain to cover his face with his hands as he continued to bow and move his lips in time with the others. After a few moments, he noticed that, in fact, Saith hadn't noticed him at all; her eyes had moved past him. With a pang, he realized she was staring at the boy who stood behind the crowd, the one with the child's mind. For Silas was certain that he was the only one not bowing, chanting, and giving thanks to Saith.

As if she could hear his thoughts, Saith frowned. She gave some sort of signal, for at once one of her guards came forward and inclined his head so he could hear. Without averting her gaze, the girl addressed him. Then the hulking boy nodded.

Through his half-shut eyes, Silas could sense rather than see that two other guards began to circle the group. Still bowing and chanting Saith's name, Silas inched his way back; he wanted to see what was going to happen next. Within moments he became aware of a small commotion in the back of the central hallway. Out of the corner of his eye, he could see the guards walking away with the simple boy, whom they held between them. Seemingly unaware of what was going on, he continued to laugh and play with his fingers.

On an impulse, Silas made a decision.

By now, the devotions had ended. Saith had begun receiving individual followers: They approached one at a time, lay facedown on the ground before her, then murmured to her in soft and urgent voices.

Silas took advantage of the moment to break away. He knew the layout of the District better than anyone; from where the guards were walking, he assumed they were heading to the hidden staircase that lay at the far end of the main floor. Making certain not to draw attention to himself, Silas found his way to the metal door and slipped inside the dark stairwell.

Although it was pitch-black, Silas could hear the sounds of the guards and their prisoner high above him, echoing down through the seemingly airless shaft, and he put on speed until he was only a level below them. They all continued upward, flight after flight. Finally, they stopped; by Silas's count, they were on the seventh floor. There was a clunk of the door being pushed open. Then he could hear the guards stepping out, dragging the younger boy with them.

Silas climbed the final steps and waited for several seconds in the dark. Then he too pressed open the metal bar that opened the door and stepped out into the hallway.

The layout was exactly the same as the hall where he lived: a square passageway with sleek wooden doors on one side and windows looking down on the atrium below on the other. Silas could see the guards on the far side of the hall, through the panes of glass. He dropped down so he wouldn't be noticed. Then he darted forward at a crouch until he made it to the corner. He took a quick peek: No one was there. As he crept down the corridor, he could hear the guards more clearly as he drew near. When he reached the next corner, he pressed himself against the wall and willed his heart to stop pounding.

He was no more than a stone's throw away. The three boys had stopped in front of the twin silver panels with the vertical seams that stood in the same place on every level.

"The elevators," Joseph called them. Unlike the rest of the immaculate beige hallway, the rug beneath their feet was blackened and filthy.

"But he a baby," one of the guards was saying. He had pushed his hood from his face; he was perhaps fifteen, with brown hair and snub-nosed features. "When my sister alive, she the same way."

He was speaking of their prisoner, who sat on the dirty ground between them. Using his finger, the boy traced pictures in a tiny patch of clean carpet before rubbing them out and starting over again.

"Her orders."

"But he ain't no harm."

The other one shrugged. "She don't want that in the District no more."

Silas became aware of the sound of the boy's breathing: noisy and through his mouth. This got the guards' attention as well.

"Better get it done, then," the first one said. He sounded resigned.

The second guard pulled something from beneath his robe. Silas realized the object was a gun. He leaned over the boy who sat between them, absorbed in his game.

Then he shot him once in the temple.

Silas squeezed his eyes shut. Trembling, he could taste the bile rising in his throat and he willed himself not to vomit.

A noise made him look around the corner again. One of the guards was using a crowbar to pry apart a set of silver panels as the other held the dead boy by the ankles. The first one gazed through the doorway of the partly open elevator. Even from where he stood, Silas winced at the terrible smell that filled the air.

"Ready?"

Together, they half dragged and half pushed the body over the threshold. The twin doors weren't fully open; an arm snagged on one and the boys had to kick and maneuver it free. A few seconds later, Silas thought he could feel the faint thump as the body hit the ground floors below. Then the two guards, working together, managed to slide the elevator panels shut again.

"I need a drink," the first one said.

"Proof? Ain't it gone?"

"I got some hid."

Both wiped their hands on their robes and clapped them to remove dust and blood. Then they headed back toward the staircase.

Silas had already retreated in the opposite direction, disappearing around the corner just before the guards appeared. He crouched low a few feet away from the door, his heart thundering in his thin chest.

After he heard the bang of the door shutting and the lumbering steps fade away down the stairwell, Silas girded himself. Then he stood up and moved out into the hall.

He walked quickly, trying not to think. At the elevators, he stopped.

The guards had forgotten their crowbar, which lay at his feet. Silas picked it up and, with difficulty, inserted its sharp edge inside the seam of the second set of panels, the way he had seen the other boy do. By rocking the heavy tool back and forth, he was able to work the doors open a few inches. As he pulled one of the panels open even farther, the blinding stench hit him so hard his eyes and nose began to water. Feeling in his pocket for a firestarter, Silas clicked the tiny wheel with trepidation. Then holding it out as far as he could, he leaned over and attempted to peer down into the darkness.

"Hey!"

As Silas whirled around, he saw one of the guards standing at the far end of the corridor. *The crowbar,* he realized with a sinking heart. The boy was already fumbling in his robes for what Silas knew was his gun.

It was impossible to run. Silas could already hear the other guard coming around the other direction to cut off any escape.

In desperation, Silas tried to fling the iron tool at his assailant. It was far too heavy for his thin arms and clattered against the wall instead. Yet the guard instinctively quailed, his arm against his face, and this bought Silas precious seconds.

Silas turned to the elevator. He had a sense of what horrors lay in its depths, and the thought of it filled him with dread. Yet he had no other choice.

Leaping through the doors into the foul darkness, Silas dropped like a stone. Behind him, he heard the gun go off.

As Esther gathered the third load of dirty bedding, she paused to push the hair back from her eyes.

Silas had not returned the night before. Nor had he shown

up that morning to help her on the sick floor. Alone, Esther brought the sheets and blankets up to the roof garden and added them to the giant metal tub kept in the corner for much-needed washing; thanks to the recent heavy rains, there was enough water to boil for laundry. She was glad for her usual chores—gardening, fixing a broken pane of glass, helping Michal and Skar pound dried beans into flour. They were a welcome distraction. Yet as the hours passed, her anxiety about the boy grew.

After the midday meal, Esther drew Skar aside to speak in private. She had told her friend about Silas's mission the day before.

"Any sign of him?" Skar asked.

"Nothing," Esther said.

Esther tried to cling to hope, for although he was young, Silas was clever and resourceful. Every time the door to the roof banged open or she heard a footfall in the corridor, she looked up, her heart pounding. Yet as the afternoon deepened and the sun grew low in the sky, there was still no sign of the boy. After dinner, Esther was supposed to teach the evening classes. Yet her mind was not on her work and she stumbled over the simple lesson she was giving the few Outsiders who had shown up.

Uri had been reading, unnoticed, in a corner of the library; now he came forward.

"Why don't you rest?" he whispered to her. "I'll take over."

Esther's initial impulse was to retreat to the dark stairwell, as she often did when she needed to think or had trouble sleeping. Yet it brought back unsettling memories—not of Trey, but of Aras. She shook off the feeling and on an impulse, headed to the eighth floor, a level below.

The corridor was dark and silent. Moonlight spilled in through the corner windows, forming gleaming pools on the carpet and reflecting off the interior windows that looked out on the dark District. As Esther paced around the rectangular hallway, she found that her thoughts kept returning to her former partner.

For weeks, she had made peace with the thought of him with another girl. Aras had moved on with his life; now she was attempting to move on with hers.

So why did he feel so close to her tonight?

Esther's bare feet were silent as she made her way along the soft beige carpet, leaving a trail of faint impressions. She closed her eyes as she walked; with her arms extended to either side, she let her fingers brush the walls, guiding her. *It was as if she too were blind like him,* she thought. And the more she thought of him, the more she sensed him materialize as a ghostly presence behind her. She could almost feel the softness of his breath on the back of her neck, the warmth of his hand as he reached out to touch her.

To warn her?

Esther's eyes popped open. She could hear it now: a faint cry that seemed to arise from the building itself. It was not a dream. In front of her, the silver panels of the twin elevators shone in the dim light. She leaned forward. Then she pressed her ear against the smooth metal surface and listened.

And she heard it again.

It sounded far away; there was no way of telling whether or not it was even human. For a moment, Esther picked in vain at the sealed doors; then she gave up in frustration. Whoever it was lay far below her, many floors down. She would have to descend to the mall to find out who or what it was.

Esther was halfway down when she hesitated. She could not go alone.

Skar was in her room with Michal, preparing to retire for the night. But when she saw Esther, she got up without speaking and slipped her knife into her pocket. From their bed, Michal watched them both, her face drawn with concern.

"Don't worry," said Skar in a soft voice. "I'll be back as soon as I can." She bent down to kiss Michal before joining Esther in the hall.

The girls leaped down the stairs, taking entire landings in each bound. Skar said nothing, but matched her friend stride for stride in the darkness.

The two girls emerged on the deserted main floor. Moonlight streamed down through the skylight far overhead, throwing deep shadows.

"That way," Esther whispered. Skar nodded and the two ran across the hall and down the twin staircase that led to the basement. After the smoothness of the dusty marble floor, the sharply grooved steps cut into the soles of their bare feet. Then they picked their way across the food court, surrounded on all sides by the soft sounds of boys sleeping, and toward the back corridor where the elevators lay.

Esther approached the two sets of metal panels. Even though they were tightly shut, the stench wafting from them was overwhelming and the air was filled with a distant hum. When she lit a firestarter and held it up, Esther saw that blackened rot seeped from both seams and spread onto the floor.

Skar was already working at one of the doors with her knife. By jamming the blade in and pushing it back and forth, she was able to separate the metal slabs a little bit. It was enough room for both girls to slip their fingers in. As the noise and smell increased, the two girls tried to force the elevator open. Pulling with all of their might, they managed to slide one of the doors open.

Inside was a nightmare come to life.

Dozens of lifeless bodies were packed together in the bottom of a dark shaftway. Freed from their prison, they now spilled out into the hallway at the girls' feet. The humming sound was that of thousands of flies buzzing everywhere.

Esther recoiled, her hands to her mouth. Behind her, she heard Skar's breath quicken.

"Help." The voice came from somewhere higher up. It was little more than a croak, but Esther knew it belonged to Silas.

"He's still alive," Skar said, her tone practical.

"Can you move?" Esther whispered to him.

"Yeah." Silas's voice was louder. "My legs hurt. But I'm all right."

The two girls glanced at each other in the flickering light. Then, swallowing hard, Esther clicked it off. Without speaking, they both knew that what they had to do would be easier in the dark.

First, Esther tore off strips of cloth from the bottom of her T-shirt, which both girls tied around their mouths and noses. Then they crouched down side by side and began pulling bodies out of the way.

It was horrific, yet the darkness made it seem abstract, as if it were happening in a dream. Esther tried to touch only fabric, robes that were dried and stiff with what she knew was blood. As they pulled, it tore in their hands, yet bodies began to slide out into the hallway, making the job easier.

Esther yanked on whatever she could grasp that didn't feel human: belts, T-shirts, jeans. Once, her hands closed on a limb that was soft and rotting; clamping her lips together so she wouldn't cry out, she adjusted her grip so she was holding only the baggy denim around it. The air was filled with the sounds of fabric shredding and bodies sliding and landing on the ground with a thump. More than once, pieces of clothing tore off in Esther's hand. At least two of them felt like partnering ties.

Throughout, Esther clung to the one thought that made it bearable: *Silas was still alive.* Were it not for that one hope, she felt she might go mad.

At long last, Esther heard something move above her. It reached out and struck her; by instinct, she grabbed it. It was a foot, blessedly moving and alive.

"I got him," she whispered. Together, she and Skar pulled the boy free. He slid down the bodies strewn in the corridor and landed on the floor before them.

Esther took out her firestarter and clicked it to make sure he was all right. The boy looked pitiful: His face was bruised and one of his eyes was swollen. Yet he was alive. That was all that mattered.

"We must go," said Skar. "Someone will have heard us."

She had put one arm around Silas; together, they were already heading back the way they had come. Esther was about to extinguish the light and join them when her eye fell on something.

It was not a body. No, this was something that had dropped to the side, a strip of blue cloth she had torn from one of the dead.

It was fabric from a shirt.

The same shirt she had given to Aras.

Esther bent and picked it up, but her mind struggled to grasp the meaning of it. Even after she clicked off the fire-starter, the pattern of the cloth stuttered and repeated in her brain like an obvious message she still could not understand.

By now, Skar and Silas had already made it to the foot of the dual stairs. Her friend hissed a warning at Esther to hurry up, yet Esther heard her as if through a fog. Thoughts whirled through her head as she tried to make sense of it all.

But there was no time to understand what had happened.

The glow of an approaching torch lit the hall, throwing ghastly light on the pile of dead.

"Esther!"

Gideon was flanked by three guards, one of whom held a gun.

Fingering the shirt fragment, Esther felt as if her life were draining out of her. For when she heard Gideon's voice—the boy she had nearly partnered with—everything clicked into place.

What the girl Nur told her had been a lie.

Aras had not left her for someone else. He was dead.

Gideon had killed him and hidden his body.

Grief and rage came crashing down on Esther like physical things; she felt as if she were drowning. She could not move and did not care or even notice when the guards surrounded her and seized her by the arms.

Gideon was in a bad mood.

He did not want to admit it, but even he was appalled by the carnage uncovered by Esther. He was aware that trouble-makers needed to be disposed of in a prompt and efficient way to keep them from spreading dissent. Moreover, he approved of the use of brutality to ensure order. *Yet the number of people Saith had ordered killed,* he now thought with irritation, *was going too far.*

He had called Saith to his tiled office to discuss this and other important matters, but the girl didn't seem to be listening. She sat on the counter, swinging her legs and humming to herself.

"Who laugh at me now?" she asked again and again. Then she giggled and swung her legs harder.

Exasperated, Gideon knew she was talking about Esther.

He had tried explaining things to the little girl. Earlier, Gideon had ordered his guards to drag the dead bodies out of the elevator and into the garage for the sole reason of ensuring that no one else discovered them. Finding out about the slaughter of so many would shake even the most fervent believer's faith in not only his and Saith's leadership but perhaps the entire system they had devised.

But Saith didn't seem to understand.

"They bad people," she kept saying. "Ain't no reason they alive."

For the first time Gideon realized that Saith was more of a risk than he could have ever foreseen. To her, other people were like toys or ants or pieces of dust; having them destroyed meant nothing to her.

Under Saith, people could be put to death for the mildest infraction or perceived flaw. Anyone who was injured or disabled, petty thieves, anyone caught fighting or causing a nuisance, people she deemed unclean in either body or mind, even someone she simply found unattractive. They had all been executed; a single kiss or lecherous glance was punishable by death. Yet most had been guilty of one thing only: disrespecting Saith by refusing to bow or carry her image, or not praying loudly enough.

Gideon found this an emotional and messy way to wield power.

He had decided to leave matters of order and enforcement to Saith; he now realized that had been a serious mistake. The younger girl had gone overboard, and her competition with Esther had become poisonous.

"So," Saith said now. "When we kill her?"

Gideon sighed. "I told you. Not yet."

The pretty little face frowned. "Why?"

"I told you, there's one last thing I need her to do."

Esther sat crouched in the dark.

From the size of her enclosure, she assumed it was a closet of some kind. Esther did not know how many hours she had been there. All she remembered was being led to the fifth floor then thrust into a tiny and windowless space.

Throughout, her mind had been whirling. She thought of Aras, and her heart was filled with guilt and grief. She felt rage, too—directed as much at herself as at Gideon. She had appeased her partner's killer; and the more she thought of this, the more it felt as if her heart would break from shame alone.

Her only hope was that Skar and Silas had escaped. But where could they have gone? And what of all the others?

Her thoughts were interrupted by the sound of the lock being undone. Then the door opened and daylight spilled in, making Esther wince.

"He want to see you," said a guard.

She was dragged to her feet; after crouching for so long in the small space, she could barely stand. Walking between two armed boys, Esther was led to the far staircase, where she was forced to stumble up the stairs.

They were taking her home.

Perhaps, she thought with sudden and irrational hope, *she would be allowed to rejoin her group. They might be imprisoned, but at least they would be together.*

Yet they turned onto the ninth floor, and Esther was led

down the hall where she had worked. With a sinking feeling, she saw that all of the rooms were silent and deserted. Feathers and bits of paper were strewn on the floor or floated in the air. And everywhere she looked was devastation.

The sickrooms were shorn of their bedding. The few medicines that Esther had collected were destroyed, their plastic bottles smashed and the contents spilled across the floor. In the learning rooms, desks and chairs were overturned, adrift in what seemed to be an ocean of paper that was torn and trampled.

Upstairs was even worse. The rooms in which Esther and her friends lived had been ransacked. Tattered remains of clothing and other belongings that had been emptied out of dressers and boxes were trampled underfoot.

Her children and friends were nowhere to be seen.

Although her heart was shattering inside her, Esther knew she had been taken here on purpose. They wanted her to be humiliated, to have her spirit broken. And so she kept her chin held high, to deprive her captors of any satisfaction. But she faltered when she saw who was waiting for them at the end of the hall.

It was Gideon. He gave the guard a brusque nod and turned to go.

"Murderer." She could not hold her tongue.

Gideon stopped for a moment. Then, snapping his fingers for them to follow, he disappeared around a corner.

"Where are my children?" Esther shouted the words after him. "Where are my friends?"

No one answered; the two boys just dragged her along with them. The Insurgent leader had disappeared through an open door and they shoved her in as well. Inside, Joseph's library was a shambles, the floor littered with books. A dying fire was burning in the middle of the room. It had already scorched the ceiling and black ash still drifted everywhere.

"Talk to him." Gideon's voice came from behind her.

A forlorn figure sat alone in a far corner. He was turning the pages of a damaged book, as if to comfort himself with a small, familiar action. Looking traumatized, a striped cat huddled by his feet.

"Joseph?"

The guard jerked her back.

"No," said Gideon. "Let her go. She got to talk to him."

She spun around and gave him a furious look. "About what?"

Gideon refused to meet her eyes. "You and he, you the only ones left who know how to work the garden." Esther's heart pounded when she heard this: *Were the others already dead?* "But he ain't saying nothing. You want him to live, he got to tell us what he know."

He nodded at the two guards, who released her. Rubbing her arms, Esther advanced into the room and knelt by the older boy's side.

It took a minute for Joseph to notice; he closed the volume and looked down at Esther. He smiled as if this were just another visit, and only then did she realize that he was too shaken to understand what had happened.

"The others are gone," he remarked.

"I know." She kept her voice down so the others couldn't hear. "Where did they go?"

Joseph shrugged.

Blindly, Esther took her old friend's hand and pressed a kiss on it. He yanked it back, unnerved by the contact as she knew he would be, and she smiled in spite of herself.

"Joseph," she said at last. "You know things about the District, right?"

He looked at her, frowning. "What sort of things?"

"About the water system. And the garden. How to maintain everything."

Joseph nodded, even as Esther swallowed hard.

"I need you . . . ," she started, then stopped. Blinking back tears, she tried again. "I need you to work on those things for Gideon from now on. Do you understand?"

"But—"

"Please listen." She ducked her head and whispered as softly as she could. "Don't teach him or anyone else what you know. Just do the work yourself. That way, you'll be safe."

He frowned again. Esther knew the others were impatient for her to finish, but she stayed for just a moment longer.

"Do you remember," she said, "when I used to visit you in Prin? When I used to bring you food?"

"Yes," Joseph said, with fondness.

"Let's think about those days. From now on. All right? Whenever we're sad."

"All right," he said. "That's a good idea."

Esther reached to give the cat one final stroke. Then she was pulled onto her feet and dragged to the stairs by the guards.

From the far end of the hallway, Gideon watched them go.

Esther had been led away too swiftly to see either Gideon or the small figure in white who had joined him. Saith was laughing to herself, a soft and throaty chuckle.

She was rocking something in her arms.

It was Esther's baby.

"Bye-bye" was all Saith said.

PART THREE

SIXTEEN

GIDEON STOOD IN A CORRIDOR OF BEIGE CARPET THAT SEEMED TO GO ON forever.

At the end of the hallway, a boy was waiting for him: dark skinned, with sunglasses and long matted locks. It was Aras. As Gideon approached, he tightened his grip on the club he carried.

When he reached him, Gideon swung his arm as hard as he could, and in the silence, he could feel the force of impact as wood hit bone. The other boy staggered heavily and dropped to his knees, bright red blossoming against the wall behind him.

Finishing him off would be easy. And yet something was wrong.

Someone was watching.

Gideon spun around and saw a figure standing at the other end of the hall.

It was Esther. She said nothing and yet he could feel her unblinking gaze of judgment burn into him.

Gideon awoke with a start.

When he realized he had dreamed the same thing for the third night in a row, he felt angry beyond words.

Gideon had had no qualms about ordering Aras's death. It had been a practical matter, the simple removal of an obstacle to his plans. True, things had not worked out the way he had hoped. Still, the boy had felt no guilt about his actions.

Until now.

He could not stand the thought that Esther, shut in a cell upstairs, now understood what had happened to her partner. It had been her own fault for spying on Gideon and the inner workings of the District. Had she left things alone, she could have continued to believe the comforting lie that Aras had left her for another girl. By meddling into the affairs of the basement, she had discovered not only the truth about Saith's rules, but also the fate of the boy she loved.

Gideon found her judgment unbearable. That she had called him "murderer"—and to his face, in front of his guards!— nagged at him, no matter how much he tried to put it from his mind. Her presence in his life—even in his mind—had become too much to endure.

He had to get rid of Esther, he thought, *once and for all.*

And yet Gideon didn't trust strong emotions, including his own. If he was to dispose of the girl, he would need to do so in a cool and regulated way. After several days of mulling over the problem, he finally came up with a solution.

Gideon had already decided that a different kind of discipline had to replace the childish and arbitrary one established by the girl priestess. This new system would create true order and stability. It would provide a way to get rid of Esther in a manner that was dispassionate, beyond reproach, and impossible to trace back to him. And it would effectively intimidate any supporters Esther might have inspired.

The new justice would be fair, rational, and consistent. Under its rules, there would be clearly delineated levels of wrongdoing and punishment. Unlike before, only the truly dangerous—dissidents who openly spoke out against the system or threatened Saith's life—would be put to death.

Esther was a dissident. It was as simple as that.

Everyone else would serve another purpose.

Gideon remembered well the plan Esther had confided in him of building smaller gardens throughout the city. The idea was worse than foolish: It was downright dangerous. Transferring control of the food supply to the mob would destroy everything he had worked so hard to build and effectively take away all of his power.

But what if it were done properly, using a bigger space that he alone controlled?

The roof of the District had long since exceeded its limit. The building itself was relatively small, after all—only ten stories high—and the garden had been designed to support a few dozen at most, not the hundreds who came each day.

Gideon thought of the huge buildings that lay only a few blocks away. The structures were so immense they appeared to touch the clouds and seemed as immovable as the mountain that lay in the distance. Made of steel and glass, they far outsized the modest District.

Gideon had decided to take over the largest of the buildings and transform it, as the previous owners had done to the District. The area of the roof would be immense—many times the size of the current garden. He would take Esther's idea of feeding the hungry, yet he would do it on a huge scale and at an enormous profit.

Of course, it would take many months of backbreaking toil. Even the first step, Gleaning the necessary steel beams, sheets of glass, and other materials, and then transporting them to the new site, would be extraordinarily difficult. Then everything would have to be carried up many flights. Only then could the real work of building begin.

Such labor, Gideon knew better than anyone, was expensive. To ask someone to perform these tasks would command many pieces of glass, far more than one could earn by selling food or other objects.

But you didn't have to pay slaves.

Under Gideon's new legal system, all those found guilty of violating Saith's countless petty and arbitrary laws would be sentenced to work, without pay, in the new building. Joseph would design the space and supervise the work.

Gideon's plan was so brilliant it almost took his breath away. And yet he hesitated. He knew that this new system had to be presented to Saith in a way she could not only accept, but embrace.

Then he had an inspiration.

What if he were to dedicate the new space to her? If the little priestess had a weak spot, it was her vanity. Would his argument be enough to mollify her?

When Gideon explained the concept of the new court and building to Saith later that morning, he was careful to emphasize this aspect of his plan.

"People come from all over." The boy leaned against the counter in the girl's private chamber, as Saith sat in a cushioned seat, one of her assistants rubbing lotion into her thin arms. "They hear about it for miles."

"And it bigger than this place?" The girl did not deign to look at him, but examined herself in the mirror.

"Three times over. It as big as the sky."

Saith said nothing for a few moments. Then she smiled.

"Then we do," was all she said.

Although Saith suggested that Gideon act as judge of the new court, he thought better of it. *Best to remove himself,* he thought, *from any appearance of personal vindictiveness.* No, someone else had to serve in his place.

Gideon already had the perfect candidate in mind.

Esther awoke to the faint sounds of moaning. Sobs and groans rose all around, seeping through the walls.

This was how she began each morning.

Esther had been alone in a dark closet for weeks. When

guards had first led her down the eighth floor, she had tried
to look around. Most of the doors on the hall were closed,
with guards stationed every few feet. Only one gaped open
and Esther glimpsed what seemed like at least a dozen people
inside, frightened and wide-eyed. She thought she recognized
one of the sick people and tried to make eye contact. But she
was hurried past before she could tell for certain that it was
him.

The entire ninth floor—where she had tended the sick and
taught classes with Joseph and Uri—had been turned into a
prison.

Esther had spent the first few days exploring her brick cell.
Although it was pitch-black, she was well acquainted with
its layout. For months it had been her supply closet, where
she'd kept medicine, clothes, and bedding. Everything had
been cleared out except the dented metal shelves. Although
they were flimsy and threatened to collapse under her meager
weight, she managed to scale them, taking care not to make
any noise. Methodically, she investigated the cinder-block
walls with her hands, running her fingers over every inch of
the painted brick. But she found no vents or ceiling panels she
could break through, no hidden airways that might lead to
freedom.

The door was made of solid wood; it would be impossible
to break down. Again and again, Esther tried its rounded metal
knob in vain, hoping that a guard had left it unlocked. She
wished she had asked Silas to teach her how to use the tiny
tools he kept tucked in the side of his sneaker.

Escape, she realized, *was impossible.*

Her only visitor was a glowering and silent boy who appeared every morning with her daily meal: a bowl of vegetables and a cup of water. A second boy waited behind him and kept a gun trained on her the entire time.

Alone, Esther was wracked by too many feelings to contain. The uncertainty of her fate coupled with her isolation in total darkness was nearly enough to drive her mad; late at night she paced the tiny room, fighting the panic that threatened to strangle her.

With difficulty, Esther forced herself to be practical. She was relieved to know that Joseph was safe, at least for the time being. Yet she still had to find out what had happened to her children and other friends.

At first, Esther attempted to communicate with her fellow prisoners in the neighboring rooms by tapping on walls. When that proved useless, she lay down and pressed her face against the plush carpet and peered out underneath the door.

Through the narrow gap, she could hear when new people were brought upstairs, their cries and murmurs as they were shoved down the hall, and the jangle of keys as they were thrown into cells. Throughout the day, many feet passed by. Occasionally someone would stumble or fall down before being yanked back up. One time, Esther found herself staring directly into the dark eyes of a little girl who lay mere inches away before she was pulled to her feet.

That image haunted Esther for days.

Just as frequently, a guard would disappear into a room, his partner waiting outside. Within moments, the first one would reappear, dragging a prisoner with him. The three would head back to the far end of the hallway, which Esther knew led to the enclosed staircase. The metal door would clang open and shut and the sound of footsteps would fade, leaving Esther to wonder where they were going and what lay in store for the unlucky soul.

Then one morning, they came for her.

It had been an unusually heavy few hours of traffic. Esther had seen many guards retrieve one or two prisoners at a time and escort them down the hall. Then, to her shock, two sets of feet stopped directly in front of her. She had barely enough time to roll away and yank back from the door before it opened.

She blinked in the sudden light.

"Get up," one of them said. When she didn't move, he reached in and grabbed her by the arm. Then he thrust something in her face: It was a white robe. "And don't do nothing stupid."

Putting on the hooded garment, Esther stumbled down the hallway, a guard on either side. Sunlight streamed in from windows at both ends; by its brightness, she judged it to be midmorning. None of the doors they passed were open, and when she tried to glance through the windows at the District below, she could see nothing.

From the dried-out carrots and rancid cucumbers she was served every day, Esther knew that Gideon and his people were having trouble keeping the garden running. For a moment, she wondered if she was being brought upstairs to work, and her heart quickened. If Gideon placed a value on her experience, perhaps he had spared her friends as well.

But once they were in the dark stairwell, one of the guards yanked her to the left. That meant they were heading downstairs. To Esther's surprise, they stopped two levels below, on the seventh floor.

It had the same layout as the floors above, yet even at a glance, Esther could see that this hallway had seen much more traffic. The beige carpeting underfoot was matted and heavily soiled.

The guards walked her down the hall. Looking ahead, Esther saw that the central door was ajar; inside, she knew, was the largest room on the floor. One of the boys tapped on it, then pushed it open.

Brilliant sunlight poured in through the oversize window that overlooked the streets of Mundreel. It made the air, already stifling, seem even hotter. Six guards stood against the wall; the two of them holding guns flanked the door. The rest of the room was filled with dozens of people who stood in silence, their heads bowed. The only sound was a faint murmur of voices that came from the front.

As Esther was forced to join the others, one of the guards handed her something: a piece of cardboard with the number 127 written on it. It made no sense to her, and she stuffed it into her pocket. Then Esther glanced at the person standing next to her. A wisp of golden hair curled out from beneath the robe that cloaked his or her face and for a second, Esther's heart lurched: *Was it Michal?* Whoever it was seemed too frightened to look up and instead turned away.

After several minutes, Esther realized they were moving forward a person at a time. She couldn't see what was at the front of the room or who was talking. But it was clear they were waiting to see someone.

With a feeling of dread, Esther wondered, *Who was in charge? And what was he or she about to do?*

As he listened, Eli stared at the top of the table and traced the grain of the blond wood with one finger.

He found it much easier not to look at the prisoners. Although everyone in the room, including him, was hooded, he could still see a bit of face once in a while: a slice of chin, the tip of the nose, a strand of hair. Even one glimpse was enough to remind Eli that these were people, not just numbers. So he tried to keep his eyes averted at all times.

The numbers had been Gideon's idea, and Eli had to admit that they helped. As each prisoner was pushed forward one at a time, Eli was handed a piece of paper that had a number written on it. Thinking of each criminal as a number and not as a person made his job a little easier. All he had to do was sit there and listen as a guard told him what the person's crime had been.

Holding hands. Being sick. Being imperfect. Not showing respect.

It was strange, Eli thought now, *to think of holding hands as a crime.* Even boys and girls who were partnered with one another weren't allowed to be together, much less show any signs of affection in public, which struck him as unnatural.

Still, he knew enough to keep such thoughts to himself.

In his new job, Eli had the power to decide what the punishment should be for each case of wrongdoing. So far, all of the people present had committed minor felonies: kissing, having a limp, not praying loudly enough. According to his instructions, Eli sentenced such criminals to a work detail. Although Eli wasn't exactly sure what that involved, he knew that the prisoners would be given food, as well as a place to sleep; and hard work, he reasoned, never hurt anyone. He had yet to condemn anyone to death and hoped he never would.

The new responsibility had bolstered Eli's spirits. Although he had stashed away a few bottles of proof, he had given up drinking after his appointment; he felt newly focused and alert.

Yet by now the room was stifling hot. The continual drone of the guards' voices was like the buzzing of an insect. Glancing out at the yellow sky, Eli eased his neck and hoped they'd break soon for a meal. He took the slip of paper handed to him: 127.

The charges against prisoner 127 were so extreme, however, that they caught his attention.

"She try to kill Saith."

Despite his own rule, Eli glanced up. So did the prisoner, who turned to the guard in surprise.

"That's not true!"

The guard cuffed the prisoner once, hard, knocking off her hood. But Eli didn't need to see her face. He would have recognized her voice anywhere.

It was Esther.

She glanced up, bareheaded and defiant, and in that split second their eyes met.

Esther recoiled. She must have known it was him, for the blood drained from her already-pale face. Although his head and entire body were heavily cloaked, Eli had never felt so exposed in his life.

A second guard grabbed Esther by the arm. Yanking her hood back up, he forced her to lower her head and avert her gaze. But it was too late. Eli's mind was already whirling with a thousand thoughts and memories.

The early days when he first loved Esther seemed so far away. So did the time after their partners died and he had dared to hope she would finally be his. She had broken his heart more than once, and more than once he had vowed to forget her.

Yet one emotion crushed all of these flickering feelings, making them seem trivial: the guilt Eli felt for having killed Aras.

He knew he had to say something, but his tongue felt dry and thick within his mouth. When he tried to speak, one of the guards leaned forward to hear. Then the boy straightened up and spoke out loud.

"She try to kill Saith." His voice rang out in accusation. "You know what that mean."

"I know." Eli felt sick, yet his senses were keen. Was this how it would end between the two of them, so cold and impersonal? He feared he could not delay much longer.

And at last, he knew what he had to do.

"I'll do it," he said. "Give the prisoner to me."

As Eli stood, everyone in the room stared at him in open surprise. One of the guards hesitated.

"You need help?"

Eli shook his head. Then, with a brusque gesture not unlike one of Gideon's, he motioned for Esther and the guard's gun.

Eli led his prisoner out past the crowd and down the hall, his hands starting to shake. Then, once he was certain they were alone, he released his grip. Pulling down his hood, he turned to face her.

"Eli," Esther said, as if her suspicions had been confirmed.

"Listen." He spoke quickly, his voice soft. "The ones going to the work details are downstairs on six. Make sure you get there without anybody seeing you and go with them when they leave. That's your only chance of getting out of the District alive."

Esther listened, her head down. "It's a lie," she said at last. "That I tried to kill Saith."

Eli shook his head. "Most of what they say is a lie. But if enough people believe it, no one will complain when you're put to death."

By now, they were standing in front of the elevators, which gaped open. Esther glanced at the carpeting, which was blackened with dried and clotted filth. The entire corridor stank of death. Then she looked up at him in question.

"Go quickly," said Eli. He felt too guilty to return her gaze.

Esther turned, pulling the hood up over her face.

"Thank you" was all she said.

Eli waited until Esther made it to the corner. He lifted a

hand in farewell; and with a nod, she was gone.

He counted a few extra moments to make certain she had had enough time to make it to the stairs. Then he took aim and fired into the empty shaft of the elevator; the blast echoed and reverberated in its darkness.

When Eli walked back to the room of prisoners, the barrel of the gun was hot in his hand.

He would stand by Gideon's side that evening when the Insurgent leader announced Esther's execution. And Saith herself would praise his wisdom and present him with a reward of forty glass pieces.

SEVENTEEN

UNDER A MERCILESS SUN, DOZENS OF WORKERS TRUDGED DOWN A BROAD avenue of Mundreel. The only sound was the clank of chains that scraped and dragged along the asphalt. Everyone was shackled to someone else at the leg, and to make certain no one tried to escape, the entire group—nearly thirty in all—was bound together with a single coarse rope knotted around their necks.

The locked iron links dug into Esther's ankle so tightly, walking was torture, and the rope scratched and chafed the soft skin of her throat. Still she gritted her teeth and said nothing. There were only half as many guards as there were prisoners, yet they were armed and watchful. Cloaked and anonymous like the others, Esther walked in silence, trying not to draw any attention to herself.

At great risk, Eli had spared her life and for that Esther would always be grateful. As he had instructed, she managed to make it to the stairwell even as the sound of the bullet meant for her rang out and reverberated in her ears. There had been such commotion on the lower floor, she found it easy to slip in among others being assigned to a work detail and, with her face obscured by her robe, to go undetected. Then, like the other slaves, she had had her head shaved and was chained to another person.

Yet ironically, Esther's survival also meant her death.

Even as she was being shackled and bound, Esther knew that word was spreading throughout the District that she had been executed for plotting against Saith. She had heard those around her whisper about it even as they were all herded out-doors together and set on their long march.

No one knew who she was, and Esther intended to keep it that way. She had nothing left—no weapons, no allies, no glass. She owned nothing now except her anonymity. It would be her one tool, she sensed, if she were to ever escape. For she still vowed to herself that she would find out what had happened to her family and friends.

From now on, she would be Hagar.

Esther had found the name weeks ago in one of Joseph's books, a dense collection of stories called *Holy Bible*. Hagar had been the slave of Sarah, wife of Abraham. Seeing Sarah's name in print had given Esther a jolt of pleasure. So she now chose an identity that would link her to both her daughter and sister, if only in her own mind.

It was her sole comfort.

Ever since they had left the District, the small girl tethered to Esther's left leg walked as if in a daze—she wove back and forth, and was then yanked back to the group by the makeshift collar around her neck. Now she stumbled and fell. The unexpected downward tug of the rope made those closest to her stagger as well. Esther was pulled to her knees, and as the cord tightened around her throat, she frantically dug her fingers under it, trying in vain to loosen it. Several more were yanked down beside her. Choking and on the edge of panic, the entire group was forced to halt.

Within seconds, a guard lashed out at the group with the buckled end of a leather belt. He pushed his way through as best he could, until he saw the cause of the holdup.

"Get up!"

As he rained blows on the still form, Esther took care to look away. This voice was already familiar to her, both piercing and guttural. It belonged to the one who led the slave masters, a boy named Jud.

"I said, get up!"

The girl stirred. Then she tried to push herself up, but she was too weak. No one in the group made a move to help her.

With a foot of rope and some chain connecting them, Esther found herself locking eyes with the girl. She was an Outsider who looked no older than Silas: nine at the most.

"Help me," she whispered.

Although it hurt to do so, Esther forced herself once more to glance away; she knew that giving any aid might threaten them both. After a moment, the girl managed to get to her feet, and the group continued its forced march.

"That way!"

Jud's harsh voice rang out in the heavy air. He was ordering them toward a large, open-walled structure, set in from the street. Esther recognized it as a parking garage.

"Faster!"

The group tried to move quickly, but it was difficult to proceed as one; people gagged and choked against their shared noose as they shuffled and stumbled toward the building. At the entrance, several of the guards untied them, separating them into pairs. Each couple was handed a length of rubber tubing and a container of some kind; Esther found herself holding an empty soda bottle. Then they were ordered to begin collecting fuel.

In Prin, people had Harvested gasoline from ancient cars and trucks, which they then traded to Levi for food and other goods. Although it was a difficult and exhausting job, his system had seemed humane compared to this. The fuel would be used by Gideon and Saith to run their generator and provide them with the comforts of electricity, yet the slaves would receive nothing in return.

Rubbing her throat, Esther glanced around. She saw at once that almost no one knew what to do. Bewildered, they wandered among the dusty cars and vans, struggling to figure out where the gas was even kept. The guards, who clearly had no better understanding of how to proceed, walked among them, lashing out. Esther winced at the repeated crack of leather on skin, followed by cries of pain.

Of all the jobs in Prin, Esther had hated Harvesting the most of all. Still, she knew how to do it; it wasn't that difficult once you understood the basics. Tapping her partner on the shoulder, Esther now indicated a hulking car in the corner that stood well off the ground on oversize tires. Experience had taught her that large vehicles often contained the greatest amount of fuel. It took her a moment to locate the unobtrusive metal flap in the side, which she pried open to reveal the familiar notched plastic cap underneath. To her relief, it was unlocked, and with an effort, she was able to unscrew and remove it. Then, as the other girl watched, Esther took the length of rubber and inserted it, feeding it out inch by inch until she felt it hit something deep in the bowels of the machine.

Kneeling on the ground with the empty soda bottle, Esther took the other end of the tubing in her mouth. She began sucking on it, deeply at first and then with caution as she sensed that the fuel was drawing closer. Yanking out the tube at the last possible moment, she stuck the end into the container she'd been given. Gasoline, clear and pungent, gushed out and began to fill it.

Then Esther froze.

Only too late did she realize she was being watched. It hadn't occurred to her that knowing how to perform such a simple chore might draw unwanted attention. Yet that was clearly what had happened.

"Smart," a voice said, "ain't you?"

When Esther didn't look up, she felt a rough hand on her shoulder that yanked her around so hard, the gas cap in her hand flew in the air and clattered to the ground. She found herself staring up into the face of the chief slave master.

Jud was probably eighteen but looked even older; his bulk was massive and the bit of his face visible beneath his hood was dense with a black beard. Hulking and vicious, the boy seemed more like a bear than a human. Esther had known many such people in her life—bullies who preyed on the weak, yet who were themselves threatened by the slightest hint of challenge from anyone beneath them.

"Go get that," the boy said, pointing at the cap.

Esther stooped to retrieve the piece, half dragging the smaller girl with her. When she stood, she sensed the boy was assessing her even more closely. Praying that he hadn't recognized her, she kept her eyes down.

"You a smart little squirrel. Ain't you?"

"No."

"What that mean?"

"It means I don't know much."

"More than the others."

"I've done it before, is all."

"Yeah? Where?"

"Someplace."

Although she kept her gaze lowered, Esther knew that the boy was staring at her from behind his hood. Despite the fetid, humid air, she felt a chill run through her body.

"What your name?"

"Hagar." The unfamiliar word caught in her throat for a second, but the boy didn't seem to notice. He nodded. Then he turned and barked at the others.

"All you . . . watch Hagar! She teach you!"

Esther's heart sank.

Although no one had paid her the slightest attention before, she now saw everyone in the garage turn to take her in: some with dull obedience, a few with curiosity, but most with open resentment. This was the one thing she had been trying so hard to avoid. She pulled the folds of her hood closer to her face as she chose another car and knelt by its side. She repeated the procedure and felt the gas rise up the tube. But this time, she secretly let the fuel drop back down to wherever it came from. When she took the end out of her mouth and stuck it into a fresh bottle, nothing came out.

Some of those watching murmured, unimpressed. A few even tittered.

To her relief, they turned away even as the bearded guard scowled at her, his fingers tightening around the belt he held. Wincing, Esther now closed her eyes and braced herself for the blow that was coming. Yet nothing happened. When she opened her eyes again, she saw that the boy was studying her, as if trying to decipher something.

"You know what happen to smart little squirrels?" he said at last. "They make trouble for others."

Without warning, he struck out and lashed the face of the

little girl chained to her side. As she cried out and fell to the ground, the boy stood over her and pointed down at Esther.

"*You* did that," he said. "See?"

Sickened, Esther nodded.

After that, she did what she was ordered to do. She taught the others which vehicles were the most promising, where to look for the metal flap, and how to feed the tubing until it met the faint resistance of gasoline. She demonstrated how to siphon the deadly fluid without swallowing any by accident. And she stood by and assisted those who needed help.

Within an hour, every empty vessel had been filled.

Throughout, Esther could feel the eyes of the slave master follow her. *The boy was not as stupid as he looked,* she realized with despair. It was as if Jud had somehow read her mind and detected the one thing she had dreaded the most. Thanks to him, everyone was aware of her by now: every slave, every guard.

How could she possibly get away?

The slaves were given only the briefest of breaks.

A guard kept close watch as one of the workers passed around a gallon jug of stale water. Each was allowed no more than a single sip; anyone who took more felt the crack of a cudgel across the shoulders. Afterward, everyone lined up to scoop a handful of cold, congealed porridge from a large pot.

Esther drank what she could, but found she was unable to eat. She still felt guilty for what had happened to her young partner; and after she made certain no one else was looking, she handed over her share. The little girl gave a short nod of thanks before cramming the paste into her mouth, swallowing ravenously. Esther could not help but notice the red welt that snaked from the child's cheek down the side of her throat.

"I'm sorry," she said.

"Ain't your fault."

After that, they exchanged a few words. The little one said that her name was Ava; Esther only just caught herself before saying her real name.

"How old are you?" she asked. A bit of porridge still clinging to the girl's chin reminded Esther of Kai and she had to force herself not to wipe it away.

"Don't know," Ava said. "Young?"

"That it! Time to go!"

After being rounded up and counted, the slaves were once again tethered together by the neck. Carrying their containers of fuel, they were ordered to continue down the sweltering street. They were soon joined by other workers, who, although shackled in pairs, were not roped together as a group. Instead of fuel, they carried lumber, panes of glass, coiled tubing, and other supplies. No one was allowed to speak to one another, and they proceeded in eerie silence.

They were no more than a dozen blocks from the District when the guards ordered everyone to stop.

Wary, Esther glanced around. They were surrounded on all sides by steel and mirrored glass, standing in a canyon of immense buildings that seemed to pierce the sky. To her confusion, she saw that the slave handlers were ordering them to approach the tallest structure, one that took up the entire block.

The building rose straight up like a cliff face, a vision of gleaming silver that reflected the cityscape around it. The tower was several times larger than the District; Esther attempted counting how many floors it held and lost track at forty. Most of the stores and businesses of Mundreel showed signs of vandalism, earthquake, and the passage of time—broken windows, cracked edifices, and collapsed walls. Yet this one was perfect, as pristine as the day it had been created.

Esther couldn't help herself; she found herself shrinking in front of its enormity and splendor. And she could sense that the others, even the slave handlers, were intimidated as well. At first, she couldn't see an entrance anywhere. Although three sets of spinning doors were set in the glass façade, they appeared locked. Then she noticed that she and the others were being led around the corner, where someone had smashed the thick glass, forming a gaping hole. Everyone edged in, shuffling their chains and staying close together.

Inside, Esther gasped.

When she and her friends had first arrived in Mundreel, the District was the most opulent place they had ever seen. Yet it was dwarfed by the sheer height and magnificence of the room they found themselves in now.

Coolness emanated from the glimmering walls that rose straight up on both sides and from the floor itself, all made of the same polished white stone. Enormous panels hung at either end of the lobby, covered with strange and colorful pictures that resembled something a child would draw. Farther back, Esther counted six separate banks of elevators; each held at least a dozen doors that gleamed silver against the white marble. An immense wooden desk faced them, its blond surface gleaming smooth and clear as a pool of water.

But the slaves had not been brought here to ogle. Already, they were being untied and herded across the lobby to an inconspicuous metal door in a far corner. Carrying her bottles of gasoline by the neck, Esther found herself pushed into a dark and nearly airless stairwell. With Ava struggling beside her, she joined the others who began trudging up the steep staircase.

Guards were posted every few levels, holding up torches to light the way. As she passed Jud, Esther saw him take note of her. "Watch her!" he yelled to the others who followed. "Do like her!"

Esther felt chilled. Jud again sought to isolate and praise her, in order to infuriate the others. It was working: Those above her glanced down with looks of hatred.

"Not fast enough! Do like *her!*"

Then she heard the lash of the belt.

The stairs seemed endless; Esther counted twenty-eight flights of fifteen steps each and there was no end in sight. At every landing, more and more of the slaves began to falter or drop what they held. The guards reassigned what each one was to carry: The younger, weaker ones were given the fuel and smaller tools, while the stronger were ordered to take the heavier lumber and glass. Esther struggled to lift a set of glass panes; although she was supposed to share the load with Ava, she knew the young girl was not strong enough. As they labored upward, she noticed that more and more slaves were being ordered to leave what they carried and return downstairs.

Finally, only Esther, Ava, and four others remained. The slave handlers who accompanied them no longer barked orders at them or even hit them with the belts they carried; they, too, seemed exhausted and out of breath. A final set of stairs led to a narrow door with the word EXIT written on a sign above it. The six were directed through the door, as the two remaining guards followed.

Gasping, Esther stepped out into the blinding sunlight of the roof. Already, the others were undoing their head coverings as they dropped their planks and building materials. With a sigh of relief, she too set down the glass panes before pushing back her hood and flexing her aching fingers, her arms trembling with exhaustion. After the stifling heat of the staircase, it was a pleasure to be back in the open. It took her a moment to register her surroundings: an immense roof that seemed four times as large as that of the District.

Then what she saw stunned her.

In a near corner, a garden was in progress. True, the glass structure was minute compared to the one at home; it held no more than a dozen long tables, unlike the hundreds that she was used to. Yet although crude, it was a perfect replica of the other greenhouse, with transparent panels set in soldered iron and a concave ceiling meant for catching rainwater ending in a large pipe that led to a tank below. The small building was still incomplete; Esther noticed that one wall consisted of nothing but heavy plastic, probably to allow for expansion. Still, her unbelieving eyes saw the tables were covered with long, dark green tubs. She imagined they were already filled with water and held the beginnings of a first crop.

It was her idea—the one Aras had first shared and that she later suggested to Gideon. The Insurgent leader had obviously stolen her plan. Yet instead of helping others, he had distorted her vision to benefit one person alone: himself.

Trembling with bitterness, Esther forced herself to look away; the sight of the thing was too painful to behold. She noticed that at the far end of the roof, a group of workers gathered around Joseph, who stood with his back to her. Stumpy weaved in and out of his feet. They were all dwarfed by immense piles of building materials: stacked glass panes, iron rods, wooden planks and beams, and tools scattered everywhere.

Before Esther could move, her heart pounding, her old friend looked up.

And stared right at her.

Joseph's eyes grew huge; his mouth dropped open in shock. Stumpy noticed Esther, as well. Lifting her tail in greeting, she began to saunter toward her.

Esther did not dare bring a finger to her lips. She could only give a quick shake of her head and mouth a desperate word: *No.*

The slave master was behind her, close enough that she could feel his breath upon her neck.

"What wrong?"

Jud yanked her around so she faced him. Esther knew that her face was pale and feared what he would read in her expression. Sure enough, the boy looked up to see where she had been staring.

All he saw was the back of a boy, walking away. A cat's tail swished from beneath his arm.

The guard turned to Esther again.

"Move, you." He had already raised a hand to Ava, who cowered in fear.

But Esther did not need to be warned twice. She picked up the heavy glass panes and carried them to the far wall.

Late that afternoon, Esther rested with the others in the shade of the building. She was still thankful that Joseph had managed to keep her secret; she didn't care to think what would have happened if he had not. A few feet away, the guards sat together and talked among themselves. Only Jud kept an eye on her.

Even though she was surrounded, she felt more alone than she ever had in her life. Esther closed her eyes, thinking once more of her loved ones. After so many days, she knew that the chances of their survival were slim. She conjured up Aras and the others who had been made to disappear and realized that it was all too likely that everyone else she loved had met the same fate.

The idea that she might never see any of them again hit her like a wave of physical exhaustion, and for the first time, she felt engulfed by a crushing sense of despair.

Then she opened her eyes.

Far in the distance, a wisp of dark smoke was curling up into the afternoon sky. *Were her eyes deceiving her?* It disappeared and her heart sank. Then another faint cloud appeared, unmistakable. It too disappeared. Then another tendril of black.

Back in Prin, this was the way she and Skar had always signaled each other.

Esther sat up, her heart pounding. The last smudge rose in the sky and was already fading; it was impossible to tell who had sent it or if it was a deliberate sign.

Esther forced herself to avert her gaze so that no one would notice what she was staring at. When she looked back a moment later, the sky was once again clear. Still, Esther felt buoyed by an irrational surge of hope.

Maybe her people were alive, after all.

And if they could stay alive, then so would she.

EIGHTEEN

As word spread, more Outsiders began arriving at the District. They traveled from miles around, all seeking the same thing:

They came for the potion that would guarantee them life.

Each morning before the rotating glass doors were even unlocked, they congregated outside. Once they were allowed in, those who had known in advance to wear white or black robes took their patient place among the worshippers. Others had to wait to purchase them from Saith's assistants, using items they had Gleaned or glass to pay for them. Only then were they allowed to join the line of chanting, bowing petitioners that by the first light of day was already snaking its way through the main hall.

The faithful waited to visit Saith in her altar, the structure on the ground floor that had once been a fountain. Sitting in a chair made of black mesh with metal legs that spread like a giant silver claw atop black wheels, she alone was uncloaked. With her shaved head and oversize black T-shirt that fit her like a dress, the girl priestess looked even younger than usual, surrounded by towering guards and a hooded assistant.

By her feet was a bucket, half-filled with bright blue liquid.

Once in her presence, a worshipper would bow low, chanting. Saith dipped what looked like an immense spoon in the vessel and scooped out some of the fluid. She would present it to the one who knelt before her; he or she would drink from it as Saith murmured the same words over and over:

"Live to get old."

The follower swallowed deeply. He or she would then turn from the altar, chin wet and eyes gleaming with desperate hope. Then each would stumble away, chanting loudly and bowing before joining the others:

"Forgive us, Saith. Clean us, Saith. Heal us, Saith. Save us, Saith."

The sound of prayer, Gideon thought with irritation, *was as insistent as the droning of bees.*

Though he was a full level away and his door was shut and locked, he could still hear the faraway murmur, rhythmic and pulsating. Even when he managed to block out the sound for a few moments, Gideon remained all too aware of the worshippers, hundreds of them.

Gideon had thought from the beginning that Saith's religion was a clever way to fool and manipulate the gullible; yet it had secretly made him uneasy. He sensed that her cult, like the money system, hung on unquestioned belief and as a result was fundamentally unsound. He had been horrified to find out exactly what Saith was now promising: not merely her blessings, but long life, if they drank her concoction.

With more and more people flocking to the little priestess each day, begging for sips of her supposedly magical liquid, it was only a matter of time before they decided to test its power. That moment would come with the next rainstorm, and after that, Saith's fervent believers would start to sicken and die. Gideon didn't like to imagine what would then happen to her, the District, or the entire life they had set up for themselves.

More and more it occurred to Gideon that Saith had begun to believe her own words: that the blue concoction she mixed from paint and clean water would actually protect people from the disease. That she was universally beloved. That she was immortal. He rarely spoke to her anymore, so he wasn't certain. For although they were still business partners, the boy now realized that Saith was becoming too unstable to trust.

And so Gideon had begun to form a change in plans.

According to reports, construction of the new building was going well; Gideon was due to visit the following day. He would have his boys drive the slaves to finish at least a section of the garden as soon as possible.

What Gideon now planned for the new space was a secret

he shared with no one: that along with a few trusted guards, he would inhabit it alone.

Saith was driving the District toward disaster: that much was clear.

Gideon planned to be long gone by the time it happened.

By the light of a single torch, Nur wadded up the cloth once more and scrubbed at the floor. The last of the worshippers had left, and now the arduous part of her day began: polishing the central hall of the District so that it would look pristine again by morning.

The girl had to work extra hard to get the marble surface spotless, leaning in with all of her weight. The harsh cleaning paste dried out her hands and made them crack and bleed. Within minutes, her back and arms were aching, and her knees bit into the hard ground as she leaned forward.

To rest, Nur sat back for a moment on her heels. From habit, she reached up to push the heavy tumble of dark locks away from her sweating face. Her hand touched nothing but air, for of course, her head had been shaved weeks before. Even though she rarely indulged any feelings of self-pity, thinking about her lost hair gave her a slight pang. Lowering her hood, the girl gazed at herself in the surface of one of the polished silver legs that supported Saith's chair.

Her reflection ballooned back at her, and Nur had to tilt her head to and fro until she could get a fair picture of how she looked.

What she saw made her cry out.

Without the lush and glossy cascade of dark brown that had once softened her features, her ears now stuck out in a ludicrous way. Her eyes looked too big and her chin too pronounced. When Nur touched her ashy cheek in despair, she saw how ugly her hand was: withered and dry, like a claw.

She did not even bother examining her figure, which all males used to stare at with desire, even Gideon. How they used to fight for her attention! Ever since she was young, her beauty had given her a feeling of power, and as a result, Nur had always felt in charge of her dealings downstairs, no matter how much the other girls looked down on what she did. *They were only jealous*, she thought with momentary spite. Yet now, she knew that no boy would ever look at her again. Thanks to Saith, she had become flat and bony, and old beyond her years.

Nur was not aware that tears were running down her face, tears of grief and anger. She was so busy peering at this nightmarish self in the silvery metal, she didn't hear the person approaching from behind. Then a sound made her turn.

A cloaked figure stood still, its head cocked.

"Oh," it said. "I didn't know it was you."

It was Eli.

Embarrassed, Nur wiped her face with her sleeve and started to lift her hood to once more cover her face.

"Leave it," he said. "It's nice to see you again."

Nur gave a damp smile. Because of the separation of the sexes, she was no longer permitted to speak to any boy. If Nur and Eli were caught right now, they would be subject to harsh punishment.

Yet Nur had not seen Eli in many weeks and had considered him a friend—one of the few she had—when they both worked downstairs. It had saddened and bewildered her that he drank so much proof; it turned him into a pathetic relic of a person, and she wondered why he had allowed that to happen. Many nights, she had had to physically roust him from his chair and help him stagger outside and back to his room.

Yet now something had changed.

He looks different, she thought. *Sober, clear-eyed, and kind.* "It's nice to see you, too."

She made room on the ledge of the fountain and the two sat side by side. Without asking, Nur extinguished the torch, and both of them kept their voices low; that way, perhaps they would be able to detect anyone before they themselves were spotted.

Even so, the two friends talked at first about trivial things, relatively safe topics: new people who had come to the District, the quality of the food for sale, the shortage of sheets to sell the worshippers.

Then Eli mentioned his new job.

Nur kept her head down as Eli told her about his responsibilities and how he alone determined the fate of dozens of criminals every day. He spoke slowly at first, as if fearing her judgment. He described the people who came before him: thieves, blasphemers, the unclean.

Then Eli fell silent, as if gathering courage. In one breath, he described how he had had to sentence Esther to death and then kill her himself.

Noticing that the boy was trembling, Nur gave a sympathetic murmur and placed a hand on his arm. The news was no surprise; she had been in the room when the message had been delivered to Saith. Still, Eli clearly felt the need to confess. "Don't blame yourself," Nur said. "You had to do it."

Eli nodded. He seemed to want to say something more about the execution, but when Nur turned a questioning look to him, he shook it off.

Eli explained that often he was left alone now, in the court. Without guards supervising his actions and reporting them back to Saith and Gideon, he had been free to make more and more decisions on his own. That afternoon, for example, he had sentenced a boy who had been accused of stealing a rotten squash that had been left unattended.

The child was no more than five.

Nur shot Eli an incredulous look. "But that not stealing. Besides, he too little to know any better."

"I know."

"So what you do?"

Eli hesitated. Glancing around, he lowered his voice even more. "I was supposed to send him to a work detail."

Nur frowned. "Make him a slave?"

Eli shook his head. "I couldn't. So I told him not to do it again. Then, when no one was looking, I set him free." He sighed. "If she finds out, though . . ."

There was silence. In the darkness, Nur heard herself speak. "I seen her mix the water."

Eli shot her a questioning look.

"Saith," Nur explained. "I seen her mix the water. She use a can of something blue. Ain't nothing magic about what she does."

Nur knew she was saying things she shouldn't, accusations that would get her executed if anyone were to find out. Before now, she couldn't trust anyone with her suspicions. Yet this boy who held such power had confided in her. She couldn't help herself; it had been so long since she had unburdened herself to anyone, and the relief she felt was almost physical.

Then Eli spoke again. He didn't sound scandalized or angry; he lowered his voice to a whisper and said something even more dangerous. "So what should we do about it?"

Nur gave a start and grabbed Eli's hand to silence him; she thought she heard something. Her heart pounding in terror, she kept still. The noise came again, and this time it was for real.

One of Saith's guards was walking across the lobby, a lit torch held high. "Who there?" he shouted.

But Nur and Eli had both sprung to their feet. By the time the guard reached the fountain, there was no sign that anyone had been there.

"Girl!"

Nur appeared at the doorway. She saw that Saith was alone, lying facedown on her bed. She was leafing through a thin book filled with colorful images: *a magazine.*

Since she had begun working for her, Nur spent most of her waking time with the girl priestess. She slept in an adjoining room, prepared her food, and attended to her throughout the day. Saith was not so much cruel as utterly unaware of the older girl's presence. Nur was nothing more to her than a piece of furniture or a utensil: something to be used and otherwise ignored. As a result, Saith was utterly unselfconscious in her presence—which meant that Nur got to see her as she really was, not as she pretended to be.

Now Saith looked at pictures in the magazine, shifting to get comfortable. With fresh clarity, Nur saw that the priestess was nothing more than a child, willful and spoiled. She threw tantrums when she didn't get her way; she was vindictive and vengeful, remembering the smallest slights long after anyone else would have moved on.

Yet Nur had to admit that the child was clever, too. She understood how frightened everyone was: afraid of water, of earthquakes, of the disease. Of dying young. So she had created a religion based on fear.

Without bothering to look up, the little girl now indicated a table across the room, covered with small bottles.

"Try something new tonight," she said.

Every few days, Nur was responsible for grooming Saith. She was ordered to use the creams and lotions that had once filled the shelves of one of the stores downstairs, supplies that were now kept locked up and reserved for Saith alone.

Nur examined the bottles, uncapping each and sniffing the contents. There were dozens of them, smelling of flowers and fruit. She chose a new one and approached Saith, who was already stretched out on the bed.

Nur stood over her. Although she knew guards kept watch outside the door, she and Saith were alone. As she opened the jar, she gazed down at the younger girl, the person who had not only taken away her youth and beauty, but also kept her as a virtual slave.

As she poured some lotion into her hands and rubbed her palms together to warm it up, the fragrant aroma of blossoms rose in the air. Saith looked oddly defenseless, waiting for her anointing to begin. Her pale and fragile limbs were like twigs, and her neck was like the stalk of a plant.

Without being aware of it, Nur flexed her fingers. Working so hard, she had grown strong; her body, once so soft and curved, was now as lean and taut as a boy's. Her arms and hands were especially muscled now; they could crush and twist.

It would be so easy, Nur suddenly thought.

Trembling, she pulled back. Instead, she placed her hands on the soles of Saith's feet. Then she began to rub the lotion in, gently and methodically.

"That good," said Saith.

Nur let out her breath; only now did she realize she had been holding it in. She continued to work in her methodical way, massaging cream over the girl before finally wiping it off with a soft cloth.

Lastly, she helped the little girl back into her T-shirt. She did not need to be told what to do next.

Nur went to the door and without speaking or making eye contact, signaled to a guard, who nodded and disappeared around a corner. Within minutes, he returned, carrying something in a wooden crate. He handed it to the girl, who brought it into the room and set it on the floor where Saith was already waiting.

The box held the squirming body of a baby with lavender eyes and a flattened nose.

Saith was so intent she didn't seem to notice her underling, much less bother to dismiss her; she just sat on the edge of the bed and stared down at Esther's child. In the meantime, Nur moved unobtrusively behind her, putting away her supplies and folding towels. She too stole glimpses at Sarah and a strange feeling rose within her.

Prior to working for Saith, Nur had never been this close to a baby. Infants had been an abstract notion, something that had never interested her much, even though other girls made such a fuss about them. Yet she was surprised to see how cunning the little thing was, with its round belly and slender limbs. Its rosy skin almost seemed translucent in the delicate webs that separated its tiny fingers; altogether it was an enchanting creature. Even though it was only a variant, Nur was astonished by the powerful emotion the child stirred in her: a need to nurture and protect that she had never felt before.

And so she was chilled by the expression on the priestess's face. There was no trace of affection, warmth, or sentiment of any kind. Instead, she gazed down on the baby with eyes that were cold and clinical. Nur was suddenly reminded of a boy she had seen once on the street, crouched over a dying snake that he prodded with a stick. Saith's eyes held the same fascination and fear, the same disgust and calculation.

In the silence, Nur slipped away.

With a sick heart, she realized that Saith was planning to do something terrible to Esther's baby.

Unless, of course, she was stopped.

Several blocks away, the sun continued to blaze down on the roof where the construction was taking place. By midmorning, the black surface had become so hot, it sent up waves of rippling air that reeked of tar and burned through the tattered soles of everyone's sneakers.

But Esther paid it no attention. She was far too concerned about the change she had noticed in Jud.

For the past two days, the slave master had been even more unreasonable in his demands, driving workers and punishing stragglers with unprecedented viciousness. Because the slaves had to carry materials up dozens of flights before they could even begin the day's work, building progress was slow. Still, it was going far better than Esther could have imagined. Under Joseph's patient tutelage, the miniature greenhouse was nearly completed.

Workers were soldering the last of the metal strips that made up the frame, and the final panes were stacked to one side, waiting to be set. Inside, the long, wooden tables held over a hundred plastic trays that were halfway filled with sterilized water. Tiny seedlings, their roots suspended in the liquid like fine white hairs, were already growing in a few of the planters: tomatoes, squash, radishes, cabbage.

Yet from the heavy, sweating face of their supervisor, Esther could see that none of it was good enough. And during their midday break, she found out why.

Jud wasn't angry.

He was afraid.

As usual, Esther had found herself on the outskirts of the group, sitting cross-legged on the hot and gritty tarpaper that lined the roof. Two of the older slaves walked among them doling out lunch: a handful of porridge and a sip of musty water from a plastic bucket. As Esther waited her turn, she kept her head down and her attention on Jud and the other masters gathered in the corner. Earlier she had noticed a messenger from the District communicate a few words to Jud before leaving. Now the boys spoke in agitated murmurs. By concentrating, Esther was able to hear their distinct voices.

"It got to be right," Jud kept saying.

"It is," one of the others assured him.

"It got to be right for *them*," Jud repeated. "He just said they coming. *She* coming. Today." As the others murmured, Esther turned away, her heart pounding.

They could only be talking about one person. *If Saith showed up for an inspection*, she thought with a sickening feeling, *what would she do? How would she hide?* Esther wore a hooded cloak, like the others, yet she knew it provided precious little cover for her face.

Their short break now over, the slaves were ordered back downstairs. As Esther descended the suffocating stairwell, she wondered why they were being brought to the lower level.

Once they emerged in the lobby, she understood.

Standing behind the immense front counter was an altar of sorts that they had started several days earlier. Its location was critical, for Esther knew that it was intended to be a prominent place where the girl priestess would sit and welcome her followers. Although they had laid the foundation, it was far from finished. Part of the problem was that Joseph had no experience or knowledge about how to construct such a thing, and so it resembled a greenhouse in miniature, made of panes of glass held together by soldered metal.

To her astonishment, Esther realized that Jud intended for the structure to be finished in time for Saith's arrival that day. She could tell by his persistent hysteria.

"Faster!" he kept screaming as he cracked the leather belt he always carried above their heads. "Go faster!"

Slaves struggled to fit panes into the metal skeleton that served as the altar's frame. A central gap was reserved for a special piece of glass: a large and thick slab, as wide as it was tall, made of a beautiful pebbled blue. Eight workers had spent nearly an entire day transporting it across the city; the spectacular panel would make a fitting centerpiece. Now Esther, Ava, and two others were ordered to pick it up and set it into to the altar.

Esther held back for a moment. She was still thinking about how to disguise herself as she watched the others approach the slab. Together, the three struggled to hoist it, stationing themselves underneath to gain the most leverage.

Anyone could see it was a nearly impossible task: The heavy slab kept shifting in their sweaty grasp. When Ava stumbled once, nearly dropping her corner, the entire piece shifted dangerously.

Then Esther had an idea. It would be risky, but she could think of no other way to avoid being recognized by Saith in the few precious minutes she had left. "Let me do it."

One of the workers shot her a mean look. "You gonna show us how?" He was breathless from lifting; his raspy voice was full of hostility.

Esther shook her head. "Let me do it *alone.*"

All of her companions stared at her, puzzled. Then the boy snorted and turned to the others. "Let her."

The three tilted the segment back to the floor and waited for Esther to take hold. Then, skeptical yet clearly curious, they backed off.

Esther faced the piece of glass. It was taller than she was and nearly as thick as her wrist. Even balancing it took considerable effort; she guessed it outweighed her by three or four times. Using all of her strength, she managed to tip the piece up on one corner as it nearly slipped from her grasp. Realizing that everyone in the lobby was now watching her, Esther hoisted the edge as high as she could. Then, deliberately, she let go of it.

And watched it shatter on the marble floor.

Everyone cried out as glass exploded with an earsplitting boom. The impact could be felt across the entire lobby as chunks and bits of blue spilled in every direction.

In the silence that followed, all eyes swiveled to the slave master.

For several seconds, Jud remained still. He hadn't witnessed what had just happened and seemed unable to make sense of the mounds of broken blue pebbles that lay scattered across the marble floor.

Then he erupted, drawing the leather belt. But before he could strike out, Esther's companions spoke.

"She did it," the boy said, pointing at Esther, his voice trembling. Ashen faced, the girl by his side nodded.

"He's right," Esther said in a level voice. Although her stomach was knotted in fear, she did not shrink back; she raised her chin in an open look of defiance, one she hoped would trigger the boy's anger. "I slipped."

Jud snorted, as if in disbelief. He began to turn away and Esther felt a fresh pang of dread. *Would he punish another slave for her behavior, as he always had before?*

Then, in one movement, he whirled around and lashed the belt directly across Esther's face, snapping her head back.

Inwardly, Esther rejoiced; she had bargained for this response. Yet the pain of it was beyond excruciating, unlike anything she had ever experienced before. As she collapsed to the floor, her arms curled uselessly around her head. She was lucky to have taken the brunt of the blow across her jaw and cheek; it had missed her eyes by a fraction of an inch. She watched as the slave master stormed off, barking at those who had witnessed the assault: "Clean this up! Now! *Now!*"

There was a long pause. Then other slaves advanced to her side in twos and threes.

Esther felt herself wavering in and out of consciousness, yet sensed the others standing above her. Ava knelt by her side. The younger girl now rested Esther's head in her lap and attempted to blot the blood with her smock.

"Please." Esther could barely speak; her jaw felt as if it were on fire. She gestured at her face, and Ava understood. She took the hem of her own garment and tore a ragged strip from it. This she wound around Esther's face before knotting it at the back.

Now, Esther thought with grim satisfaction, *she was safe.* And just in time.

"She here!" she heard a guard yell. "Saith is here!"

Saith and Gideon stood on the far side of the lobby and surveyed the workers, who had hastily raised their hoods to cover their heads.

"Show respect." Jud's whisper was harsh. In response, all of the slaves put their fingers to their temples and began to bow again and again. Even so, more than a few dared to keep their expressions hard and full of contempt.

Esther stood in the back row, her swollen and aching face concealed by the rag. She felt not only shaky but nauseated as well; she prayed she didn't become sick or draw any further attention to herself. With gratitude, she noticed that those on either side of her now stood close by, including those who had despised her only moments before. With their support, she was able to stay erect. As she bowed with the others, Gideon's eyes skittered across the assemblage but didn't stop on her.

For her part, Saith seemed unimpressed. She glanced at the stacks of lumber, glass, and other building materials that sat unattended near an inner staircase. Although the slaves had scrambled to clean the lobby before her appearance, heaps of debris, broken glass, and dust were still everywhere. The little girl sighed with dissatisfaction and addressed Gideon.

"When it be done?"

"Soon." Red-faced and sweating, Jud was much taller than the priestess. Still, Esther could tell by the way he hunched his shoulders and leaned forward he was trying to make himself appear smaller and more humble. But the little girl acted as if she hadn't even noticed the boy as she glanced up at the majestic ceiling.

"He say they on time," Gideon replied.

"They better be." Saith sounded sleepy.

At this, Jud glanced up, a flash of panic in his eyes. "I show you how fast we go," he blurted. "We hold a contest. See who the best."

Saith shrugged, not displeased. Taking her lack of negativity as a kind of enthusiasm, Jud brightened; Esther could see his pathetic smile.

Within moments, the slave leader had ordered two chairs set up for his esteemed visitors by the mouth of the enclosed staircase. As Saith and Gideon sat, the boy then ordered the workers to file past, one at a time. "Which two you want?"

As Esther passed, she made sure to favor the side of her face that was covered. For a second, she felt Saith's gaze fall upon her, but then it moved on. Saith chose two of the older slaves, both boys. They were ordered to each pick up a heavy length of lumber and race each other up the dark and stifling stairwell to the roof. After depositing their loads, they were then to race back down. The winner would be given a reward and the loser punished.

"But be quick," Saith said.

"You heard her!" Jud yelled. "Fast!"

As the boys shouldered their heavy loads and staggered toward the stairs, Esther could hear Saith chuckle. Because they couldn't reach the ground, her little legs swung back and forth; she was clearly enjoying the spectacle. Gideon had already left his seat and wandered away; Esther assumed he was bored or maybe even disturbed by the childish and needlessly cruel display.

After several minutes, Esther could finally hear the sound of someone descending. One of the slaves burst out of the door, empty-handed; he was gasping for breath and nearly staggering. A moment later, he was followed by the other, equally as exhausted. The loser was told to await his fate. Then the winner was ordered to approach Saith.

She handed him a tiny hard candy.

And so it went for at least an hour: Two by two, slaves were ordered to pick up heavy panes of glass, pieces of lumber, or bags of cement and race each other up the endless staircase. While Saith opted for the strongest-looking slaves at first, she soon grew bored and began picking more unlikely contestants. For one turn, she selected two of the youngest workers, a boy and a girl who were no older than six or seven, and ordered that each one carry a heavy brick. By the time it was over, only the boy emerged; and he too was rewarded with a tiny sweet.

Esther was among the last chosen. When she was called, she saw that her opponent was a fellow slave who had once been especially hostile to her, a thin and pale boy around her age. He had been kind after she had been knocked to the ground; standing next to her in line, he had briefly allowed her to sag against him. Yet from the look in his eye, Esther could tell his only concern was not being punished. Each of them was ordered to pick up a sack of cement. Then, at the signal, they were told to begin.

The boy bolted off up the dark stairwell, taking two steps at a time. With the heavy bag slung across her shoulder, Esther toiled upward in silence. The air was so stifling it was hard to breathe, and her legs soon burned and trembled. She tried counting the floors to take her mind off how exhausted she was and how badly her face hurt: twenty-eight, twenty-nine, thirty. There were seventeen more flights to go.

Then she stumbled; her foot touched something soft and she nearly fell. Putting aside the bag, Esther reached forward to see what it was. Her competitor lay sprawled at the top of a landing, the bag of cement by his side.

Esther prodded him. "Are you okay?" she whispered.

He didn't reply.

There was nothing she could do. Esther continued upward

until she reached the roof, where Joseph waited. Her old friend could not risk questioning her, for there were others around; he expressed his concern by meeting her eye and raising an eyebrow. She gave a slight shake of her head in reply before dumping the bag in the corner. Then she turned and headed back.

Free of the massive weight she carried and walking downstairs, Esther at first felt wonderfully light. Then the effort became more and more painful. By the time she stumbled back into the lobby, her legs wobbled so badly she could barely stand.

Yet she had won. And as a result, she too found herself face-to-face with the little girl.

The strip of cloth was now soaking with perspiration. Esther feared it clung to her features and showed more of her face than she cared to reveal. Looking up, Saith began to hand Esther a sweet. Then, abruptly, the little girl glanced away.

"That enough." She tossed the candy across the room, where it skittered on the dusty marble. "You get them."

As exhausted as they were, everyone scrambled for the treats. Esther was not hungry, yet knew she would draw unwanted attention if she held back. As she got down on her knees and fought for a few pieces, she overheard Saith.

"Get the rest over with."

Jud obeyed, yelling at the guards to help him bring forth the losers. One by one, each was pushed against the central counter and hit once, hard, across the back with his belt. Saith had kept a few candies for herself; as she watched, she sucked

on them. Yet before Jud was even halfway through, she seemed
to lose interest in the diversion.

"That it," she said to Gideon, who had rejoined her. During
the spectacle, he had apparently climbed the stairs to the new
garden by himself; now, his face was impassive. Saith bent her
head close to his and spoke a few words. At one point, she took
the unfinished candy out of her mouth and flicked it away.
Then she started out of the room, not waiting for anyone.

As Saith disappeared, Gideon addressed Jud in private.
Esther could not hear what he said, until he turned to leave.

"You hear her?" he said. "Get it done."

Jud nodded silently as Gideon moved ahead to catch up
with Saith.

Esther was relieved she hadn't been recognized. Yet something told her that it was the least of her worries.

After Saith and Gideon left, Jud ordered everyone back to
the roof.

He moved to the only shaded area under a crude tent and
sat heavily on one of the two chairs. Jud was normally in their
midst, cracking his belt over the shoulders of anyone he perceived to be weak or slow. Yet he now sat unmoving for so long
that everyone began casting anxious, sidelong looks at him.

Finally, one guard gathered the courage to approach. Esther
couldn't hear what he said, but she saw Jud gaze up at him, his
face a frightening mask of rage and mortification. He didn't
bother to whisper, and his voice could be heard by all.

"We got to go faster."

"But ain't possible."

"Something slow us down." Jud's bloodshot eyes flickered over the workers toiling at the far end of the roof. Then he came to a decision. "The little ones. We got to get rid of them."

The other boy blinked. "Get rid of them? What you mean?"

"Kill them. That way we speed up."

Esther inhaled. Although it was clear that everyone on the roof had heard, no one reacted; the only sound was the clanking of tools and the rasp of metal on the tar-paper roof. The suggestion seemed both too monstrous and too nonsensical to be real. Everyone's eyes were focused on the other guard, who was silent for a long moment.

At last he spoke. "You going to do that?"

"No," Jud said. "*You* going to."

After a second, the guard nodded. Yet when he walked back to the other guards, Esther noticed that his face was ashen. He consulted with his peers, but spoke too softly to be overheard.

Then he emerged from the huddle.

By now, the slaves had stopped working. The roof was so silent everyone could hear the squelch of the guard's sneakers on the hot tarred surface as he approached. As he walked, he hiked up his robes and his right hand went to his back waistband.

"All right." His voice dull, he nodded at the smallest workers, who huddled together in terror. There were eight of them, the youngest no more than six or seven. "Some of you got to come with me."

None of them moved. The boy raised his voice. "You hear? Got to come with me—"

A clear voice interrupted him. "You don't have to."

Startled, the guard glanced up.

Esther had risen to her feet. She spoke loudly enough so that everyone on the roof could hear. "It's all up to you."

"*Shut up and sit down!*" screamed the guard.

From the corner of her eye, Esther could see Joseph quail as he stared at her, his eyes round with terror. *Of course Jud and his boys could shoot her dead,* she realized. *Everyone else as well. After all, they had weapons, and the slaves had none.* But there were worse things than death. If even one of the children were to go along with his or her destruction without questioning why, then they were all doomed.

She could not allow that to happen.

"That boy over there?" Esther crouched in front of the youngest and indicated the slave master with a nod. "He says he's got all the power. But that's only true if you believe him. If you don't, he's got nothing."

A murmur rippled through the slaves.

"Little ones . . . on your feet!" The guard acted as if Esther hadn't spoken. He pointed at a tiny girl with enormous eyes. "You first!"

The child stared up at him, terrified. She seemed about to rise. Then she couldn't help it: She glanced at Esther.

"He says he's in charge." Esther spoke in a soft voice. "But that's only if you let him order you around." Holding her gaze, the girl gave a slight nod. She didn't move.

By now, the whispering among the slaves had grown more agitated. Esther didn't blame them; if her plan backfired, she was putting all of their lives at risk. And yet she was aware of a basic and more practical truth: *Jud needed them.* He needed them to finish building the altar and the roof; without them, he alone would face Saith's wrath. Esther realized that this did not give her and her fellow workers much power; still, it was something. And none of them had anything left to lose.

"Listen to her," someone said.

"Stay where you are," called another.

"Get up!"

The guard was desperate. Esther could tell from the look in his eyes that he didn't want to carry out his orders; he was acting from fear alone, making him nearly as vulnerable as the slaves themselves. Knowing this, Esther met his eyes in a silent appeal. The guard started back, shocked, as if she had somehow seen inside him. But he didn't have time to respond.

"Out of the way."

Jud had arisen. With one forceful movement, he shoved the guard to the side. Now he faced the assemblage, the belt in his hand. There was a new depth to the anger in his voice: It was filled with pure hatred.

"You gonna get a *lot* of people killed now," he told Esther.

But what Esther saw in the slaves' faces was something new. This time, there was no fear, no blame, no apathy. Instead, she saw fury . . . and rebellion.

Even killing them all would get Jud nowhere.

For a moment, Jud quailed, then he abruptly changed tactics. Stepping forward, he kicked his way through the crowd until he reached Esther. Then he grabbed her by her arm and dragged her out before the others as he fumbled with his robes.

In one motion, he pulled a small gun from the waistband of his jeans and raised it to Esther's temple.

"*Now* things go faster," he said.

The slaves erupted.

Bursting up off the floor like a single creature, they rushed forward with a roar of anger. Within seconds, they had knocked and trampled Jud to the ground, twisting his weapon from his grip. Then they turned their fury on the stunned guards, punching, kicking, and pinning them to the ground. The boy who had been ordered to kill the youngest struggled to retrieve his gun, but a boy punched him in the stomach, allowing a girl to wrestle it away. The incensed mob swarmed across the roof, destroying everything in its path.

Slaves seized every weapon they could tear from their captors—whips, belts, clubs, guns—and soon the air was filled with the sound of screams, beatings, and the occasional bang of a pistol.

Esther was stunned by the fast-moving melee and found herself unable to do anything about it. She felt that she had pulled an obstruction away from a river and now the force of the flood was beyond stopping. Stumbling backward, she found Joseph, who stood on the other side of the roof, pale and unmoving. One hand pressed to his mouth, he clung to his cat carrier so tightly Esther could hear the plaintive cry of the animal inside.

Before them, a crowd had collected around something on the ground. For a second, the mob parted, and Esther could see a bloodied Jud. Two slaves held him down, but there was no need; his body was broken and unmoving.

"Stop!" Esther cried. She strode forward and attempted to push through the hysterical throng.

Above the din, the slaves somehow heard her voice and obeyed. Some of them straightened, backing off. The smallest one turned, her face vacant, a smear of blood across her cheek. But they hadn't finished with their destruction.

As the workers began to shove past her in the opposite direction, Esther was at first puzzled. Then she understood where they were directing their rage: at the greenhouse, nearly completed.

"Let's tear it down!" one boy shouted, and his words were met with cheers.

"Tear it down!"

"No!" Esther shouted.

They chose not to hear. Within seconds, they had descended on the thing they had spent weeks building, wielding hammers and clubs and their fists. The air was filled with the deafening sounds of smashing panes and cracking wood. Splinters of glass glinted on the tar-paper floor; entire tables were knocked over and their tubs tumbled to the ground, splashing their contents everywhere.

Esther stood to the side. She was shaken and sickened by the destruction she had brought about; at the same time she was glad that they were free. Yet for how long? They could not take the risk of remaining.

Already, the workers were slowing down; they stood, vacant eyed and delirious, the worst of their energy spent. "We have to go," Esther called out. "Now."

The slaves blinked and wavered in the purple-and-orange light. Then, obedient, they allowed Esther to steer them toward the stairwell, dropping their tools as they went.

Overhead, the sun was setting, which was good; Esther knew they would need the darkness to hide them and cover their tracks. What's more, she could now make out something that filled her with the only hope she had left:

A smoke signal, faint yet high in the sky.

NINETEEN

AFTER FEEDING THE FIRE MORE DAMPENED WOOD, SKAR SCANNED THE
pale yellow haze of the late afternoon sky. Other than a faraway
flock of birds, nothing stirred. She saw no answering plume of
smoke rising from the city below. Once again, she experienced
what had become a familiar reaction: a stab of disappointment
followed by stoic resolve.

*She would not give up trying to contact Esther until she knew for certain
that she was dead.*

It had been many days since she had last seen her friend, on
that terrible night they discovered the unspeakable secret in
the District basement. After half dragging, half carrying Silas

up to the lobby, Skar had waited, expecting her friend to follow. Finally, she whispered to the boy to go outside. Skar had
then bounded up the ten long flights back to her home two
at a time, for she knew Gideon's boys would soon be on their
way. In the precious minutes she had gained by her speed, she
was able to gather Michal, Uri, and Kai, whom she quickly sent
downstairs to join Silas. Yet, search as she might, she had not
been able to locate Joseph or Sarah. She was still looking for
them when she'd heard the Insurgent guards burst into the
hall. Only then was she forced to leave, waiting for the moment
the coast was clear before escaping to the stairwell.

In the confusion, Skar had been able to slip undetected
across the lobby and out into the night. Silas, Michal, and the
others were waiting for her across the street, trembling with
fear and dismay as they huddled together in the shadows of a
neighboring building. Skar knew that it would be minutes until
Gideon realized they'd escaped and sent his boys out to hunt
them down. So with a heavy heart, she had taken Kai in her
arms, and ordered her friends to follow her as they fled into
the night.

Because Silas knew the layout of the city better than anyone, Skar had asked him to guide them. With a crescent moon
lighting their way, he had led them north, toward the shad-
owy mountain that loomed over the rest of the city. As they
climbed uphill, Uri thought he recognized some of the streets
where he, Saith, and their friends had once lived. But they did
not stop. They now realized they could no longer trust anyone else. Silas led them even farther, to the distant side of the

hill, until they reached a neighborhood of two- and three-story houses and small businesses.

There, Skar found a storefront on the ground floor of a brick building. Taking a quick look inside, she saw that it seemed clean and vacant; even the glass windows were still mostly intact and had large, incomprehensible words painted on them: ST-VIATEUR and BOULANGERIE. The remnants of a peculiar five-pointed symbol could be seen on one window; adorning another was a picture of a round foodstuff with a hole in the middle. Skar ordered everyone inside, and at once they curled up on the dusty floor, Michal cradling Kai in her lap. Before long, all were asleep except Skar, who stood by the window until dawn, keeping an eye out for anyone who might have followed.

Later that morning, Silas Gleaned the other stores that lined the street and came back with a few crucial items: a fire-starter nearly full of fuel, a firebowl, a bucket, a plastic bottle. Uri immediately went out in search of water to boil and filter, while Skar and Michal continued exploring the narrow streets, bringing Kai with them.

On the mountain's peak, the three had come across a spectacular building they hadn't noticed the night before. Only one story high, it had a massive roof made of red tile and large doors of broken glass on all sides. Within was an immense room, with a vaulted ceiling and a giant glittering construction of glass shards that hung high overhead. Dust motes danced in the light that poured in on all sides. Kai, enchanted, had clapped his hands, laughing at the echo; then raced across the smooth floor, scattering pigeons that flew into the eaves, cooing.

Michal watched him for a moment before turning to Skar. "Can't we stay here instead?" she had begged.

Although it was undeniably beautiful, the wide and empty expanse had made Skar uneasy. "It's too obvious a place. . . . It would be the first place anyone would search," she said. "And there's no place to hide."

"But look." Michal had already found that the large doors opened onto a terrace. She called to Kai, who ran past her onto the flagstone surface. Beyond the white cement fence that encircled its perimeter lay the entire city of Mundreel spread out beneath them, the massive buildings as tiny as Kai's toys. Michal had lifted the veil she always wore to feel the mountain breeze.

Skar had joined her. Yet she was not admiring the view; she had already noticed something in the distance. Although they were too far away to say for certain, she thought she recognized a distinctive building. It was made of a glittering yellow material that reflected the sky. If so, that meant she knew where the District was. . . .

Within moments, the variant girl had dragged out some old bedding she had seen inside the large room. She placed it in the center of the terrace, then dug the firestarter out of her pouch. It had taken several moments for the mattress to catch fire; the shredded white plastic that covered it crackled and melted at first, refusing to light. But at last the stuffing beneath it had ignited and soon the entire thing was ablaze, sending up foul-smelling smoke.

Holding Kai back from the flames, Michal had watched her partner questioningly.

"For Esther," was all Skar replied.

"What if it draws someone else?"

Skar had only shrugged. The other girl nodded with sober understanding.

That was more than three weeks ago.

Even now, Skar followed the same routine every morning. At dawn, she went hunting with the bow and arrows Silas had Gleaned for her. Then, with her freshly killed prey dangling from her belt, she climbed to the mountainside terrace, gathering whatever she could find on the way that would burn: bits of furniture, discarded clothing and books, rotted wood. After building a fresh fire, she would watch the horizon.

But there was never a response.

Skar didn't bother tormenting herself with possibilities. Although she did not know why Esther had not followed her that night, it was not in her nature to dwell on what might have happened. All she knew was that she had complete faith in her friend's resourcefulness, strength, and determination. She also understood that if Esther were still alive, nothing on earth could keep her away from her children and loved ones. She would spend every waking moment searching for them, and so it was Skar's obligation to provide her with a sign.

Yet after so many days, Skar was growing uncertain.

Brooding, she now sat alone on the white stone balustrade. Her knees were drawn up to her chin as she stared down over the city. Behind her, the fire sent thick black smoke wafting up

into the purple-and-orange sky; the sun was close to the horizon and soon it would be time to return home for the night.

More and more, Skar wanted to return to the District to
find out for herself what had befallen Esther. It was all she could
do to keep herself from slipping back at night and breaking in.
Yet she was aware that even when hooded, she was far too
noticeable to casual onlookers. She also knew that although
she had struggled to teach the others how to hunt, Michal,
Silas, and Uri were still clumsy with the bow. Nor did they
have any knowledge of how to track, stalk, or hide.

In short, Skar could not afford to let herself be caught.

Resigned, she was about to get up and return home.

Then she froze.

Something or someone was nearby. Skar had heard the
crackle of a broken twig, seen a movement in the branches out
of the corner of her eye, and sensed a sudden light muskiness.
Was it a curious animal or child drawn by the fire?

Or was it someone more dangerous?

Skar tensed. Although she wasn't much of a fighter, she
hoped to escape without being seen. She slithered to the
ground in a single, silent move. Then she crept along the stone
fence, trying to slip away undetected. She was almost at the
end when an unfamiliar voice rang out.

"Hold it."

A boy stepped out from the trees. In the glare of the setting
sun, his white clothing seemed to give off a brilliant light. Still,
Skar could see clearly enough to realize that he held an object
pointed at her.

It was a gun.

Skar straightened and turned to face the stranger. The boy lowered the weapon.

"I know you." He sounded surprised.

And as he stepped forward, Skar finally saw who it was.

Trey stood before her, the assassin who worked for Gideon. His face looked thinner than when she had passed him that night on the District stairs. Yet he was unmistakable in his white clothing, with the curious white stripe in his dark hair.

"What you doing up here?" With a single movement, Trey returned his weapon to its hiding place.

"We left the District," replied Skar, choosing her words with care. Trey didn't appear to be hunting them down; after all, he had put away his gun. Still, she had no idea what allegiances he still held or what price, if any, had been placed on their heads.

"So did I. Me and Gideon, we had a parting of the ways." As he spoke, the boy gazed beyond Skar, as if expecting to see someone else with her.

"Yet you are still in Mundreel," she said. "Why?"

Trey shrugged. "Thought I could get me more work out here. But it hard. Nobody got anything to trade: no food, nothing. Nobody want anything except to go see that little girl and get saved."

Skar shot him a quick look. *Was he testing her?* Keeping her face neutral, she nodded, revealing nothing.

The boy indicated the fire. "What that?"

Skar followed his gaze but looked back at him, not answering.

He persisted. "You trying to signal someone?"

The girl wasn't certain, but thought she detected something in his voice—a flicker of vulnerability—and so she decided to take a chance. Keeping a close watch on his expression, she spoke in a flat and deliberate voice. "I'm trying to find Esther."

The effect was unmistakable. At the mention of her friend's name, Trey gave a start and glanced up. His face flushed.

In an instant, he looked like a young boy. And in that moment, Skar understood.

"Can you help us?" The question rose to her lips before she knew it. She still couldn't tell whether she could trust the killer, yet she was desperate enough to take a chance. "I last saw her many days ago, when we escaped. It's impossible for us to go back. . . . I think Gideon's boys may still be looking for us."

"So she alive?"

"That is what I need you to find out."

Trey said nothing, gazing at the ground.

Skar wondered why he hesitated. Then, with a pang, she remembered that he was a hired hand, someone who only worked for pay. She wracked her mind for what she could offer. "We don't have any glass," she said at last, "but if you bring us news, we will give you food and water to last you many days. I promise."

Trey flashed her a wounded look. "I don't need pay," he said, spitting out the words.

For what felt like the first time in weeks, Skar's heart

expanded within her and she smiled with genuine warmth.

"I understand," was all she said.

Trey took time to reload his weapon, then took off into the night. Skar watched him from the terrace, a flash of white disappearing into the forest below.

Long ago, experience had taught her to expect the worst. Yet for now, at least, she was filled with a strange new hope.

Stars lay scattered across the night sky. Far beneath it, the silence of the dark streets was broken by cries and the sounds of destruction.

Esther kept close to the edge of the building. Behind her in the shadows, she could feel Ava tremble as she pressed against her. Around the corner, they could hear the smash of cudgels and the sound of people screaming. The acrid smoke of torches hung heavy in the air.

Once she and the slaves had made it to the street, the reality of their freedom hit them. Many of them turned to one another, hugging or slapping one another on the back as they shouted and wept with relief. Buoyed by their victory, they lingered on the sidewalk. Some picked up bricks and stray tools from the street and threw them at the lobby doors and walls, laughing and cheering at the sound of splintering glass.

But Esther knew there was no time for celebration. Although it was nearing the end of the day, she was sure fresh teams of workers were still due to arrive with materials. It would be only a matter of minutes before someone discovered what had happened. And, once word of the rebellion spread, Gideon's guards would be out in force, searching for the escaped slaves.

But Esther had no idea it would be so soon.

She'd been able to convince only Ava to join her and Joseph. Although all three of them were weak and shaky, she had taken them by the hands and forced them to run with her, leaving the joyous cacophony behind. She'd hoped that while there was still light in the sky, she had a chance of pinpointing the location of the smoke signal. Perhaps she could even build a fire of her own in response. Yet no sooner had they gone three blocks than she heard the faint sounds of celebration turn to screams of terror.

Clearly, Gideon's guards had arrived, and from what Esther could discern, they were suppressing the uprising with swift brutality.

Now, the three shrank back in the shadows as they heard someone approach, running fast. A slave boy, the one who had been the first winner of Saith's contest, rounded the corner. When he saw them, he shot them a look of desperate appeal. But before Esther could pull him to safety, a guard caught up and bashed him over the head with a metal club. The boy pitched forward and collapsed at their feet, shuddering and twitching. Then he was still. Ava gave a choked cry and Esther put her arms around the girl, silencing her until the guard moved on.

The three of them hid in the shadows like that for an hour, listening to the sounds of the crackdown that raged around them. Only when it finally seemed to taper off did Esther dare to peer around the corner. What she saw sickened and horrified her. By the light of the new moon, she saw dozens of motionless heaps on the sidewalk—the bodies of slaves.

"Don't look back," she whispered to Ava.

Joseph was quieting the mewing Stumpy. "Esther," he whispered, "we must go."

At the sound of the strange name, Ava looked up questioningly.

"Esther?" she repeated. She shook her head, bewildered. "Gideon kill her long ago. Why he call you that?"

Esther did not explain or even respond; there was no time. Once more taking the hands of the others, she raced with them through the silent streets.

Soon, they made it to a different neighborhood, one that was far from the enormous skyscrapers, and they could no longer smell the lingering stench of the torches. But still she urged the others along.

Finally, Ava could run no more. She stumbled in the dark and then fell to one knee, nearly dragging the other two down with her. Esther attempted to carry the girl, but she, too, was exhausted.

"Okay," she said. "Let's stop for the night."

By now, they were in what seemed to have been an industrial section of town, surrounded by large buildings, abandoned trucks, and empty lots with rusted chain-link fences. Esther found a structure where the massive door was already rolled halfway open, allowing the three to duck under. Although their sneakered feet made no noise on the cement floor, their whispered voices echoed in the immense space.

Esther was wary. Long ago, Skar had taught her to avoid open spaces in favor of nooks that were small and hidden, invisible to the casual glance. Yet she had detected no such shelter nearby. Walking in small steps with her hands held in front of her, she felt her way across the cavernous room. She found a short set of steps in the corner that led up to an elevated platform against the wall.

It would have to do.

Ava was so exhausted she dropped to the hard floor, and within moments she was sound asleep. Joseph, too, drifted off, snoring intermittently, one arm draped around the cat carrier. But Esther was too keyed up. By now, her eyes had adjusted to the near-total darkness. The only thing she could make out was the horizontal band of night air visible under the door, discernible by the faint moonlight outside. She stared at it for what felt like hours.

And then Esther started.

She could have sworn she saw a dark shape scuttle across the strip of gray air and then disappear. The skin at the base of her neck prickling, Esther sat up. All of her senses straining, she automatically placed her arms around the sleeping people on either side of her.

Something scrabbled against the cement floor: nails clicking on the hard surface.

As Esther rose, another creature appeared at the door opening, and then another. By now, she could smell a pungent tang, faint yet so sharp she could almost taste it. She heard something else, as well: a loud panting. A new vibration stirred the air: the throaty growl of many animals that were clearly watching her . . . and waiting.

Trembling, Esther stepped to the edge of the platform. In the murky light, she saw she was facing a sea of shadows: At least eight wild dogs stood in the gloom before her. Like all cowards, the animals were attuned to the presence of anything more vulnerable than they were.

They had detected Ava, tiny and defenseless as she slept. Or was it Stumpy, who now stirred in the carrier and hissed?

"Shoo . . . get out of here!" Esther spoke in a harsh whisper. She was about to clap her hands, but thought better of it; if she awoke Ava, her screams would almost certainly trigger an attack. Instead, Esther made an abrupt and sweeping gesture with both arms to get rid of them. The dogs nearest her quailed and shrank back. But the pack did not retreat. One of them, a rust-colored mutt with matted fur, bared its teeth and advanced.

Esther felt a trickle of sweat run down her back. Moving in a deliberate way, she walked to the steps and started down, again trying to appear bigger than she was. She didn't want to get too far away from the others; doing so would leave them open to a sneak attack from the side. Instead, she would try to assert her dominance by confronting the reddish dog, who she sensed was the leader.

She stood one step above the ground, gazing down into its glittering eyes.

"Go on," she whispered. "Get out!"

Her plan backfired.

Esther's stare seemed to infuriate it further. Coiling itself back on its haunches, the dog sprang forward and launched itself at her throat. Esther, stunned and terrified, stumbled backward and fell onto the cement stairs, one useless arm held up in protection.

Then an explosion occurred.

Something barreled across the dark garage. With a loud yelp of surprise, the red dog swiveled in midair; then, growling and snapping, it began fighting with the creature that had attacked it. The two bodies thudded to the ground no more than a foot from Esther, who watched in amazement.

There was no contest. The second animal was much bigger and within seconds, it towered over the first one, which squirmed on its back, baring its throat and belly in abject defeat. The victor growled deep in its chest, placing its jaws for one second over the other one's muzzle as if in final warning, then it let go.

And turned toward Esther.

The girl remained frozen where she had fallen, but she was no longer frightened. Although the past few months had been cruel to her old friend, who was much thinner now and walked with a limp, she still recognized him.

"Pilot," she whispered with a feeling both of sorrow and wonder.

Aras's dog walked over to her and leaned heavily against her as she took him in her arms. His fur was dusty and matted and she could feel his ribs etched in sharp relief against his side, yet his immense tail thumped as he pushed his face against hers and licked her again and again.

Then she sensed his muzzle searching as it pushed against her hip.

Confused, she dropped her hand to her pocket. Realization hit her as she reached in and pulled out what was inside. It was the tattered rag she had recovered from the elevator: the piece of blue cloth that had once belonged to Aras. Pilot nosed it violently, snuffling as he breathed in its smell.

And then he began to howl.

The room resounded with the grief-stricken cries of the animal as he mourned his lost master, now gone forever.

TWENTY

ESTHER STOOD AT THE BASE OF A BROKEN STAIRCASE THAT LOOKED AS IF it led to the sky. Embedded in the side of the mountain, the ascent appeared not only endless but impossibly steep. Yet after hours spent leading the others through Mundreel, she felt certain that they were at last close to the source of the smoke that billowed high above them.

Joseph seemed well rested after a night of sleep. Even Pilot stood by her side, eager and panting as he awaited her orders. But Ava, who looked paler and more fragile than ever, drew a shaky breath as she gazed upward.

"Don't think I can." Her voice was barely audible.

"Come on," Esther said. "We'll help you."

"Your friends. They at the top?"

Earlier that morning, Esther had attempted to build a fire in order to send a signal of her own. Yet without a firestarter, she had been at a loss. She'd tried striking a spark between two rocks as she had seen Skar do many times, but it was no good. She would just have to locate the origin of the signal and hope for the best.

Still, she spoke with confidence, because she had no other plan. "They can feed us and take care of us. We just have to get there first."

The dog had already climbed the first few steps and now turned back, as if waiting for them to follow.

"See?" Esther said. "Pilot says you can do it, too."

She knew her joke was silly, yet it cheered the girl, who smiled for the first time that day. Ava had initially been terrified of the animal, and with good reason; although loyal to his owners, Pilot was vicious and unpredictable. Yet perhaps sensing how vulnerable the child was, he was now on his best behavior. He even allowed Ava to hold on to his back, gripping his dusty fur for support.

Esther took the girl's other hand, which felt hot and papery in her own. With Joseph and his cat carrier bringing up the rear, they began the arduous journey up the stone steps, which soon gave way to wooden planks.

Their footing was unstable and the steps were punishingly high. Many were warped or cracked and the ancient nails that held them in place squeaked and groaned. As the sun beat down on them, Esther and the others clung to the bent and rusted banister for support. At times, the stairs gave way altogether and they were forced to pull themselves over the dusty incline hand over hand.

Yet with each painful step, the smoke grew closer.

Esther kept her eyes on the ground beneath her and focused on moving her feet; it was the only way she could bear to continue. Behind her, she could hear Joseph toiling upward, matching her step for step. With her left hand, she still kept tight hold of Ava. By now, Esther was practically dragging the younger girl upward. Finally, Pilot scrambled ahead. When Esther raised her eyes, she saw he stood at the top, gazing down at them, impatient. He even wagged his tail.

With that, Esther pulled herself onto the final step. Ava dropped forward upon the ground as Joseph, still gripping the cat carrier, joined her.

Esther saw that they were now high above the city of Mundreel, which spread out behind them. They stood before the wide expanse of what had once been a public park. Brown and straggly growth filled a haphazard field that faced a dense forest.

To her disappointment, Esther saw that although they were closer, the smoke was still farther away, rising from above the treetops. She estimated they had at least another half mile to go.

Behind her, Joseph had struggled to get the younger girl back to her feet. By now, Ava was barely conscious. Esther bent over and took her on her back, hoisting her leg with one hand while gripping her opposite shoulder with the other. When she straightened, she felt as if she were carrying hundreds of pounds, even though Ava was not much more than half her weight.

The heat of the sun and the effort of carrying Ava made it seem as if the child was burning up; within seconds, Esther's back grew even slicker with perspiration. Yet she continued across the park grounds and into the deep woods that surrounded them, the dog by her side and Joseph trailing behind. As she picked her way through the tangled undergrowth, she managed to keep an eye on the ephemeral gray trail in the sky.

At last, she saw where it was emanating from.

Deeper in the woods, the remains of a fire smoldered in the center of a wide stone terrace, set in the side of the mountain. Behind it loomed a large building, ornate yet in bad repair.

Esther turned to Joseph and gestured for him to be quiet. Without making a sound, she then slipped Ava from her shoulders and onto the mossy ground. She clicked her tongue softly; Pilot's ears perked up at the familiar command. Then, moving with great care, she and the dog made their way closer.

Peering through the dense foliage, Esther saw no one at first. Then a figure stepped out from around the building, dragging a tree limb.

It was Skar.

Even as the variant girl looked up, Esther had burst from her hiding place and was racing toward her. Pilot exploded in joyous barking as he ran with Esther. She flew to her oldest friend and leaped into her arms.

They stayed like that for what seemed minutes, and although Skar rarely cried, her face was soon wet with tears, both hers and Esther's. Finally, she was able to pull back and look into the other girl's eyes.

"It is good to see you," the variant said, with her typical understatement. Esther smiled.

"You, too," she said.

"We did not know what had happened after that night. After Gideon and his boys arrived."

Esther shook her head. "Eli saved me. He's in charge of sentencing, and he . . . I have him to thank."

Skar was letting Pilot sniff her hand; now the dog even deigned to allow her to stroke him, lowering his massive head. "But that was weeks ago. Where have you been since then?"

For a moment, Esther thought of the crack of Jud's belt, the backbreaking labor in the new tower, the brutal attack by Gideon's guards. She could not bear to recount any of it, at least not yet. She shook her head. Skar nodded with understanding; then she placed a soft palm on Esther's wounded jaw.

"It's all right," Esther said. "It'll heal." She took Skar's hand away and squeezed it. "But tell me about you and the others. Did everyone get out? Are you all well?"

Skar smiled. "We are. But—"

Then she smiled. Ava and Joseph had emerged, timidly, from the underbrush. Skar had already run forward and was embracing the older boy, who kept his arms rigidly at his sides.

Still, he beamed the whole time.

After a quick introduction, Skar took Ava herself, lifting her onto her strong back.

"Follow me," she said.

Skar led them down streets, cutting past backyards and through sections of forest until they finally emerged onto a sidewalk. Esther saw they were in a business district of brick buildings, two and three stories high. They stopped in front of one and Skar nodded.

Inside, the smell of roast meat hung heavy in the air. A small group was seated on the floor, finishing their midday meal: Michal, Silas, Uri.

And Kai.

"*Mama!*"

With a look of amazement, the little boy stood up, food still pasted around his mouth. Then he ran to her. Forgetting her exhaustion, Esther bent low and scooped the delighted child into her arms, pressing kiss after kiss upon his soft and sticky face. She could not squeeze him tightly enough. He too clung to her, giggling and squealing with joy at the feel of her mouth on his neck.

The others surrounded her as well, laughing and exclaiming as they hugged her. Esther tried to greet them all in turn but the whole time, her eyes kept roaming through the empty storefront. At last, they landed on Skar.

"Where's Sarah?"

The chatter died down as one by one, her friends averted their eyes. Finally, Skar spoke.

"They have her." Her expression was grave. "Saith and Gideon."

Esther felt the floor shift beneath her. "But . . . but you said—"

"I did not mean to lie to you. But it was important to get you to safety first." Skar sighed. "I am sorry, Esther."

In an instant, all the strength that Esther's friends had given her seemed to vanish; her knees buckled and she sank to the floor, still holding Kai. Numb, she sat like that for what felt like hours. She listened to Skar describe the onslaught, their escape, and how they came to their new refuge.

"Then I must go," Esther said. She struggled to rise, but Skar put a hand on her arm, restraining her.

"You are much too weak."

"I don't care. I have to find her. I—"

"We will find out where she is soon enough. I have sent someone to the District."

Esther glanced up sharply. Her eyes flickered to Silas, who looked as surprised by the news as the others.

"Who?"

"The boy with the white hair. Trey."

Esther drew a deep breath; at first, she thought she had misheard. "Trey? When did he . . ."

"He left only yesterday. But if anyone can find out what is going on inside the District, it is he."

After a pause, Esther nodded. Although the odds seemed grim, she knew that her friend was right: Trey was more than capable. Knowing that he was at that moment searching for news of her child, Esther was comforted . . . so much so that for the first time in what seemed like weeks, she allowed herself to feel a sudden and fierce stab of hunger.

"Please," she said, "if there's anything left . . . we're starving."

Michal began serving what remained of their meal, and Uri fetched clean water from a bucket in the corner. Joseph accepted his portion and fed Stumpy a chunk of it, having freed her from the carrier. Then he began eating ravenously, cramming roast rabbit into his mouth. Esther waited to take her own until Ava was served. Then she made certain to feed Pilot before starting to eat as well.

"Here," Michal said, as she bent over the smaller girl, holding out a haunch of meat.

Then she stopped. With a cry, she jerked back so fast she dropped the food on the floor.

On the underside of Ava's outstretched arm was a round purple mark, small yet unmistakable: a lesion. *That explained the heat,* Esther realized with a pang as she remembered the thin body pressed against her back. *The girl was burning up with fever.*

"You can serve her," she said to Michal, with more force than she had intended. "It's all right."

But she could see stubborn dismay on Michal's face. Silas, too, had begun to back away, pressing his arm against his mouth and nose; even Skar appeared uneasy. Esther retrieved the food from the ground and, brushing it off, handed it to Ava. The girl whispered her thanks. Then she lowered her eyes and began to eat.

Esther was exasperated. She knew that nothing she could say would ever convince her friends that the sick posed no threat, that their fears were unfounded—not even the fact that she herself was still alive.

Then someone cleared his throat.

It was Uri. Like Joseph, his mentor and friend, the boy seemed ill at ease speaking to a group. His thin neck was flushed a dark red and he worked his hands, twisting his fingers together.

"Esther's right," he said. "I don't think you get sick that way."

Because Uri was normally so silent, the others paid attention.

"Some diseases you get from people." Uri looked as if he were addressing the floor. "We all know about those. The ones where you sneeze or cough . . . if you're sick like that, you pass it to others. But some illnesses, you don't. Like a headache. A cut that doesn't get better." The others nodded as they digested his words. "That's because we get sick from all kinds of things. Bad food. Animal bites. Not always people."

Now he raised his head so that everyone could hear. "This disease comes from water. That means it's safe to be around someone who's sick." He indicated Ava, who stared at him without comprehension. "In fact, the more time we spend with them, the less likely we'll get sick. It makes us . . . immune."

Finished, Uri glanced away. Joseph was looking at him with an expression of pride on his face.

Esther thought over Uri's strange words: the idea that

spending time with the dying kept one from getting the disease. Could it be true? She saw the others looking at Ava quizzically, considering his odd ideas.

After a whispered discussion, Ava was allowed to remain in the store: She was given space in the corner, far from the rest. Within minutes, heedless of the stifling air, the girl was fast asleep. So was Joseph.

Michal had taken Kai; she, Skar, and the others had slipped away to give the three some much-needed quiet. Esther had curled into a ball on her side, when she felt something bump against her.

It was Pilot, nosing her cheek. She put her arms around him and burrowed her face into his dusty fur.

Soon, they, too, were asleep.

Esther felt someone touch her arm.

Fear exploding in her chest, she bolted upright, her arms covering her face. It took a moment to realize she was no longer in slave quarters and that Jud wasn't standing over her, brandishing his belt.

Kneeling in front of her, gently shaking her awake, was Skar.

"Sarah is alive," Skar whispered. She gestured to the door.

All of the day's events came rushing back. "Sarah." Esther's voice was a croak, and she stumbled to rush outside.

Lit by the setting sun, Trey was leaning against a rusty and dented car. When he saw Esther in the doorway, his face lit up; for a moment, it seemed that he might rush forward and seize her in an embrace. Then he looked away and cleared his throat as if uncomfortable.

"Your friend in there said you was still alive," he remarked in a neutral voice. "Had to see for myself. 'Cause that sure ain't what they say back at the District."

He looked much the way she remembered, with the white strip in his dark hair. He was leaner than before, his face more creased. *It was becoming to him,* Esther had to admit; she was glad to see him. Yet there were so many emotions to take in now.

"Sarah," she said instantly. "She's still alive? What did you find?"

"She alive. But ain't that simple. They holding her."

"What do you mean?"

As Trey talked, Esther crouched down to pat Pilot. The animal had come out to investigate the stranger and although he growled at first, he stayed close to Esther. Occasionally, she scratched his stomach, something he loved. But mostly, she listened.

After finding a white sheet to cover himself, Trey had found it easy to slip into the District. Inside, things were much worse than they had been when he'd left only weeks before. The worship of Saith had become even more crazed than ever. The pilgrims who arrived every day waited for hours to see her. Praying and bowing, they wound their way around the lobby in a seemingly endless line. Then they were given a sip of colored water that the girl promised would give them eternal life.

"I tasted some," remarked Trey. "Waited my turn so I could see what was up. It ain't proof, but it close. Water with something nasty in it."

But that was just the beginning. After listening to her speak and talking to a number of her most devout worshipers, Trey realized that Saith *no longer saw herself as just a priestess or seer. She claimed to be transforming into something greater than that . . . something that was no longer human.*

She was becoming God.

Esther gave Trey a sharp look. "And Sarah?"

Grim, the boy shook his head. "I couldn't get much information, but Saith planning something. I heard everyone say the same thing." When he finally met Esther's eyes, his expression was full of anger and contempt. "She aim to do something with your baby. Something bad."

Esther said nothing.

She was swept up with a feeling she had never experienced before. It went beyond rage or hatred or the fierce need to protect. It surpassed even the love she felt for Sarah, Kai, Skar, and her friends.

In a moment, her world, which had never before been simple or easy, became stunningly clear, and for the first time, Esther saw everything as if it were laid out beneath a brilliant light. On one side was Saith and all that she represented: greed, cruelty, and pride. Saith stood for death, for innocent blood being shed, for lies and madness and grief.

On the other side was everything else: not just Esther's family and friends, but everyone who lived. She did not need to know them—their lives, their joys and struggles—to understand their worth. As flawed as people could be, she was fighting for every single one of them.

Then she felt something. Trey's hand was intertwined with hers.

Esther did not remember moving, but a second later she was in his arms. She pressed her face into his shoulder and then his chest. He smelled of fire and smoke and the outside world. Her lips brushed the taut skin of his neck, then pressed upon it. She moved her mouth to his, exploring. His arms went around her and clasped her fast.

Kissing Trey was an exquisite relief after all that she had endured. For a moment, she yearned for him, was tempted to move even deeper into his embrace, and to hide herself in him. Yet she found herself resisting.

She and Trey were united in a crusade. There was no time for this now. After their mission had been completed, they might be able to afford the luxury . . . but only then.

Esther forced herself to pull away. "Let's go," she said, and he nodded, with reluctance.

When they reentered the storefront, Michal had Kai on her lap and was preparing dinner as Uri boiled water in a fire-bowl. Although Ava was still motionless, Joseph was awake and drinking from a plastic bottle.

Everyone looked up as one and faced Esther for instructions. It was clear they could not make a move without her.

Yet Esther knew that she no longer mattered. Even if she died, it would be all right. The cause would outlive her. It was the newest and most exhilarating feeling of all.

"All right," she said. "Here's what we're going to do. We're going back."

TWENTY-ONE

WHEN GIDEON RETURNED TO THE DISTRICT AFTER INSPECTING THE NEW building, the setting sun threw brilliant light that cast deep shadows behind him. As he brushed past the guards who opened the lobby doors, he seemed cold and impassive.

Yet secretly, he was exhilarated.

The construction had gone exactly as he had planned. Although Joseph's understanding of building was primitive at best, he had still managed to oversee the completion of a small section of roof. This had been Gideon's goal from the start: that the workers finish a single piece of the garden as quickly as possible. All that Gideon needed for now was something that could comfortably support a few people.

One of those people, of course, would be him. The others would be his guards.

Watching Saith, Gideon was convinced that she had no idea what he was planning. He had gambled on the chance that she would be so distracted by the altar in her honor, she would not notice what was actually taking place on the roof. The crude shrine had served its purpose.

Gideon would be ready to leave the District that night. Traveling with him would be three of his most trusted aides, who would patrol his new home, work the garden, and see to his needs. As far as Gideon could tell, the time had arrived none too soon.

His guards, ever watchful, had informed him only days before of something he had long dreaded: The first of Saith's pilgrims were becoming sick. Giddy with the promise of eternal life, they had ventured back onto the streets of Mundreel to test their new invulnerability by doing stupid things: drinking runoff water, wading in whatever streams they could find. Gideon recalled the brief yet fierce shower earlier that week. He could only imagine how the foolish and hopeful had stayed outside in the deadly downpour merely to flaunt their convictions.

Apparently, he thought with a grim smile, *the disease itself didn't care about Saith's promises or her magical blue water;* instead, it had made its usual swift and inevitable progression. Now, dozens of her disciples—bewildered, frightened, and clearly dying—were starting to return to the District in greater numbers each day.

They were there to demand not just an explanation, but a miracle.

It was all, Gideon thought with distaste, *so pathetic. And so predictable.*

According to Gideon's informants, Saith's panicked guards were dealing with the problem the only way they knew how: with a trip to the eighth floor and a bullet to the back of the head. Yet clearly, such actions could not continue much longer. Every day, more and more of the dying were showing up at the front doors of the District; very soon, it would become impossible to dispose of them all that way. It was only a matter of time before word spread . . . and Gideon could only imagine what the reaction of the crowds would be.

He smiled. Within hours, such things would no longer be his problem.

The boy now stood alone in his room. Although moonlight shone through the skylight far overhead and filtered down to the basement, Gideon sensed it was still too early. He had told his three guards to move out together when everyone was asleep. He would go first; they would follow, transporting all of the glass in as many trips as it would take.

Idly, Gideon picked up a few items then set them back down. There was nothing he wanted; he had never cared much for luxuries, and objects held no sentimental value for him. As for clothing, what he wore on his back would do. Certainly, if he were to ever want for anything in the future, he would soon have the means to acquire it.

Gideon realized that there was one thing that he wanted to

bring to his new home. His notebooks, filled with figures and inventory lists, might come in useful. He searched his meager shelves for a few minutes before recalling that he had left them locked in the tiled office upstairs.

The District was mostly silent. Yet as he approached his office, his hand already digging for the keys in his pocket, he stopped abruptly.

He thought he heard something coming from within the locked room.

But that was impossible, he thought; he allowed no one inside. Leaning forward, Gideon pressed his ear against the wooden surface and listened. The sounds were muffled yet distinct: an odd splashing and a voice murmuring low. Trying not to make a noise, he inserted his key into the brass opening.

Then with one swift gesture, he twisted it and shoved open the door.

At the far end of the room, Saith stood over one of the white sinks. Too late, Gideon remembered that she possessed the only extra key. She was bent forward at the waist, splashing in the white basin, which was partly filled with water. A gray plastic bucket sat by her feet. The girl was washing what seemed at first to be a doll, until he noticed it was moving. To his confusion, Gideon registered what it was.

Esther's baby.

The mutant infant lay placidly on its back in a shallow pool of water, blinking its strange eyes as it beat the air with tiny fists. Saith was using a plastic cup to scoop up water and pour it over the child, talking to herself as she did.

"What you doing?"

Gideon's voice echoed in the tiled room. Wincing at the sudden noise, the baby jerked its head in his direction. But Saith turned with a smile, as if expecting him.

"I make it clean. See?" With a cooing sound, she poured something from a nearby bottle, which she rubbed into the child's pale skin. Even from where he stood, Gideon could smell the sickening scent of flowers as suds foamed up. "It nice and clean now."

Gideon pursed his lips. He was not interested in Saith's little-girl games, and within a few hours, he would never have to deal with them again. Without a second glance at her, he turned to his notebooks, which were stacked against the wall. After he picked them up and leafed through a few to make sure that everything was in order, he turned to go. Then his eye fell on the pile of glass that glittered in the corner. Although he was not sentimental, he could not help himself. On impulse, he scooped up a handful of the smooth green shards and slipped them into his front pocket.

"You want to know what I do?"

Gideon started. As always, Saith's tiny, high-pitched voice had a drawling, singsong quality that made it compelling.

"No." Gideon turned and started heading back out. Tired of the girl's manipulations and game playing, he was looking forward to leaving her forever.

"I make it clean for the ceremony."

Her words had the desired effect. Although Gideon hated being drawn in by her, he could not keep from asking:

"Ceremony? What ceremony?"

She smirked. "The one that make me God. I kill this baby, then I gonna live forever."

For a moment, Gideon felt as if he was going to vomit. He had no sentimentality about infants, certainly not mutant infants. Yet Saith's bizarre plan revolted him in both its senselessness and cruelty. For the first time, it dawned on him that the girl was not merely grandiose, but insane.

She actually believed what she was saying. And that made him shudder.

Head cocked, Saith was watching him, her eyes glittering like black stars. "I know what you do," she said unexpectedly.

"What?"

"You know." Her voice was still lilting, but now it sounded insinuating. "I know you think you move to the new place by yourself. Without Saith."

Gideon felt his face flush as he took in her accusation. *How did she know?* He began to stammer out a denial, but she continued to speak over him.

"You think I don't see what you do. You think I stupid. Maybe even that why you build that altar. So I don't see." Helpless, Gideon could only gaze back at her as she continued. "But boys tell me things. That slave master? He tell me everything."

Jud. Gideon swallowed hard. He had to force himself to remember that she was just a little child, that he was the older of the two, the more powerful. He had the upper hand.

But did he?

"So what you aim to do about it?"

Saith cocked an eyebrow as if the question was impertinent. "Maybe I move there myself," she drawled. "Maybe soon . . . after the ceremony. That what you aim to do, ain't it? Leave without saying? That why you take those books. Well, maybe I do it. I move there instead of you."

She gave a smile that was both sweet and self-satisfied. *She was missing a tooth,* Gideon noted, *which made her seem even younger than she was.* Suddenly, the boy felt as if the ground had begun to crumble beneath his feet. In the next moment, he was filled with a rage so violent, he thought he would choke on it.

Blood rushed to his hands. Without thinking, Gideon took a step in the girl's direction. But even as he did, he heard a sound behind him.

Two of Saith's guards stood in the entrance. As if in warning, one kept a hand idly at his waistband.

Slowly, Gideon forced his arms to his side. Saith was no longer looking at him. She had lifted the baby out of the sink and was drying it on a towel as she cooed at it.

Their meeting was over. He had, he realized with a sense of disbelief, *been dismissed.*

As he walked with faltering steps to the doorway, he heard Saith's voice at his back.

"Ain't you clean now?" She gave a throaty little chuckle. "Ain't you pretty?"

The door closed behind him.

* * *

Minutes later, Gideon emerged from the hidden staircase at the end of the lobby.

Now that Saith was onto his plan, he had no time to lose, and he couldn't afford to be caught disobeying her laws about comingling of the sexes. So, he took care only to advance when he saw that the coast was clear.

He headed toward the store on the fourth floor that adjoined Saith's quarters.

Seeing that a light was on, he waited behind a corner until two hulking guards walked past. Then he darted into the small room.

By the glow of a torch, a girl, short haired and thin, stood with her back to him. She seemed to be examining different bottles and jars that were arranged on a glass table. Then she turned, and when she saw him, she gave a cry of surprise. Gideon silenced her with a finger to his lips, and gestured out the door at the guards. She nodded in understanding and fell silent.

Nur looked different—so much so that for one heart-stopping moment, he thought he had made a mistake. He had not seen her for several weeks, and during that time, she had undergone a terrible transformation. Gone was the vibrant, luscious, and pretty girl he had been expecting—the one who had once teased his feverish imagination. Now noticeably thinner and with her beautiful chestnut hair shorn nearly to her skull, she looked exhausted, haggard, and older.

Sensing his dismay, Nur recoiled. Then, turning away, she

fumbled with her hood and attempted to draw it over her face.

"Don't," he managed to say.

She froze where she was.

He crossed to her and, summoning all of his willpower, took her by the shoulder and gently turned her back around so that she faced him. Since any kind of physical contact made Gideon uncomfortable, it would have been hard enough to touch her like this even in the old days. Now, he had to force himself to hide his disgust.

With difficulty, he smiled.

"You look good," he said. "As good as ever."

She winced as if struck. "You lie."

"No," he insisted. "You pretty."

Tears brimmed in her eyes. Then she wrenched herself away as they spilled down her wasted cheeks and she began to sob.

Gideon had hoped that Nur would be upset, but he hadn't realized how bitter she would be. Seeing her now, her beauty gone, he realized he had seriously underestimated her reaction to what had happened under Saith. He understood that Nur had had a treasure stolen from her, not one that could be tallied and entered in a book, like glass, but one just as valuable.

Still, her pain was to his advantage.

"I been thinking of you," he continued. "All the time. The way we used to be."

As she wept, Nur gave a mirthless laugh. *Even so*, he noticed, *she was listening*. He racked his brain for more compliments.

"I think of your face," he said, stumbling over the words. "Your body. How you let me watch you."

She shot him a look through reddened eyes, and Gideon realized he had struck a nerve.

"I miss talking to you," he said. "You the only one who ever understood me. I miss you."

A smile flickered across Nur's face. "Me, too."

"You been up here too long," he said. "I want you back. This time for real."

The girl didn't say anything for a moment. "What you mean?"

"I mean . . ." Gideon let out a breath. "I want you be my partner. My queen."

To his surprise, Nur didn't break into a smile or attempt to hug him. She continued to stare at the ground, as if the pattern of tiles fascinated her. Then she spoke. "How I know you serious?"

Gideon was flummoxed. "B-because," he managed to say at last. "I told you how I felt."

"Did you?" She glanced up at him, and he was startled by the hardness of her expression. "So how come you leave me up here all this time? Make me work for that girl who treat me so bad? How come you forget me?" The boy tried to answer, but she wouldn't let him; the accusations were now tumbling from her lips as if they had long been held back and finally allowed to burst forth. "You told me before we be partners. Then Esther come around. After that, Saith. All the time you don't come to me. Not even downstairs, where all the boys come. Why would I trust you now?"

Because Gideon had no defense against what she was

saying, he acted purely on instinct; he had no idea what else to do. Forcing down his distaste, he reached out and took her clumsily in his arms. At first, she struggled against his awkward embrace; then she stopped. Suddenly, she was clinging to him and burying her face in the side of his neck. She was crying again, but this time he sensed it was not from anger but for release.

"I saved you," he said. The stubble of her hair felt unpleasant against his lips, and he was keenly aware that her thin body, shaking with sobs, was bony, hot, and sweaty. Still, he could tell it was the most effective thing he could do. "When she found you and brung you upstairs? She wanted to kill you. I saved your life."

Nur could only nod.

At last, she pulled back to look at him. Her nose and the rims of her eyes were pink, and a trail of mucus gleamed beneath one nostril; still, she looked happy.

"You take me away from here?"

"Yeah. This time, I promise."

"Where we go?"

Briefly, Gideon told her of the new building. Nur listened, smiling, then spoke. "When?"

"Tonight." He paused. "Only there something I need first."

The girl shot him a questioning look.

Gideon had taken a corner of his robes and was using it to remove something from his pocket. He handled the object gingerly: a small glass vial that minutes before he had filled up on the moonlit roof. It held an inch or so of dirty water that he had drawn from the immense tank where rain was collected prior to being boiled.

"I need you do something," he said. "For both of us."

As always, Saith's room smelled of flowers.

The little girl appeared at the doorway. Wearing an oversize robe of a soft and slippery fabric, she frowned at what she saw. Nur had dragged in a small metal tub, which she had filled with warm water. Now she knelt by its side, stirring it with one hand as she poured in powder from a small plastic jar.

"What that?" asked Saith, her nose wrinkling.

"It a special bath." Nur had managed to whip the crystals into a glistening white froth. Wiping the sweat from her brow, she sat back on her heels, waiting.

Saith sniffed. "Where you get the water?"

"From the reserves."

Nur knew better than anyone that water was strictly rationed. There had been a heavy yet brief rainfall the week before; that was nearly gone and there was now precious little to drink. That she had squandered so much of it on something as frivolous as a bath for a single person was beyond indulgent. Yet it was exactly the extravagance of it that she secretly hoped would appeal to the priestess.

And she was right: Saith smiled. Then she slipped off her robe and stepped into the tub.

Nur was waiting as the little girl leaned back. She was already working some special soap into a lather, which she began massaging into the child's head.

"Harder," said Saith.

Nur continued to rub the girl's scalp, using all the skill she had to make the child relax. And it worked: Saith grunted once or twice with pleasure and sank deeper into the water. Soon she was nearly asleep. Occasionally, Nur was aware of a figure moving past the screened doorway: Four guards surrounded the entrance. Other than that, the room was silent but for soft and rhythmic splashing sounds.

The jar of rainwater was in the front pocket of Nur's robe. When she moved, it bumped against her thigh, reminding her of its presence. She had promised Gideon she would do it. Their future together depended on it. No one would ever know; unlike, say, drowning the child outright, it was something she could accomplish surreptitiously, without drawing any attention or suspicion to herself. Even with armed guards a few feet away, the risk would be minimal.

Yet now that the moment had arrived, she felt sick with doubt and anxiety.

"That feel good," said Saith at last. "Now wash it off."

Nur dipped a plastic bowl into the bathwater and poured it over Saith's head again and again until every trace of soap was gone. Then Saith stirred in the tub and stood.

"Dry me," she commanded.

Nur hesitated. If the girl got out of the water, it would be too late.

For a second, Nur shuddered to think what would be her fate if she were caught. But then she noticed something.

Saith was turning this way and that, admiring her pretty

little body in the long mirrors that hung along one wall. With her gleaming skin and damp hair fresh and soft from the bath, the child looked perfect.

She was so lovely, Nur thought with a stab of bitterness.

She took out the bottle from her pocket, unscrewed the lid, and poured the contents into the tub.

The murky rainwater swirled and blended. As Nur lifted a towel and draped it over the little girl, the invisible poison made its way to a new victim.

TWENTY-TWO

A WEEK LATER, IN THE MIDDLE OF THE NIGHT, THE CALL OF A SINGLE BIRD echoed through the steel and glass canyon of downtown Mundreel. Its faint cries carried across the dusty marble lobby of a huge white building called "museum." There in the high-ceilinged space, more than two dozen people, a dog, and a cat lay motionless, fast asleep.

Only one person was awake.

Esther had spent the night huddled near a lit candle, por-ing for the hundredth time over the odd picture that Uri had sketched for her of the District. This "diagram" was meant to depict all ten floors of the building, as well as the surrounding block. After studying it, Esther found she was able to follow the layout of the floors, the locations of the doors, the stair-wells, entrances, and exits. With Silas's help, Uri had been also able to add useful details: where Saith's altar was, where she slept, and where her many guards stood lookout.

The guards were the most worrisome factor.

Esther was all too aware that by comparison, hers was a small band, made up of the sick, the young, and the starving. They were sparsely armed with only the makeshift weapons they had been able to Glean from stores and homes: table legs, bricks, broken glass, household utensils. Saith's and Gideon's boys were not only older, stronger, and better trained; they outnumbered them and carried guns. Esther knew that the only advantage they had was the element of surprise; without it, their attack would lead to certain slaughter.

She could not allow that to happen.

In the past, Esther wouldn't have bothered to plan anything. She would have confronted Saith on her own, slipping into the District on impulse and without any thought or strategy. Back then, she was reckless and confident enough—*foolish enough,* she realized now, ruefully, *to throw herself into danger without any thought of what might happen.*

Esther realized she could no longer afford brashness. She now had the weight of many people's lives on her shoulders: not only her family and friends, but the individuals they had added to their numbers in the past three days.

Recruiting more people had been Skar's idea. At first, Esther had disagreed with her; she didn't know whom they could trust and who might be a disciple or even a spy of the girl priestess.

"We are only nine," Skar had argued, "and four are little ones."

Although she was still doubtful, Esther had finally seen her point.

She and her friends began their search for recruits by canvassing the area where they had first met Saith and Uri. The ravaged neighborhood was not far away, on the other side of the mountain.

When they arrived, the narrow streets of modest buildings were even more desolate than Esther remembered. Without hesitation, Uri had led them to his old home, a sagging gray house with two stories that stood in the middle of one block.

The boy had looked in through the splintered entrance, which was missing its door. "Hello?" he called. When there was no reply, he glanced at Esther, who nodded.

"Wait here," she told Skar and the others. With Pilot by her side, she and Uri slipped inside.

The air had been stifling hot and smelled of dust, mouse droppings, and, above all, something sweet yet sickening. Esther recognized it as the smell of death, of bodies decomposing. She felt the hair on the back of her neck rise as Pilot growled, straining forward against his chain. He led the two deep into the darkness, pulling her with sure steps. In a dim, unfurnished room, something glittered. As her eyes grew accustomed to the light, Esther realized that three people were watching her.

They were alive, but just barely. At least one was in the

final stages of the illness, a motionless child cradled by another. Ordering Pilot to sit with a click of her tongue, Esther dug into her bag for a bottle of water. Uri was already walking among them, looking for a familiar face.

"What you want?" The boy who spoke sounded hostile and suspicious, his voice little more than a cracked whisper. He sat with the dying child in his lap, a dirty blanket draped over his shoulders.

"This is Uri," Esther said. "He comes from here."

No one responded.

Esther tried again. "We're looking for folks to help us."

"Do what?"

"Do away with Saith."

This was, Esther knew, *a calculated risk: These could be the girl's sup-porters.* And in fact, the information received a visible reaction: All of them murmured, and the boy with the blanket sat up.

"How you do that?"

Esther noticed he had asked "how" not "why"; *that was promis-ing,* she thought. Still, she herself wasn't sure of the answer. All she said was, "Are you interested?"

The boy exhaled. "She the one got us sick."

Esther knelt close. She struggled to uncap the bottle, but the boy grabbed it from her. He unscrewed it and took a long drink of water, the muscles in his throat working. Handing it back, he gave her a brief nod of thanks. Then at last he spoke, and Esther was filled with mounting horror.

Days before, he and his friends had gone to the District in search of the miraculous liquid provided by the priestess. Like most of his friends, he had been skeptical at first. Yet as the blue water burned his throat, the boy had inexplicably been filled with a sense of both light and heat. He was caught up in a feeling of euphoria and then total belief.

After that, no one took precautions any longer; why did they need to? When the rain came, they didn't hide from it. Instead, he and his friends stayed outside, laughing and drinking from the sky itself.

The first lesions appeared two or three days later. One by one, they became ill until all seven had been stricken. And now they were the only three left in the household.

"So I come," he had said. Although his voice was faint, Esther could hear the anger that lay beneath it. "The others too far gone." He indicated the child in his lap and his voice softened. "I think she gone by tonight. But I the last one who got sick. So I still got strength."

In this way, Esther and her friends gathered up soldiers for their army: one at a time, entering homes, meeting the sick and the frightened, and hearing their pitiable tales of outrage and bitterness. Not everyone they met was sick, yet each had lost partners, friends, and relatives to the disease, all because of their belief in Saith and her magical potion. As a result, they were desperate not only for the water and food that Esther and her friends offered, but the chance of retribution.

Esther and Uri managed to enlist eighteen in all.

Silas led the newcomers in Gleaning excursions into homes and stores. Then they forged crude weapons from what they were able to salvage. As Trey taught them the basics of hand-to-hand fighting, Skar hunted from dawn until dusk to keep their growing numbers fed.

Three days later, they were finally ready.

Within the next hour or two, they would make their way to the District, less than a mile away. Disguised in white and black robes, they would join the crowds of worshippers that flocked to its doors every day. Once inside, Esther, Skar, and Silas would each take a small group in different directions throughout the lobby and basement; at a given signal, they would disarm guards at their posts. In the meantime, Trey would make his way upstairs and deal with Saith single-handedly.

If possible, he was to take her alive. The same applied to Gideon. Trey had argued with Esther on both points, but she had been adamant:

Enough blood had been spilled. She did not want to add to it.

Although Esther's plan was simple, she continued to agonize over the unknown. She had focused all of her energy preparing for Saith's guards, whom she knew were armed and loyal to the girl they served. Yet she did not know how great a danger the rest of the District's inhabitants might pose. Inside, people were still true believers who had traveled far and considered it a privilege to be under the same roof as their idol. Esther couldn't predict to what lengths they would go to protect the girl they were convinced was holy.

She would just have to trust in luck. And as she came to that conclusion, she found herself thinking of someone else.

Eli.

As far as she knew, he was still in the District. Thinking of him now, Esther had a strange twisting feeling in her gut.

Her old friend had deliberately turned his back on her and the others months ago. He had acted out of his own free will when he chose to side with Gideon and, by extension, Saith as well. He had served as their judge, upholding their cruel and senseless laws, and sentencing her and countless other innocents to Shunning, slavery, and worse.

And yet he had saved her life.

Esther could still remember the boy he had been back in Prin—the one who had once asked her to be his partner. Since then, they had traveled many miles together and had both suffered terrible losses. She had been able to recover from her wounds and, in so doing, had grown stronger, even wiser. Yet somehow, he had not been able to do the same.

Eli was not a bad person, she thought now, *yet he was fragile. And didn't the strong have an obligation to look after the weak?*

Pensive, Esther folded up the map and slipped it into her jeans. The air was so heavy, she wiped moisture from her forehead. Then she sensed someone watching her. Trey sat up a few feet away.

"You all right?" he whispered.

She nodded. But, even in the dimness, she saw the boy shoot her a questioning look as if sensing her apprehension.

Esther surprised herself by saying: "It's Eli." Trey was silent as he slipped his weapon out of its hiding place and examined it quickly and methodically. "Before we go in," she went on, "I want to get him out. He can't take care of himself. The longer he's there, the more danger he's in."

"He mean that much to you?"

"If nothing else," she said, "I owe him something."

Trey nodded. If he was taken aback to hear her concern about the unsteady boy who had once guarded the basement drinking room, he didn't show it. He got to his feet. "I'll go."

Esther shook her head. "He's my friend, not yours."

She attempted to stand, but Trey held her back. "Then nobody's going nowhere . . . not now, anyways. When we get there, there be plenty of time."

"But—"

Trey shook his head. "Best thing you can do now is get some rest. You ain't slept all night, right?"

Esther shrugged. Yet even she had to admit that the insides of her eyelids felt raspy, and a sudden wave of exhaustion made her light-headed.

"I wake you in an hour."

Esther didn't want to agree. Yet no sooner had her eyes closed than she felt someone shaking her.

It was Skar. Behind her, the sky had brightened; it was nearly dawn. Esther could detect the clatter of everyone getting ready.

For a moment, Esther was disoriented. But she rose, trying to get her bearings. There was a growing humidity in the air, the type that precedes storms. "Where's Trey?"

"He's gone. To the District, to get Eli."

Esther stopped, as a surge of annoyance swept over her. "He lied to me. We agreed that—"

Skar squeezed her arm in sympathy. "He said that we could do without him. But we couldn't do without you."

Esther fell silent.

She could only hope that it was true.

A mile away, another person had been unable to sleep. As he had for days now, Gideon paced the lower floors of the District, his thoughts in a constant whirl.

He had been this way ever since he'd found out about his new home. On the same night Nur had poisoned Saith's bathwater, one of his guards had awoken him with terrible news. There had been a slave uprising at the construction site, with dozens killed. Unable to believe it, Gideon had hurried to the building.

What greeted him was a scene of total destruction. By moonlight, he saw that the surrounding streets were littered with the bodies of slaves and slave masters alike, indistinguishable in the gloom. Up on the roof, the tar-paper floor was littered with the shattered remains of the greenhouse. The long wooden tables had been upended, their boards splintered and cracked, and the green plastic troughs lay broken on the ground, their fragile crop already withered and yellowing like so much dead grass.

Worst of all, Joseph—the only person in Mundreel with enough knowledge to rebuild the thing—was gone.

If Gideon was devastated by the violent end to his plans, he did not let on to his guards. By the time he had made it back to the District, he had already begun rethinking his options.

He would continue to stay at the District with his boys. The old garden was still functional; somehow, he would have

to find workers to maintain it. His only challenge would be sur-
viving the upheaval that he felt certain was about to take place.

For Saith was dying.

The day before, Gideon had noticed a glassy brightness to
her eyes and a flushed appearance that indicated fever. The
girl priestess had begun to wear a billowing white cloak that
tellingly covered her arms and legs. Although she continued
to receive disciples (*fewer each day*, Gideon noticed), her guards
now kept visitors at a distance. They also whisked her away the
moment she grew tired. Yet their loyalty had its limits; Gideon
was amused to note that none of her guards dared to stand
close to her any longer or touch her with their bare hands.
When they were forced to approach her, they covered their
mouths and noses with their arms.

Although the plans for his escape had been upended,
Gideon didn't regret ordering Saith's poisoning. With her
health declining, he felt a deep sensation of relief. He hadn't
trusted himself to appeal to the masses, and so he had allowed
two girls, first Esther and then Saith, to be his public face. Yet
Saith had climbed too high, with disastrous results.

And so, he thought, *had Esther.*

With Saith vanquished, Gideon felt that he was finally exor-
cising the ghost of Esther as well. Even though he had had her
killed weeks before, her memory still haunted him, appearing
in his dreams when he least expected it. *He would*, he thought,
be free at last of her lingering and disturbing presence. And without any
female to drag him down, he could finally live the life he
deserved.

Nur, of course, remained. With a pang, Gideon recalled that he had promised her a lot in exchange for Saith's death. It had perhaps been a stupid blunder to offer such a deal, yet he had been desperate. *Still*, he thought, *she would be easy enough to handle.*

Gideon's pacing had taken him to the main lobby. It was now early morning, and through the main glass doors, he saw a crowd already waiting in the street. Even from this distance, he could see that many of them were obviously ill: Held up by friends, their faces were hollowed out with pain and fever. He felt a wave of contempt for all of them. They were waiting to see Saith, no doubt, to demand an explanation, an apology, or, just as unlikely, a miracle. Instead, her guards would take care of them, as they had so many before. This dance would continue until the crowd grew tired of the betrayal and decided to take matters in its own hands.

He turned to go, leaving the sight of them behind.

Then he stopped.

His eye had been drawn to a slight figure in the street, standing apart from the others. Studying her, he saw that she was just a thin girl, and draped in a white hooded robe. Gideon laughed to himself and shook his head. *His victory over Saith had driven him a little crazy*, he thought. *It was making him hallucinate.*

But the laughter died on his lips as the girl glanced up. Gazing directly at him, she seemed to hear what he was thinking . . . and his heart stopped.

It was Esther.

Although he could see only a sliver of her face amid the folds of her hood, Gideon would have recognized her anywhere.

Esther appeared to be talking to someone next to her, a person who kept his head down. Then the crowd shifted and the two figures disappeared from sight.

Gideon staggered back a step.

Esther was still alive. But how was that possible?

Gideon forced himself to find blame. Anger, unlike fear, grounded him and gave him direction.

It was clear he had been betrayed. And the only person who could have done it was Eli.

Gideon had given the boy one last chance, and as payment for his kindness, Eli had conspired against him. He had never ordered Esther's execution and shot her himself, as he had claimed. He had given her some lighter sentence, one that had allowed her to escape with her life. And why? Gideon could think of only one reason: that Eli was still in love with her, a cowardly, disgusting motivation.

Whatever she was planning, Esther had to be stopped. But first, Eli would pay for what he had done.

Gideon would make sure of it.

TWENTY-THREE

ELI CROUCHED BEFORE THE FREESTANDING COUNTER, HIS HANDS PLACED on the bottom drawer. The twin metal knobs felt smooth and cool to the touch.

Then with great difficulty, he forced himself to let go.

His last few bottles of proof were stashed inside. When he had quit drinking, the idea of "forever" had seemed too hard to bear. As a result, he had kept these last flasks, just in case. Now he was sorry he had saved them, for it was too great a temptation.

Several nights ago, Nur had come to see him and confided in whispers that she had poisoned Saith. Although he was shocked by her cold-bloodedness, Eli concluded that it was a good thing; Saith's death would save lives and end all kinds of suffering. Yet it raised disturbing questions as well. What would become of Nur, the last friend Eli had in the world? And how would Gideon respond? With the priestess gone, Gideon would have complete and unchecked power. What would he do with it?

All of these unknowns made Eli deeply uneasy. Although it was early morning, he longed to soothe himself with a drink, especially when faced with the most unnerving question of all:

What would happen if Gideon found out about Esther?

Eli knew he was only tormenting himself by asking it. After all, no one had seen Esther escape; their secret was surely safe. Yet he also knew that with Saith dead, he would most likely be relieved of his job. As the system fell apart, who knew what buried truths might surface? Uncertain, he once again lowered himself in front of the cabinet and placed a hand on the drawer.

Then he froze.

He thought he saw a white shape move behind him, reflected in the polished band of metal that edged the counter. Unnerved, Eli stood and swiveled around, his heart thundering. Like all of the stores in the District, his room had no door, just an entry that was open to the atrium. Downstairs, he could faintly hear the sound of the crowd outside, disciples clamoring to be let in. But other than that, he sensed nothing.

The boy gave a shaky laugh and turned back to the drawer. *Perhaps he needed that drink more than he thought.*

Then, as if from nowhere, a hand clapped over his mouth

and something that felt like an iron band tightened around his neck.

Terrified, Eli tried to scream as he clutched impotently at the arm that cut off his breath. Then he heard a voice close to his ear.

"I ain't gonna hurt you. Just be quiet."

Eli stopped struggling, and as his assailant released his grip, he whirled around to confront him.

The hired gun called Trey stood in front of him. Eli gaped at him, but the other boy's expression was unreadable.

"Let's go," Trey said.

Eli hesitated, his mind whirling. He glanced over Trey's shoulder to see if anyone was behind him, a trap waiting to be sprung: There wasn't. Even so, Eli backed away, frightened and suspicious.

"Who are you working for now?" he asked.

"No one," said Trey. "This is for Esther. She wants you out of here, before we attack. We're outside—dozens of us."

Eli felt as if the ground had opened underneath him. "But . . ." he began, aware that he was flushing a deep red. He was stunned to learn that Esther not only was thriving but had returned to the District to wage war against Gideon and Saith.

Yet what disturbed him the most was the fact that she intended to save him.

No one except Eli and Gideon knew the truth about Aras's death. The guilt of it still tormented him, and now it filled him with fresh despair. Would Esther want to rescue him if she knew that it was he who had killed her partner in cold blood?

Did Eli deserve to be saved?

Trey glanced up. Then Eli heard it, too. Someone was approaching from down the hall and moving fast.

Trey shot a look at Eli. "It sound like you ain't got much time to decide."

He took off and disappeared around the corner. After one more moment of uncertainty, Eli ran after him.

Trey had already vanished. Panicked, Eli glanced around. He saw the boy in white beckoning from farther down the hall. When Eli caught up, Trey grabbed him hard by the shirtfront.

"Keep up," he ordered. Then he began to run.

Eli, who hadn't moved quickly in months, was soon panting and drenched with sweat. Trey yanked him down the hallway, darting in and out of stores and behind columns. Within seconds, they had made it to the hidden staircase at the far end of the corridor. Inside, the darkness didn't make Trey slow down; in fact, he took entire landings in a single leap. As Eli was dragged behind Trey, he stumbled more than once and nearly broke his neck.

Soon, they had reached the lobby; Trey opened the door a crack and peered through. Two guards passed by outside and as Trey ducked back, he tugged on Eli's arm as a warning to stay quiet.

Trey waited until the pair had disappeared. Then he shoved open the door and tried to pull Eli out into the corridor with him. But the other boy stood as if rooted to the spot.

"You all gonna fight Saith's guards?" he said. "You can't win." Eli wrenched his arm away from Trey's grip. "Wait here."

Then, before Trey could stop him, he took off up the dark stairwell.

Eli didn't know how he was able to run so quickly up the stairs that seemed so steep and endless. Yet he knew exactly where he was headed: a small room on the eighth floor. He burst out onto the hall, which was blessedly empty. Then he found what he was looking for.

Minutes later, he reappeared in the lobby, where an impatient Trey was still hiding, waiting for him. Eli gasped for breath, his heart pounding. Trembling with exhaustion, he nearly dropped the large cardboard carton he was carrying.

Trey glanced inside before looking up. Something like admiration flashed across his face.

"Is that everything they got?" he asked.

Eli nodded. "I think so."

Trey nodded once. "Nice," he said.

The container was filled with dozens of unopened cardboard boxes. And within each were hundreds of copper-plated bullets.

The two boys made it to the side exit. Across the lobby, Trey could see that a huge mob had gathered outside by the front entrance. There looked to be close to a hundred people milling about, far more than Esther's meager army, yet they were indistinguishable in their hooded robes as they pushed and shouted.

Then he heard the thud of footsteps approaching fast behind him.

His heart thundering, Trey attempted to pull the door open

wide enough to squeeze through. They had only a few seconds: Three guards were running across the lobby, coming straight at them with their weapons drawn.

Trey was already fumbling to retrieve his gun when Eli turned to face them.

"Don't be crazy," Trey snapped as he pulled him back. But the other boy shook his head.

"The only bullets they've got left are in their guns," he said. "Once those are gone, you'll be clear."

Trey began to reply, but Eli had already taken off. A shot rang out, then another; both were instantly followed by the crack of the bullet hitting marble and skittering across the floor. But Eli, zigzagging toward the other end of the atrium, was right: He had managed to draw their attention and their fire.

Trey cursed under his breath; he had no choice but to take the chance the boy had given him. He pried open the side door. Then, still carrying the box, he squeezed out and onto the street. Behind him, he heard three more shots in quick succession, then silence. Only then did he dare to glance back, and to his relief, he saw Eli trailing him.

Gideon spun in a circle, unsure where to go.

Eli was not in his room. As infuriating as that was, he realized that he had a far more pressing problem. Even from where he stood on the second floor, he could clearly hear the commotion from outside. The mob sounded as if it had doubled or tripled over the past few minutes alone. More and more former disciples were gathering every minute, all of them screaming Saith's name.

It was only a matter of minutes until they broke in. Once that happened, there was no telling what they would do.

As for Saith, she seemed oblivious to the disaster that was unfolding outside.

She appeared to be going through with her lunatic ceremony up in her chambers. As odd-smelling smoke wafted down through the District, Gideon could hear steady chanting, praying, and the beating of some kind of drum. He couldn't believe that she hadn't heard the noise from downstairs, the shouts and the breaking glass. Even her followers, the devout who lived inside the District and prayed to her each day, were sneaking away in two and threes, despite the harsh punishment that such disrespect would surely bring. He saw them gathered in corridors and on the stairwells, whispering to one another or heading downstairs to see what was happening.

Gideon had always known some kind of reckoning was coming. Yet already this seemed larger and far worse than he had ever imagined.

And it was all because of Esther, he thought grimly. It was clear that she had planned everything, amassing a mob to take her revenge. Because of her, what would have been a protest had turned into a full-fledged revolution.

Gideon couldn't understand why Saith's guards weren't suppressing the uprising. Early on, he heard a few shots from the sentries downstairs, but after that, nothing.

He himself would not make the same mistake.

Gideon called together his boys—his four strongest and most faithful—and ordered them to follow him up the enclosed staircase. He had one of them stop on the eighth floor to empty the supply closet. The rest of them followed him up to the roof. He would station three of his men in the top of the stairwell; the fourth would stay with him in the garden. Their orders would be to fire on anyone who attempted to gain access.

Yet moments later, the fourth guard appeared on the roof. He reported that the closet was empty; the entire cache of ammunition—thousands of bullets—had vanished.

Gideon felt a little faint. Without weapons, he and his boys were trapped. When the revolutionaries finally broke in—and that became more likely with every second—he too would be destroyed.

He had to keep Esther's mob from breaking into the District.

The only question was how?

Out on the street, Esther was trying to keep her people calm. Heavy air hung over them like a blanket and dark gray clouds had thickened overhead. A ragged excitement buzzed through the crowd, like flames licking the edges of a dry field.

Once it ignited, she didn't know if she could control it.

She and her army had run into others like them, dozens of former followers of Saith who were now sick as well. Bewildered and furious, they clustered outside the glass doors, frantic to be let inside and given an explanation. Earlier, Esther had ordered her people to stay calm, not speak to anyone, and keep their weapons hidden until it was time to strike. Yet it was clear that no one was obeying her.

Someone from her crew had told one of the others what they were planning; as the word spread, a new restlessness took control of the crowd. "Let us in!" shouted one girl, her voice shrill. "Where is Saith?" demanded another. "Bring us to her!" Still the guards inside did not remove the bar that kept the revolving door from turning; they stood stone-faced, their guns by their sides.

Esther exchanged an uneasy glance with Skar.

"What happens if we can't get in?"

Skar shook her head; she clearly knew no more than Esther.

No sooner had Esther spoken than one of the people hurled a chunk of mortar. It bounced harmlessly off the glass wall, yet the small action seemed to unleash something. The crowd surged forward as one, screaming and shouting. They pushed their way into the round entrance and tried to force the doors to turn. A boy picked up a rusted piece of metal from the street and smashed it into the façade again and again. A spiderweb of white cracks formed as people cheered him on.

The guards inside shrank back. Then one of them fumbled in his waistband. Drawing out a gun, he aimed it at the assailant and Esther flinched. But when he pulled the trigger, it didn't go off. He paused to double-check it, turning to the boy next to him, who did the same.

Moments later, Esther saw a lone figure emerge from around the corner.

Trey was running to join her, a battered cardboard box under one arm. He was glancing back, and a moment later Esther saw who was following him.

Eli appeared around the side of the building. Yet even as Esther called his name, he stumbled and pitched forward. As she ran to catch him, she saw that the back of his shirt was black and glistening.

For the second time in her life, Esther held the boy in her arms. He was struggling to say something, his fingers fluttering as he attempted to pull her close.

"What is it?" she whispered, trying to hear his words.

But even as she stroked his face, trying to give him a moment of relief, a series of violent spasms shook the boy's body.

After that, he was still.

Esther looked up at Trey for an explanation. The boy in white shook his head.

"He drew the guards away from me. Without him, they'd still be armed." Trey sighed. "Looks like he took their last bullet."

But there was no time to react.

By now, the crowd was crazed. A heavy wind had begun blowing, gusting grit and whipping everyone's robes. Two boys had grabbed a short silver pole, one with a metal head and a cracked glass face, something found on every sidewalk. Holding it at their waists, they swung it back before smashing it into a wall of the District. The cracks that were already there widened, and a hundred more formed. A few additional blows and they could break their way in.

Esther heard a strange noise far above: the explosion of glass smashing. An instant later, someone on the ground screamed.

A girl pointed upward, her mouth open in horror. Esther looked up as well and recoiled. What she saw was unbelievable.

Someone had broken through the greenhouse and leaped from the roof.

Everyone shrank back as the body hurtled straight down at them, tumbling midair in a shower of broken glass as its tattered robes fluttered. It hit the sidewalk with astonishing force; the ground jolted as the pavement cracked beneath it. Those standing closest to it shrieked as they were splattered with blood and gore.

Esther had both hands pressed to her mouth in shock. Less than three feet away, the body had landed facedown, covered in glistening shards with one arm bent backward at an angle that made her feel faint. She steeled herself and took hold of his shoulder. Flipping him over, she stared into the face of an unfamiliar boy with a snub nose and curly black hair. His expression was strangely serene: It seemed as if he were only sleeping. But that wasn't the only shock.

His arms were covered with lesions.

A girl behind her let out a cry. "He was sick." Frantic, she backed away in terror as she tried to wipe the blood from her face.

As word spread, panic began to fill the air. Esther tried to make sense of what had happened. *Had the boy leaped because of the disease? But why now?* Then a teenage girl next to her grabbed her arm and pointed upward.

Another body was falling toward them. Seconds later, it was followed by a third.

Everyone scattered. They flattened themselves against the sides of the building or crouched behind abandoned cars, fighting one another for cover. All eyes were wide with horror as they followed the bodies plummeting to the ground, landing with one deafening explosion after another.

By now, the sidewalk was stained red and heaped with carnage, glinting with broken shards, but Esther didn't care. As the wind whipped her hair, she examined the bodies. Like the first, both showed signs of the disease: wasted limbs covered with purple lesions. But one also showed advanced signs of decay.

The realization hit Esther like a physical blow:

The bodies had been dead long before they hit the ground. Which meant only one thing: Someone was throwing them off the roof. The corpses were being used as weapons to drive the revolutionaries away.

The tactic was working.

Everyone around Esther was screaming, pulling off their robes as they frantically attempted to wipe themselves clean. Dozens had already fled, including all of Esther's recruits. The sidewalk was littered with their abandoned weapons.

The uprising was over before it had even begun.

Even Esther's friends seemed to surrender where they stood, trembling and splattered with filth. Esther saw Michal tugging Skar's hand, begging her wordlessly to find shelter. Skar glanced at Esther, who just nodded, giving them permission to leave. Skar signaled the others, and one by one, they picked their way across the street and disappeared around a corner.

Esther remained where she was.

Trey was the last to leave her. He met her gaze and gave a faint smile. He held out a hand, but she didn't take it. Then he joined the others, his footsteps crunching on broken glass.

Now it was just Esther, alone.

She stood with her chin high, gazing upward. She was certain that Gideon must be watching—either from the roof, where he had ordered the attack, or from one of the lower floors. Wherever he was, this was how she wished him to see her: defiant and unafraid, even in defeat.

Then Esther heard it: the first rumble of thunder.

Transfixed, she stared up at the sky. A brilliant fork of light split the gray and yellow, and moments later, a deafening roar boomed through the streets of Mundreel. When the rain began, it did so in a burst: A dense veil fell in sheets and waves, drenching everything in its path and filling the air with a heavy thrumming sound.

Esther didn't move. Although she could hear the screams of others as they took refuge in buildings and parked cars, she stood and marveled at the strange feeling.

She had never before felt the rain, had never experienced the tickling sensation of a thousand warm drops bouncing off her damp skin, running through her hair and down her back, dripping into her mouth and eyes. Her sneakers were filled with water; her feet squelched with moisture. Laughing, Esther pulled down her hood and raised her face to the heavens as her robes grew heavy and sodden.

Days ago, she had listened to Uri's strange words in their refuge on the mountain; since then, she had thought about them many times.

Yet it was only now that she truly understood it in her bones: *She was immune now. The rain could no longer hurt her.*

Lowering her head, Esther shook her hair hard so that drops flew. Then she blinked through the water that dripped into her eyes. Through it, she glimpsed her friends, huddled together for shelter in the doorways of neighboring buildings. When she caught Uri's eye, they both smiled; then he nodded.

Dozens of people stood only a few feet away from Esther, on the other side of the glass, openmouthed with wonder. All of them wore the white and black robes of Saith's followers, some with their hoods down. A few even leaned their hands against the partition, as if to get closer.

They stayed like that for an endless moment. Even after the rain stopped and the sun began to break through, Saith's people stared at Esther, occasionally turning to whisper to one another.

Others also began to appear around her, emerging from

buildings in tentative twos and threes, stepping carefully through the moisture. They stopped and stared at the drenched girl before them.

Esther pointed to the District, and said, "Let's go."

Now they would follow her anywhere.

TWENTY-FOUR

"*Forgive us, Saith. Clean us, Saith. Heal us, Saith. Save us, Saith.*"

Saith winced.

The chanting voices that she normally found so soothing were much too loud, even unpleasant. She had stationed two boys with metal pans on either side of the altar who struck them rhythmically with wooden clubs; now she regretted that touch. Combined with the dense and pungent smoke that wafted from firebowls placed around her room, the noise felt like a metal spike passing through her burning temples. She rubbed her head, feeling the dry, papery skin beneath her fingers, and again tried to concentrate.

She was burning up with fever.

Shaky and weak, the girl tried to focus, to find once more the divine conviction deep inside her, the unquestioning sense of self that for months had ruled everything she said and did. But right now she felt nothing except pain, heat, and a bone-crushing exhaustion. She grasped the heavy knife with the black handle, the silver blade printed with the strange word SABATIER; it felt like it weighed a thousand pounds. As she attempted to hoist it, everything swam in front of her eyes: the lines of hooded acolytes kneeling on the ground in front of her, bowing in unison, the guards on both sides, and the white billows of smoke. The only thing she could do was stare at the thing that was closest, the object that rested on a low table before her: the mutant baby named Sarah.

It lay on its back on a white towel. Burbling and kicking its bare legs, it tossed its head from side to side, its strange lavender gaze flickering around.

The infant gave a passing glance up at the priestess, and when their eyes met, Saith felt a shock that momentarily snapped her out of her dizzy spell. For an instant, she could once again feel the deep wellspring of bottomless power that lay deep within her, crackling like lightning, and inwardly, she was swept by relief.

All she needed was to sacrifice and bathe in the blood of an innocent, and it would be done.

Summoning all of her strength, with shaky hands, Saith again raised the weapon.

Then she hesitated.

Beyond the chanting and rhythmic beating of the gongs, she heard something else far-off; it was jarring and strange. Saith recognized it: the sound of a large mob, angry and energized. She was not the only one who had noticed; several people in her audience seemed distracted. Some even paused in their repeated bowing, stopping to whisper to one another and cast furtive looks over their shoulders. To her disbelief, one disciple even arose and slipped away, followed by a second and then a third.

It was outrageous. "Stop," Saith tried to say. Then she raised her voice, to sound commanding and awe-inspiring, but the word came out no louder than a whisper. "Stop!"

No one seemed to hear. In desperation, Saith turned to the guard closest to her, hoping he would intercede. She was astonished to find him openly gaping at the entryway. The chanting faltered as one by one her followers stopped bowing and sat up. Within moments, Saith found herself facing a sea of the backs of people's heads. She heard one word repeated again and again:

EstherEstherEsther.

Saith blinked. *Why were they saying that name? Her enemy was dead, had been dead for weeks.*

Then Saith shook her head. It was beneath her to pay attention to this disruption, whatever it was. She would demonstrate the kind of power she had by ignoring it.

Once again, Saith lifted the blade.

But as she did, a girl with dark, matted hair materialized

in the doorway. Paying no attention to the solemn ritual taking place, much less to Saith, she stood there, breathless and laughing. The haphazard chanting stopped altogether. Even the guards stopped banging on the pans so they could hear.

"It's Esther," said the girl. "She come back from the dead. She here!"

Saith's hand began to tremble; she felt as if she would faint. Her mouth opened and shut without a sound. Then she turned to tell her guards to seize this lying intruder. They would not only punish this girl for her sacrilegious behavior; they would make an example of what would happen to those who showed a god such disrespect.

But all in the room had risen to their feet. Talking loudly, laughing and exclaiming, they began to leave the room. Even her guards did nothing to stop them. In fact, they looked torn. Huddled at the doorway, they gazed out as if they yearned to see what was going on. And then, with an impulse greater than obedience, duty, or even fear, they too fled.

Saith was left alone.

Unnerved, she had a sudden and terrible presentiment: She was the one who was dead, not Esther. And that could not be.

Trembling with fresh anger, Saith stood. The knife slipped from her grasp and fell to the floor with a clatter. With dull, unseeing eyes, she stepped over the baby. Then she stumbled down the aisle.

With great difficulty, the girl made her way through the vast atrium of the District. Her tiny bare feet hardly left an impression on the dusty floor. Delirious, she felt as if she were floating; the entire building shimmered around her with waves of scorching heat. To escape the unbearable temperature, she pushed back her hood; soon, she tore away her robes altogether, leaving them piled behind her on the ground. Wearing only a voluminous black T-shirt that hung to her bony knees, Saith no longer cared that the signs of her illness were visible to all.

She clung to the greasy metal banister and even so, nearly fell down the stairs; still, she managed to right herself and keep going. Although her legs were like lead and she felt as if her entire body were on fire, Saith was fueled by something more powerful than sickness: curiosity.

She had to see Esther for herself.

Saith reached the main level and rested against the cool marble wall. There, blinking to adjust her sight, she saw what she had been fearing: A massive and jubilant mob filled the lobby and spilled out the doors onto the sidewalk.

They were gathered around one individual. The person, a female, was using language that Saith had never heard before, strange words that made no sense: "immunity." "Exposure." She realized that the girl was talking about the killing disease, saying that there was now a way to prevent it.

Preposterous, Saith thought with contempt. *The fools.*

When the priestess finally made her way to the center, she saw that the girl was in her teens: thin, with dark hair shorn close to her head. And it was no wonder the others kept their distance: the creature dripped poison. Her wet clothes clung to her like a second skin and in the rays of sun streaming in, she seemed to radiate a brilliant light.

Esther.

It was impossible.

"It ain't real," Saith whispered. No one heard. She had to conjure all her strength. "It a trick. A spirit."

Those closest to her turned to see who had spoken. Falling silent one by one, they recoiled in shock and horror when they realized how far the disease had progressed.

Saith could no longer read the expressions on people's faces; she could only make out flickering shapes, advancing and receding. Yet she knew they must be smiling at her, bowing to her in deference and support.

The demon pretending to be Esther strode forward, its dark eyes snapping with anger. "Where's Sarah?"

Saith found the energy to laugh. Although she could barely see, she could still hear the urgency in the other's voice. *That meant the ghost was frightened,* Saith thought with satisfaction, *and fear meant weakness.*

The creature now towered over her. *"Where is she?"*

Saith smiled through discolored teeth. Then she pursed her lips. Her answer was a long, thin line of spit propelled with surprising force.

It sprayed over Esther and splattered those standing behind her.

The group fell back with a gasp. Then, as the spectators wiped the foul liquid from their faces, something inside them snapped.

The crowd's murmur rose to a bloodcurdling roar of fury as

months of long-buried hatred and fear erupted. Their enemy was before them: alone, unguarded, and vulnerable. Before Esther could stop them, the mob charged as one toward the tiny girl.

"No!" Esther shouted, but they did not hear.

In a second, they were upon the priestess and she vanished under their numbers. Dozens of people made up this blind swarm of rage, snatching, punching, kicking.

Though she kept shouting for them to stop, Esther could no longer see their target. All she heard was a single, piercing shriek. Then, abruptly, it was cut off, its echo piercing through the marble halls. And even then, the mob kept tearing at what wasn't there, crazed by the smell of blood and revenge.

Frozen with fear, Gideon heard it, too.

He was alone on an upper landing, gazing down. From his vantage point, he had seen the terrible inevitability unfold: Saith working her way into the center of the mob and the furious crowd turning on her as one, a pack of wild dogs descending on a single prey.

Even he was taken aback by the unmitigated rage of people who had once professed their love and adoration. Already, they were turning on the hapless guards, who were now unarmed and outnumbered; the atrium rang with the sound of their screams. He knew he would be next. Within minutes, they would hunt him down as well, with Esther leading the way.

Where could he go?

Gideon ran through the empty corridors, his sneakers

squeaking on the marble floor as he skidded around corners. One quick look over the railing told him what he had feared: The doors were now guarded by Esther's people. He could already sense the mob starting to spread out, moving upward into the building; by his calculation, he was ahead of them by perhaps two or three minutes at most. The District was enormous, and he knew its intricacies well. Every hiding place he considered, he rejected out of hand.

But as he ran past Saith's former chambers, he stopped. Since they had finished with the girl, perhaps he would be safe there. Venturing in, Gideon found it in shambles, as if its former inhabitants had vacated suddenly.

The room had been set up in a bizarre way for Saith's ceremony, with pots and smoldering firebowls on either side of her throne. In front of it was a low table. And lying on it was a child, wailing as it kicked its rosy limbs.

Esther's baby.

Gideon stood there, staring at it. His only emotion was overwhelming relief: This was a valuable good with which he could bargain.

He swept the infant up in his arms.

The boy had never held a baby before. The thing was warm and slippery; as it kicked its tiny legs and struggled in protest, it began to slide from his grasp. Frantic that he might accidentally kill it, Gideon tightened his hold. As if sensing his discomfort, the child began to cry even harder.

Attempting to muffle its screams against his chest only seemed to make the child cry louder. Gideon had to rock the thing clumsily in his arms to pacify it. Then the boy peered outside of the room. He ran for the corner stairwell and slipped inside.

Climbing the long, dark flights to the roof was twice as hard when carrying a wriggling infant. Occasionally, he heard doors clang open below him and footsteps thunder up or down a flight. When that happened, he had to stop where he was and bounce the child in order to silence it, his heart pounding in his chest.

Minutes later, soaked with sweat, he finally reached the top. He pushed open the heavy metal door and stepped out into the blinding heat. Hot air gusted in at him from the immense opening smashed into the glass wall. This was where he'd ordered his guards to break through so that they could hurl the dead bodies down at the protesters below.

The hole still held glass fragments. He brushed some aside and, with the blanket guarding its naked skin, propped the child against the edge. If anyone came near him, a single move would send it over.

Gideon caught his breath and prepared to wait.

TWENTY-FIVE

IN THE UPROAR, ESTHER COULD NOT FIND OUT WHAT HAD HAPPENED TO Sarah.

A few spoke of a ceremony upstairs. But the details were conflicting and confusing, and when Esther ran upstairs to Saith's rooms, she saw that they were bare.

She seized the knife that lay on the ground and examined it closely, even pressing it to her nose. To her immense relief, the blade was dry and clean; there wasn't even a trace of blood. And when she laid her hand on the table, she could have sworn it was still warm. Yet there was no sign of the baby.

Skar appeared at the door, her face etched with concern. "Gideon is not to be found."

Esther nodded. "Why don't you check from the basement and work your way up? I'll start on the roof. Wherever they are, I think she's still alive."

Skar nodded and both girls took off in different directions.

Esther made it to the hidden staircase. Taking a deep breath, she plunged into the suffocating darkness and bolted up the steps. Within seconds, she reached the tenth floor and then the roof.

When she pushed open the metal door, she was momentarily blinded by the piercing sunlight. Blinking rapidly, she forced her eyes to adjust.

That was when she saw them.

Halfway across the tarred surface, Gideon stood as if awaiting her. And there was Sarah: crying, red-faced, but very much alive.

A hot wind gusted across Esther's face, blowing grit. She noticed that the boy was standing near an enormous hole in the glass wall, broken fragments still glinting beneath his feet. Her heart lurched as she realized that he was keeping her child balanced somehow on its jagged edge, only a blanket protecting her soft skin.

The two stared at each other for a long moment.

Esther knew that she had the advantage. Saith and the guards were dead and the District had been overthrown. It was clear the boy was afraid; there was no other reason for him to threaten Sarah. It was the only leverage he had left.

Yet even as she stood there, her knees weakened at the sight of her child, so tiny and unknowing. Nothing else in the world was more important. She would do anything to save her child . . . anything at all. And looking into his eyes, she understood that he knew that too.

"What do you want?" Despite her best efforts, her voice cracked.

The boy said nothing, waiting to hear what she would offer. So Esther continued to speak, stammering as she tried to keep the shakiness from her voice.

"You'll be safe. . . . I won't let anybody harm you. You can stay here. You can have all of this"—she gestured at the garden, the entire District beneath them—"and we'll help you get it back to running order. Then we'll leave you alone. I promise."

Gideon smiled.

"That generous," he said. "But it ain't what I want."

Esther swallowed. "Then please," she said, "step away from there. I can't think with her like that."

He complied. Hoisting the child onto his hip, he walked to the center of the roof. Esther moved with him, although he was careful to keep the skylight between them.

"You ain't like Saith," the boy remarked. "She got no understanding of power. . . . It like proof to her. Make her drunk, then sick. That what kill her. Those people down there, they only helped."

Esther nodded. She was only half listening; she had her eyes focused on Sarah, measuring the distance between them. As if reading her mind, Gideon edged away so that he stood directly across the glass field from her. Then he spoke again, his voice casual.

"What I want," he said, "is to stay. Only this time, it ain't just gonna be about running things. It be you and me."

Esther blinked; she wasn't sure she understood what he was saying. "You want to be partners?"

"You don't believe me?" With his free hand, he dug into his pocket and pulled out a palmful of sparkling glass. There were so many pieces that several spilled onto the ground. He displayed them, sending glints of green against his face.

"Look," he said. "This show you I'm serious. You can have this and more . . . all you want. I give you everything I got."

Esther glanced up, and for the first time, she stared deep into his eyes, gray and fathomless. With a sense of shock, she realized that Gideon meant what he said.

He *did* want to be her partner, and not just because it would help his glass scheme. He loved her and had all along; she was the one thing he craved most in the world. And yet he did not know how to love. All he knew of love consisted of what he held in his hand.

For a moment, Esther felt pity for him. But not enough to make her negotiate—not for a minute.

"I don't want it," she said.

Then they both heard something at the same time.

Distracted, neither had noticed the person who now stood

at the door. It was a girl Esther only vaguely recognized. She was scrawny and pale, her hair cropped short. Yet her dark eyes burned with fury.

"I heard what you promise," Nur said.

Before Gideon could reply, the girl rushed forward. Seizing him by the shoulders, she struggled with him as Esther darted to the boy's side and snatched Sarah out of his arms. Then Nur shoved him, hard. Gideon lost his balance and with a cry, he stumbled backward onto the skylight. One foot and then the next punched through as he plunged downward in an explosion of glass, the pieces in his hand scattering everywhere.

Yet Gideon did not fall.

With bleeding fingers, he managed to cling to the rusted metal railing that edged the skylight as his body swung below, his legs kicking in vain to gain a toehold. Colorful shards continued to rain down on the District, dropping to the marble floor ten flights down.

As Nur backed away, her face triumphant, Esther froze, staring at the scene.

Gideon's eyes found her. "Help me," he gasped.

Esther did not want to save him. But she couldn't let him die, either. Placing Sarah down, she sat on the gritty tar paper in front of him and braced both feet against the iron railing. Then she reached out.

"Hold tight," she said.

Gideon's eyes met hers: The pupils were dilated in terror. She saw that the cords of his hands were sticking out like ropes, his knuckles white. He swallowed hard and his eyes flickered to her right hand. With a sudden movement, he snatched it with his left and Esther felt herself nearly yanked over the edge, as well. Pushing as hard as she could with her legs, she tightened her grasp and began to pull.

It was working. Gideon used his other hand to pull himself up. His chest was drawing even with the roof, when Esther sensed a sudden change in the air.

It was an eerie vibration that she felt rather than heard, a strange thrumming in her bones. It came from low to the ground. Whatever it was drew closer and as it did, she suddenly understood.

It was Pilot.

The dog crouched low to the ground no more than a foot away from her, his ears flattened close to his skull, his yellowed teeth bared. Esther was astonished; the animal had never shown any aggression toward her. He was growling so loudly she could feel his hot breath on her neck.

"Easy, boy," Esther said.

The dog hesitated. Then suddenly, he sprang forward and sank his teeth into Esther's arm.

"*No!*" she screamed.

She lost her grip of Gideon, and, flailing, he dropped backward. His other hand popped off the railing, and, shrieking, he disappeared from sight. An eternity seemed to pass in a vacuum of sound. Then a great explosion was heard that echoed upward from the District's main floor.

Pilot let go of Esther's arm. He hadn't hurt her; in fact, his teeth hadn't even broken the skin. As if abashed, he now butted his head against her, whimpering as he tried to lick her face.

Tears starting, Esther patted him. And then she gathered Sarah into her arms.

TWENTY-SIX

THE GIRL RAN ACROSS THE BROKEN ASPHALT.

Small for her size, she darted barefoot from shadow to over-hang through the empty streets of Mundreel, her dark limbs flashing in the early morning light. Behind her, a telltale sound revealed that she was being followed. She shot a quick glance behind her and sped up.

Trying to lose her pursuer, she rounded one corner and then another. Spying an opening between two buildings, she raced into its dark recesses and advanced three paces before stopping. Facing her was a dead end, the back wall of a build-ing. The footsteps drew even closer.

She hesitated.

Then, gritting her teeth, she ran forward, leaping upward at the last second as she clung to the sheer expanse. Her fingers and toes scrabbling for a purchase, she began to scale the bricks, awkwardly at first, and then faster than a lizard.

The one in pursuit caught up to her seconds later and stood below, panting. He was openmouthed with amazement.

"Hey," called Kai. "That's cheating!"

At his voice, Sarah stopped climbing.

She twisted her neck around to gaze down on her brother and laughed, showing tiny, pointed teeth. "You have to tag me," she called. "And you didn't." Letting go of the wall and pushing away at the same time, she dropped easily to the ground. "So I win?" She smiled up at him, her lavender eyes crinkling in the morning sun.

"You win." Rueful, Kai laughed as well as he bent over, catching his breath. He was still winded from stalking his little sister through the city streets; she had more energy than anyone he knew, even their mother. "Who taught you that? Was it Skar?"

Bashful, the four-year-old shook her head and shrugged. "I just did it."

Esther and Skar played with both children every day, devising long and engaging games through the ravaged streets and buildings of Mundreel. They were the kind of pastimes the two girls used to invent for themselves back in Prin.

Yet from the beginning, it was the little girl who excelled.

It was true that Kai was fast and tireless, as well, yet he had to practice over and over until he mastered each technique. For Sarah, everything came naturally. And she delighted in it all, as if the world with its obstacles were a giant playground devised for her entertainment.

An hour later, the children entered their home. As their laughter echoed in the vast space, they noticed their mother and her friend watching them from two levels up. Esther waved at them as they disappeared into the corner staircase. The older girls marveled at how Sarah forced her brother to catch up.

"She didn't get it from me," Esther said. "It must have been from Caleb."

Skar smiled. "The skill was from him. The stubbornness was from you." Then she squeezed her old friend's shoulder with affection. Skar went off to begin her day's work, and Esther started up the stairs.

It was too early for the place to be crowded, yet she knew it would be soon.

The days of the District as a marketplace were over. Gone were the luxury items, the soft and expensive articles of clothing, leather goods, and household objects. The stalls with merchants hawking their wares were a distant memory, as were the glass fragments themselves. Yet every day, dozens showed up, strangers as well as familiar faces. They still came to trade, but it was no longer just goods that they dealt in. They brought with them ideas, knowledge, and information.

The empty stores were now classrooms and workshops, where anyone with a skill or area of expertise could share what he or she knew: not only reading, history, and science, but art, music, and storytelling. Craftspeople revealed what they understood about building and repairing, cooking and irrigation, metalwork and carpentry.

With their help, each year, the library had continued to grow. As word of its existence spread, new visitors brought in hundreds of books, magazines, and other artifacts from miles around. The library was open to anyone who could read, and those who could not were welcome to learn from one of the teachers trained long ago by Joseph, Uri, and Esther.

The place where Saith had once received her visitors was now nothing more than an empty fountain, cracked and forgotten. Yet the need for spiritual comfort was real: More and more, Esther sensed that there was a force greater than she was, and she knew she was not alone in believing this. Although it was nothing like the grand altar Gideon had once planned, she had decided early on to set aside a small room on the ground floor. There, anyone who chose to could quietly pray alone or in groups.

The roof garden had become a model for others; Joseph still used it to show Outsiders how to design and construct them. There were dozens of flourishing greenhouses spread across the city, growing food, purifying rainwater, and supporting anyone who was willing to put in the work.

And, from the start, Esther had encouraged Uri to continue his scientific research.

Working alone, the boy had come up with an idea that he thought, risky as it was, would prevent the killing disease. Uri took careful scrapings from the lesions of a dying boy; then, without telling anyone, not even Joseph, he administered them to himself through a shallow cut in the arm. After waiting several days, he stood out in the rain, as Esther herself had done. Like her, he turned his face to the poisonous stuff, letting it drip into his open eyes and mouth.

Esther was horrified when she found out. Yet by the time he told her, it had already been a full week since his exposure and he had not yet fallen ill. After a month had passed, he began offering these "inoculations," as he called them, to their friends.

Not surprisingly, most people were frightened and suspicious at first. And he was too late to save those who were already dying. But the continued health of Skar, Joseph, and the others who had received the treatment started to win over even the most fearful. Within months, dozens of new people were vaccinated. The results were extraordinary; there had been virtually no new cases in months.

In time, Esther sensed the disease would be vanquished for good.

Yet despite the newfound stability of the District, the girl was aware it took constant vigilance to maintain it.

Every few months, it seemed, an interloper would appear who wanted to take it over, using either subterfuge or physical force. Esther had learned from painful and bitter experience that doing nothing in the face of aggression could be disastrous; it wasn't enough merely to do good. Turning a blind eye to Gideon's plotting had led first to his cruel and unjust exploitation of the monetary system and then to Saith's horrific rule.

Esther could never forget that it had also led to Aras's death.

Knowing this, she and the group of elders with whom she now ruled the District—Skar, Joseph, Silas, Trey, and Uri—had figured out how to deal with such troublemakers. Early on, they had conferred in private and had discussed the possibility of punishing and even imprisoning them. But remembering how Saith had been corrupted by absolute power, they ended up voting unanimously simply to Shun these miscreants forever.

Esther was not afraid that the criminals would return, seeking vengeance. After all, she and the others could defend themselves if they had to. And she would have help doing that.

"Hey!"

Esther turned as she saw Trey coming around the corner, his back to her. He had his fists up, pretending to spar with Kai.

"Almost!" he called.

Kai jabbed at him, and Trey dodged the punch before reaching out and mussing the boy's hair. Then he turned and kissed Esther before starting back toward the children's school, which he ran with Michal. Kai jogged to catch up.

Esther knew that the gunman no longer carried his weapon, but kept it hidden in their room, in case of trouble. Yet he had never used it in the four years they had been partnered.

The girl continued up the stairs. At last, she reached the library and stood in the doorway, watching.

Joseph spent nearly all of his time there, cataloguing new books, accompanied by Stumpy. By now, he had a few silver threads in his dark hair, and the feline also showed signs of stiffness in her joints.

"You wanted to see me?" she asked.

Joseph looked up. He was poring over one of his handmade calendars, concentric circles on a wooden board punctuated by different-colored marbles set in shallow depressions. Stumpy rested in his lap, dozing. Joseph seemed particularly excited about what they denoted, muttering to himself.

"I thought you might want to know," he said. "I was going over some dates, and it turns out . . . though I can't be sure . . ."

"What is it?" she said, with more affection than impatience.

"I don't know the exact date, but it's soon. Either that, or it's happened already."

Joseph went on, discussing at length the challenge of pinpointing exact dates in the past, and accounting for something called a "leap year." But soon it became clear what he was trying to say.

"Happy birthday," Joseph blurted out.

Esther was twenty years old.

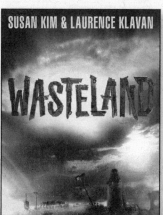

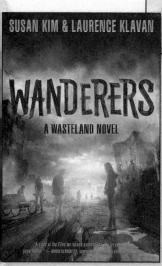